Quantum Nightmares

Quantum

Jose M. Rodriguez Jr.

short strories

Nightmares

FLARE BOOKS

El Paso, Texas

Published by Flare Books.

© 2025 Jose M. Rodriguez Jr.

For further information, write to info@catalystpress.org.

You can find out more at catalystpress.org.

In North America, this book is distributed by
Consortium Book Sales & Distribution, a division of Ingram.
Phone: 612/746-2600
cbsdinfo@ingramcontent.com
www.cbsd.com

First edition, first printing
1 3 5 7 9 8 6 4 2

ISBN 978-1-96351-121-5
Library of Congress Control Number 2025936338

Cover design by Enzyme

CONTENTS

Prologue: The Grays

IT WAS A SIMPLE ITCH THAT STARTED IT—the panic, subtle at first, slow, dull. The bridge of Betty Hill's nose was begging to be scratched, and when she tried to satisfy the urge—eyes still closed in that lazy realm between sleep and consciousness—she realized her arms were tied down. She tightened her eyes shut, afraid to see what in her mind's eye was evidence of an abduction.

She tried wriggling free, thrashing her hips, realizing her legs were also strapped down. She stopped squirming. Caught her breath. Regained her composure.

She opened her eyes slowly.

Where am I? Betty thought. She couldn't remember being strapped to a cold steel table in what appeared to be a hospital setting of sorts, but unlike any hospital she'd ever frequented. The brightly lit room had curved walls and high ceilings with hanging lights that dangled like the branches of a weeping willow swaying slowly in a lazy wind. A luminescent wave pulsated along the branches in a dizzying spectrum that changed from blue to purple, orange to red—every color represented in their turn. The wave of changing colors was shiny, almost glittery, as it ran along the branches.

Betty couldn't be sure, but she had a sense that the luminescent wave was actually a *bioluminescent wave*, that it was the lifeblood of the room in which she was being held captive, that it was alive.

A holographic 3D imaging of Betty's cardiovascular and nervous systems rotated at the foot of the table. Her vitals were listed on the side of the hologram. Her BP was a little high, per usual. She looked to see if there was a blood pressure cuff on her arms. There wasn't.

The technology before her was terrifying; it was terrifying because she knew it hadn't been invented yet. The rotating holographic 3D imaging at the foot of the cold steel table she laid on was light years ahead of the technology of the 1960s.

As she fought through the fog of her intellect, fragments of memory returned slowly, incrementally, pieces of a jigsaw puzzle in a flash of light. The last thing she could recall was driving with her husband Barney as a bright light followed their car.

"It's probably just a helicopter," Barney had said as he looked, in- *credulous, in the rearview mirror. The light followed them for another twenty miles. Betty's fear grew with every mile mark they passed. She begged him to do something, anything. "It's just a light, honey," he'd said. But he couldn't stand the fear emanating from her eyes and when he finally turned off route 30, the bright light turned as well. There was no question about it. The light was following them. It suddenly increased speed and was right atop of them. Then the bright light pulsated, and a blinding blanket of white light surrounded them, swallowed them.*

That was the last thing she remembered—the blanket of white light, and as she tried wriggling free of the restraints, she cried out, "Barney, are you there?"

Only the echoes of her scared voice answered back, slapping against the curved walls, surrounding her.

A seamless door hissed open. In walked two tiny beings. At first glance, Betty thought they were children, but as they approached, she realized these peculiar entities weren't human at all. She could hardly believe her eyes. She was consumed utterly by fear. She thrashed and kicked and screamed until a notch the size of a cigarette pack latched open at the head of the steel table and, from tiny spigots, a yellow mist was released into the air. Betty was suddenly calm as a Buddhist monk. She watched the two beings' approach with perfect fascination now.

How odd, she thought, *how fabulously curious, these tiny beings.*

The tallest one was four feet tall; the other was six inches shorter. Their skin was an incandescent gray. It appeared smooth and moist, like a frog's hide. They had long, spindly arms; short legs extending from a tiny trunk; and an enlarged, bulbous-shaped head resting on long, skinny necks. Their massive, almond-shaped eyes were dark and soulless, and their mouths were nothing more than tiny slits.

Hello, the leader said, *I am this ship's captain.* He motioned to the shorter being. *This is my chief medical examiner.*

Although Betty acknowledged she should be scared, terrified even, she couldn't bring herself to partake in any fear-based emotions. She observed them just as objectively as she would a rising sun. They were so tiny, these creatures, their anatomy so different from humans. Her face reflected off their black-mirrored eyes like a still lake on a moon-drenched night. To her surprise, she didn't see fear in her face.

I must be going mad, Betty thought. Then a revelation. *What was in that mist?*

No ma'am, the mist was not a hallucinogen, the medical examiner assured. *It simply augments the dopamine inhibitors in your brain.* His tiny mouth didn't move, but Betty could hear him all the same.

Betty giggled loudly. Her giggle slingshot around the curved walls and met her ears, making her self-conscious. "How'd you do that?" she asked. "How'd you talk without moving your lips?"

Thought transference, the leader thought. He nodded at the medical examiner who consulted the rotating holographic scan at the foot of the table, and the scanning ballooned ten feet high by five feet across. A vertical bar with green numbers counted rapidly from zero. The medical examiner returned the leader's nod. Everything was working smoothly thus far.

We are in a unique position, ma'am, in dire need of help, the leader thought, *and you are in a unique position to help us. But we cannot, no,* he paused, tilted his head, *we will not proceed unless you comply.*

The green numbers were at eighty percent and climbing rapidly.

"Comply with what?" Betty could hardly believe that she could be of any help to a species that had conquered interstellar travel.

It'd be easier to show you, the medical examiner thought.

The numbers turned red, blinking ominously at one hundred percent. The symbiotic download was complete.

Betty's assertion that the ship was alive turned out to be true. The table she was strapped to absorbed her genetic makeup, plotting a map of her brain to better interface with. The leader nodded at the chief medical examiner, who did something or another on the holographic imaging, and Betty received the following upload to her consciousness:

By the turn of the twentieth century, humanity had made great strides in the advent of technology. The industrial revolution inundated the world in a technological renaissance, the likes of which hadn't been seen since the first man harnessed fire. In less than one hundred years, humanity took quantum leaps far exceeding any comparable timeline in history. Trading their horse and buggy for locomotives, their locomotives for cars, their cars for planes, and their planes for spaceships.

Drunk on hubris alone, they found themselves floating in the cosmos. From the dizzying heights, they saw their cities lit up like an ocean of dancing stars—godlike, indeed.

Their technologies became so advanced, it soon replaced the basic know-how their ancestors took for granted, and the rudimentary skills which got humanity to that juncture and bridged the gap to the height of their arrogance slowly disintegrated. They disgraced that pioneering first man and forgot how to make fire.

Eventually, there were no more farmers, no fishermen, no carpenters. But allow me to regress.

Betty's eyes flickered about as her subconscious mind interfaced with the quantum computer, and she was physically there to witness what the voice in her head spoke of.

In 2060, following the worst of three global pandemics that decimated the human population over the span of thirty years, scientists developed a homogenized serum, extracted from the mesoglea of an immortal jellyfish. The super-antibody concoction rendered illness obsolete. It was the greatest medical innovation in history and certainly the most far-reaching since the discovery of the germ. The world dubbed the medical marvel "Ambrosia" a worthy designation which meant "immortality" in ancient Greece and was purported to be the food of the gods, the nectar of immortality.

The population boomed, and for a fleeting moment, humanity lived in blissful harmony. But it didn't take long before the honeymoon phase boomeranged into a lingering hangover period. Although humanity had beaten sickness, its sole benefactor—death—was still lurking about the dark night like a famished vulture patiently awaiting its next feast. And feast it did. For humanity hadn't anticipated the strenuous effects an exponentially growing population would have on the planet's food stores. Death, the great equalizer, restored balance.

Many died from starvation—too many.

Once again, the citizens of earth looked to their scientists for answers. "We have defeated sickness," they cried, "but our children still battle starvation."

The call to arms was answered in 2065 when physicists created a whole network of quantum computers capable of godlike knowledge. They named the AI consultant "Oracle" and in utter desperation, the decision was made to take the human out of human error. Humanity turned over every major decision to the Oracle's infallible care, ushering in the AI initiative, which resulted in 3D replicators printing food and fully automated AI systems capable of plowing fields.

The GPS and self-driving technologies boasted the lowest margin of error and highest yields in the planet's history. The system was so safe and effective, it was immediately installed in every car, plane, and boat. Within a generation, humanity had forgotten the intricate nuances of how to farm and drive effectively. Within two generations, they had forgotten the abilities altogether.

With nothing but time on their hands, the now free farmers, pilots, and captains became AI's greatest advocates. This was the catalyst to fully integrate technology into every viable facet of society—which, in hindsight, was the beginning of their demise. But first, it ushered in a golden age comparable only to the great industrial revolution of the twentieth century, and like the industrial revolution, the new golden age culminated with humanity in the stars.

With their quantum computers devising all manner of technological innovation, every industry was eventually usurped by machines. 3D printers oozed out entire neighborhoods before construction workers could lay the foundation to just one home. Factories never slept and production increased tenfold in the first quarter alone. Before long, doctors, lawyers, and cops became automated, redundant and unemployed; so too did garbage men, fast-food employees, and clerks of all varieties.

Without the need for a workforce, the global economy pivoted, and humanity set their sights inward toward their spirits and outward toward the cosmos.

They became obsessed with ancient origin stories and scoured the planet for evidence of an ancient progenitor race. This became their unified purpose—to meet their maker.

National borders disappeared as they turned over every stone and searched the deepest crevices of every ocean and cave for mention of the star people that came down and jump-started humanity. With the Oracle's knowledge and guidance, they invented sophisticated submarines capable of deep-sea diving. In this way, they found the fabled cities of Atlantis and Lemuria.

Then the Oracle told them to focus their ground-penetrating sonar on the rolling dunes of every desert where they found thousands of missing pyramids and even the fabled hall of records, an ancient repository of earth's hidden history spoken of by the sleeping prophet—Edgar Cayce.

After the deserts, they scanned the thick canopy of the Amazon rainforest and discovered the legendary city of El Dorado, where they stumbled upon gold and knowledge. So much knowledge.

In rapid succession, they discovered ancient ruins and pyramids on every continent. Each discovery pushed back humanity's origins further than the last. But there was no discovery more revealing than what they found in Antarctica—earth's oldest and most grandiose pyramid, twice the size of the Great Pyramid on the Giza Plateau.

It was, however, also covered in Egyptian hieroglyphics, a strong indication it was likely the pyramid from which all other pyramids derived their uniformity.

When every square inch of the earth was scanned and plotted, and there was no more knowledge to be had, humanity put their accumulated texts into their AI database and awaited instruction.

The Oracle's instructions were rather unambiguous; humanity was to follow in the footsteps of their maker and become a space-faring species. They explored the moon first, then Mars, Phobos, and Europa. In short order, they explored every planetary body in the solar system and stumbled upon ancient ruins in these places, too. Each place left a breadcrumb to the origins of humanity.

The debris of evidence suggested these ancient peoples killed each other in a cataclysmic war that spanned the entire solar system. The presence of pyramids, monoliths, and Egyptian hieroglyphs proved beyond a shadow of a doubt that a select group escaped the destruction and were the progenitor race the ancient texts speak of. Earth was the spoils of the victor. They first touched down in Antarctica circa 250,000 BCE and fanned out from there to warmer climates, eventually instructing the ancient peoples of Sumer, Egypt, Asia, and South America, in every discipline.

Although these finds were rich in knowledge, they lacked a certain credibility that could only be gleaned from a survivor. After finding nothing but destruction and ruins on Pluto, the logical assumption was that if there were any survivors left, they would be found outside the solar system. And with the Oracle's blessing, humanity decided to leave its cradle—the Milky Way Galaxy.

The Oracle was designed with one prime directive: the continuation of the human species was paramount in any decision-making process. As such, it was the Oracle's contention that so long as the earth remained habitable, a fingerprint of humanity should remain. A global lottery was instated to decide who would stay and who would go. And it was so. Half the population remained on earth while the others became space-faring nomads. They left their home with the promise to one day return.

As time passed and generations died, a growing resentment developed between the separated humans like a petty sibling rivalry gone awry. Like most mutual resentments, each waited on an apology that never came, and the animosity was left to fester. The time between communications became few and far between and, ever stubborn, neither party budged until they crossed that invisible line of estranged relations and became nothing more than an afterthought, old acquaintances, strangers.

However, for the humans on earth, this lapse in time without so much as a progress report wasn't entirely intentional. In 2130, a massive solar flare fried the power grids on earth, effectively sending them back to the stone age. The Oracle was among the casualties, and without its guidance, the humans on earth very nearly went extinct trying to relearn the rudimentary skills they had forgotten in the process of turning their lives over to the care of the machines. With the fabric of society broken down, pockets of humanity survived in small clusters, slowly relearning how to make fire and the like.

The space humans didn't fare much better. The further into the cosmos we traveled, the more the composition of our physiology changed. It became apparent, rather quickly, that human physiology was not equipped to sustain the expanded rigors of space and zero gravity. At the Oracle's behest, we started augmenting our bodies with AI technologies.

We exchanged organs for pumps, wires for veins, and eyes for optical lenses, capable of seeing in all spectrums. Each generation tinkered more than the last until we were more machine than human. It was an inevitable transition, the Oracle explained. Man was built with a low tolerance for limitations, the driving force of society. Ancient Egyptians had prosthetic hands. Cochlear implants replaced hearing aids; Lasik replaced ocular lenses. Man has forever tinkered with their bodies, and we were no different. Our post-biological physiology became absolute when we implanted neuro links in our brains to communicate telepathically. But we didn't anticipate that when we became symbiotic with the Oracle, we relinquished our right to remain symbiotic with source.

It was then—when it was already too late—that we realized our meddling with nature had rendered us sterile. Procreation had become a small miracle in the large space fleet. To offset this unforeseen anomaly, we endeavored to create designer babies in labs. The experiment was both a smashing success and a miserable failure. The first generation was a genuinely incredible species, capable of amazing feats. God-like, even. We were, however, wholly sterile.

In accordance with its prime directive, and to ensure the continuation of the species, the Oracle had no recourse but to abort the mission of exploration, the mission for man to meet their maker. We returned home to a foreign and desolate land.

Vegetation had swallowed the buildings, and sparse human populations scattered the wastelands. There was no discernible order to their congregation other than most of the villages set up near fresh bodies of water. The rest followed herds of wildlife, reverting to their hunter-gatherer ways. Indeed, they looked like rabid cavemen and had long forgotten most of their past.

What was remembered, however, passed down orally by each succeeding generation, was the promise of the return of their sky brethren. But over the years, the stories developed a certain mystique contrasting with truth, and we became like gods to them. So, they hunted and ate and mated and looked up to the heavens and waited on the return of their gods.

After 4,576 years in space, our physical appearance had been drastically altered. The zero gravity had made the tallest of us four feet tall and our muscles atrophied into spindly twigs. Our travels had taken us to cold and dark places. Our eyes acclimated, became enlarged and darkened, our skin taut and gray from lack of sunlight. Because of the vast difference in our physical appearances and our divine-like abilities, when our ships descended from the heavens, earth humans thought the prophecy fulfilled, and then history repeated itself.

Akin to when Cortes landed in South America, earth humans revered these tiny, gray beings, with magical-like abilities, as gods. They threw precious gems at our feet and pelts around our shoulders; a welcoming, albeit surprising turn of events. We thought it would take some convincing to mend the looming animosity that wasn't there.

We took advantage of the circumstances and tried mating with them. It was, however, a careless and unfortunate oversight.

In our time spent as interstellar globetrotters, we acquired natural antibodies from exotic fauna and flora life. Conversely, due to the diluted efficacy of the Ambrosia antibodies inherited from our ancestors, earth humans were unable to fend off any novel diseases, and by the time anyone considered quarantine, it was already too late. A galloping fauna disease raped its way through their ranks, and the few remaining earth humans were utterly wiped out.

With earth humans dead and gone, and our festering inability to procreate, the fate of humanity seemed destined to a singular outcome—extinction.

Once again, the Oracle came to the rescue, suggesting time regression as our only viable option. We had picked up bits of knowledge on the matter in our travels but never had the opportunity to attempt such an audacious endeavor as it requires a complex system that augments the energy from a planetary body in conjunction with the sun of which it orbits. Now that we were back on earth, we had both.

We identified ancient sites on earth's ley lines that optimize the earth-sun marriage's geomagnetic energies. These places are susceptible to function as portals during certain times of the year.

We decided to utilize the strongest vortex, The Gateway of The Gods in Puma Punku, and put our machines to work. They gutted the melted infrastructure and replaced the wires with advanced quantum fiber optics capable of harnessing the sun's immense power. In this way, we created a stargate that allowed us to navigate time and space.

We have traveled back in time many thousands of years because we need your help—if you are willing.

The instantaneous upload was an immersive virtual experience complete with sensory systems, indistinguishable from reality. Betty was back on the steel table in less than a second. Her resting heart rate climbed to two hundred BPM, and her BP approached stroke level numbers. The medical examiner did something on the rotating holograph, and the steel table Betty laid on turned into red mercury. A medicinal liquid absorbed through her skin and her vitals stabilized in an instant.

"Was ... was that *real?*" Betty said between staggered breaths. "I felt like I was *there.*"

You were, the leader thought. *In a manner of speaking. Your brain cannot distinguish between reality and the quantum field any more than it can between reality and a dream.*

Betty examined their large, mesmerizing eyes. The experience she just had made her aware that they were seeing her in different spectrums, and she now also knew that their intentions were pure. They meant her no harm.

"So, you are us from the future," Betty said, "and you need my help to ensure the continuation of the human species."

Yes ma'am, the leader thought.

"I'd love to help," Betty said, "but I can't possibly imagine how."

We need permission to extract your ova, the medical examiner thought.

"My whata?" Betty was confused.

Your egg cells, the medical examiner thought.

Though the quantum vision she just had didn't last more than a second, in the quantum realm, it lasted many years. She felt a close connection to these majestic beings, and she was besieged with a fierce longing to help them.

"I'm happy to help," she said, not fully realizing what she was doing.

As soon as she agreed to help, a medical team of four gray beings walked into the room. Two of them were four feet tall; the other two were six inches shorter. Levitating trays floated in between them, and as they approached, Betty noticed tools that resembled dentistry equipment. They split into two teams of two. One team further prepared the instruments while the other team examined Betty. The leader grabbed a clipboard and flipped through the pages.

I must first warn you, the leader thought, *you may experience some side effects from the procedure.*

"What kind of side effects?" Betty asked apprehensively.

One gray shone a bright light into her mouth, eyes, and ears while the other counted vertebrae. Betty winced at its cold hands. The gray retracted, rubbed its hands together for a few seconds, then continued the process with fingertips regulated at the optimal temperature of 98.6 degrees Fahrenheit.

We must put your eggs into a quantum incubator, the medical examiner thought, *which will connect you to the quantum field in a major way.*

"So, what's the problem?" Betty couldn't see the relevance.

The grays assigned to the tools had completed their setup and stood by waiting, while the ones examining Betty tested her reflexes, rotating and tugging at her extremities.

Well, we don't know yet, the medical examiner thought. *You will be our first—our Eve.*

"I like the sound of that," Betty said.

But the Oracle has given us explicit instruction to warn you that since we are mucking about in the quantum field, the medical examiner thought, *and your subconscious mind operates solely in this realm,* he paused, *you will likely experience some incredibly vivid dreams.*

Dreams, Betty thought, almost amused. "That's not so bad," she said.

Well, we say dreams, the leader thought, *but it will be more like the immersive virtual experience you just had. Since everything that has ever happened or is going to happen exists simultaneously in the quantum field of the Akasha, you will, in fact, be time-traveling; you will be unable to distinguish a separation between your life and the people and animals you will be connected to. You will see through their eyes. Their experiences will become your own, and really, there is no predicting what you will dream.*

"That sounds like a grand time," Betty said.

Indeed, the leader thought, *unless, of course, they are nightmares.*

There was no way to be sure—for his mouth was too small to tell decisively—but Betty thought she saw the slightest semblance of a knowing smirk tug at the corner of the leader's tiny mouth.

How suspicious, she thought as the calming effects of the mist wore off.

The medical examiner and the leader shared a curious glance, and another mist released into the air. Betty welcomed the deep solace that accompanied it.

So, do you consent? the medical examiner asked opportunistically.

Betty Hill was a good woman, a noble woman. She dedicated her life to the pursuit of helping others. She was a social worker and an active member of the NAACP, and she wanted nothing more than to help her future relatives.

"Anything I can do to help," she said, "is just fine by me."

Splendid, the medical examiner thought. He pulled a page out of the clipboard and told her to sign on the dotted line.

Betty grabbed the paper and gave it a once-over. "What's this?" she asked.

This one, the leader thought, *is a research and development compliance saying you are in fact aware that you will henceforth have intimate ties to all of humanity, along with infinite alternate realities since we're delving into the quantum field.*

Betty signed the paper, and the other team of little gray beings went to work. They grabbed their tools. Scraped her fingernails. Swabbed her mouth. Scrubbed skin cultures into glass containers.

The medical examiner handed Betty another sheet.

"And what's this?" she said as one of the gray's cut a lock of her hair and placed it into a container.

Run-of-the-mill NDA, the medical examiner thought, *we can't have you remembering any of this, so,* he paused, *we must mind-wipe you.*

Betty's head snapped sharply.

It's a harmless procedure, the medical examiner assured, *you will remember bits and pieces but not enough to piece anything together absolutely. Unless, of course,* he looked at the leader nervously, *you get hypnotized.*

The team of grays wrapped up the systematic process. They placed a large syringe at the end of the table and left the room with the various samples.

After Betty signed the NDA, the medical examiner waved his hand, and everything went black.

Betty and Barney Hill found themselves back in their 1957 Chevrolet Bel Air. The clock read 12:30 a.m. They could not account for the last two hours, and they were thirty-five miles south of their last known location, going in the opposite direction. They had gone backwards somehow.

It was dark. They were on the side of the highway. Crickets sang from the sea of tall grass a few feet off the shoulder of the road. The air was warm, inviting.

"What the hell happened," Barney said.

As if to answer the question, a bright light exploded from the right. There, forty feet into the grass, parked on the ground as if it were just another car, was a massive saucer-shaped vehicle, which elevated ten feet off the ground, spinning, glowing. There was a row of windows that went around the equator of the ship, and in the windows were small people waving bye. Then the vehicle shot vertically at impossible speeds, disappearing in the canopy of stars above.

They were in a daze the rest of the drive, and when they got home, they noticed several peculiar occurrences: both of their watches had stopped working at 10:30; the top of Betty's shoes were scraped as if she had been dragged somewhere; and her new dress was torn in several places.

Betty was too tired to piece everything together: the spaceship, the missing time, the torn dress. It was all too much and would have to wait until the morning to delve into.

She placed her torn dress into the closet and laid in bed. She tossed and turned until a wave of exhaustion hit her with force.

She slipped into REM like a warm blanket, and a paralyzing anxiety enveloped her with the decision she was being forced to make.

The Gender Reveal Party

IT WAS UNSEASONABLY HOT FOR EARLY APRIL. Last night's rain hung in the air, rising off the earth in hazy plumes, drenching everything in a fresh layer of condensation. In direct sunlight, the temperature was unforgiving. But under the shade, it was divine. And shade is where this story takes place—shade from the massive canopy of an eastern cottonwood tree, to be exact. The tree sat in the middle of the backyard as it had sat for many years past. It was a massive tree with a base diameter the size of a monster truck tire, thick and ancient and full of life as a family of hatchlings could attest, tweeting and twirping in their nest on the long branch that dangled over the picnic table, their constant cries a beautiful backdrop noise as they vied for Mama's attention.

The sun's rays winked through the thick canopy of dancing leaves. The light breeze carried hints of nearby juniper and fresh-cut grass upon its ethereal wings.

Yes, by all accounts, it was an utterly perfect day for a gender reveal.

The party stirred with great excitement on this most joyous of occasions. An assembly line of giggling children weaved between the talking adults, slithering about like an accordion snake, only stopping to throw blue and pink poppers at each other's feet in the massive fenced-in backyard, which was outfitted in pink and blue streamers, balloons, hanging paper flyers, pom-pom flowers, and garland strings. The pink and blue were equal in representation. Every decoration carefully alternated between each color so that everything blue was married to its pink counterpart. There was a perfect symmetry to it, a certain familiarity that made one feel safe.

The gender reveal planner had truly outdone herself; everyone thought so. It's all they spoke of as they sipped coffee from their pink and blue booty mugs, which doubled as perfectly charming parting gifts.

"Just look at these adorable little booty mugs," Mrs. Robinson said.

She held the little pink mug before her face, meticulously regarding it as if it were an ancient relic unearthed for the first time in millennia. Then, looking at the blue mug her husband drank from, thoughtfully, she said, "Do you suspect we're gonna have a snip it or plug it kinda day?"

"Ray and Shirley say it could go either way," Mr. Robinson said with a subtle shrug.

Ray Anderson was grilling in the far corner. His wife, Shirley, busied herself filling booty mugs with coffee and handing out cleverly themed *hors d'oeuvres* like baby pigs in a blanket. They stole a glance at each other, eyes twinkling as if their souls were on fire, burning brightly, twin flames united, an eternal love. They were the kind of couple other couples either envied or despised, but for the same reason: theirs was a storybook love. They were also the expectant parents of the child being celebrated at the gender reveal party and host to said event.

Ray placed the burgers and dogs in a plastic container and gave it to his Domestic Android System, who placed a lid on the container and brought it to the serving table.

"Lu-nch ... is ... re-dee," the DAS said in a monotone voice, its pixelated eyes scanning the faces in the crowd for one reason or another. The Andersons were upper-middle class and while most homes were host to the older model DASes—the clunkier, clumsier ones—the Andersons were fortunate to afford one of the newer model DAS. At 6'0, and 90 lbs., the new DAS was shorter and less girthy than its predecessor. It had a sleek, streamlined skeleton with extra power to the digits which made for better dexterity. Its head was essentially a small, oval-shaped screen with a pixelated face.

The children screamed and ran to the line like famished savages.

"Slow down, little ones," Shirley said. She winked at her husband. "There's more than enough for everyone."

"Why didn't you let your DAS grill, Ray?" Mr. Robinson asked. "Mine cooks, cleans, and has even given me a handski when my wife had one of her timely headaches."

Everyone laughed as Mrs. Robinson hit her cheeky husband playfully on the arm.

"Soon, you won't need a wife at all," Ray joked. He winked at Mrs. Robinson to ensure she knew he was joking. "I let mine do most things," he said. "Heck, it even tuned up the zero-g converter in my antigrav last week—it was flying funny. I just love grilling. There's something very—" He paused, looking for the right word. "—*primal* about it."

Ray nodded, approving. Yes, primal was applicable, what with the proliferation of DASes and 3D replicators. Cooking had become a lost art, and grilling was all but extinct. He even had to special order the grill he currently played on because the newer grills were built with a digital interface only compatible with the corresponding homes' DAS. He'd paid extravagantly for the alterations and the permit. But he was old enough to remember what authentic, charcoal barbecue tasted like, and though replicators were remarkably similar, they lacked a certain degree of smokiness that could only come from real smoke. The consensus seemed to be that it was worth it.

Two birthday cakes sat on the picnic table in the middle of the yard. The one on the left was decked with blue icing. Its opposite was dressed in a bright pink fondue frosting. Perched atop each cake stood the number seven. Written in white coloring on each cake were the words, "Happy 7th Birthday, Jesse." The only distinction between the cakes aside from the coloring was the letters under the greeting: on the blue cake, it read xy; its pink counterpart read xx.

Feeding the kids was a simple enough task. The lot of them enjoyed their burgers and dogs without the exhaustive burden of choosing accompanying condiments.

"Chew your food, Taylor," Mrs. Marshall said to her three-year-old. "It isn't going anywhere."

After the last child ran away perfectly content, the adults congregated to the line, which moved sluggishly as they placed their burgers under a roof of lettuce, tomato, and onion, then doused it in their choice of condiments.

But it was the New Chicago dog bar at the end of the table that was really slowing down the line.

"I can't wait to see what they pick," Mrs. Jackson said. "I can hardly stand the suspense," she added eagerly, and as she stared at the small medical tent tucked away in the corner of the yard, she wondered if the procedure hurt terribly. *I'm glad I'll never have to find out,* she thought with a shudder.

"What do you think your little Drew will pick," Mr. Robinson asked. "They'll be seven next year, right?"

"Yes, they will be, and it's hard to say really," Mrs. Jackson said. "Like little Jesse Anderson, it could go either way."

Mr. Robinson nodded in agreement. "My Sammy was the same just a few years ago," he said. "We didn't know what she was going to pick 'til she did. I'd half hoped she'd pick xy." He paused thoughtfully, then: "But I can't say I'm disappointed she picked double x. Little girls love their papas 'til they're old n' gray." He looked at the ground resentfully, eyes growing big with tears, heartache. "Little boys go off and fight in wars as my Angel did."

"He died for a noble cause, your Angel did," Mrs. Jackson said, putting a kind hand on his shoulder. "Those naturalists are stuck in the past." She turned her head and spat on the ground.

At the mention of naturalists, there was a sudden shift in energy spawned forth by patriotic fervor; an aggressive and palpable shift that started in the pits of their stomachs and rose to their chest and rose and rose, until their fingertips tingled with a burning desire to defend their way of life. Everyone but Mr. Robinson felt it. It was always the same for Mr. Robinson. People didn't speak to him if not to express pity in some form or another. It was exhausting to him, all the sad eyes, the hushed whispers, the sudden and sullen silences when he walked into a room, as if his son's ghost walked alongside him, a preview of what was to come for those with kids currently fighting on the frontlines. He pulled out his flask, poured a drink on the ground for his dearly departed son, then took a gulp of heavy scotch and stepped forward a few inches as the line progressed.

"My Cameron is joining the fight next year." Mrs. Davis had just finished preparing her hamburger and was presently waiting in the line for the New Chicago hotdog bar. "He says he can't *wait* to kill some naturalist rebels." She paused, nodding to herself with far eyes, then: "It should be a choice, after all."

"*A choice it should be.*" This from everyone within earshot range.

A wave of excited murmurs started at the front of the party and made its way to the lunch line. An older gentleman came waltzing in with a young boy on his heels. Every time the older man took a step, a light hissing was heard, birthed by the hydraulic pistons in his leg, a prosthetic android.

"What are *they* doing here?" Mrs. Jackson said in disgust.

"Be nice, Susie," Shirley said, "my father is too old to change."

"He should be too old to have kids then," Mrs. Jackson said with her hands on her hips.

Shirley looked at her with smiling eyes and gave her a knowing smirk. Her eyes said, *I agree.* But her lips said, "Perhaps. In any event, you all be nice to my little brother now. He's only four and innocent in allathis."

A little boy came running up to Shirley and jumped excitedly into her arms. "Hey, Jacky boy, goodness, have you gotten big." She ticked his belly playfully and said, "Run along and play with the other kids now."

Baby Jack's countenance suddenly changed. He went from all smiles to a grave, terrified look, full of ambivalence and fear.

"But they don't like me," Baby Jack said. His shoulders slumped forward, his face sank, eyes on the ground, tears threatening to escape.

"Sure, they do." Shirley rubbed her little brother's back.

"*Naha,*" he said, "they were calling me names like naturalist and natty at the last gender reveal, and no one would play with me."

Shirley examined the playing kids. Her child, Jesse, and their best friend Bailey played with gender-neutral dolls while others kicked a soccer ball around. She noticed a few kids pointing and snickering at her younger brother, causing a primal wave of mama bear anger to stir in the pit of her stomach.

"I'm sorry to hear that, little man," Shirley said, "but you mustn't give 'em that power. You must be brave. Besides, Jesse will be there for you this time."

Little Jack's eyes lit up at the mention of Jesse. He always looked up to his older neicew.

"Do you know what they're going to pick?" Jack whispered with raised eyebrows. Shirley looked at her little brother's face brimming with genuine curiosity.

"I don't. But I rather like the surprise," Shirley whispered. "Now run along."

Jack scurried off and found Jesse to wish them a happy birthday. Jack was a dying breed in the New Republic of America. Very few women had natural pregnancies anymore. Most of them received testosterone/estrogen treatments aggressive enough to offset the natural biological makeup of their fetus.

The gender modification treatment program had been around for twenty-five years. The result was four generations of born hermaphrodites.

"Hiya, doll face." Jack Sr. kissed his daughter on the cheek. "Boy, it's a scorcher," he said as he removed his purple heart WWIII cap and wiped his brow.

"Heya, Pops," Shirley said, "how goes it?"

Never one to shy away, Jack Sr. let his daughter know exactly how it went. "These fuckin' fanatics won't leave Jack Jack alone. He's getting bullied every day," he said vehemently, thrashing his arms at the sky, pointing at unseen enemies. "Goddamn school is a breeding ground for little shits. I'd kick their asses myself if I weren't certain to be euthanized."

"Don't do anything stupid, Pops," Shirley said. "Jack needs you."

"I've got it covered." He wriggled his eyebrows in that coy way he used to at the breakfast table when Shirley was in middle school and, after his wife departed for work, he'd alert the school she was "feeling ill" and they'd spend the day either playing magnetic golf, hoverball, or, when she hit high school, underwater speargunning.

Shirley was afraid to ask what "I've got it covered" entailed. But her face must've hinted at inquiry, because Jack Sr. leaned in and whispered, "I'm paying the Larson boy on the down low to protect him."

"You are *not*."

The caravan of laughing tykes cut through the talking adults like an ancient river cutting a mountain valley in half. Running anchor on the commode was a pudgy boy with bright red hair. He was the biggest kid at the party and was out of shape, leaning over, huffing, puffing. The rolls on his arms shook as he coughed. The kid's name was Sam xy Larson. When Sam stopped coughing, he was delighted to see who was before him. "Hey, Mr. Jack," he said with one of those goofy, conspicuous looks kids accidentally portray when they're in on a secret or prank; guilty and culpable and it was obvious to anyone who cared to notice that they were up to no good. Sam then ran off with his fists clenched, chasing away a band of would-be bullies from Jack Jr.'s area, duly fulfilling his bodyguard duties.

Shirley's gaze slowly went back to her father. Her head tilted; a serious look transformed her face, her aura, from giddy happiness to a stern cautiousness, visible to the eyes, palpable to those with the sight. She spoke the next words slowly, quietly: "And what do you think they'll do … when he gets in trouble for beating a kid up and tells on you?" she asked.

He shrugged and said, "I'll jus' deny it." He had this blasé demeanor about him that was enviable and dangerous in equal measures. Shirley wished she didn't put so much stock in the opinions of others. She wished she could have her father's bravery, saying what she wanted, when she wanted, expressing her opinion as an individual instead of conforming with the mob rule. But, then again, where some people saw bravery, others saw carelessness. Not only was it unpopular to speak so brazenly and openly against certain aspects of the New Republic of America, but it was also dangerous, too. Rumors of government plans to quell dissenters had already been circling for several years. Leaked documents containing names and lists and locations of "internment camps" where they planned on rounding up those they deemed worthy enough to "reeducate" and plug back into circulation after they'd proven they would no longer be a problem. But for those already too far gone to be considered salvageable, well …

Shirley had spent a great many night trying to convince her father to tone down the pro-naturalist rhetoric. But he was too old to change. Stuck in his ways with what he fancied an inalienable infringement on his rights to foster opinions—popular or unpopular—a right he fought for; a right he was ready to die for; a right that was slowly disintegrating with each passing day.

But a gender reveal party wasn't the venue to pick a fight on such matters. Shirley bit her tongue, too, but she couldn't remove the disapproving look in her eyes. It was a peculiar look that Jack had rarely seen from his oldest child, whose chipper disposition came stock with the baby who was all smiles, a bundle of joy really. The look penetrated a myriad of paternal insecurities forcing him to further argue his reasons.

"You don't see him coming home every day, Shir. His confidence is shit," Jack Sr. said. "It breaks my heart to see the little man just so."

The disapproving look on Shirley's face melted away, replaced with that mother bear anger once more. She was old enough to remember how bad it had gotten before the gender modification program equaled the playing field. She saw a group of kids huddled around a table, whispering, snickering, gawking at her little brother. She recalled doing the same thing to a girl named Beth Cassidy in seventh grade. Beth took her own life that same night, but the guilt haunted Shirley to this day. The gender modification program was instituted the following year.

Yes, the disapproving look had changed indeed, and Jack Sr. saw an opportunistic window to better argue his reasons.

"I tried doing it properly, kiddo, I *did*," he said in earnest. "I talked to the parents and when it continued, I talked with the school board, but they disagree with the Republic's decision on letting us old-timers choose. They think I'm a naturalist. Which I am but that's beside the—"

Shirley grabbed her father's arm and led him next to the medical tent. "What is *wrong* with *you*?" she asked.

In a world that boasted intercontinental maglev bullet trains and flying cars, the medical tent—perhaps the most important aspect of their society—was small and modest; ten square feet with an arching ceiling that apexed in the middle so it looked more like a carnival tent than a medical one. The walls were made of a thick, white canvas and the door flapped in the wind, exposing a tray with an array of surgical tools and a small operating table in the middle.

Jack Sr. was uncomfortable being so close to the medical tent. Shivers ran down his spine. *Absolutely barbaric,* he thought.

Shirley knew he wasn't listening, so she snapped, "*Dad.*"

"*What?*"

"You can't say shit like that here, Pops."

"Why not?" he said, slowly raising his arms at his side. "This is still New America, is it not?"

"Everyone here is a choicer." Shirley's patience was running thin with her father. It seemed the older he got, the less he cared about conforming and as time progressed, the accepted tolerance for such behavior was on the decline. Soon it would be illegal to speak those words and she didn't want her father euthanized. She tried appealing to her father's humanity instead, her father's experience with war: "Some of these people's kids have died fighting naturalist rebels," she said.

Jack Sr. looked up to a sea of eyes squinting hatefully at him. Some would look away when he looked at them. But many refused. They just kept on squinting hatefully at him. "I didn't mean nothin' by it," he said, "all's I'm saying is that the school is like a prison yard for Jack Jack. And the fuckers won't protect him, so I had no choice but to buy him some protection." He paused for effect, then with the most serious look Shirley had ever seen on her father's face, he said, "It was either that or kill a kid, Shir."

Shirley knew her father well. He was a good man. An honorable man rich with integrity. He could be stubborn in his ways, sure, but not maliciously so. He was more often misunderstood than anything. But she also knew he *would* kill a kid to protect Jack Jr. and that he was just trying to mitigate circumstance to avoid having to personally get physical.

"I understand, Dad. Can we talk about this later, please? Just make sure there's no proof of your little shady dealings with Larson."

"I'll cancel the checks," Jack Sr. said with a smirk.

Shirley's hands went to her hips. She tilted her head, unamused. "I'm serious," she said.

"Sorry," Jack Sr. offered.

"You will be if his uncle finds out," Shirley said, scoffing. "Seriously though, you couldn't find a kid who has ties in the Mars or asteroid mining business? You had to pick a kid whose uncle is head of the New Chicago Department of Euthanasia?"

In 2075, the biggest problem any government faced was combating overpopulation. To this end, the New Republic of America implemented a controversial program to rid itself of certain undesirable demographics: rapists, pedophiles, and murderers were euthanized outright; any senior citizens deemed a danger to themselves, or others, would be put on a termination list where they'd adhere to a point system. Walking around naked was one point. Driving around aimlessly was ten points, which just so happened to be the ceiling.

Rounding out the euthanasia list was anyone with a terminal medical condition who wished to end their suffering. Mercy suicides, they were called. Everyone assumed, by the direction things were going, that naturalists, or anyone else deemed a threat to the New Republic, would soon be joining the list.

Jack Sr. looked at the ground and sunk in like a dog that had just soiled the carpet. Shirley felt bad. She knew firsthand how cruel kids could be. She also knew he meant well.

"I'm over it, Pops," she said. "Wadasay we get you some grub, yeah?"

The hissing hydraulics followed Jack Sr. around, an audible shadow. She sat him down then introduced him: "Dad, this is the Jacksons," she said, pointing, "and the Davises," point, "Robinsons. Everyone, this is my father." A few people nodded their heads at him, but most paid him no mind.

After Shirley brought her father the plate, her attention was caught by a woman standing alone next to the medical tent. The woman was very official looking. She was decked in black slacks and shoes and wore a standard issue federal government gortex coat with the words "GMB" in gold letters embroidered on the back. Her name badge read Officer Biles. She flailed her arms, trying to get Shirley's attention. Once they locked eyes, she tapped her watch resolutely. The party had to adhere to a strict itinerary, Biles was there to ensure as such. Shirley looked at her watch. *Where has the time gone?* she thought.

"Okay, everyone, please listen up. This is Officer Biles," Shirley said.

"She is a coordinator slash auditor with the Gender Modification Bureau. Please give her your undivided attention."

Officer Biles cleared her throat then: "Under the authority of the New Republic of America and in accordance with the Gender Modification Bureau, case number 92515903 shall commence in thirty minutes." She pivoted and spoke to the other half. "After Jesse has picked a gender nomenclature, we'll sing happy birthday to him or her and welcome them into the fold." After a brief pause, she added the bureau's motto. "Any day is a great day for a gender reveal," she said. "It should be a choice, after all."

"*A choice it should be*," droned everyone in unison.

Shirley clapped her hands and jumped and squealed, excited. She ran to her husband, who was huddled in a corner with a few of the other fathers watching the Cubs game on a small device that projected a hologram of the game that was so real, you could almost smell peanuts and crackerjacks.

What an utterly perfect day, Shirley thought.

The entire party was lively but for Jack Sr.'s table, where an uncomfortable silence loomed about. When the DAS brought fresh drinks to the table, Jack Sr. excused himself to use the restroom. During his tour in China, an android soldier had shot his kneecap off. He'd had problems being around them without a certain level of anxiety ever since.

When he returned from the bathroom, everyone stopped talking.

"No, you ask him," Mr. Davis whispered to his beautiful wife.

"Ask me what?" Jack Sr. said.

"Oh, nothing pertinent," Mr. Davis said, meekly.

Jack Sr. took a bite out of his New Chicago dog. "Oh, come off it, man." He wiped his mouth with a napkin. "I doubt you pulled such a beautiful wife by being so timid." He winked playfully at Mrs. Davis. "Just ask. I promise I won't get offended by the question if you promise not to get offended by the answer."

"Fair enough. Why didn't you guys conform?" Mrs. Davis asked eagerly. "Was it *really* just the age bit? Or was it personal preference? Or what?"

Jack examined the faces at the table. The hatred he was so used to seeing was no longer in their eyes, just genuine curiosity. The oldest person, Mrs. Davis, was in her early thirties, so they all had lived most of their lives in the new system. It was hard for them to fathom anyone going against the grain, not following the herd. Jack considered playing it coy, mysterious; but he thought maybe if he could convince the parents of the kids bullying his son that they were good people, they could assert some authority and end the madness.

"Welp, my wife and I were 2020 babies," he said. "I remember when all this talk about gender neutrality started, and I understand the reasoning behind it. I do." He looked at the ground, eyes vacant, remembering. "People used to treat the LGBTQ community in the old America like they were lepers. Suicides were at an all-time high. Family and friends often did not even know a kid was homosexual until they found their cold dead bodies. And there were lots of bodies."

"One hundred and fifty children a day, right?" Mrs. Davis asked. She was the resident history teacher and was enthralled thus far.

"At its height," Jack Sr. said, nodding. "But even just one is one too many."

The heads at the table all bobbed at the same time, giving Jack the impression the picnic table was a boat that just hit choppy water. Mrs. Davis in particular was touched by Jack's sincerity.

"Around the time I was in fifth grade," Jack Sr. said, "they surpassed veterans for the highest demographic of suicides—not something to boast about. Each year that number climbed steadily. It was an epidemic of the soul. Poor children, killing themselves because they saw no end to their torment."

He often worried his son would succumb to the same fate. Whenever Jack Jr. had a difficult day at school or came home early because no one would play with him, those were the worst days. If he were too quiet in his room, Jack Sr. would make a reason to come in, any reason at all. He always feared he'd find his son dangling from a rope. But usually, he was just crying into a pillow.

"I've seen firsthand what being an undesirable outcast does to a kid's confidence and self-worth, and I agree they should've done something—but to make everyone hermaphrodites until seven and then allow them to choose the gender they identify seems a bit ... *extreme*. No? The source of the problem was the bullies, not the sexual orientation of the kids they were bullying."

"Yes, but it should be a choice after all." This from Officer Biles, who was hovering about the table.

"A choice it should be," said everyone but Jack Sr.

"Do you not know the retort?" Officer Biles asked, squinting at Jack Sr. with a penetrating gaze.

"Yes, it should be a choice. Of course, it should be," Jack Sr. said nervously. "I've known men so feminine; it boggles the mind to think God would be so cruel. As if on the day they were born, the spirits went into the wrong bodies, and you'd have a six-foot-five, three-hundred-pound beast of a man with the mannerisms of a woman."

"The human spirit is both male and female," Officer Biles said, "so why can't the body be, too?"

Jack looked around the table, thinking, grinning. "You promise you won't get offended?" The picnic boat crested on another wave, as they all nodded in agreement. "I'm a naturalist at heart."

There was a minor uproar. Everyone raised from their seats. Napkins were thrown. Food was dropped. Drinks spilled.

"I knew it," some said. "Unbelievable," said others. "In this day and age?"

Officer Biles's face was ever placid. She stared at Jack, eyes vacant, distant, as if she were in the middle of a particularly mundane daydream. He couldn't get a read on her. It was mightily unnerving for Jack. *Could I get in trouble for this?* he thought. *Of course not. It isn't illegal to be a naturalist if you aren't a terrorist. Not yet.*

Self-preservation prompted him to explain himself out of the self-imposed hole.

"But I'm not a fanatic," Jack Sr. assured. "I'm just ... old school, s'all. I believe everyone is beautiful no matter what race, creed, or sexual orientation they identify." He could tell he was losing the support of his lone ally, Mrs. Davis.

"Us deciding not to take the hormones was a thoroughly considered choice," continued Jack Sr. "My wife, God rest her soul, was in menopause and couldn't receive the treatment—it's a marvel she got pregnant in the first place. We would've had an abortion if it wasn't outlawed outright in the 2040s. And when we discovered Jack was a boy, the doctor said she was too old to take the estrogen injections to offset the testosterone and grow both parts. He said it'd kill her. But in the end, it was the birth that did her in, and ..."

Jack Sr.'s voice broke off as the speakers on the drones hovering over the party came to life with a special report:

The New United States Congress has just passed a bill in a unanimous decision to extend the gender modification program another twenty-five years. The bill will remain the same with a few amendments—the Gender Modification Bureau has recognized your grievances of the lack of options for preapproved unisex names. As such, the list has been bolstered with twenty-two additions. We will be sending this list out presently.

At that moment, everyone's smartwatches vibrated and buzzed.

"Kelly, Stacy, Charlie ..." Mrs. Davis read from her smartwatch. Her voice broke off as the report continued.

The new amendment also stipulates senior citizens will no longer be exempt. They will conform or be euthanized. Speaker of the house Chad Hutchins had this to say, "While we are sympathetic to our elderly citizens, we decided to include them into the fold for their safety and the safety of their children. They were the only ones exempt in the previous bill, and while most elderly citizens are barren, about one percent do retain the ability to procreate in their later years. What time has shown us is that there's been a pronounced uptick in adolescent suicides among the population of children born from these elderly parents. When we started this program, it was to protect all our children—sadly, we have failed them. The inclusion of the elderly is an attempt to remedy this. No child shall be left behind. All pregnant mothers will receive the offset treatment regardless of age, or, they may choose to be euthanized.

In other news, terrorists from a naturalist rebel cell bombed several gender modification treatment facilities in a well-coordinated attack across all twelve districts. The cowardly acts left twenty-five dead and ten injured. Only a few months ago, they ...

Shirley hurriedly consulted her smartwatch and muted the drone home entertainment system's speakers. She swiped down on the screen. The drones descended to the ground, retracted their wings to digest the sun's rays for future use.

"Hey," Jack Sr. said, "I was listenin' to that."

"Are you sympathetic to the naturalists' cause, sir?" Officer Biles asked. She scrutinized his purple heart WWIII hat as if he should be ashamed.

"That's *absurd*," Jack Sr. said. "Did you not hear what I just said?"

Officer Biles didn't answer. No one said a word. Even the kids stopped playing. Everything so quiet, still; the air suddenly seemed more humid, oppressive. Five seconds passed and still, no one moved or spoke. Everyone was scared that Officer Biles would enact an executive order and have the DAS euthanize Jack Sr. on site. Which was just a Barney way of saying execute.

Utter silence can be the loudest noise ever conceived in awkward moments, when time stands still, seemingly in reverse, stretching three seconds to feel an eternity.

It was Mrs. Robinson who was brave enough to speak first.

"My parents were at the first rebel attacks twenty-five years ago," she said.

"The naturalist rebels were then what they are now: religious fanatics hellbent on the sanctity of the Holy Bible," Officer Biles said. "The church started the first conversion therapies in the 2010s. They shamelessly sent their youth to exorcise the evil, homosexual tendencies out of them. But a person cannot change who they are at their core. A zebra cannot remove its stripes. Nor should they have to."

She examined the faces at the table. Gender Modification Agent duties entailed a wide scope of responsibilities. The most important being, of course, gender reveal party planning. But they had other duties that some would say were just as important. Such as the dissemination of knowledge and information. They were part of a select few who were allowed in one of the twelve citadels. Everyone else had to take them at their word. They were the new keepers of knowledge, like the priest and shamans before them. Knowledge was power and the New Republic of America preferred to keep their citizens ignorant, docile, and complacent. But even Officer Biles didn't know if what she read in the history books was what really happened or a propaganda campaign as those naturalists' vermin claim. She had her doubts. But she wouldn't dare voice them.

"After their mind control, talking therapy, and behavior modification programs failed in conversion, they started using testosterone and estrogen treatments. It was out of their barbaric and criminal trials of injecting children with hormones that the gender modification program was born. We used their research as a basis for the hormone treatments during gestation. And now we live—" she said, raising her arms to the side, spinning slowly in a circle, "—in a proverbial utopia, where everyone is who they feel they are at their very core. No one is ostracized. No child is left behind."

"*Almost* everyone," Jack Sr. said bitterly.

Shirley winced at the overt jab.

"Do we have a problem, sir?" Officer Biles took a few steps in his direction, flexing her authority.

"Can I offer anyone a drink?" the DAS asked. Its camera and sensory systems detected dilated pupils, sweat glands perspiring, rapid pulses, heavy breathing and body heat rising. All telltale signs of an impending altercation of which it had been programed to deflect. It attempted to provide a buffer to a tense situation. "Would anyone like to hear a joke," said the DAS; the pixels on the face screen stretched to show a hearty smile. The DAS didn't wait for a response.

"A naturalist priest and a polar bear are—"

"Not now, DAS," Shirley said, shooing him away. "It's time."

The coordinator looked at her watch, then at Jack Sr., then back at her watch. She didn't like him, but she was duty-bound to stick to the itinerary.

"Okay," Officer Biles said, "let the reveal begin."

There was a wave of excited cheers as Shirley consulted her smartwatch again. The drone entertainment system awoke from its short hibernation and flew about the party, recording for posterity. She scrolled up on the smartwatch. The Cubs game on the holographic device turned into a live stream of her in-laws in New Jersey.

"Hello, Raymond," Ray's mother said excitedly, "where is my birthday grandsaughter?"

Jesse Anderson threw down their gender-neutral doll then ran to the hologram. "Here, put this on," Shirley said, handing her saughter a light nylon hat with accompanying suctioned gloves that could interface with their grandmother's system. They put the system on and wrapped their arms around an imaginary person. They closed their eyes, feeling the warmth that only a loving hug could provide. Grandmas always gave the best hugs.

"Now, doesn't that feel nice," Grandma said. "My, can you feel that love?"

Officer Biles interrupted the nice moment when she clapped her hands loudly. Silence ensued. "Well, ladies and gentlemen, boys and girls, the time we have all been waiting for has finally arrived." She stuck her arm out and reached for Jesse Anderson, wiggling her fingers as if she were in a Broadway musical.

"The sensory system, dear," she said. "Take off the hat and gloves."

Jesse removed the sensory system and ran awkwardly to the coordinator. They were an introvert at heart. Everyone knew that. And all the unwanted attention made them ever more uncomfortable.

Officer Biles took a small silver marble from her pocket, held it at arm's length, and let it go, but it failed to adhere to gravity's all-encompassing grasp. It floated about and set out to record the event for the census department.

"This is Care Coordinator Julie Biles of the New Chicago District Gender Modification Bureau." She glanced at her watch. "Date is April 9, 2075. Time is 13:00 twelfth district standard time. And we are here at the Anderson residence where little Jesse Anderson will finally reveal which gender they most identify. The DAS is on hand with the surgical tools. The surgical station is all sterile and prepped to either snip it or plug it."

She had coordinated many gender reveal parties in her time and knew the monotonous introduction by heart. But then came the most rewarding part of her job. "Jesse," she said, "can you open your eyes wide and allow the marble to scan your retinas, dear?"

The flying marble descended until it was eye level with Jesse Anderson and then emitted a red laser that scanned and cataloged their retina fingerprint for the system.

"Okay, Jesse," Officer Biles continued, "your mother tells me you're quite shy so, I'll try and make this as painless as possible." She looked at Jesse with kind eyes. "Have you thought about which gender you most identify with?"

"Yes," they said.

"And have you made a decision?"

"Yes."

"Would you like to share with everyone?"

Jesse thought about it for a second then shook their head.

"It's okay, honey." *Only about half the kids choose to announce their picks*, Biles thought. "I would be nervous, too," she admitted. "How about this—wadayasay we use the cakes to make the decision? Does that sound like a fun game?"

Their eyes lit up, they shook their head up and down, nervous, excited, scared.

"Okay, I'll tell everyone to close their eyes, then we'll all count down from ten, and when we open our eyes, you'll be at the cake you most identify. Then we'll sing happy birthday to you. Does that sound like a good plan?"

They nodded a child's nod and admitted timidly, "Yeah, it does."

"*We're going to the cakes for decision, people,*" Officer Biles shouted. "You ready, Jesse?"

It suddenly was a game to them. They no longer dreaded the attention but rather enjoyed it. "Let's do this," Jesse said, uncharacteristically confident. Ray and Shirley beamed with organic pride.

"Everyone, close your eyes," Officer Biles said. "*Ten, nine ...*" Everyone joined in the countdown.

Jesse shuffled their tiny legs to the picnic table and laughed and waited for everyone to finish the countdown. They grew impatient and joined in, "*Three, two, one ...*"

When everyone opened their eyes, an exploding burst of cheers rocked the backyard in New Chicago. "You go, *boy*," Grandma screamed from the hologram. "Give him back the sensory system; I wanna hug my grandson." But no one could hear Grandma; she may as well have been in New Jersey.

Officer Biles gave the DAS a preloaded command, and an array of strategically placed nodes shot out of the ground like a sprinkler system, as baby-blue confetti fell from the sky, released by the drones. The confetti were made from a metamaterial mined from a cave in the Arisa Mons mountains on Mars. When combined with a few terrestrial chemicals, their featherily composition made for perfect confetti; the lightest thing ever created by man. The air filled with these tiny peanut-looking snowflakes, scarcely not a space between them, drifting, falling, floating. The kids squealed as they chased the confetti around like bubbles.

Officer Biles had outdone herself indeed; she basked in the raining confetti.

Ray and Shirley ran to their new son's baby-blue-clad table, and the three hugged joyously. "I'm so proud of you, son," Shirley said.

"Did I make the right choice, Mommy?"

"Oh honey, it's not my choice to make," Shirley said. "Only you know who you are inside."

Ray took a finger full of blue icing and smeared it all over his new son's face. "Come here, you," he said.

"Are you proud of me, Daddy?" Jesse looked up, his eyes full of desired acceptance.

"I would've been proud with any choice you made, kiddo," Ray said stoically.

Officer Biles just loved to see the face of a new gender, but she had an itinerary to adhere to and interrupted the revelry.

"Okay, everyone," she said, excited, "it's time to sing happy birthday to Jesse xy Anderson. Are we ready?"

Screams.

"Happy birthday to you ..."

Jesse xy Anderson looked around at all the happy faces. He couldn't fathom what it was he was so scared of. *Even Uncle Jack is having fun, playing with his new friend Sam xy Larson and Sam is older than Jack, so he must be pretty cool,* Jesse thought.

"Happy birthday, dear Jesse xyyyyyyy ... happy birthday to youuuuuu."

Jesse balanced himself on the table and blew out his blue birthday cake amid a round of claps. The DAS cut the cake while Ray and Shirley handed out the plates.

"I'm so sorry, Ray," said a drunk Mr. Robinson. "Maybe the war will end by the time he comes of age." He took out his flask and took another gulp of scotch.

As Jesse xy Anderson sat down to eat his cake, he noticed his mother and father talking with the coordinator and DAS near the surgical tent. Suddenly, he remembered altogether what had frightened him so. It wasn't the attention or even the choice as most people suspected. For he didn't mind the attention all that much, and he had long since known which gender he identified with. It was the surgery that followed the choice—the snip it or plug it dilemma—that haunted him so. It was a well-guarded secret that only about half the kids who picked xy truly identified with it. The others were just too scared to snip it off. His best friend Bailey, now Bailey xy, had done the same thing the previous year.

It would hurt more to get it snipped than it would to get it plugged. *It was his choice after all.*

The nightmare haunted Betty's thoughts throughout the day. She couldn't explain it, but she knew the nightmare happened or would happen in some substrate of reality. In this realm or another. She could feel the poor child's timid acceptance, his uncanny logic. She grieved for the child who would have to spend the rest of his life in a body he didn't identify with, in a system created to avoid just that. The irony was gut-wrenching.

Later that night, Betty found herself sitting on the porch swing, thinking about the nightmare she'd had last night. She swung on the swing until the steady rhythm lulled her into REM, and she found herself staring into a cloudy eyeball in the sky.

Dog Day Afternoon

Sara Munson sipped her tea, trying to admire the sun as its crown peaked over the sea of rolling black hills which, from this distance, looked more like mountains, black, majestic. The warmth radiating from the mug was refreshing in the otherwise brisk morning air, which formed droplets of condensation upon the new day, drenching everything in a fresh layer of dew.

Once, when she was little, she asked her mother, "Why is it sometimes wet like this, Mama?" Her tiny brain unable to process water without rain. "It's Mother Nature giving her children a bath," her mother replied.

For some reason, that'd stuck with her all these years. There was something so fantastically quaint about the explanation, like a real-life fairytale.

Of course, real-life Mother Nature can be the biggest bitch of them all.

She'd already been sitting on the patio deck for forty-five minutes as part of a morning ritual advocated by her therapist, Dr. Hooper. Per the good doctor's advice, she tried starting her day with intention. "An attitude of gratitude" was the official wording. But when she woke up every day next to her husband—a man she loathed beyond comprehension, whose very presence disgusted her—that was a tough ask. The few times she was able to distill gratitude upon her waking moments was when he was passed out on the couch.

After the gratitude bit, she went downstairs and found that not only did her oldest daughter, Bella, fail to clean the living room—even though Sara explicitly told her to as she went upstairs for the night—but that the living room was dirtier then when she went upstairs. Much dirtier. There was so many clothes on the ground, you could scarcely see the floor. It was so blatantly dirty, in fact, it was hard for Sara to believe Bella hadn't done it on purpose to make a statement.

They used to get along brilliantly, Sara and Bella, but the power dynamics changed in their relationship when she became a teenager. And what used to be a loving, reciprocated bond between mother and daughter became a dysfunctional shitshow of a relationship—a running game where each player played a move, the opponent countered, and whoever won that round was the Alpha until the next match. It started off innocently enough, but things escalated quickly, and Sara had a very real, very healthy fear that Bella would come home one day pregnant just to win the game. The clothes on the ground were Bella's latest move, prompting Sara to miss the days when disciplining a wayward child meant leaving a mark. She didn't want to hit her children. She truly didn't. But she'd exhausted every other option. She was officially at the end of her rope.

As she waded through the moat of clothes, she cringed when she went into the kitchen to put a kettle of water on the stove only to see that her son, Jacob, hadn't done his chores either. The sink looked like the before effect of a Dawn commercial. Unlike her daughter, though, Jake's insolence wasn't malicious, just pure laziness. Which somehow seemed worse to Sara than the blatant disrespect exhibited by Bella. It was Sara's contention that the sole job of any parent was to raise decent, semi-responsible kids who would, as adults, realize the value of hard work, or at the very least not be lazy. She didn't even pass her own bare minimum metric of good parenting. She was failing at motherhood. And she was failing miserably. She squirmed to think what others thought of her.

The entire time this was all going on in her head—when she woke up to her least favorite person in the world, when she walked through the blast area where the clothes grenade went off, to the disgusting kitchen, she had her headphones on, listening to positive affirmations in the background, but her kids' missteps were too big a slight on her ego for the affirmations to have any effect.

She went outside on the patio deck. The moisture in the air hit her like a mac truck, reminding her of a fond memory: "It's Mother Nature giving her children a bath." She sat down and tried meditating for ten minutes, but her attention bounced from one matter to the next: *I hope Jacob put the clothes in the dryer. Do I have enough gas to get to work? I wonder if Butters will feel anything.* The innocuous thoughts were tethered by an incessantly recurring theme that sprouted deep in the pit of her stomach. Springing forth out of her subconscious mind like roots busting through a seedling, bleeding into conscious thought, exploding, screaming: *Fuck my life.*

After a few minutes of trying to herd her wild thoughts, she gave up the meditation attempt and tried writing in a gratitude journal but after struggling to come up with the minimum of five things to be grateful for, she became discouraged and her default setting activated, zombie mode, sending her mind spiraling down a despairing road of negativity. A few minutes passed before conscious thought returned and she found herself doodling rudimentary sketches of her Shih Tzu, Butters, asleep at the foot of the sliding door.

"Get it together, Sara," she said to herself. She was determined to complete *at least one* of the morning tasks.

Presently, she was attempting a grounding and mindfulness exercise that was supposed to force her to be present. But her mind kept steady, pulling her to the distant past or pushing her to the immediate future. A ceaseless tug-of-war match which was the reason, her therapists said, "behind your anxiety and depression."

Sara couldn't fathom why or when she had given up on happiness. Probably not long after she gave up on her dream of being a writer. And as she observed her life objectively—a middle-aged woman, unhappily married with three entitled and ungrateful bratty children—she knew she had settled and settled hard.

A born and bred Midwesterner, Sara never understood the utility of therapy. Still, she had cousins who left South Dakota for California and swore by its efficacy like devout followers of some unnamed religion. Mostly she feared what others would say if they found out. The prevailing school of thought in the surrounding areas regarding mental health was to stuff your feelings down deep and *never* talk about them. Indeed, seeing a therapist was considered a sign of weakness. Sara was convinced Midwesterners were cut from a different cloth, woven by pride, grit, and maybe just a smidgen of masochism. Because to a Midwesterner, suffering is healing.

Sara had subscribed to the school of hard knocks until a few months prior when she started having generalized anxiety, compounded by debilitating panic attacks. She watched her mother go through a similar episode at around the same age. Sara's father had cheated on her mother, who subsequently had a short bout with depression before taking her own life. Sara had always fancied herself stronger than her mother, until adulthood drowned her in crushing waves of lonely despair.

She heard the birds chirping; she could feel the light breeze bring the sun's rays to her like a divine gift, and yet she felt utterly hollow. She closed her eyes and felt the warmness of the mug she gripped in her hand. She tightened her grip then released it. She hadn't realized how tense she was until she started doing progressive relaxation techniques. Next, she tightened her core and released it. Her thighs. Calves. Feet. Then her whole body. Fully realizing the individual parts of her. Connecting her. Making her whole. *The knee bone is connected to the elbow.*

Progressive muscle relaxation was the last step in her regimented morning rituals. For the past six weeks, as perennial as the morning sun, she awoke one hour earlier than was customary. Before her husband awoke and demanded his work clothes and breakfast; before her kids awoke and the circus of finishing homework and getting them dressed, fed, and off to school began.

"People's days tend to go how their mornings go," Dr. Hooper said in that first meeting. "If you're like most other Midwestern housewives, you work all day, then you go home, and your *real* job starts. You have no time for yourself," he said, squinting his beady little eyes. "Give yourself this *magnificent* gift."

This line of logic was perfectly sensible to Sara. But she was beginning to feel like a failure even in trying. She had nearly made peace with how empty her life was, and a slow resentment was percolating toward Dr. Hooper for giving her a false sense of hope.

She cursed his name as the beautiful sunrise rose by degrees and shone its beautiful rays over the beautiful rolling black hills of South Dakota.

She was surrounded by so much beauty. But that which was abundant in nature was lacking, naturally, within her.

Her husband's alarm blared through the cracked window. He snoozed it quickly and slipped back into REM. Sara knew she only had another eight minutes of this morning routine, advertised as an alleged utopia by her therapists before her daily Cinderella-esque tasks commenced. She smirked as the catchy jingle from the iconic movie ran through her mind: *Cinderelly, Cinderelly, dressed in yelly, Cinderelly.*

The smirk quickly turned into a frown as she identified with its uncanny lyrics.

She despised her life, and if not for her kids ...

The last memory she had of her mother was trying to wake her.

Sara was eight when it happened. Her mother had chased a bottle of alcohol with a bottle of Xanax, stated the coroner's report, and "laid next to her daughter to hold and scar her with finality." An accurate albeit presumptuous prediction. It was bad enough that she killed herself. But when Sara awoke in her cold, dead arms, it compounded Sara's hatred for her. And as much as she despised her life, she could never be so cruel to her children.

The alarm buzzed once more then the room came to life as her husband turned on the bedside lamp. She could see his profile running a hand through his graying hair. Even the sight of his shadow showered her in disgust. There had never been any love between them, so there was never any love lost. His sentiment was that she trapped him with a baby sixteen years prior. They had been little more than disgruntled roommates who occasionally fucked ever since, an unforgiveable sin of the flesh, which was "The worst kind of sin," according to her mother. "Sin of the flesh." Sex without love seemed exceedingly worse when the unrequited love came from her husband. But it did spawn two more children to tend to: feed, bathe, shower, nap, burp; the list endless. And through all of it; every diaper, every practice, every waking moment, Sara did it all alone, her husband watching from the shadows, sneering. From the day Jacob was born, she'd considered herself an honorary member of the coalition of single mothers.

There must be more to life than this, Sara thought as the bell clock perched on the table wailed incredulously, shaking off the morning dew like a dog shaking dry. Her fortress of morning solitude was over. She felt worse than before she started, only more tired.

Sara suddenly had the dreadful impression she was being watched; that sixth sense, that sickly feeling in the pit of your stomach that you get when you see those red lights and slam on the brakes and your tires screech, and your heart's racing and you rear-end the car ahead of you. She cinched her robe and straightened her hair, suddenly insecure. She pretended to stretch her back, rotating her torso, looking first in her husband's window, then over the picket fence. She switched sides and looked at her neighbors' houses. She was alone.

Just as her heart rate plateaued, she heard it. Loud and concise and unmistakable. It was a laugh; of that she was certain. A high-pitched cackle that sounded like a witch taking a moonlit stroll on her broomstick. She looked up and that's when she noticed it, for like the laugh, it was concise, unmistakable—there was only one cloud in the sky, and it was in the shape of an eyeball.

She rose from the wicker chair, equal parts scared and curious. It was a massive eyeball complete with an eyelid, iris, and even eyelashes. The detail was remarkable. She spun around in circles to see if anyone else had seen it, but, as she had already concluded, she was alone. She gawked at the curiously shaped cloud as it hovered ominously over her house. She felt its presence penetrating her, probing her, judging her. Then, with unmistakable clarity, the eye cloud winked at her.

Startled, she dropped her mug of tea. It shattered as it met the deck.

"*Shit*," she said, bending over and picking up the glass. She looked back up when she heard it again—the slightest whisper of a maddening laugh riding the rising wind before dispersing the cloud in a puff of smoke. The wind shook her body like a pile of leaves dancing in the laughing wind. She dug her palms in her eyes, rubbing hard. And when she looked at the sky again, it was a pristine virgin blue, without a cloud in sight.

Great, Sara thought. *I'm losing my mind.*

—

She was greeted with a rare apology when she went inside: "I'm sorry, Ma," said Jacob. "I fell asleep." Just as Sara suspected—he forgot to transfer the laundry over. *God, I hate Mondays,* Sara thought. She would have to wear an off-color pair of scrubs again. Something she had been warned against more times than she cared to recall.

"I asked you to do *one thing,* Jake," Sara said, gritting her teeth. "Just *one* thing."

"*Technically,* it was two things," Jacob said. Sara squinted hatefully at him. "I know. *I know.* Transferring a load of laundry isn't a chore." He stepped closer to her. He was tall for a sixteen-year-old. Even by his father's mammoth family genes. Which produced five boys all north of 6'2. Luckily that was all he'd inherited from his father. *That and his laziness.*

He hugged her tight and whispered into her ear, "I'm sorry, Ma."

She wanted to forgive him, but there wasn't a shred of remorse in his voice. Not to mention instead of looking her in the eyes, he had his eyes down as he fondled his iPhone. Sara refrained from snatching it and throwing it at the wall. She tried a breathing exercise instead, focusing on the rising and falling of her stomach.

"Don't be reactive to outside stimuli," Dr. Hooper had said in their last session. "You and you *alone* dictate your emotions. Don't give anyone or anything else that power."

Easier said than done, Doc, Sara thought then, as she did now.

"Can you sign this for me, Mommy?" This from her youngest child, Jenny.

In most families, the youngest is usually the sweetest. Not at the Munson residence. Jenny was the problem child of the family. Any time Sara received a call from the school, she knew Jenny was freeing frogs from the science lab or unionizing the less popular kids to combat bully mistreatment. The latter incident earned Jenny a two-day suspension for "inciting a riot" in the cafeteria. Sara remembers hearing Jenny screaming in the background, "*There's strength in numbers,*" as she spoke with the principal on the phone. She let most of the shenanigans slide because she was proud of her daughter for taking a stand in her convictions, perhaps even a little jealous.

She snatched the paper out of Jenny's hand and stared into her eyes, peering into her soul, determining what noble cause she had decided to champion this time.

"I've got detention tomorrow for boycotting the cafeteria's disgraceful recycling policies," Jenny said. Her weight shifted nervously as if she were trying to balance her mother's wanton temper.

Sara took a deep breath. "Why are you *just now* showing me this?" she said under her breath. But she knew the answer—if Jenny had shown her, she would've been grounded for the weekend and unable to attend the sleepover at her best friend's house.

"We'll talk about this later," Sara said. She hated grounding her children, mainly because it meant they would be home sulking, making her miserable life all the more miserable. She knew if she grounded Jenny, she would bend to her parole request by Wednesday, if not sooner. Thereby defeating the purpose of discipline.

She heard the front door open and close then her husband's car turn over before he roared out the driveway without uttering a word to her. *Love you, too, you miserable fuck,* she thought.

"Where's Bella?" Sara asked.

Jenny and Jacob answered with shrugs, heads tilted down, eyes glued to their phones. They went to the kitchen and ignored the impressive spread of bacon, eggs, and French toast that Sara had made, congregating around the toaster instead, waiting on Pop-tarts to emerge.

Ungrateful little shits.

"Bells! *Bella.*" Sara took the steps two at a time. "I swear to Christ," she growled, "if you're still in bed, I'm going to lose my shit."

Sara struggled to open the door. She thrust her weight against it and found Bella squirming out of bed. A mountain of dirty clothes blocked the door; the room looked as if a tornado funneled from the ceiling and tossed the contents haphazardly about.

Growing anger stirred in the pit of Sara's stomach. How Bella had so many clothes was a wonder. Sara certainly didn't buy them. And she knew her husband hadn't. She just hoped her daughter wasn't stealing them, or worse. *What do teenage girls do for money these days?*

"I'm up, I'm up," Bella said. "I was just resting my eyes." She stretched and yawned.

"Didn't I tell you to clean your room *two nights* ago?" Sara asked. "And what's up with the living room? Huh. You tryna tell me something?"

"I think it speaks for itself. No?" Bella sat at the edge of the bed and removed a crusted mucus from her eye.

Speaks for itself? Sara couldn't believe Bella's brazenness, her gall. She wanted to pull a handful of hair from her scalp.

"N'how can you expect me to clean my room when we have to put my poor little doggy down tomorrow?" Bella exaggerated a frown. Sara knew she was using humor to deflect. She knew that out of all her children, Bella was going to be the most distraught over the death of Butters, who was Bella's birthday present when she turned seven. They were inseparable until she turned thirteen, then she suddenly was at a loss for time to play with her.

Bella put the back of her hand to her forehead and tilted her head back in a dramatic gesture that reminded Sara of a daytime soap opera she used to watch; the acting was so horrible; it was addictive to watch. "I'm inconsolable," Bella said.

Sara put her hands to her hips.

"I'll do it tonight," Bella said. "I promise."

"You've got eight minutes to get to the bus stop."

"That long," Bella joked. "Wake me up in three minutes then." She prostrated herself back on the bed.

"Hurry up, *please.*" Sara looked at her Fitbit. "I can't afford to drive you to school again today."

"Can you get my clothes out of the laundry, *pleeeeeaaassee?*"

"Jake forgot to transfer the load."

That made Bella pop out of bed as if it had spontaneously combusted. "But *Ma,*" she cried as she rummaged through the carpet of dirty clothes, "I had the perfect outfit picked out."

"I'm sure you can find something to wear in that statement you made in the living room."

Bella sniffed a pair of panties, made a sour face, threw them over her shoulder.

And when she looked at her daughter's indecisiveness over what to wear, Sara knew she would have to take Bella to school. She knew she would be late for work. Again.

To her credit, though, Sara did rather well accepting it. Only one aspect of her therapy sessions came easily to Sara—the acceptance part.

"You can't control the weather or how bad the Bears suck." Dr. Hooper laughed as if this were an inside joke with himself. "You can't control the traffic or other people's behaviors. Sometimes, all you can do is accept—*it is what it is*—and move on." He nodded, his droopy earlobes shaking like flabs of arm fat. "Dwelling on *anything* has zero utility."

Of all the woo-woo talk about positivity and catching, checking, and changing her thoughts, Sara could readily accept that bad things would always happen to her. Her shadow was cast by Murphy's Law, following her around like a gypsy curse.

The thought of a gypsy curse reminded her of something. She ran out of her daughter's room. "I'll meet you downstairs," she said over her shoulder. "We need to be gone in fifteen minutes."

"Thanks, Ma," screamed Bella, coordinating a halter top with something or another.

Sara skipped the last three steps and landed in dog shit, slipping, hitting her head on the bottom step. Blue and purple and pink stars flickered and blinked in her mind's eye.

"*Goddamn it, Butters*," she growled fiercely but quickly felt awful because she knew Butters couldn't help it. The Munson family had just recently discovered their ten-year-old Shih Tzu had colon cancer, a brain tumor, heart murmurs, and spots on her liver. She started having seizures the week prior. The appointment was already made to put her down Tuesday morning.

Sara saw Butters cowering in the corner.

"It's okay, baby girl," she said sweetly. "I'm not mad at you."

Sara picked herself up and realized she had slid in the mess; her pants were covered in shit. Literally. She took a deep breath, slid her pants off, held it with two fingers as if it were roadkill, then chucked them down the basement stairs. But they stuck to the wall. She laughed maniacally. *Of course, it'd stick to the wall.*

She slammed the door and ran to the calendar on the refrigerator. Today was circled in red with a big smiley face. Today was the one day of the year Sara looked forward to. Today was the town fair. A sudden wave of primal lust enveloped her, directly succeeded by overwhelming sadness as she noticed an ominous red x on Tuesday and the word "Butters."

Bittersweet, indeed.

They were ten minutes late getting on the road because Bella couldn't find her book bag, and they had to stop for gas. Sara activated her drone mode and drove on autopilot.

She had been so busy hating her life, she hadn't realized that today was the carnival. Desire filled her body as she thought of Raul, the sexy Roman gypsy she'd been having an affair with for the past five years.

With less than one thousand people, Rolling Hills, South Dakota perfectly captured all aspects of small-town America. The town was at the tail end of a tristate tour of a traveling circus that boasted audacious claims of fifty towns and cities in two months, staying for two or three days then packing the caravan and moving to the next site. Their presence marked the beginning of summer for the residents of Rolling Hills, as they always pitched their first tents on Memorial Day weekend. Because it was the first stop, they stayed for four or five days. Which meant four or five days of orgasms for Sara—a justifiable reprieve for enduring another year with her husband who hadn't touched her or even looked at her in years.

Every year they would come into town, her husband home on the couch drinking beer and sulking in self-pity. She would give her children some money, bid them farewell and they'd run off without even thanking her. Then she'd go to the gypsy's tent, and there he'd be—this exotic-looking Arabian prince with his young, chiseled body and long, thick eyelashes that had caught her heart like a Venus flytrap. Having been attentionless for so long, she rather liked the attention Raul gave her body.

And boy, do I need a release, she thought.

—

Sara glanced over at Bella, her heart aching with a bittersweet mixture of maternal pride and longing. Her daughters were growing up so fast, finding their own independence, slipping away from her grasp. She sighed, pushing the thoughts of Raul and the carnival to the back of her mind as she tried to focus on the present. She knew she had to maintain the facade of a loving mother. Her heart could be elsewhere, marooned on an island of despair, sustaining off hopes and dreams and perennial visits from the Gypsy cuckold. But her mind; her mind had to stay on point.

The car continued its journey, the hum of the engine a background to Sara's racing thoughts, as she mentally prepared herself for a day filled with mundane responsibilities and a night of forbidden pleasures.

"You okay, Ma?" Bella said somewhere in the background of her mind. "Earth to Ma. Mom!"

"What?" Sara swerved the car to the right. "Did I hit something?" She glanced in the rearview mirror.

Bella giggled. "Nooo," she said, examining her mother. "You just had this faraway look on your face."

"Yeah, I'm sorry," she said. "I was just thinking about putting Butters down tomorrow." She took stock of her body.

Nervous twitches of anxiety vibrated her legs and hands long outside expected time.

Bella's lips pursed and twisted to the left. "Ummm, that's not the look I'm talking about."

"What look are you talking about then?"

Bella thought about it before giggling and saying, "Longing."

"Puh, longing? Gedafagoutahere." Sara felt her face flush. "I haven't longed for nothing but sleep and peace and quiet for years."

Bella studied her mother and after realizing she didn't care, she went back to her phone without saying anything.

"Are you and your sister coming with me to the fair tonight?" Sara asked as she plotted her escape.

"No offense, Ma, but we're too old to be going with you."

They pulled up to the school and joined the accordion dance of cars coming and going.

"Can you just give me the money *now*, and I'll give Jake and Jen their cuts at lunch," Bella said.

Even better, Sara thought. She was at the head of the suburban caravan now. She pulled over, rummaged through her purse, and handed Bella eighty dollars. She tried hugging Bella, who winced and recoiled.

"Really, dude," Sara said, equal parts amused and hurt.

Bella plugged her nose and said, "You smell like shit, Ma."

"Well, that's just not nice at all."

"No, dude, lowkey," Bella said, turning her head to the side and gagging. "You got some shit on your back."

Bella laughed and got out of the car.

"Don't pull out," Sara said under her breath. "Please, God. *Please.* Don't pull out.*"

Her eyes dropped down to the speedometer which informed her she was going 70 in a 40. A surge of anxiety shot through her stomach and rose to her chest in sputtering waves. She glanced in the rearview mirror and the sheriff's car that was hiding under the billboard sign pulled out hot, its blue and red lights flashing on a beat to Sara's anxiety.

"*Goddamnit*," she growled. She signaled right, merging with the shoulder of the road. The tires kicking up great big billows of dust in the car's wake. She came to a stop. She slammed her hands on the steering wheel and glanced at her disheveled look in the rearview mirror. She started playing with her hair.

The sheriff's car pulled up right behind her. She tilted the mirror and when she saw who it was, her heart fluttered a beat. *I may just get out of this with a warning yet,* she thought. She pulled her breasts up, perkiness defeating age, gravity; put her game face on, determined to flirt her way out of the ticket.

Deputy Cane Rose moseyed out of the vehicle and closed the door. He put his visor hat on and made his way to the driver side window, which Sara had already lowered, saying, "If all I had to do to see you in that uniform is speed a lil, well, then—"

"License and registration, please." All business, Deputy Rose had a determined look on his face, placid, uninterested. It wasn't always like that, though. Once upon a time, he was madly in love with her. But that was a long time ago.

Embarrassed by his aloof response to her attempt at flirting, Sara nodded dutifully and reached into the glove compartment. Empty single shots of Captain Morgan and Smirnoff fell to the bed of the passenger side floor. *Shit*, she thought. She completely forgot about her cache of empties, last week's lunch leftovers. Her registration was buried under the graveyard of empty bottles. There were at least twenty Captain Morgans and another ten or so Smirnoff vodkas on top. She cupped a handful, and they cascaded to the ground. In Sara's mind, the noise it made when it hit the ground sounded like the click of handcuffs locking—foreboding, inevitable.

She found the registration and tried slamming the glove compartment shut, but bottles blocked the locking mechanism. She threw the door down and brought it back up in a fluid motion and it clicked shut.

"I can explain the bottles," she said, turning toward Deputy Rose, who was leaning in the window, sniffing for alcohol on Sara's person. But when she turned around, his face a few inches from hers, him advancing, she thought he was trying to kiss her, and she puckered her lips and leaned in to kiss him.

He pulled away, a disgusting grimace on his face. "What the fuck, Sara," he said, wiping his lips with the back of his hand.

"I'm *so sorry*," she said. "I thought that … I mean you were leaning in and … I thought that … *shit* … I'm sorry."

Sara had dated Deputy Cane Rose back in high school for a year before she grew bored and left him for her now-husband and Rose started dating her best friend, at the time that is. They had been married for fourteen years. Happily, it would appear. Sara was forced to watch their Hallmark-card family grow in numbers and happiness because he coached Jacob's baseball and soccer teams. And she trolled him on every social media platform he had. He was perfect in every way, and every time Sara saw him, she slipped into a mini depression begotten by titanic regret.

"Please don't tell Cheryl," Sara said. She could see her reflection in the blue-tinted aviators. She looked pathetic.

Deputy Rose grimaced. "I'll be back in a few minutes," he said before walking away shaking his head.

She spent the first five minutes sweeping up the empties and throwing them in a plastic bag. Ten minutes passed. She looked in the rearview mirror, wondering what was taking so long. She looked at the clock on the dash. It read 9:45. She was already forty-five minutes late to work and she still needed to get home and change clothes.

She fumbled through her purse for her phone when Deputy Rose finally emerged from the car. He had papers clutched in his hand, and Sara knew exactly what the papers were. *I can't even talk myself out of a ticket anymore*, she thought. Hers was the kind of beauty that was legendary in the small town she called home. Even in her early thirties, she was stunning. She'd gone most her life using her beauty as a weapon, a utility. But now, it would appear, her beauty was no longer an asset. She didn't quite know how she felt about that.

He walked up to the door and handed her a ticket. She glanced at it and laughed nervously. "*Five hundred dollars*," she said, throwing her arms up. "I was only going thirty over the limit."

"Forty over the limit," he corrected her. "And you're lucky I'm not arresting you for the empty alcohol bottles." He handed her another piece of paper, the one that she needed to bring to court. "Now, since you were twenty-five over the limit, you *must* go to court on the date posted." He pulled his lips back and added, "They're going to suspend your license, Sara, and you'll have to get SR22 insurance. I wrote down all the information on the back."

"Suspend my license?" she said. "How am I supposed to get to work?" She suddenly felt nauseous at the thought of her husband having to take her to work every day.

"You can drive yourself to work," he said. "Just have Peggy sign the paperwork and send it to the DOT. But if I catch you driving anywhere else, I'll have to write you another ticket."

The ticket was a magnificent cherry on a shit-sandwich of a morning.

—

"Is everything okay?" The charge nurse glanced at her watch as if to validate that Sara was over an hour late.

"I just had to rush home after dropping Bells off at school and I gotta speeding ticket on the way here." She produced the speeding ticket as proof, but the charge nurse didn't even glance at it.

"Why'd you have to go back home?" the charge nurse asked.

"My dog has all kindsa cancers; she's incontinent," Sara said. "I slipped on her shit this morning and I *thought* it was only on my pants, but realized as I was dropping my daughter off that it was on my top as well." After an uncomfortable pause, she added, "We've got an appointment to put her down tomorrow. Butters, that is. Not Bella. Could you imagine." Sara smiled weakly then looked sullen, distraught, hoping the loss of a family dog would incite kindness.

The charge nurse's light green top matched her light green bottoms beautifully. Her name tag was perfectly centered. Her starched pants crackled as she walked, and her hair was in a nice, neat bun. She looked prepared for a military class A inspection.

Conversely, Sara had on a wrinkled multicolored flower top and wrinkled Sponge Bob bottoms; she forgot her name tag at home in the pockets of the shit-covered pants, and her hair, frizzy and unkept, looked like she just sat in the front seat of the world's fastest rollercoaster.

The charge nurse cleared her throat then sipped from a white coffee mug that read WORLD'S BEST BOSS in bright red letters. "How long," she said, sipping her coffee, "have you been with us, Sara?" Another sip.

But Sara didn't hear the question. She was busy with an internal dialogue about the pretentiousness of owning such a coffee mug when something caught her eye. Something ominous, familiar.

Behind the woman's desk stood a large full-body mirror where Sara saw the ghastly reflection of a large eyeball staring at her. It was a hazy silhouette of sorts; translucent like how ghosts are depicted in cartoons. Aside from its apparent lack of mass, the eyeball was perfectly defined. Though the cloud eye she encountered earlier was massive, it lacked a certain degree of definition this eye had. She couldn't be certain, but Sara sensed it was the same eye.

It was a beady little brown eye with little whiskers for eyelashes; a thin, crescent-shaped eyebrow was penciled in above the eye and the wrinkled eyelid was smothered in so much blue eyeshadow that it looked like a four-year-old playing dress up. But it wasn't a child. It was an adult. It was a woman's eye. Sara knew that empirically.

Aside from the physical evidence, Sara, somehow, someway, could feel a feminine energy shooting out from the mirror in daggers; a fierce motherly sort of love like a mama bear protecting her cubs from a lioness. Sara being the lioness. But that didn't seem entirely correct. There was something missing in the hypothesis. And when the eye squinted hatefully, Sara was more able to pinpoint the source of the energy. It wasn't motherly love. It was a jealous lover kind of feeling, primal protection; an envy as old as Cain.

"Well?" The charge nurse raised her arms at her sides as if she were receiving the holy spirit.

The disembodied eye, the woman's eye, winked playfully, a youthful twinkle turning the otherwise hostile appendage into something benign, then it disappeared in a puff of smoke just as it had done earlier when it was a cloud eye.

Sara squirmed in her chair.

The boss cleared her throat, bringing Sara back to real time. She looked at the now-empty mirror and composed herself. "I'm sorry," she said shakily, staring at the empty mirror. "What did you say?"

"How long have you been with us?"

Sara mulled it over for a few seconds. "Like five years," she said. "Ish."

The woman rocked in her chair, reached into a filing cabinet, took out a stack of counseling statements she had written for Sara over the years. "Do you know what these are?" she asked, knowing full well Sara did. Sara nodded. "These are writeups for not wearing uniform-colored top and bottoms, tardiness, too many call-offs, not wearing a name tag, messy and unpresentable hairstyle." She nodded at Sara's sloppy uniform. "And that's just to name a few," she added.

Sara sat silently, longing for tonight's release.

The woman reached into a different drawer and retrieved another stack of papers. "Do you know what these are?" she asked, motioning to the pile of papers. Sara remained silent.

"These are applications for very willing, very competent CNAs," she said. "One of them is my niece."

She wants to replace me, Sara thought.

She forgot about the inexplicable events she'd experienced that day, the eye that seemed to be following her. She lost the fear and anxiety; they turned into rage. She wanted to cheetah-jump across the desk and skull-fuck her boss with a dirty plunger. But she composed herself.

"I'm sorry, Mrs. Crawford," she said in her practiced fake voice. "I've just been so stressed."

"Yes, your dog's sick. I get it. I do." The woman looked at Sara, incredulous. "But be that as it may, this is still your final warning," she said. "You are on probation for the next month."

Just then, Sara heard the slightest whisper of a maddening laugh echo from the mirror.

"I mean it, Sara," she cautioned further. "If you get even one more writeup, I've gotta fire you."

Sara nodded and left the room, lost, confused.

Sara managed to escape the rest of the day without incident. She felt like there was a target on her back and very nearly quit several times but thought better of it.

She just needed to make it to tonight.

She just needed a release.

She just needed Raul.

Sara's husband was working on his car when she pulled into the driveway. He took one glance at her, chugged his beer, then went back to refurbishing his 1979 Mustang. She struggled to get the door open with her arms full of groceries.

"It's *okay*," she screamed. "I got it."

He answered with a grunt and a smirk. One of the bags broke when she entered the house where she saw Butters laying on the couch. "You don't know how good you have it," Sara said. "Wish I could lay around all day doing nothing." Butters sighed heavily then went back to sleep.

On the fridge was a note from the kids. They had already left for the carnival and would be back at 11:00. *I bet they didn't even do their homework.* She snatched the note off the fridge, set it on the table. The red mark on the calendar caught her eye. She felt better just looking at the smiley face, marveling how something so simplistically innocuous could also be so seductive, incite so much emotion, so much passion.

She started preparing dinner but quickly realized the only person home to cook for was her husband, so she put away the groceries, stole some mini shots of Captain Morgan from the fridge, and took a shower.

Raul had gifted her a rose pendant necklace a few years prior, probably some cheap prize winner in one of the other carnival tent games. She didn't care. It was the only romantic gift she'd received in over a decade. She ransacked the house looking for it but realized Bella had probably borrowed it again.

That first time, five years prior, Sara had been caught entirely by surprise; swept off her feet, as they say. The night didn't start off like that though. Within five minutes of being at the fair, her kids ditched her for friends. Sara was left alone, depressed. Raul, a sexual predator in his own right, saw the interaction transpire like a hawk prowling in the clouds; he saw the brokenhearted look in her eyes when they took her money and sprinted away. He observed her from the shadows for a few moments, her awkward, indecisive gestures: starting left toward the beer garden, stopping, turning, walking toward the Ferris wheel, stopping, turning, looking, waiting.

Earlier in the week, her hairdresser had convinced her to cut her long dark-brown hair into a pixie cut. "It'll accentuate that beautiful face of yours, *girlfriend*," he'd said. And he was right. Sara had the perfect face for a pixie cut. Couple that with her bright blue eyes and a corn-fed Midwesterner body, she was an attractive enough woman and usually, she was the most beautiful woman in the room.

But you wouldn't have guessed so that night, judging by her timid, self-conscious uncertainty. She had a certain vibe about her that many unhappily married women have, eager to please, to be seen.

Raul saw all of this and thought, *Low-hanging fruit.* He knew she would be simple enough to seduce.

He whistled at her, then waved her over. She walked to him with an awkward shuffle it seemed. "Yes?" she said, her voice low, shaky.

"May I readjur pom?" he asked in a thick accent.

"Oh, no, thank you." She put her hands in her pockets nervously, then her hips, then they went to her hair, her eyes growing big when she remembered she'd cut it. She felt stupid, not knowing what to do with her hands. Before she knew it, her arms were crossed on her chest, ridding herself of the "where do I put my hands" burden.

Then, pitifully, she said, "I already know what my life has in store for me."

Raul smirked, his eyes beaming with inner joy, confidence. Very discreetly, Sara looked him over. His skin was olive brown. His thick, jet-black hair was slicked back, culminating in a skinny braided ponytail. He wore a light white button-up shirt that swayed in the wind, the sleeves rolled up to show muscular forearms and tattoos. His pants were a few sizes too small, hugging his legs, exposing an endowed bulge. Everything about him was exotic, sexual. His smirk widened to show a perfect smile.

"I's on z'house," he said. Interest piqued, Sara went into his tiny tent. She was floored when she stepped inside, thinking the inner dimensions would be commensurate with the outside. But the space inside was impossibly massive, easily triple the size it should be.

There was a stocked minibar to the left, a whole living room arrangement to the right, complete with a couch, love seat, recliner, coffee table and television. Directly ahead was a door to what Sara could only presume was a restroom.

The entrance had a small wooden table with a chair on either side facing each other; there was a glass ball perched in the middle of the table and a stack of tarot cards placed neatly next to the crystal ball.

Her jaw hanging on the ground, Sara stepped back outside, circling the tent, counting. She counted seventy-five paces diameter. She went back in and was again floored.

There was no plausible explanation to explain the impossible discrepancies other than …

"Iss magic," Raul said with an accent that sent shivers down Sara's spine. He motioned for her to sit down and what she thought would be a brief if not interesting encounter ended up being the most intimate experience she'd ever had. But not intimacy in the physical sense. Not that first year. That first encounter, Raul wooed her soul.

The magical tent's scope seemed to include time as well as space. They talked for what seemed hours and hours and every time Sara looked at her watch, she was giddy to find that time had literally frozen still.

She hadn't talked with anyone, *really* talked with anyone, in a very, *very* long time. He made her feel special that night. Seen. Loved.

They spoke of life and fears and dreams and everything in between. To Sara, it was as if their souls were two rowboats drifting a dark, cold, vast, lonely ocean—each going with the tide of life, independent from the other, but somehow, someway, irrevocably the same, defying all odds of time and space and finding each other and it felt like God had made one with the other in mind, such a perfect fit, symmetrical.

By the time they said their goodbyes, Sara was already madly in love. Her rational mind knew it was impossible to love someone you only just met. And yet, there it was: that inescapable doey feeling stirring in her stomach like a flock of migrating butterflies; the feeling consumed her entirely—body, mind, soul.

The circus rented the lot for five days, two more than any other site on their tour. From there the caravan headed south, dwindling in size with each stop as the carneys disappeared at rest stops and gas stations, all the way down to St. Louis, where it called home. But for those five nights in Rolling Hills, they weren't nomadic rolling stones, but welcome guests. The citizens opened their homes to them, treating them as family.

Sara spent the next four nights having wild, tantric sex, her soul intertwining with his, becoming one.

"Ju meet here nex' year on annie-ver-sorry, jes?" This from Raul on the last day of the tour. A team of teenagers were busy loading a nearby RV with Raul's belongings.

Sara had been crying all morning. She blew her nose into a napkin. "Anniversary?" She laughed nervously. *That sounds so official*, she thought.

"If ju wan," he said with smiling eyes, batting his long eyelashes, then kissing her with such passion, she felt like she was on the cover of an exotic novel.

Sara's childhood experience with cheaters made her despise them. And the days following his departure, those feelings returned in full force, along with a growing disgust in herself. She made every effort to quell her guilt with grand romantic gestures that were both spontaneous and thoughtful, but her husband shot her down at every turn. He made her feel dumb, inadequate.

She made a vow not to go back to his tent the following year. But as the months passed and the predictably monotonous routine of her life unfolded in a depressing loop, all she could think about was Raul. Her husband stopped celebrating her birthday and their anniversary the year after Jacob was born. With no vacations on the horizon, and birthdays and holidays both empty, meaningless days, the town fair had become the only thing she had to look forward to.

And, on the anniversary, she decided to go.

"I know ju'd come bock," Raul said. He looked upon her intensely, examining her, savoring the view. "Ju change jur hair, I saw."

Sara blushed a child's blush. She *had* changed her hair. Her husband didn't even notice. It felt good to be noticed again.

What followed was a hot, steamy, five-day sexathon.

Every year since, for five days at the end of May, Sara and Raul made it their mission to beat last year's orgasm number, a daunting task they were both happy to oblige.

She pulled up to the carnival, took a sip out of her airplane shooter. The summer breeze smelled of cotton candy and funnel cake. She sat there with her windows rolled down, listening to the bustling sounds, utterly content.

The setting sun still had another forty-five minutes of life left. *I'm early,* she thought. His tent usually catered to drunken patrons and didn't even open until dusk, when the adults came out.

She checked her stash of little alcohol bottles. There were four more Captain Morgans and one Crown Royal.

She uncapped a Captain Morgan, took a swig, chased it with warm Sprite.

A van pulled up next to her. The sliding door crept open, and a happy family gushed out, excited for the night's possibilities.

God, I hate happy people, she thought.

She decided to drink her self-loathing away.

Forty-five minutes and five bottles later, Sara emerged from the car, stumbling, committed. She donned her hoodie and made for the tent, a swarm of butterflies fluttering about her stomach. She stopped at the porta-john to freshen up and stole a glance at herself in the foggy mirror. Although she felt mightily justified in her promiscuous endeavors, she still felt guilty. "Don't you look at me like that," she said to the opaque reflection and walked out.

She knocked on the door and walked in. It was markedly different. An interior entrance displayed a door of colorful beads. "These are new," she said, brushing them with her fingers. "Did your wife buy them?" she teased.

The beads functioned perfectly as a door, and she couldn't see beyond. When she passed through them, she stopped dead in her tracks. The room was completely different. There was no minibar, nor was there a fully furnished living room. The dimensions were perfectly sensible for a small tent. There was a small wooden table in the middle of the tent with two chairs on either side. That was it.

A short, pudgy woman twenty years her senior sat in the chair that faced the door, gazing into the crystal ball. She had beady little brown eyes with so much blue eyeshadow, it looked like a five-year-old had applied her make-up. Her eyebrows were penciled in. She was hunched over a crystal ball. She looked up, a mischievous smirk tugging the corner of her lips.

"Jus' on thime," the old woman said. "I been watch ju." She let that sink in, then: "Please seat."

Every fiber in Sara's being screamed for her to run. But she didn't. She needed to see Raul first. *Just once.* She sat down slowly, deciphering the woman's broken English. *I been watching you,* Sara thought as she scanned the small room. *The fuck does that mean?*

The only other thing aside from the small table and chairs was a massive aquarium that was behind the woman, home to a giant, yellow python.

"Raul tell me ju have fling, jes?" the old woman said.

Sara suddenly felt nauseated. Not from embarrassment but from sheer anger.

Who was this woman to take away the only thing I have? she thought.

"Ju've say nothin' for me?"

Sara studied her. She was old and gray-haired. Deep wrinkles crisscrossed her pruned face, and Sara thought she looked like how a testicle might look if it were soaked in water for too long. Her head had sunken into her shoulders a few inches like a scrotum retracting in the cold. *Why would Raul tell this woman about our affair?* Then a revelation—*Could it be possible? Would the beautiful and young Raul marry such a beast of a woman?*

"Who are you, and where is Raul?" Sara demanded.

"I am—" the old woman pulled her hand to her chest, "—Raul's wife." She studied Sara's figure. "I see why he like ju *Pizda*," she said. "Pretty face, jung body."

Sara had to take shit from her boss. She had to take shit from the father of her children. And on occasion, she even had to take shit from her children. But she didn't have to take shit from this little old lady.

"What happened to Raul?" Sara said urgently. "Where is he?"

"That's what ju have say tu me?" the old woman asked. "The wife of the man ju've been *schlepping?*"

The alcohol-lubricated years of pent-up anger and resentment boiled to the surface. She thought of the morning she found her mother's cold corpse. She thought of the perfect man she left her miserable husband for. She thought of the job she hated and the life she hated and let loose. "I have nothing to say to you, ya nasty old witch," she said. "That man is the *only* good thing in my life. Now where ... *the fuck ... is he?*"

"Welp, he *sss*lithers about like a snake somewheres, I'm sure," the old woman said with a devious smirk.

"Look-it, lady, I don't have time for this."

"Ju have to get back to jur family, jes?"

Sara didn't like her tone. "You don't know me," she snapped. "You don't know what my life is like. Who are you to judge me, Quisimodo?" Liquor made the words come out easily. "Yes, I slept with your husband, but it was *so* much more than that, he understands me."

Sara suspected she would regret being so mean.

The old woman's smug expression changed as she thought of the energy her husband exerted on this woman, this stranger; she grew very bitter and mischievous.

"Does snake look like ju know, jes?" The old woman threw a hitchhiker thumb over her shoulder toward the aquarium. "Take good look."

There was something deeply majestic and beautiful about the snake. Sara noticed it had long, thick eyelashes.

She leaned in, squinting.

The old woman jumped across the table and smeared cake frosting that smelled of frankincense, wormwood, and dog shit all over Sara's face. She laughed maniacally then pinned Sara down like a schoolyard bully.

"Ju sleep wit' a snake and leave me wit' scraps like a hog," the old woman said. "I steep ju in cake and leave ju strapped like a dog."

Sara managed to squirm her way out of the old woman's domineering posture and escape unscathed. When she got home, her husband was on the couch, passed out with Pizza Hut boxes and beer cans strewn about the living room as if it were a college dorm.

"Fuck my life," Sara whispered.

Her hair was sticky from the icing. She crept upstairs and took a shower. It was only 8:45 p.m. when she got into bed.

As she welcomed sleep to sweep her away, she mulled over the events of the strange night. *What the hell was that all about?* she thought. *Hogs and dogs and cakes and snakes—snakes.*

"Hey Siri," she said, "do snakes have eyelashes?"

"Here is what I found about snakes having eyelashes," Siri said.

Sara scrolled through the pictures and confirmed what she suspected was true—they did not. *How odd,* she thought.

She twirled the rose pendant necklace Raul gave her that was inside the cake the gypsy smeared in her face. *How the hell did she get my necklace into a cake?* Sara was confused. She struggled through the drunken haze and tried to remember what the old woman said but she was unable to.

She rolled the pendant necklace in her fingers and drifted to sleep.

Sara's head felt as if it had been split in half when she awoke in the backseat of what seemed to be a car fit for a giant. Her breaths were shallow, hasty; and she had an unadulterated desire to lick her belly.

"D'you think she'll be back?" Bella asked.

"I don't know," her father admitted.

"She wouldn't just leave us like that. Would she?"

"I don't know," her father repeated. "There was a rumor she was having an affair with a carny." He lifted his hands off the steering wheel and threw them up. "Maybe she finally left me. I've been expecting it for years now if I'm being honest."

There was a long pause.

"She promised she would never leave us," Bella said. She stroked the rose pendant necklace she had found wrapped around Butter's neck.

When Sara tried to speak to her daughter, only barks came out.

"It's okay, Butters," Bella said, leaning back and looking at Sara. "It'll all be over soon enough."

Betty awoke from the timeless dream at 3:00 a.m. She had only slept for a few hours, but it seemed like a lifetime—another's lifetime. Am I going mad? she thought. She tried confiding in her husband, but he tried to convince her it was nothing but an incredibly vivid dream. She considered seeing a therapist but feared she would be committed to a mental institution, and, for some reason, she felt like seeing a therapist was weak; she guarded her pain, her suffering, for in it, was a healing power.

That night she fought sleep as best she could, but she found herself humming a song she had never heard before, a maddeningly catchy chorus, boring a hole in her brain, driving her violently mad.

Crazy Shark

McCANN GLANCED AT THE CLOCK ON THE DASHBOARD. It read 3:23 a.m. He and his partner, Perez—a feisty little Dominican who wouldn't hesitate to punch you in the throat if you called her Puerto Rican—had just finished their third cup of coffee of the night, which—if not for sweet old Mrs. Clawson calling at 10:08 p.m. about her neighbor's loud music—had been utterly uneventful, a welcoming reprieve after six hellish days of unsolved break-ins and robberies.

The seconds from 12:00 a.m. to 6:00 a.m. carry a different length depending on activity level, and when not immersed in conducting the duties of the job, that length can seem immeasurable, particularly brutal if spent in bad company. Luckily, McCann and Perez shared no such problem. They'd known each other for the better part of their lives. It was like a smooth dance, their partnership, a delicate and precious blessing that neither took for granted, each knowing when to talk and when not to talk, when to press or to give space, complimenting each other's personalities and temperaments, their strengths and weaknesses, forging a bond that was both rare and cherished.

"One hand washes the next." That was the password they used to enter the fort they'd built in the woods that cut the town in half when they were seven years old. Twenty-six years later, it was as true now as it was then.

On a slow night such as tonight, they passed the time talking about the Cornhuskers bowl prospects or reliving the glory years of Osbourne and Frasier/Kramer, online shopping, debating theology, telling dirty jokes, comparing bucket lists, etc.

Tonight, they argued over the nuances of job security regarding gender.

"I'm jus' sayin' chicks are more emotional, s'all." McCann said this as if it were the only school of thought available, shocked that he even needed to present an argument.

They used to pass the time fucking. Sometimes, three, four times a night. In the backseat of the cruiser, against the dumpster in the back alley behind O'Malley's, in the drunk tank at headquarters, seemingly intent on scratching *fuck everywhere* off both their bucket lists. But Perez's boyfriend had proposed a few weeks prior and while she considered cheating on her boyfriend perfectly acceptable, cheating on her fiancé was *no bueno*.

And while McCann argued a case for the emotional superiority of men over women—he, himself, was eternally hurt, lashing out like a passive-aggressive toddler in need of his pacifier. Her love was like crack and he, an addict.

"C'mon. Just one *more* time," he'd begged her the previous Friday in the abandoned parking lot of the auto shop that'd closed its doors in 2020 at the onset of Covid. *Why else would we go to our favorite spot if not to*—

But despite McCann's sentimental attachment to their favorite spot, he failed to consider that there wasn't much to the small town of Flint, Nebraska, which offered a gas station, a small hardware store, post office, and a courthouse which doubled as a jail. Sandwiched between Lincoln and Omaha like a sweaty taint, Flint was so small that if you blinked while driving, you'd find yourself in another town, just as small, just as forgettable, swallowed by a sea of waving corn stalks on either side.

When Perez refused his desperate chivalries, he called her a "selfish spick cunt" and she gave him the shiner that still lingered and stung every time he put concealer on. But the sting to his black eye was nothing compared to the sting to his heart. Every time he put the concealer on, he was forced to remember the lessons she'd given him as she concealed the hickeys on his neck over ten years prior:

"All's ya gotta do is dab it ... that's it ... just dab it, lightly," she said, straddling his naked lap, her nipples caressing his chest as she leaned forward, her warm flesh intertwined with his, a lock and key, so perfect, so right.

"23, dispatch." The radio mounted on the dashboard danced and twinkled in red and green lights, festive as it was lively.

McCann pushed the memory away and said, "That's why men make better cops. We're jus' more 'motionaly stable."

He nodded at Perez with utter finality and removed the walkie from its brace. Then, into the walkie: "Dispatch, go for 23."

McCann was squinting at Perez and never one to back down, she squinted right back. He didn't actually believe the nonsense he was spewing about men being more emotionally stable, for he himself was an emotional wreck, but—like when he called her a "selfish spick cunt"—he knew the overt slate would dig under her skin and take root in her ego, clawing, gnawing, begging for an argument, which, inevitably, begs for reconciliation.

He was weaponizing her feisty temperament to instigate an episode of passion—love. Hate. Anger. It didn't matter to him. It was all passion.

He wriggled his eyebrows, and she smiled the smallest of smiles, barely perceptible but for the eyes.

"We gotta call from Jerry, *implorin'* us to check out a lot at Happy Homes," said Francine.

McCann and Perez shared an amused look. McCann spoke into the walkie: "*Implorin' us, eh?* Look at you, Fran, with your fancy pance words. Don't forget 'bout us common folk when you finish your degree."

Covering dispatch was Perez's baby cousin, Francine, who'd been having a tough go of it of late and had severe self-esteem issues. Perez was fiercely protective of her, and McCann looked at Perez when he talked, hoping to see in her eyes a reflection of what he felt in his heart for her, hoping she'd give him an approving smile. He'd do anything to see that smile.

He was an objectively good-looking man: tall, stocky, he had all his hair and teeth—which in Flint is better than most prospects—but his pappy always told him, "The way to win a woman's heart, *n'keep it,* ya see, is to make her smile more than you make her cry, sonny boy."

And Perez was smiling, a beautiful, evanescent smile, light seemingly exploding in a coronal halo about her angelic face. Only she didn't hear him, and the light wasn't an internal radiance, but the phone she held as she scrolled exotic pictures of St. Thomas, Bermuda, Jamaica, and other honeymoon spots.

McCann took her phone and chucked it on the ground. And when she opened her mouth to unleash the sassy Latina spirit that made for such passionate lovemaking, he put his finger over her mouth, moving it playfully back and forth as if his finger was lipstick, nodding at the radio with a sly smirk. When you've spent as much time together as these two, first as friends, then lovers, and now partners, you develop a symbiotic relationship that requires little speech. They knew each other's grunts, moans; they knew what the other was thinking simply by their posture. And Perez's mind translated the smirk and nod— *You gotta hear this.*

She sighed heavily and turned her attention to the radio, her stunning profile accentuated against the passenger side window.

Regal and legendary, she had the face of a goddess and the body of a porn star.

"Why does Jerry implore us over to check out Happy Homes," McCann said, holding Perez's gaze, lost in her large fiery brown eyes. "Did he get ripped off again?"

Two months prior, Jerry called emergency dispatch where McCann was stationed for the night. Jerry made such a fuss over the incident that McCann decided to enlist Coon and Boon, two of the bigger surrounding towns, for help as well.

"Send everyone," Jerry had said in a panic. "And please … *hurry.*" So ominous, so loaded with the probability of disaster—that little two-second pause between please and hurry—it's what compelled McCann to make the call to Coon and Boon; it certainly wasn't what Jerry was saying, because McCann didn't understand half the shit Jerry was going on about and he damn well should've known better.

But that pause was so fucking … *convincing.*

Perez was the first on the scene and instead of clearing out the call, she decided to give McCann a proper lesson on procedural call vetting. "You'd better call Denning, too, Mac," Perez had said, fighting through the urge to laugh; her voice, serious, sincere. "I don't think Coon and Boon will be enough."

Then she went offline. She and Coon and Boon and she even got Denning on board. Everyone went dark, ignoring dispatch, driving McCann mad with perilous possibility. And just as McCann was about to leave the station and head to Perez's last known location, four sheriff's vehicles—all distinct makes and models and with different colors and words, representing the surrounding towns—snaked around the gravel road off Route 30, kicking up dust as the earth met the sun and the moon and the stars in that quiet twilight moment when the sun breaks the surface to the east casting light on the rest of the falling cosmos.

Perez was the lead vehicle. She pulled up, smiling. Jerry was in the backseat, eyes big, hands behind his back, thrashing back and forth. The back window was lowered; McCann could scarcely make out what he was saying.

Perez got out of the car, smile brighter than the rising sun.

"What the hell happened," McCann said. Though this wasn't the first time Jerry had played him, he declared then and there it would be the last time.

Perez put her hands on her hips and said, "Well, Jer here seems to think that we're the Better Business Bureau and called because he thinks Baby John John shorted him on a sack."

"He did short me, Goddamnit. I'ma call the FBI on you, too, Dani, 'restin' me for no reason ... no reason at all ... I got the right to bear drugs if I done made it m'self." Jerry had waived his right to remain silent and he went on like that for the rest of the night, regurgitating a litany of ill-advised legal defenses that he'd learned from other meth heads, who are, many of them, self-anointed jailhouse lawyers, which would explain their extensive arrest history.

News of McCann's blunder spread fast, reaching Chris Bane, the Attorney General of Nebraska, who sent him a sticker of the Better Business Bureau to put on his desk, one of those given to children when they visit on field trips.

It was a small town, and McCann caught shit from everyone. But there was only one person he cared about.

Perez was a country girl raised on country values and raised to like country men. The few city boys that settled in their small corner of the world— "Running away from drugs or problems," her mother always said—never stayed long enough to realize they were the problem before they sourced it outside of themselves and went to pollute the next town with their presence.

She wasn't attracted to them anyways. She liked big burly tough men, men with thick beards and hair on their chest, men who chugged beer and knew their way around a farm, and McCann was convinced that this, above all other reasons, was what put him out of contention for her heart resolutely, the reason Perez decided to marry that twat instead of him. He'd been made to look weak. His persistent insecurities, never a problem before then, were now the wedge that drove Perez further away, not the fiancé, according to McCann, who suddenly felt as if he was the subject of another joke.

How stupid do they think I am? he thought. *And using Jerry again to deliver it? Poor choice, Asshole General Bane.*

"Please keep traffic for matters that are serious, Fran," McCann said into the walkie with as much authority as he could muster. Jerry had played him, had turned him into a laughing stock. Never again.

Once shame on you, he thought. *Twice shame on me.*

"This is serious, boss," Franny said.

"What's he sayin'?"

Please ... help.

"Well ... I ain't entirely sure."

"Then it ain't exactly an emergency, now is it, Franny?"

Perez hit McCann on the thigh hard.

"He's goin' on 'bout kids, sir," Franny said. "The kids are hurt, the kids are n'danger. And music. He's worried the music will hurt the kids? I don't know. But it sounds serious."

Please ... help.

Rubbing the knot out of his thigh, McCann said, "Tell him to call DCFS 'cuz I ain't gonna fall ..."

Perez snatched the walkie from his hand. "What's his position," she said, staring out the passenger side window, intentionally avoiding McCann's eyes because she knew he'd be squinting playfully and saying with his eyes—*See, girls are more emotional.* The thought of it made her smirk.

She loved McCann. He was employed, nice, funny, he had all his hair and teeth—which in Flint is better than most prospects—and he was great in bed. But any chance they ever had at happiness passed them by long ago and though she cherished their long friendship, they had no future aside from the occasional hookup.

Besides, she was no longer attracted to him. He was too timid now, too sensitive, too insecure. The alpha male gene she'd gravitated toward before was gone, and another alpha took his spot: Attorney General Bane. She didn't have the heart to tell McCann that not only did she call it off with her fiancé, but that she was transferring to Omaha at the end of next month to move in with Bane, but not before they went on a little vacation.

"Corner lot," Francine said. "*Janet's* lot."

"At least this'll give us an excuse to pop in," Perez said to McCann, who nodded. "We're enroute," she said into the walkie. Then, after a few seconds, when McCann opened his mouth to say something: "Not a fuckin' word." He smiled and she smiled and then they drove in silence.

They were at the trailer park in a few minutes. It was a large complex. Twenty acres of dense bungalows and singlewides with a few doublewides spread intermittently like bars of gold in a field of shit. An overwhelming majority of the residents rented both the trailer and the lot, but a few of them owned either one or the other.

A new resident, Janet Bigelow, had just bought the two corner lots, and she put up six more trailers since she moved in three months prior.

"It's my land, innit?" That's what she told McCann when the landowner called complaining of the new trailers. "And the law says I can do wit' my land as I want, now go on, git."

Of course, she was right. Legally the landowner didn't have a leg to stand on. The lot fell into unincorporated limbo, it dwelled in that gray area where residents could tell you to get fucked if they so wished, unless, of course, they require taxpayer amenities like firetrucks and ambulances. And when Perez said, "At least this'll give us an excuse to pop in," she was talking about the sheriff's mission to rid his town of Janet Bigelow and her band of merry squatters—

"I don't care how you do it," he'd said. "Just getter done."

On the downlow, he'd promised McCann a raise if he got the job done, a raise his crippling ego desperately needed.

For two months McCann spent his off-duty hours watching the lot in a trailer owned by the PD, but aside from the overall sketchiness of the lot and its residents, it didn't share the telltale signs of a trap spot.

Traffic was low, most people that stopped stayed for days if they left at all. They were always doing some kind of construction, bringing in supplies and tote boxes, but they always left with the same tote boxes. And the few people that McCann pulled over after leaving either didn't have drugs on them, or they had very little and would rather take the time than turn snitch and conduct a controlled buy on Janet Bigelow. He was shocked, *shocked*, that he was unable to catch a felon with drugs and one strike left. It was unheard of.

He often imagined Janet taking people's keys like his mother used to do when he was in high school.

"I'm a MADD mother." She used to say this with a grave expression, squinting, frown scrunched in, as she went around the house filling drinks and taking keys. "You, too, Jerry. I love you, honey, but I'm a Mother Against Drunk Drivers."

Only in McCann's mind, Janet wasn't letting the people leave with drugs.

Well, played, Janet, he thought. *Well, played.*

For the first time in a long time, McCann was grateful for Jerry. He could almost forgive him. Almost.

It was dark. A lonely streetlight buzzed with an electrical hum above them, gnats and mosquitos flying and buzzing about. The next streetlight was twenty meters in either direction, lighting enough to realize just how little you could see. There was a barrel fire in the far-right corner of the land with a few people around it, but aside from that, there didn't seem to be much traffic.

"So how you wanna play this?" Perez said.

Though McCann's ego could use a pedi and a medi (shit, a facelift too) to help him feel better about himself, he was not the one on administrative probation. Perez had another forty-seven days remaining on her ninety-day probation for an incident where she "accidentally" slammed a man's head through the driver's side door when he left his two-year-old in the backseat. The only reason she wasn't arrested was because they agreed to knock the child endangerment down to a misdemeanor if he didn't press charges. If she could make it forty-seven more days without incident, then she could put in for transfer to Omaha PD.

"We use the kid angle," McCann said. "Simple health and welfare."

"Just a couple of concerned neighbors."

"*Howdy-do, neighbor.*" They said this at the same time and laughed at the same time. It was an inside joke regarding a horse and a drunken man who was utterly naked but for the boot on his left foot.

"Remember when he ..." They didn't see Jerry until he was pounding on Perez's window. She screamed. McCann laughed, but only to hide the fact that he screamed, too.

"You *mother fucker.*" Perez lowered her window. "Don't ever do that shit again, Jer."

"I get an award for this?" Jerry skipped the pleasantries and went right to work. He started doing the contortionist bit that he was known for, it was even included in his rap sheet under identifying marks, the meth in his blood moving his torso and arms awkwardly as he twisted and turned. He stared at Perez with little patience, then. "I get an award for this, r'not, Dani?" There was desperation in his voice and in his eyes.

"What are you talkin' 'bout?" Perez was confused, mostly because she couldn't imagine Jerry possessing any form of civic morality. She imagined him getting an award from the mayor and had to reroute her thoughts because if she went down that road, she'd be laughing all night.

"An award for what?" she said, confused.

"He means a reward." McCann looked at the streetlight when he spoke. He could hardly stand to be in Jerry's presence.

"S'what I said, innit?" Jerry said. "I getta reward for this, yeah?"

Jerry's arms flailed like balloons full of water, one of those gyrating blowup dolls at cellphone stores and headshops. "'Cuz all 'em tweakers ain't gonna like that I blew up they spot."

He had this entitled bewilderment playing in his eyes, such seriousness, such earnestness. It took everything in Perez not to burst out in a fit of laughter. She grabbed McCann's hand and squeezed hard. He knew the gesture. She was teetering on the brink of hysteria. He squeezed her hand. They looked at each other from the corner of their eyes. McCann nodded. *Put your game face on,* he said with his eyes. *We'll laugh about it later.*

McCann cleared his throat and said, "What tweakers?"

"*All a'em.*" Jerry threw his arms up as if he were including the whole world, pointing toward the corner lot, spinning in circles, delirious, desperate, his eyes bulging from his head like a cartoon character.

McCann shined his floodlight on the path to the corner lot and the light enveloped six naked people—four men and two women. They looked at the light, confused, scared, having sex in the dark. The light was too bright, and they couldn't see, but someone on the left screamed, "*5-0.*" And there was a great ruffling as the bed of leaves was disturbed and McCann swiveled the spotlight to see a dozen people scattering like rolypolys hiding under an upturned rock. It was like something out of a horror film, the final scene when the protagonist finds the vampire lair and must kill the minions to get to the boss. Only they didn't stand and fight. They scurried about, their hands full of innocuous items, bumping into each other like a team of cops trying to capture Charlie Chaplin.

"It was *Jerry.*" The voice came from the left. "*Jerry called 'em.*"

McCann shone the light in the direction of the voice, where a man tried escaping with a disassembled vacuum cleaner which proved difficult in the leaves, so he threw it over his shoulders and ran up the steps into one of the smaller six trailers, like a kid playing a game of tag and the trailer was base. There, he was untouchable.

Neener neener neener.

"A*www, man.*" Jerry was twirling in circles, head toward the sky with an agonized look on his face. "I told you they was gonna know."

The news of his betrayal would spread fast, and Jerry would be excommunicated by every meth head in Flint and the surrounding areas. They were like a club, the meth community, a club with one rule only: *never* snitch. He'd betrayed that covenant and by the end of the day, he'd be a man without a tribe. He rolled on the ground crying.

"I *knew* I *shouldina* called you guys."

McCann didn't feel bad for him. Not even a little. He'd grown up with Jerry. They played little league baseball together and then at high school. McCann was a decent third-base man with a wide stretch and a rocket for an arm, but Jerry made first team all-state at short stop three years in a row. He had Big Ten scouts watching him play; his agility, his speed, his reflexes, all coveted traits; he was naturally ambidextrous, and batted .350 righty, .333 with his left.

But meth had flooded the streets of Flint, Nebraska. And because of its wide availability, kids skipped marijuana and experimented with meth instead. Jerry was hooked right away. But McCann didn't like the way it made him feel, the way he'd be up for days, the way he'd spend ten hours watching porn, beating his dick until he either bled or came.

And the more meth he did, the more disconnected from reality he became.

McCann remembers very vividly the last time he used: it was Halloween 2008, and his tolerance had built up rather quickly, such is life. Jerry—who'd graduated to IV use (such is life)—convinced him to slam a thick .30 cc rig. His arm burned like battery acid as the meth entered his veins, the fire spreading up his arm toward his heart, snaking around his armpit, and when it hit his chest, it took his breath away and for a second, he thought he'd die right there. Then came the cough, an uncontrollable cough that pierced the very bottom of his esophagus and came bursting out his mouth in sputtering waves.

When the burning subsided, and the coughing, he was left with a feeling of utter despair.

"It was *too* much," he kept saying, trying to remember if he'd ever heard of anyone overdosing on meth. "It was too much, Jerry. *Too much.*"

But Jerry was preoccupied with his own emergency: using a phone app that purported to locate hidden cameras, he swept the basement, certain that his girlfriend had strategically planted at least one hidden camera.

McCann acclimated after a few minutes, Goldilocking from too much to just right. He fed off Jerry's fear and utter certainty of the hidden camera, joining him in the fun and games, downloading the app and meticulously scanning every square inch of basement. *Did I scan that already? Yes? Oh well, I'll do it again.*

There was nothing more satisfying in the world to do than what he was doing right then and every time their phones approached an electronic device, the barometer in the app picked up radio frequencies and Jerry and McCann thought it was hiding a hidden camera and they gutted the fucker, neither of them knowing what they were looking for, but certain they would find it.

"Is this it, Jer?" McCann said, holding up the innerworkings of the gutted tv.

"Surely is. You see how it's got words on it? That means someone else put it there."

Three hours later, after every inch of the basement had been scanned and every device had been vetted and destroyed, the ground covered in chips and mainframes and other functional components, a technological graveyard.

The novelty wore off and Jerry went to ensure the upstairs was free of cameras, too.

And with the certainty of privacy—*no cameras down here*—McCann found it perfectly sensible to jerk off. He found a delightful porn video but then found another and another. Another. Before long, there were fifty-six tabs open on his phone, all of them containing certain attributes that demanded his attention, but too many good options to pick from—*if only I had fifty-six dicks*—trying to get in stride with the circle and twist motion he favored while flipping through the videos, appreciating the variety but not spending too much time on any one video, no lubrication, twisting and turning, skin-burning, every so often seeing fairies and shadow people in the corner of his eyes, disregarding them because *at least they're not recording me.* Flipping through another tab, an hour passed. Two. Four. *Fuck this.* He snuck in the bathroom looking for Vaseline, lube, lotion, soap, *anything*. He found a lonely pink bottle with a woman's smooth legs hiding under the sink behind a stack of toilet paper. *Perfect.* He went back to playing bleed or cum.

He'd been up for four days, the lack of sleep contributing to the shadow people and fairies, a normal occurrence when sleep-deprived, as natural as floating specks and dots. But then, somewhere between reality and psychosis, he had a dream; a terrible, terrible dream; or at least he thought it was a dream; a vision, perhaps; a premonition—whatever it was, he thought it really happened—he thought he'd killed a kid.

He came to, pants around his ankles, right forearm throbbing, muffled moans of ecstasy coming from his phone which was under him and so hot it was almost burning his taint. He hit the side button on the phone, putting it to sleep (poor thing'd been working for hours). Silence.

He looked about him, trying to remember where he was, who he was. When one is on a cycle of sleeping only a few hours every four days, their mind's ability to retain memory has a lagging system, and upon waking, it takes a few minutes to remember anything.

He repositioned himself on the bed of discarded technology. A sharp burning sensation shot through his groin, and he noticed his dick was red and raw and shedding skin like a snake, his pubic hairs wet and shedding in patches, the acidic smell of female hygiene triggering memories of his childhood and his mother's lady preparation. It was a very particular smell, and it wasn't the pleasant smell of strawberry or raspberry as the pink bottle would have you think. He wiped his dick and screamed. He'd lost the game. He bled. He bled very badly. But the game appeared to be fixed because what he thought was lotion was something else entirely.

He glanced at the bottle and read the label: *What the fuck is Nair?* He picked it up, fuming as he read its function, the deceiving sketch of a woman with perfectly moisturized legs. *There should be a fucking warning label on this. Skeleton, cross and bones. Smiley face with* two red x's for eyes. *Something other than the sketch of a woman with perfectly moisturized legs.*

He considered suing the company: *No sir, I don't know what perfectly moisturized legs look like in a drawing, but I know what they should not look like.*

As he contemplated how his testimony might transpire, it clicked, just like that, a flash, a moment of cosmic knowledge inserting into his consciousness. The time lag on his mind had caught up, ending the memory embargo, and as the dreadful reality of his situation settled in, utter dread and guilt and shame enveloped him.

What the fuck am I doing? he thought shamefully. *Jerking off when I killed a kid last night?*

He gathered himself, crying, grabbing a pillow, wiping his discarded pubes on it so it looked like a wet dog laid there, pulling his pants up, wondering how long it'd be before he became someone's bitch in prison, giving out handskis for protection?

He grabbed his phone and glanced at the open tabs: *doggystyle compilation, busty MILFS, stepsister fucks stepbrother* ... and the shroud of filth and disgust deepened, it deepened so much he could hardly breathe.

There was a dead kid somewhere. Of this, he was certain. How the kid died, he did not know. But a small voice in his head kept saying, *Vehicular homicide.* He cried harder, forgetting he did not even own a car. The guilt encapsulated him. It's all he could fathom. And the shame. The utter shame of it. *Oh my god and the poor kid's parents?* His mind created various tidbits of the kid's life, things only people that knew the kid could know: *he was eleven, turning twelve this winter. He had a crush on his best friend's mom and sister. He liked to watch movies, comedy and horror, he liked canned Chef Boyardee and playing sports. He wanted a Nintendo 64 for Christmas. And he's dead.*

McCann would've bet his life on that last bit. It was empirical.

He grabbed his phone, considering if he should get high and jerk off one last time as a free man, but decided that he didn't have hours to waste. The sooner he turned himself in the better it would look, and besides, *if they knew I was jerking off while the poor kid laid dead somewhere on the side of the road, they'd think me deranged.*

Again, he thought of the poor kid's parents. He cried some more. The guilt and the shame ate at him and then came the fear: *They can see my search history.* He scrolled the tabs and the desire to jerk off again activated a deranged compulsion and obsession far surpassing depravity. He quickly factory reset his phone, took out the battery, hid the battery in the back right pocket of a coat hiding in the back of the closet—*just in case they try to track me*—and then washed the phone under a faucet before smashing it with a piece of what used to be a television but what Jerry called a "Transmiterator."

He found Jerry upstairs coloring masterfully in a coloring book, so immersed that he scarcely noticed McCann, who demanded to be taken to the police station at once for the murder—*or was it homicide?*—of an undetermined eleven-year-old boy. *Soon to be twelve.*

Two things happened that day: it was the last time McCann ever used meth. And it was the end of McCann's and Jerry's fifteen-year friendship spanning back to when they were five years old.

With the fear and memory of committing a murder that he never committed, McCann was scared straight. It seemed so real that he could hardly believe it didn't happen and often he imagined another McCann paying for the crime he most certainly committed in an alternate universe.

Jerry, on the other hand, stayed the course. He honed the fierce competitiveness that made him such a great baseball player and strived to be the best at anything he did. That included meth.

Perez got out of the car and walked to Jerry slowly, bending over, approaching him like a wild animal, hand out, speaking gently:

"It's okay, Jer," she said. "Everything's gonna be okay, hon." She started rubbing his back softly, the same way she used to do in high school when they dated for two years, back when he was an all-star shortstop. She'd always had a soft spot in her heart for him, her first love. But the good-looking, funny, sweet, charming Jerry she once knew had been relegated to skin and bones, scars, and fresh scabs all over his body from "digging the bugs out," the teeth currently in his mouth paid for in full by the good people of Nebraska.

"You mentioned somethin' about kids. Jer?" Perez kept right on rubbing his back.

You're wasting your time, Dani, McCann thought. But he was quite certain now this wasn't part of an elaborate joke.

At the mention of kids, Jerry sat upright, in a panic, as if he suddenly remembered that he forgot to shut the stove off. "She's got the kids up in the main trailer," he said.

"Who does?"

"Janet, *the bitch.*" Jerry started mumbling something or another about the decline of quality drug dealers, about how they took advantage of people's time, and how, "If McDonald's treated 'em cusmers like this, well, then, I'd just go to Burger King, I don't care how good dem chicken nuggets are, I would ..."

McCann got out of the car and circled around to Perez and Jerry. "Slow down, killer," he said. "What exactly did she do?" He stared at Jerry on the ground. *That could've been me,* he thought.

"She went crazy, is what she done did ... *crazy* ... letting her kids listen to that fucking song over n'over, usin' it as a babysitter, she was. I told her. I did. I says, 'That song's gonna drive ya crazy, Jan,' but she never listens to me." He looked at Perez with hopeful eyes, then: "Am I gonna get an award for this?"

"He's fuckin' useless," McCann said. *Why are we here?*

He took out his flashlight and spun around slowly, taking in the scene. There was a stillness to the night, peaceful, serene; but there was something else also, layered like the tater tot casserole his grandma used to bake when he was a kid, the one with the Fritos and meat on the bottom, and lettuce and tomato on top. He had a feeling that all wasn't as it seemed, that the stillness was misleading, hiding something bad, something nasty, a trick; like vegetables in a perfectly good casserole.

The tire swing swayed as the soft breeze blew gently, kicking up the top layer of leaves briefly before dying down. The man with the vacuum from earlier opened the blinds and looked out, a set of binoculars wrapped around his neck, and a military grade set of night-vision goggles strapped to his head. McCann laughed. He remembered how he used to get high with Jerry and play with those.

Stay on point, he thought and kept walking, looking.

In many ways, the set-up and function of the corner lot resembled a small-scale slave plantation, with the main house in the far corner and six smaller ones (three on either side) within a call's distance, the meth heads checking in regularly to see what errands needed to be done, taking orders from the main house. It was the only lot that had grass, though he could barely notice because of the thick blanket of leaves which had started accumulating dew on this brisk autumn morning. There were four big oak trees, one on each corner, protecting the lot from an unforgiving sun under a canopy of shade. The trees were fifty feet apart, with five-fifty cord pulled taut, and a few pairs of old jeans hanging on one.

McCann stepped closer. Leaves crunched. He heard something. Faint. Indiscernible. It was coming in the direction of the main house. He took another step. *Is that ...*

"But, Dani, you don't get it, they ain't gonna sell me *fuck all* now." Jerry had pulled himself from the ground, crushed leaves stuck on his clothes and in his hair, crumbling off as he moved his hands, hurriedly pleading his case. He was a few feet from Perez, puppy-dog eyes, looking like a spoiled child who knew which parent was the pushover.

McCann took another step. He unbuckled his holster, hand hovering, flashlight on a swivel, moving forward.

"The least ya'll can do is pay me reparations for ..."

"Shut him *the fuck up.*" McCann was trying to listen.

Perez was about to sneak Jerry a twenty spot and tell him to scat when she noticed McCann advancing stealth-like.

"Watcha got, partner?" She left Jerry with his pockets open. She took out her flashlight, unbuckled her holster and filed in next to McCann, walking slowly, knees bent, head on a swivel. A light breeze from the east carried on its ethereal wing's music, a very particular, very popular song, a child's song. They took a few steps more then stopped, tilting their heads, capturing the noise in their ears.

"Is that 'Baby Shark'?" McCann said. He didn't like kids much. They were a perpetual cycle of need personified—feed me, bathe me, burp me, change me, rock me, watch me. He was too selfish to give another human being that much attention. And he knew it, too. But that's not what he'd told Perez five years prior, right before she left him. He had a healthy fear of becoming a father. His parents fucked him up all kinds of a ways from Sunday and he didn't want to pass that dysfunction on. Which, to him, at least, seemed the most selfless thing to do.

And rather than giving the woman he loved the thing she wanted more than anything, McCann martyred himself, sabotaging his relationship with Perez and forever placing himself in a zone that neighbored the friend zone.

Though, to be fair, he had a valid argument. His father died of cirrhosis of the liver when he was ten, but not before putting in years of abuse, beating McCann's ass for reasons that eluded him even to this day.

His mother was also an alcoholic, though her drug of choice was meth. When he was seventeen years old, she left him for whichever drug dealer she'd been fucking that week. *Bob? Or was it Rob? Maybe Bobby? Billy? Brent?* ... It didn't matter. She'd left him with no money or food in the fridge and never returned. He didn't even know if she was still alive.

To the rest of the world, McCann projected a tough and macho man incapable of being vulnerable, or showing weakness, but inside, he was an emotionally stunted man, a child in a man's body, with enough insecurities to fill an Olympic-sized pool.

"That's what I been tryna tell yas." Jerry's eyes bulged, fear filling them like helium filling a balloon. "The music *made her* do it."

McCann looked at him closer. It wasn't fear in his eyes. It was grief.

McCann turned slightly to meet Perez's eyes. *Made her do it?*

They pulled their guns from their holsters at the same time, nodding, synchronizing. They linked up back-to-back, Perez covering the rear, sweeping the lot in a 180-degree circumference, conscious that all the meth heads here got their meth from the main house, ready to shoot a slave that was loyal to their master. McCann covered the front half, hunched over, knees bent, flashlight resembling a lighthouse as he made wide, steady sweeps.

They were fifty feet away. The trailer seemed massive in the corner, a menacing beast of a structure that could fit two of the smaller ones in its belly.

The music was unmistakable now.

McCann was made to watch the sherriff's kids one night while he worked dispatch, and he would never forget that maddening tune.

Baby Shark, doo-doo, doo-doo.

For hours, he endured its insufferable singing. It was seared in his mind for days. He found himself humming it in the shower, while eating breakfast, or watching the game.

Twenty feet away.

The big house was the only trailer in the lot that was horizontal from the entrance. The other six were diagonal, staggered, perhaps strategically, perhaps not. It had three exits. One on either side and in the middle a sliding door—which McCann stared at, ten feet away—with a massive deck that was undoubtedly the handy work of one of the savvier meth heads. The deck was freshly painted. It had a picnic table tucked in the right corner with a retracted umbrella jammed in the middle. A gas grill was in front of the picnic table, the plastic cover reflecting the porch light with unusual brightness.

Baby Shark, doo-doo, doo-doo.

"Dispatch. 23," McCann said into his shoulder.

"23, dispatch."

"We're on location. I'm 'bout to knock but the music is blaring, and I doubt if they'll hear. I'll keep you informed."

"Copy, 23."

McCann stood at the bottom of the steps. A thick blanket prevented prying eyes from looking inside. They looked at each other, smiling, acknowledging the irony of having a Baby Shark blanket covering the glass. McCann climbed the steps, Perez by his side, an odd mixture of adrenaline and anxiety mixing in her blood, tingling her fingers and toes. She looked at McCann and nodded. He knocked. Waited.

He knocked again louder. And again, nothing. One more time, he knocked. And he got the same result. He tried the door. It was locked. He looked down at Perez, her neck straining to meet his eyes. He gestured his head to the left. She nodded.

They descended the steps and peeled off, McCann right, Perez left. They went around the trailer, searching for unusual activity, but there was none to be had. They met in the middle. Perez was getting worried. From all outside appearances, there was no cause for worry. But there was something severely wrong here. Of that she was certain.

"C'mon," McCann said. They went to the door on the right and knocked. Twice. Thrice. But all they heard from the inside was *Baby Shark, doo-doo, doo-doo.*

Perez jumped the steps. "Wadawe gonna do if they don't answer?" McCann knew from her voice and demeanor that she was worried.

"Wadaya think we're gonna do?" he said, smiling at her. She smiled back. God, he loved that smile. He would do anything to see that smile every day.

They went to the back door and knocked.

McCann leaned his head and spoke on the walkie. "Dispatch. 23."

"23, dispatch."

"We're gonna breach," he said. "You wanna send some backup?"

"23, dispatch," Franny said. "Trackin'. Go for breach. Backup will be there shortly."

McCann looked at Perez who had this look in her eyes, wild and unhinged. Despite her small stature, or perhaps because of it, she was the toughest and strongest person he'd ever met. He may not be the one she went home to every night, but she was his ride or die, now and forever.

She closed her eyes and rolled her shoulders, a familiar gesture she also did when she was getting annoyed. How many times had he seen her do that? How many calls? McCann laughed lightly and said, "Easy there, tiger. We're not going to Ed's tavern." She opened her eyes and let out a loud guttural laugh. It was another inside joke, one of the many they shared together. Her smile was brilliant under the soft lighting. Her posture loosened. She needed that.

"Okay. I sweep left, you sweep right." She nodded. "And don't do anything you can't come back from." He held her eyes, nodded seriously then. "Forty-seven days. Remember."

How could she forget? She'd be on a sandy beach somewhere in the Caribbean, ordering drinks from the swim-up bar and getting couples massages with AG Bane.

McCann knocked one more time for the birds.

Baby Shark, doo-doo, doo-doo.

He took a step back—his shadow casting on the wall, short and small, completely disrespecting his 6'4 stature. Then he put his size 13.5 boot through the cheap door. His leg shot through and got stuck. He jumped up and down on the other foot as he tried to maintain balance. Perez wrapped her tiny arms around his back and pulled hard, her laughs barely audible under the blaring music.

Working in tandem, McCann was able to free his leg. Pieces of refurbished wood hit his chest and fell to the ground. He laughed. She laughed. And if not for the loud noise informing those inside that they had visitors, they would've laughed and shared a beautiful moment together, adding the lovely memory to a long list of lovely memories and another inside joke that they both cherished dearly.

Later, his eyes said.

He stuck his hand through the hole, unlocked the door, and threw it back. A foot in the door, his feet stopped working and his heart sank.

The trailer had an open layout, with a massive living room that was easily half of the 1200-sq footage claimed in the title, with a small kitchen to the left which bled seamlessly into the dining area.

To the right, a narrow hallway led to three bedrooms and one bath. But, in typical trap house fashion, the open layout seemed convoluted, the floor covered to the ceiling in boxes and crates and tools and electronics and toys and any innocuous item one could fathom.

There was an electric generator on the left, which was reported stolen the night prior by Fred Astaire on 1st avenue. Car radios and GPS systems and jewelry. They'd found who was behind the rash of robberies that'd hit the small town. But that's not what caught his attention.

The ceiling was caked in a thick yellow film, a dreadful combination of tobacco smoke and meth smoke with splashes of red interspersed.

A rat with a five-inch tail navigated past a stack of DVDs and ran toward the bedrooms.

The air was hot, humid, the smell toxic, unbreathable (literally). On the dining room table that connects the kitchen with the living room, there was an elaborate contraption of clear tubes and beakers running up and down, swooping left and right into vats like some eccentric game of mouse trap. On the left, bottles of Drano and other cleaning products. The right side was reserved solely for the main ingredient: Sudafed. Boxes upon boxes stacked together to form a mountain—Mount Decongestion.

All of it made for a scene straight out of *Hoarders,* but it *still* wasn't the reason McCann's feet stopped working at the doorway.

The reason his brain refused to tell his feet to take a step—he would later admit as he drank himself into oblivion—was fear, pure and simple.

Perez bumped into him, then pushed past him, gasping, and wrenching when she saw what had McCann so shook. But instead of fear, a primordial mutation activated some ancient maternal gene inherited from her animal ancestors and her body injected with anger, adrenaline. Purely instinctual, she took off running into the hallway, bumping into a stack of old *Maxims* and *Playboys.*

McCann wanted to follow Perez, but he couldn't take his eyes off it, the horror of it, the untenable horror. He closed his eyes but that only seemed to make it worse, pictures flashing seemingly on a beat to the music, the fucking music burning into his ear canal and settling in his brain, mixing with the vision like a macabre, synchronized Christmas light show.

Baby Shark, doo-doo, doo-doo.

He opened his eyes, searching for the stereo that delivered the vile song, a song that would henceforth activate his PTSD and send him into an immediate and unforgiving panic attack which could only be alleviated with alcohol and copious amounts of benzos—Xanax. Klonopins (forgotapins as he would come to call them), Valium .... *All of them? Yes, doc, please*—that the precinct shrink will later throw at him after declaring him unfit for duty and putting him out to pasture, medically retiring him at thirty-three, broken.

The sound system was immediately to his left. He lunged forward and kicked it, breaking the expensive-looking face. But that's all it did, break the face. The music still surrounded him, coming from every angle, mocking him, haunting him. He looked up at the corner and realized it was a state-of-the-art Bluetooth system worth, easily, a couple of thousand bucks. Janet probably got it for an eight-ball from one of her slaves when they stopped by with one of those tote boxes.

And that's when McCann realized that the cult that was slowly forming on the corner lot at Happy Homes Trailer Park was being fed an endless supply of meth by Janet Bigelow. But she wasn't selling it, she was cooking it. That's why traffic was at a minimum. That's why they couldn't pull someone over as they left and with the threat of prison force them to make a controlled buy from her. That's why Jerry feared for his life, and rightfully so. He'd bitten the hand that fed him, literally. Him and at least thirty others.

McCann pivoted and unplugged the device, but even then, he still heard the catchy song playing in the background of his damned soul, distant, obstructed, almost as if it was playing in the other room.

McCann realized it *was* coming from the next room.

Baby Shark, doo-doo, doo-doo.

"*Shut the fuck up.*" In the twenty-six years that McCann had known Perez, she'd screamed like that only once before—thirty-four days ago, right before she slammed the head of a man twice her size through the driver side window.

Women are more emotional, McCann thought in the back of his mind. *That's why men make better cops.*

A sudden fear washed over him, a fear that Perez would do something stupid, that she would do something that she could not come back from.

He turned toward the hallway and saw it—

"*The music made her do it,*" Jerry's words rang in his mind.

The baby was on the coffee table, naked and disemboweled; the large intestines, a long thick wet rope strung five feet toward the ottoman where it wrapped around the neck of Janet's four-year-old daughter, her little eyes bulging, unblinking. Blood covered everything in a five-foot radius. There was blood on the floor, on the couch, even splashes on the ceiling. McCann couldn't fathom how so much blood came from such a small body, then he realized that the body attached to the four-year-old seemed …

A blanket was draped across her chest, covering her lower half, which seemed to lack a certain degree of dimensional mass, dropping off at the hips to the same level as the ottoman.

Baby Shark, doo-doo, doo-doo.

This from Janet in the back room.

There was a loud smack, the deep resonance slapping down the narrow hallway. "*One more time,*" Perez screamed. "Say that shit *one more time* and you're *fucking dead.*"

Janet found a loophole. She didn't say the words, instead she hummed the tune. "*Hmhm hmhmhm hmhmhmhm hmhm hmhm …*"

"*That's it.*" A loud smack. Another one. Then the paralyzing sound of the hammer of an unseen gun cocking, shaking McCann's knees, making his legs wobbly, a decibel measured in terror alone.

"*Don't do it, Dani,*" McCann screamed. He ran with noodle legs toward the hallway, stumbling into the couch, the dead children a few feet away, and though he didn't want to look at the mysterious bottom half of the four-year-old, the need was far greater. He yanked the blanket off.

Everything below the upper thighs was missing, sloppy jagged cuts made by a serrated blade, blood soaking through the ottoman and onto the floor.

"*Hmhmhm, hmhmhmhmhm, hmhmhmhm …*"

Smack. Grunt. Maniacal laugh.

"What the fuck is *wrong with you?*" Perez cried.

Thud. Moans. Humming.

"*Hmhm-hmhm hmhm hmhm hmhm hmhm hmhmhmhm …*"

Incoherent whispers.

The incoherent whispers scared McCann to his core.

"*No, Dani.*" If not for McCann being intimately connected to Perez ever since she moved in across the street when she was five, he might've mistaken the whispers as a hissing radiator, rustling leaves, rats scurrying about; but he knew that it was in fact Perez praying to be forgiven of her sins.

A dreadfully accurate image slid into the screen of his mind's eye: Janet on her knees, hands behind her back, eyes big as tire hubs, bleeding profusely from several head wounds, and Perez standing over her, gun aimed at Janet's head with one hand, and with the other, rubbing her Saint Mary pendant, the one he gave her when they graduated high school together.

"Every time I touch it to pray, I'll think of you," she'd said, "so that you and Mary will forever be with me, watching me, guiding me, protecting me."

Girls are just more emotional than guys.

A passing thought, whimsical, automatic. Oh, but even he knew that was bullshit, because even then, and even though he didn't see it with his own eyes, he knew the love of his life was mere seconds away from spraying Janet's brains across the cheap vinyl walls that were coming apart at the seams; he couldn't help but feel a sense of pride as the moon's rays cut through the partitioned window, meeting the pendant's silver surface before bouncing off in an array of oscillating slices that shimmered and shimmied about.

"*Dani.*" McCann turned his head and vomited as he ran down the hallway, coffee and donuts trickling down the wall. He stopped at the end of the hallway. Four doors, all left ajar, teasing him with options. He pushed the first one open, a bathroom. He was surprised how clean it was given the state of the rest of the trailer.

"*Answer me, Dani,*" he screamed as he careened down the hall.

He was about to throw the second door back when he heard unhinged laughter—the laugh of a mad person—from the door at the end of the hallway.

Then, *Baby Shark, doo-doo, doo-doo.*

A loud, deafening *bang,* followed by a soft thud.

Ringing silence.

"Dani?" Hesitantly, McCann put a finger on the door and pushed slowly, walking into the room with maddening slowness. Janet splayed out in the middle of the room, brains, and blood all about her, hands over her head, a bloody saw to her left, rudimentary painting of massive, cartoonish shark teeth covering the lower half of her face in what appeared to look and smell like kiwi. It would later be determined that she didn't kill her children in some drug addled, violent killing spree. She killed them by accident. She was just trying to get them to go to bed and she used the shark bit as a way to relate. When they didn't believe she was a real shark she fetched the dull saw and proved them wrong.

Perez was standing with her back toward the door, breathing heavily, gasping for air, crying, gasping, crying.

"It's okay, Dani," he said stepping forward. "You got her. She can't hurt anyone else." McCann hugged Perez gently, squeezing. "It's okay," he said.

Hmhm hmhmhm hmhmhm hmhmh …

Perez started humming absently, eyes vacant. McCann shook her but she only stared at him with big empty eyes and kept humming the song; a song she would never stop humming, not through any of the psych evaluations, not through any of the court proceedings, no matter how much McCann begged, she kept on humming her way to a free stay at Happy Family retirement home for the rest of her life.

Attorney General Bane never visited her, nor did the twat fiancé. But McCann did, he visited her every day, no matter how much it broke his heart. She was his ride or die.

One hand washes the next, now, and forever.

She'd sit there, staring off in the distance, a heartbreaking placidity to her face and eyes, humming along to the permanent elevator music in the purgatory that had become her life.

Hmhm hmhmhm hmhmhm hmhmh.

Black-Eyed Children

"**B**LACK-EYED CHILDREN." *That's what residents of a small rural community just outside Pekin, Tennessee has taken to calling them. Named so for their dark, seemingly soulless eyes.* "Eyes that'll make ya believe in the devil," *said Dorothy Boyd, a retired English teacher from Pekin High. But Dorothy wasn't the first to report such peculiar occurrences, and it seems she certainly will not be the last. Reports have been trickling with alarming regularity concerning these terrifying, otherworldly encounters.*

The modus operandi? A simple, neighborly knock. That's right. A knock. But like all knocks, these ones, too, beg an answer. It is an answer that this seasoned reporter isn't wholly sure we're ready for. The consensus seems to be that these black-eyed children initiate contact by knocking on the door at all hours of the night, asking to enter the house and use the phone, using any number of fabricated emergencies as an excuse to get their foot in the door and wait for their parents. But it's not what they're saying that is disturbing so many Pekin residents, it's their appearance and demeanor that has so many people concerned. And perhaps more shocking than their appearance ... is their disappearance.

Monica Krutsch, an owner of the local bakery, had this to say about her encounter: "They knocked on the door and asked to come in, but in this really scary, really monotone voice, almost like they was robots or somethin'. They said they were in an accident down the street, and I thought they were just frazzled. Ya know? Like in shock or somethin' like that. But just as I was about to open the chain link, somethin' deep inside urged me to turn the porch light on and that's when I saw 'em for what they was."

What's that?

"I reckon they're demons. Yep. Demon is the only word that comes to mind. I felt, in a very profound sort of way, that if I let them in, they were gonna eat my soul. I know that sounds a bit dramatic, but it was like I could hear their thoughts, feel their intentions, sense their evil."

What happened, next?

"Well, there was no way I was gonna let 'em in after seeing those eyes. Not alone, anyways. So, I ran upstairs to get my husband—who was madder than a rattlesnake that married the garden hose that I woke him—and when we came back downstairs, they was gone. Both a'em. Just like that. *Poof.* It was as if they was never really there. The thing of it is, though, they was there, and we had the first heavy snow fall of the year that eve'nin—six, seven inches, thereabouts—and there shoulda been a buncha footprints scurrying about this way and that, but my steps and entryway were nothing but untouched virgin snow. Clean as a hound's tooth it was."

Mrs. Krutsch isn't the only person to report such oddities in the presence of black-eyed children.

"They said they was stranded by the side of the road," *said Justin Thompson, an auto-mechanic at Jerry's Auto, who incidentally record-ed his interaction on a doorbell camera.*

"They said they needed to use m'phone. But somein' didn't feel quite right 'bout 'em, ya see? Somein' 'bout their faces and in their manner-isms and whatnot was all … *wonky*. But they was still jus' kids and my dearly beloved Betty would roll right on over in her grave if she saw me shut the door on a coupla defenseless kids on account that they scared me to the dickens. And they did too. Scare me that is. Ain't afraid to admit it, either."

What happened next, sir?

"I was getin' there, darlin'. Now let's see. Where was I. Oh, yes. I handed 'em my phone through the chain link n'left to give 'em a sliver of privacy and not two minutes later did I come back, and they done got *gone*. Never seen anything like it in my life, I reckon. But I got it all on camera, y'see."

Tell me more about the camera.

"Welp, the same night, my neighbor died in the house over yonder, ya see, and the nex' mornin', the cops came a knockin' on this here door 'cuz they found my phone, 'within arm's reach of the corpse.' So, I says, 'What phone?' Ya see, darlin', I'm gettin' up there in age, and don't fancy them phones like you latter generation, attached to your hands they are.

I use it so rarely I didin' even 'member givin' it to the kids 'til just then. So, I shows the video to the deputy, and right there on the video ya see me givin' m'phone to these two kids with their faces all fuzzy and pixxeated."

You mean pixilated?

"S'wat I said, innit?"

Yes, of course. What happened next, Mr. Thompson?

"*Butkus.* That's what done happen. They just up n'disappeared."

Define disappeared.

"They was there one moment, with their faces all funny-looking and pixxeated, I left to give 'em some privacy, just like I says, then the porch light done tore slap up, ya see, there's some frisky wires in there somewheres huggin' and touchin' and I been meanin' to fix it, but they flickered like they always do—but they only flickered for a second, mind you—and when the lights come back on, the kids was gone. But the time sequence never stopped, ya understand, darlin'? On the tape, that is. And so, we know the flicker was only for a second. *Only a second.* That's all the time they needed t'just ... *vanish.*"

What happened next?

"Well, I been takin' this new medicine that does wonders for my gout, y'understand, but it makes me tired as a dog in heat. I was so tuckered out that I done forgot 'bout the kids on the potch. I fell sleep on my *lazy-*boy—Doc says it's good for lombar, ya see—and nothin' else happens on the tape 'til sheriff department showed up the next morning."

What was your neighbor's cause of death. Officially?

"*O-fficially?* Welp, o-fficially, the cause of death was undetermined, I reckon. Yep. Undetermined. But me, personally, I 'spect foul play."

Why's that?

"The belle was only thirty-two, thirty-three, thereabouts. She did Pil-*otees* and yoga and meditated and drank kale smoothies, for chris' sake. *Kale smoothies?* Had me drink one, one day, too, and I says, 'What in *tarnation* is this, darlin'?' Thick as molasses it was, and tasted like a dog's *bee-*hind, if you don't mind me sayin'. I felt it was my duty as a *Southerna,* and as a *humin bein',* to teach her how t'make a proper drink fit for human consuption: some good ol' southern tea.

"Aside from her questionable taste in drinks, the woman was healthy as a mule. N'if you subtract health problems from the 'quation, that sorta narrows down what happeneda that nice young lady, I reckon."

I'm told you have your own theory on what happened. Don't you, Mr. Thompson.

"Yes ma'am. I surely do. I'm damn near certain those damn black-eyed bastads went to her house after mines and they… they up n'*took her soul.*"

Took her soul?

"If I'm lyin', I'm dyin.'"

Took her soul? Black-eyed demon children? Inexplicable disappearances? This all sounds like a fanciful plot to the next Stephen King novel. That is until you dig a little further, gather enough information, ask the right questions, and dots start connecting. Upon request, our investigative team dug deep into Tennessee's past, gathering a comprehensive list of all deaths in the state spanning back to 1795 when Tennessee administered its first census. Those numbers—unbelievable as they are—tell a rather grim story: that over the past five years, there's been an astronomical proliferation of undetermined deaths to the sum of two thousand percent. No, viewers. There isn't anything wrong with your television set. You heard that correctly. Two thousand percent.

In 2018, the number of deaths classified as undetermined was 350—around the national average, sitting snug in the middle at twenty-six. As of today, June 7, 2025, we're sitting at 6,035 undetermined deaths. A staggering, albeit humbling number. But not a high enough number alone that would warrant the attention this story has gotten from concerned citizens and government agencies alike. What is truly peculiar is that every state in the nation has increased at the same rate and Tennessee currently still sits in the middle of the pack at twenty-three, and the year isn't even halfway over.

What could account for such a drastic increase over such a short span of time? We turned over every rock, chased every lead, explored every possible angle, trying to find correlations for everything from toxic waste in water to vaccinations. But the only thing of note that has happened during that period is that the first encounter of these black-eyed children was reported by Demetrius Gates. That was five years ago. Almost to the date.

"There was two a'em. A littlein' and a bigin'. Say 'bout ... sixteen. Maybe seventeen. The tyke maybe six, seven. Thereabouts. I knew somethin' was off 'bout 'em right from jump. They eyes was pitch black, right? No ... wadaya call 'em in the middle? The color bit? Yeah, tha's it, no irises. No nothing. Just straight black. Like two black marbles polished to the dickens. I called the sheriff and told 'em, I says, 'Hurry on up, George, ya hear?' But—God as my witness—as I was talking on the phone, they disappeared right there n'front of me."

That must've been terrifying.

"Yes ma'am. It surely was."

I'm to understand you have a message to our viewers.

"Yes ma'am. It seems to me like the only persons that survive an encounter withese black-eyed child are the ones that refuse to let 'em in. I don't think they can enter a home without an invitation like in one of 'em vampire movies or somethin'. N'lookit, hon, I know they *look* like they's children, and they be sayin' they in trouble and they need help, but they ain't *neither*. The people of Pekin need to understand that, ya hear? *They ain't neither.* We are good, hord-workin' folks, always tryna help a neighbor. That's what I love 'bout living round these parts, these my stompin' grounds and I ain't never gonna leave n'there ain't nothin' no black-eyed children can do ta make me, ya hear?

"But I will urge yawll, whateva ya do, d'not let those children into yo house. Because I reckon, they ain't *really children.* They're soul-eating demons."

In other news, the truck drivers' union is still on strike, making it the five-hundredth day without resolve, causing the country's food storages to plummet to an all-time low. FEMA is sending out—

The pixels in the old, worn-down tube television collapsed in the middle of the screen, a vortex of colors before disappearing with a loud static pop.

What has the world come to? Nancy thought. *Soul-eating demon children? There's evil everywhere.* She made a solemn vow to say a prayer for them later that night.

Shaking her head in disgust, she set her husband's plate on the dinner tray in front of him, his robust stomach protruding from his greasy overalls, stained and potent, an odd combination of mustard and oil. Brent adjusted his reclinable chair to the upright position, placed a napkin in his collar and lap. The delicious smell of cooked meat wafted in the air and met his appetite, glands salivating, stomach gurgling in a preemptive celebration. There, on the plate, was what looked like a massive turkey leg, boiled, seared, then doused in a thick layer of barbecue sauce. Just the way Brent liked it. He was famished and with the empty stomach came a dilapidated state where even the idea of cordial pleasantries seemed like foreign concepts to him, something he'd seen on television, maybe even partook in once or twice, but certainly not anytime soon.

He could hardly contain himself. But when he went to pick up the leg, Nancy smacked his hand and said, "Grace first, dear."

He nodded and sulked as she left to get her own plate, returning shortly. She settled into her chair, upright and snug, wiggling her hips just so, the chair hugging her rear end like a tightly fitted dress. She nodded at Brent, who closed his eyes and said, "Thank you for this healthy bounty, dear lord, and thank you for their sacrifices."

They opened their eyes and dug in, ignoring the napkin cuffed in their collars, licking their fingers savagely, slurping, sucking bone marrow from the massive leg bone.

The cuckoo clock in the living room announced the time: 10:00 p.m. Immediately after, a mechanical arm lowered the arm to a stenograph and a vinyl record serenaded them from the corner, its staticky background a throwback to happier times, bountiful times. Brent was a brilliant engineer; he rigged the stenograph to be activated by the noise of the cuckoo bird.

"This is the last of our meat," Nancy said, sucking the bone marrow out of the leg bone as if there was a pot of gold in the middle.

Brent sighed heavily, annoyed. "Y'think I don't know that, woman?" he said. "Who's the one that always gotta lure 'em n'kill 'em n'butcher 'em? Huh?" He blew a steam of hot air from his nostrils, shook his head in agitation. Nancy was always nagging him, always finding it necessary to verbalize things that were implied, always micromanaging him, and she knew all the right buttons to push.

"Now don't take ya anger out on me, ya hear." Nancy looked at him with hurt eyes; eyes that were the same shade of yellow as the thick layer of toe jam that'd accumulated around her nails like barnacles under the belly of a massive ship; eyes that lacked a certain degree of humanity; evil eyes.

"The ice cream truck was my idea, wannit," she added with her nose in the air. Her tone was whiny and pleading in equal measures, like a child trying to prove their worth to their older siblings, pleading their case to be worthy of playtime.

They sat in silence for a spell, thinking, enjoying the luxury of a full stomach—which had become increasingly rare of late—when there was a knock at the door. Brent looked at the grandfather clock in the corner. It read: 10:14.

They shared a curious glance. Nancy moved the television tray then inched off the recliner slowly, silently. She tiptoed to the door, back hunched over as she tried to look through the glass which was obstructed by a blind. She peeked through the blinds and gasped when she saw who it was. She put her hand to her mouth. She hugged the door with her back, a wicked grin playing at the corners of her lips, reaching her yellow eyes as she licked her chapped lips.

Her demeanor was intriguing to Brent, who said, "Well, who the hell is it, woman?"

"Why, I think ... I think it's two of 'em black-eyed demons the news was going on 'bout?"

"What in the Sam Hill is a ..." But even as the words left Brent's lips, he remembered the news report and could hardly believe their luck. He had gotten mad at Nancy earlier because she was right— she was a nagging record player, but she was right—they *were* out of meat and worst yet, the season had changed since their last kill, and it was too cold to go hunting in the ice cream truck without causing suspicion. He been racking his mind for solutions when destiny delivered the answer to his door.

He looked at his wife and she looked at him, having a nonverbal conversation, getting on the same page. He nodded at her. She nodded back at him. Their eyes connecting their actions with their fate.

He put a hand over his mouth and pretended to breathe heavily, then gestured his head to the right. Nancy understood the instruction. She launched off the door and practically skipped to where he'd nodded, disappearing into an adjacent room.

Another knock. Louder. Impatient. Robust.

Brent stood up and ran a hand over his overalls, covering it in grease and barbecue sauce as he tried ironing out the wrinkles to look more presentable, more trustworthy; he glided over to the door, suddenly feeling younger with the prospect of fresh meat. He peeked through the half-moon shaped window and laughed when he saw it was them. It was really them. Just as Demetrius Gates had said: Two children. One younger. Maybe seven or eight. The other sixteen, seventeen. An odd pair, they were. Brent figured the younger one was just like his wife's pleading whine from earlier, begging to play with his older brother, trying to prove his worth, that he was cool enough to hang.

The kids were decked in black slacks and a black hoodie donned over the crown of their heads with eyes the color of a black lake which shimmered as the porch light met them. There wasn't much meat on their bones to speak of, but they would have to do. The younger one was about four feet, nine inches, which would make for a sizeable femur bone, much bigger then the three foot five-year-old they had just sat down to eat.

Brent removed the chain link, unlocked the dead bolt, swung the door open wide and gestured for them to come inside before they read from the familiar script of possible emergencies.

"You guys must be freezin'," Brent welcomed them, even though it was a pleasant night for late October, with Halloween only a couple of days away. The two kids looked at each other, hesitantly, bashfully. The older one gestured his head in a manner that seemed to signify the end of whatever this was. But Brent grabbed them by the shoulders and corralled them in before they had a chance to balk and run away. He shut the door, checking to see if anyone noticed the rare arrival of guests at the Anderson residence, but all he saw was an empty, dark street with a small patch of flashing orange and black lights from his neighbor Mac, who married a woman that always went over the top with decorations. Particularly with Halloween, for it was her favorite holiday.

Brent noticed she'd put up a new decoration: a floating ghost with arms that flailed and gyrated and danced, and suddenly, Brent felt like dancing himself. He closed the curtain, turned around and regarded the two children the way a slave auctioneer might regard a new stock; the way the witch from Hansel and Gretel might regard them. He went around the children in a half circle and stood at the foot of the door, blocking their exit.

"C'mon in now, fellas," he said. "We ain't gonna hurcha."

The children left the safety of the front entrance, shuffling along in small, mechanical steps. Their faces were expressionless, their eyes as dark as the earth's deepest cave. They stopped a few feet into the room. Then, as if choreographed, they said in a very dry, very robotic voice, "May we use your phone." They said this in unison perfectly. Brent admired their determination as he could tell they'd practiced extensively on synchronizing the time just right, not to mention tone and tempo, which were both flawlessly identical. He almost felt bad for what was to come next. *Almost.*

Brent grabbed the big one under the arm and led him to the reclinable chair. "You just sit right on down while I fetch ya that celly, ya hear." He disappeared into the same corridor that his wife had disappeared. She met him at the door, already wearing her gas mask. She handed him his. He donned it then flipped the light switch five times, initiating the sequence that triggered the release of silo gas, which came out the vents in great big plumes, quickly filling the room in a foggy haze.

The boy collapsed first. The smaller ones always collapsed first.

"It ain't rocket science, Nancy," Brent had said the last time they'd deployed the same tactic a year and a half ago at the onset of the truck drivers' union strike, when they were able to lure the Chavez kids with promises of chocolate chip cookies and fresh lemonade. "They faint first 'cuz they's closer to the vent s'all."

The teenage boy stood and started for the door. He staggered along, his rubbery legs wobbling, threatening to collapse underneath him like a fawn taking their first steps. After a few veering steps, he fell on his face.

Brent and Nancy worked with their gas mask on, checking the kid's bodies for any phones or identification. They didn't have either. Janice removed the hoodie from the smaller kid.

"Well, now, wait a dagon minute," she said. "Is that—"

She licked her fingers and removed black Kiwi from the kids' eyelids. Then she stuck her finger into his eyes and removed black eye contacts.

"—It is," she said.

"Who is it?"

"The Jackson kid from a few blocks down."

"I know 'em?"

"I don't think so."

Brent looked at them, scoffed, then said, "Po'or bastads picked the wrong house t'prank."

He found himself wishing the neighborhood kids were real black-eyed children; with the Chavez kids still missing, they were bringing a lot of heat and attention to the neighborhood. Of course, this didn't stop him from continuing, but, as he worked, he found himself wondering what a soul-sucking demon child would taste like.

They dragged the bodies to the basement door. Brent hit a lever and the stairs turned into a slide and the bodies slid down into the basement.

Brent hit the lever again. The slide turned back into stairs, which he took, one at a time, whistling dixie. He dragged them to the back room and placed them on meat hooks. Then he sharpened his butcher knife and prepared to drain the bodies.

Untitled YouTube Commercial Script

(SCREEN PROLIFERATED WITH GREEN, FLASHING $ SIGNS.
CUT TO ME IN DAD'S MANSION.)

If you're a loser and *don't* wanna make thousands of millions of dollars a year in passive income, doing nothing but this *one, simple, easy to learn, full-proof technique*—then go ahead and just exit this video. Go ahead. I'll wait.

(TICKING CLOCK)

Now that we got rid of the *losers*, we can get down to bizzness. If you're still here, it's because you wanna know how I can afford this sick-*sick* house.

(ZOOM OUT, PANORAMA LANDSCAPE OF HOUSE. SHOW PERSONAL
CHEF COOKING IN THE KITCHEN. THEN SHOW STATE-OF-THE-ART
GYM, WALK-IN CLOSETS, GAME ROOM, MOVIE THEATER, BOWLING
ALLEY, INDOOR SWIMMING POOL AND BASKETBALL COURT. FADE
OUT TO ME AT DAD'S DESK IN FRONT OF COMPUTER.)

I need you to do me a favor—just look at this. I want you to see this. You gotta see it to believe it. There's really no other way. Lenny, zoom in closer will ya, so they know it's real. That's my boy Lenny. He used to be my drug dealer, but now he's my bizzness partner. Closer, Len. Lil' bit more. That's too close. Back up just a hair. Good. *Boom.* There it is, *right there.* You see *that?* That's *real* money. You see the time and date and deposit. I made $59,000 in *just* twenty-four hours using a safe, foolproof technique that allows your money to work for you. It's so easy, a Packer fan can do it.

(CUT TO TEN-CAR GARAGE—REMEMBER TO EDIT OUT "FORECLOSURE" SIGN)

I used to be a loser *just like you*, working a dead-end job that I hated, living paycheck to paycheck. I couldn't keep a girl for more than a few months and every time they left me, they always gave the same reason—"You have no ambition, no drive, no future. You're a *loser*." I was totally miserable, lonely, and ... *hungry*, because there were times when I had to decide whether to pay my rent or buy food.

But that's all in the past. Now, I absolutely love my life. And you could love yours, too.

(CUT TO ME IN DAD'S PORSCHE)

Do you wanna be like me? Do you wanna live like me? I have three Ferraris and two Porsches. Big deal. That's *nothing*. I got three mansions, and two of the *biggest* chinchilla farms in Thailand where I own a sweat factory that makes the world's *softest* coats at the world's *lowest* price. Now, don't you worry, we don't just kill 'em for their pelts, we also make hotdogs in the same factory. That's right. My chinchilla game's on point, son. We skin 'em, then fillet 'em. We don't waste notta no-*thing*.

I went from being a loser, to the chinchilla king of Asia. We just opened another factory in the Philippines, too. That's right—chinchilla in Manilla.

I met my soulmate on Ashley Madison. She's from Belgium. She's *super*-hot—and she makes me waffles every ... *single* ... morning. *Homemade*. There's a language barrier, but that just means we never fight. That's right. You heard me—we have yet to fight even once. It's a nearly perfect situation I got going, and you could have it too.

I'm not lying when I say, I have it *all*. I've got the cribs, the cars, the clothes. I vacation every month to somewhere exotic and learn other cultures—just last week, I was in Detroit.

And I know what you're thinking— "This dude's full of poop. If he was making that much money, why *on earth* would he tell anyone about it." Well, I tell you this because it's lonely at the top, where all the winners are. It's the bottom that's crowded, bottom feeders fighting for scraps. And I can tell you're a winner because only the losers who don't wanna ball out have clicked off this video.

D'yaself a favor: if you want my life, if you want to be like me and get filthy-*filthy* rich doing absolutely no work—literally a something for nothing, full-proof plan—then click on the link below, and that'll send you to another link, which will send you to another link, and the next link will send you to the last one—then alls ya gotta do is plug in your information and get put on our "Super-Duper Baller Status VIP" list. It really is that simple.

And don't worry, we're not gonna charge you a *dime*. We ask for your card information as a formality only, we just need to verify who you are, because we don't make this offer to just anyone, we must vet our potential partners in this exclusive opportunity, which will be un-available in twenty-four hours—that's right, twenty-four hours. Don't let this golden opportunity pass you by, an opportunity that's better than buying Google, Amazon, or Netflix stock twenty years ago. A bold statement, you say? Well, I say, fortune favors the bold.

Stop being a loser. Stop living paycheck to paycheck. Stop buying Belgian waffles in the box when you can have the real deal. Click on the link below, provide your credit, or debit information, along with your date of birth, social security number, the city you were born in, the high school you graduated from, and your mother's maiden name. It's *that simple.*

The life of your dreams is just one click away. So, click on the link below. Change your life.

And don't forget to like, comment, subscribe, and push your notifi-cations for all my latest content.

RPCD: Reincarnation Pre-Crime Division

TODAY WAS A BIG DAY FOR *HIM* AND *HIS* CREW—today was their twenty-fifth mission. If they make it back to base alive, they've earned the right to go home as heroes, poster boys—they've earned the right to spend the rest of the war drinking martinis and soliciting donations at high-rolling fundraisers, raising money for the war effort.

If they make it back to base.

But therein lay the problem. Between them and their desired goal lay a treacherous wasteland of a sky, a perilous landmine bursting with patches of black explosions—the smallest, the size of a basketball; the biggest, the size of a sedan. Thousands upon thousands of them, polka-dotting the sky, no discernible order to the madness save for the unified goal to destroy, to kill; the spaces between the black explosions, less than free air. Far less. Patches of light blue sky hiding underneath the dark plumes of death like a man buried alive—life under death.

The plane shakes violently, the flack surrounds them, almost swallows them whole.

He rubs Shakira, *his* lucky hula girl on the dash, shaking her hips to the beat of the bumpy ride.

He looks to the left, three B-17's staggered in a diagonal line. Same for the right. With *him* at point—just one squadron among thirty—two-hundred-ten Boeing B-17s altogether, harbingers of death. That wasn't counting their escorts, the P-51 mustang fighter jet—there were another one hundred of those, smaller, faster, deadlier in a manner of speaking. The B-17 was an immense marvel of engineering, a flying fortress, built to carry massive payloads and drop it right on Jerry's head with an accuracy so tight, it was said that a well-trained bombardier could land his payload in a pickle barrel—a claim that spawned an endless supply of sexual innuendos amongst the dark-humored airmen. *You can land your payload in my pickle barrel anytime, Major.*

The P-51s were escorts, there to protect the B-17s, to ensure mission success—mission success was paramount above all else, including human life.

This particular mission was the most brazen endeavor ever attempted in the short history of aerial combat. Three hundred and ten planes, spanning hundreds of miles. Their objective—to level factories, railroads, bridges, communication towers, farms, U-boat dens, and any other high-value infrastructure assets that would cripple the German economy and end the war, once and for all.

It was the greatest show of force ever assembled in its time, a feat surpassed five months later, on June 6, 1944, when the allied powers stormed the beaches of Normandy.

The P-51s were spread evenly about the B-17 squadrons, which were seven deep and flying in staggered formations in the shape of a chevron. From the ground, it looked like the sky was full of shooting arrows. The sheer size covered the sky from horizon to horizon. What an impressive marvel to see—the flying armada—unless, of course, you were a Nazi.

"Ten miles to drop." This from the ship's navigator, Lieutenant Jones, over the comms.

Ten miles is an eternity when you're sitting on eight-thousand pounds of high-grade explosives, swimming in a sky full of flack.

The plane shakes violently. An alarm sounds. Smoke grabs *his* attention from the left. "Fires in engines one and two," *he* says. "Turning 'em off and feathering."

"Napoli's hit, sir," said Sergeant Jackson, a proud country boy from Alabama who manned the bottom turret.

He looks to *his* right where a mangled B-17—named "Orphan Maker"—was nosediving to bathe eternally in the Rhine River.

"It's going—" Jackson stops talking as the B-17 flies into a particularly unlucky patch of flack that seems to encompass the size of a professional football stadium.

He watches, seemingly in slow motion, as the plane breaks into three pieces, the right and left wings completely detached, spinning, smoking, ablaze. The body is also on fire, but *he'd* seen worse—*he'd* experienced worse. And *his* good friend, Salvador Napoli, was as good a pilot as any *he'd* ever seen.

"C'mon, Sal," *he* says under *his* breath. "Bail. Sound the alarm n'bail."

He watches the body nosediving, waiting for—

A nearby explosion shakes the plane violently.

The cacophony was maddening—the flack, the explosions, the alarms, engines three and four laboring to compensate for the other two engines, Jackson's whimpers over the comms—but all *he* hears is ringing silence—it seems to surround *him*, the ringing, envelop *him* like a vicious tidal wave pulling *him* into the sea.

He watches "Orphan Maker" intently, praying to see parachutes, but none were deployed.

Finally, it crashes into the water.

He had friends on that plane, good friends. They were all dead now, the whole crew, ten of the 100th Bomb Brigade's finest.

He wants to cry. *He* wants to go home to *his* wife and kids. *He* wants to curl up in a ball and scream until *his* lungs burn and *his* throat bleeds and there's nothing left inside but revenge, deep and visceral, the want for it, the need for it.

He pushes forward. *His* crew is depending on *him* to lead, the troops on the ground are depending on *him* to blow the ball bearing factory to smithereens.

"No ball bearings, no war machines," Colonel Lemay had said in the briefing.

I'm gonna kill every last one of you Kraut fucks, he thinks.

He looks down. The tail of "Orphan Maker" sticks out of the Rhine River, smoking, as if the river were having a morning cigarette. *He* says a silent prayer for the fallen and vows revenge.

He notices that the fires are out in engines one and two. *He* presses the lever and feeds the gas back into them.

The plane skips then rides smooth.

And they ride like this for what seems an eternity, watching other B-17s get hit, P-51s, too, dodging flack, never knowing if the next explosion will be the last one.

—

The sky clears. *His* stomach tightens. *His* legs shake. And *he* gathers a gulf of bravery to push forward. They made it through the areal land-mine alive. But now comes the real challenge. The *Luftwaffe* are preci-sion fighters and are harder to evade than the crapshoot logic of flack, which is a volumes game—flood the sky with explosions and pray you hit something sort of thing.

The flack always stopped right before the *Luftwaffe* attacked, the Jerrys on the ground don't want to take out their highly-coveted air force with friendly fire.

"Look alive, boys," *he* says over the system. *Look alive.*

He looks over to *his* left, where great big puffy clouds lined the morning sky—the kind that look like rolling hills of cotton candy, the kind that look like they might taste like marshmallows if he were to take a bite.

The sun rises on the east horizon, its complete mass just now breaking the earth's crust, shining its rays upon the living and the dead, equally, indiscriminately.

The majesty of it is stunning; *he* marvels at the dichotomy between the last few miles, the vast difference that acts of man can make to de-stroy something so beautiful, to tarnish something so sacred.

He looks to *his* right where another B-17 plugged the hole where "Orphan Maker" was, tightening the ranks, getting ready for—

"*Bogey ten o'clock high,*" Sargant Miller calls out from the top tur-ret, just one of seventeen fifty-caliber weapons, covering the whole clock. The sound of bullets whizzing by, puckering the sphincters of everyone on board. "*He's coming in hot,*" Miller screams gratuitously. A terrifying streak of glowing hot lead walks up the body of the plane.

"It's time to punch in and go to work, boys," *he* says.

The top turret lets loose, spraying the encroaching fighter jet along the fuselage. It explodes instantly. The crew of "Flack Shark" shout, feigning victory short-lived.

That was only just one *Luftwaffe*, a scout, perhaps. They had just crossed into the heart of Germany, with one goal—to destroy lives and cripple infrastructure. They knew they would meet heavy resistance, but thus far, aside from the flack, it's been quiet. *Too* quiet.

Then *he* sees them. *He* knows Miller sees them, too, because he says, "Oh, my—"

Yes, they knew they were going to meet heavy resistance. But this—

—There, in the distance, endless lines of exhaust are streaking the sky like shooting stars, hundreds of them. *He* swallows the rock that forms in *his* throat and rubs Shakira again. *Just one more show, baby, he* thinks. *Get us through just one more.*

Half of the P-51 escorts speed up ahead of the convoy; they were going to try and clear a path for the B-17s.

Godspeed, he thinks.

Half of the *Luftwaffe* mirror the P-51s. The opposing air forces meet somewhere in the middle and what ensues is the deadliest dogfight of WWII, trading bullets and rockets, maneuvering left and right, climbing and diving, spitting lines of fire from their noses and sputtering rockets from their bellies.

The sky is a massive crossing checkerboard of exhaust-lines indistinguishable from the clouds, with planes occupying the spaces.

Planes start to drop from the sky like flies. Parachutes deploy on both sides, nearly atop of each other. *He* sees falling men fumbling in their jackets, trying to get their service revolvers ready, for when they land, their enemies will be neighbors within a stone's throw distance.

"Looks like they got the invite to the big dance," said *his* co-pilot, Captain Hendrix III. "'Catch 'em with their pants down,' *my ass.*" He was referring to what Colonel Lemay said during the briefing, and was only saying what everyone else was thinking, but it was *his* ship, and *he* didn't like whining on *his* ship.

"Don't get butthurt because you never got invited to any dances, there, Henny-hunny." *He* blows a kiss at Hendrix, who forces a smile and nods.

The battlefield in the middle settles, a swirling vortex of exhaust-lines and no planes, only descending parachutes riding the wind like paper bags.

The streaking exhaust lines of the rest of the *Luftwaffe* were set up higher than them, giving the *Luftwaffe* the advantage. They start descending, breaking off into teams of four or five like packs of wolves. The *Luftwaffe* had been at war now almost four years. Their pilots were seasoned vets. Conversely, this was the maiden mission for many of the 100th. The crew of "Flack Shark" was the last remaining crew out of the original eighty-two that stood up the 100th air squadron. The rest were either prisoners of war, killed in action, or missing in action.

They close the gap.

"Wadasay, there, boys?" *he* says, feigning confidence. "One last rodeo for the road?"

"Fuckin' A, right, Major."

"Yes sir."

"For 'Orphan Maker.'"

"'For 'Orphan Maker,'" *he* concurs. The consensus was clear—they were going to finish the mission or die trying.

The *Luftwaffe* start picking off the P-51 escorts one by one.

The planes look like birds at play, chasing each other, spitting balls of fire from their mouths.

Everywhere about *him*, bullets and rockets and planes and exhaust. Sweat stinging *his* eyes, the smell of smoke and burning oil and gasoline turning *his* stomach.

A squad of four *Luftwaffe* focus on *his* B-17. *He* looks around. They seem to be attacking the lead B-17's first, the planes with high brass. *Pretty smart for a Jerry, he* thinks.

When the leaders go down, the next rank must step up, and they aren't always as poised as the leaders.

"*Rocket two o'clock high,*" Jackson calls out, then lays on his fifty-cal, clipping the fighter that sent the rocket, sending it plummeting to the earth.

The rocket is ten meters away, screaming toward them, a zipping messenger of death.

"*Hold-on,*" *he* yells, engaging the flaps on his wings at half, stalling, and the rocket flies a few inches ahead of them, hitting a P-51 instead. The P-51 starts to tailspin before the pilot ejects, shooting into the sky fifteen feet and deploying his chute.

"Two miles to drop," calls out the navigator.

The *Luftwaffe* miss them on the first pass. They go down the line, attacking the next squadron, and would be turning around to go back home soon.

Another streaking line of exhaust from the front—the P-51 escorts return pass. They will meet the Jerrys on their return somewhere towards the back of the convoy.

This was the most dangerous part of the journey—with no escorts, the turret gunners had to be on point.

"Wolf pack, seven o'clock low," calls out Staff Sargant Bowe, the tail turret gunner. "I count 5." He starts laying into his gun, the ear-piercing noise and vibrations, the sound of metal shells hitting the ground—all of it, a welcoming nuisance.

"Six," Miller corrected from the top turret—the best seat in the house. He lets off some rounds. "They're too far to hit," he says to the other gunners. "Conserve ammo, but keep 'em honest."

"One mile to drop."

"Pilot to Bombardier," *he* says.

"Bombardier to pilot," says Second-Lieutenant Brady.

"You ready, Hank?" *he* says.

"Let's give 'em their Christmas presents early, Major."

The crew screams to the violence of it. They would miss the birth of their first-born children for the chance at revenging the deaths of their friends.

"Pilot to bombardier, the plane's yours," *he* said. "Aim true, brotha."

"Roger, sir," Brady said. "Plane's mine."

"Approaching drop," said the Navigator.

"Opening bombardier doors."

The vacuum seal is broken, their ears pop. It suddenly drops twenty degrees, the frigid air cutting into any exposed skin like sheets of sandpaper.

The bulk of the returning *Luftwaffe* approach from their return. They break off into teams and pick off the straggling B-17s who weren't in tight formation.

The B-17 on the left flank gets hit with a one-two combination of rockets. It wobbles, descends. Smoke. Fire. It was in bad shape and would have to bail. The bombardier doors open, and the bombardier releases the bombs early. They don't hit their target, but they level an area spanning ten square blocks in the middle of downtown Berlin.

The plane continues to descend rapidly.

Men falling out of the bombardier doors like care packages. Some of them have parachutes open, some don't. All of them are terrifed to their core.

The rest of the crew, including the pilot and co-pilot, shoot out the doors.

The sky is full of men falling, friends falling, brothers.

The *Luftwaffe* open fire at the men dropping in the parachutes, aiming not at the men, but at the chutes, ripping holes in the fabric, causing them to plummet rapidly to the ground, until—

I'm gonna get you schnitzel-eating fucks.

"Now," says the navigator, "drop the bombs now."

"Roger that," Brady says. "Bombs away."

There were only two remaining B-17s in his squad. They both hit their targets. The crew of "Flack Shark" had done the impossible. They finished twenty-five missions. "Way to go—"

"*Rocket, seven o'clock low,*" screams Miller.

A deafening explosion rips a hole in the tail, killing Bowe in the tail turret instantly.

The bottom ball turret detaches and starts plummeting to the earth like a massive beach ball.

The plane starts spinning. Stabilizers and gyroscope compromised.

Another rocket blows a hole in the body, starboard side, sucking navigator Jones out in a flash.

Alarms. Screams. Howling winds. Spinning. Freezing. Hard to breathe.

The gyroscope fights maddeningly to keep her steady, but without a tail, it is impossible.

He hits the bail alarm and says, "Pilot to crew, destroy the Norden bombsight, eat the orders, and bail ship. I repeat—*bail ship.*"

The remaining crew start scrambling. *He's* fighting with the controls, trying to level her out.

A blur from the left—an enemy fighter walks in a streaking line of bullets, destroying the first and second engine. They ignite.

"Fire in engines one and two," says Hendrix III.

"Roger," *he* says. "Killing engines. Feathering." *He* flips some switches, stopping the flow of gas to the engines, attempting to smother the fire.

In rapid succession the remaining crew start jumping ship.

His mouth full of paper, chewing orders, Jackson goes first.

He leans over and sees a steady line of parachutes descend over enemy territory—six altogether.

Rest in peace, Bowe. Rest in peace, Miller. You, too, Jonesy. I love you guys.

In his mind, *he's* already formulating the letters to their families, something he had been fortunate to avoid up to that point. A miracle really.

"What about you, sir?" Captain Hendrix III says.

"I'm right behind you." *He's* finally stopped the plane from spinning but, with only two engines, it's veering to the left, banking hard. Hendrix shakes *his* hand and disappears into the belly of the beast. *He* sees Hendrix's chute deploy. *He* exhales deeply, suddenly aware that *he'd* been holding *his* breath.

He's alone, descending rapidly. *He* looks up, there's only one remaining B-17 from *his* squadron. *He* looks to *his* left and right to see only a few more. They were spread out like a herd of injured antelope trying to outrun a pride of lions.

From the rear, two rockets hit the plane—one on the right engines and one on the fuselage, exploding on impact.

The remaining *Luftwaffe* attack *him,* mercilessly opening fire. *He's* utterly defenseless.

The hills are too bumpy to land, *he* sees a body of water in the distance, a small lake. *He* turns engines one and two back on and banks to the right, hard.

He heard it before it hit—the sputtering high-pitched whistle of the incoming rocket. It rips the plane in half, the bottom flying to the right. *He's* cold. The engines die. *He's* gliding now, descending at a sharp angle, *he* nearly breaks *his* arms trying to keep her level. The oxygen tanks were in the bottom half of the plane. *He* can't breathe.

Cold. Falling. Gasping for air.

Nosediving right into—

The water hits *him* like a freight train. *He's* concussed. Little dots appearing in *his* vision. A piercing ringing. The nose of the plane starts sinking. *He* tries to eject the seatbelt but it's stuck, frozen. The cold water seeps in, numbing *his* extremities as *his* blood distributes to *his* core to protect the vital organs. *He* fights with the seatbelt, but it won't budge. *He* takes a big inhale as the water reaches *his* neck. The plane breaks the surface, *his* whole body is submerged in the freezing water.

He still fights with the seatbelt.

"Don't worry 'bout it, Corporal, when I go, it ain't gonna be because of a faulty seatbelt." That's what *he* told the lead mechanic, Corporal Chavez, not twenty-four hours ago.

A fucking seatbelt? he thinks, infuriated with *himself,* the carelessness of it, the oversight, the failure to pay attention to detail—everything *he* harps on *his* crew about, *he'd* failed to do *himself.*

What a dumb fucking way to die. A seatbelt. A fucking seatbelt? If only I had a—

Amid the shock and the concussion and the grief, *he'd* forgotten *he* had a knife tucked away in *his* boot strap.

He lifts his leg. *His* fingers inch down *his* shin. *He* feels the handle. *He* removes the knife.

The plane shifts on the bottom of the short channel, rocking the plane hard.

He drops the knife.

He looks up. Light gleaming in slashes as it cuts through the surf, getting fainter as the plane rocks, lulling *him* to eternal sleep.

He swallows a mouth full of water. Coughs. Gasps. Inhales. Swallows more water.

His last act as pilot of the "Flack Shark" is to punch *Shakira* in the head, knocking her off the dash.

He laughs in *his* head.

A seatbelt? he thinks. The utter stupidity of it had a morbid sort of poetry to it.

Flashing black dots encompass *his* vision.

His heartbeat lulls then plummets.

Three, two—

He dies.

Marshall Vincent Ferguson started from his nightmare with a jarring jolt. He clutched his throat, gasping, remembering.

"You okay, boss?" This from his partner, Marshall Ryan Johnson, whose face was a mask of worry, intrigue.

Fergie looked up, confused. He'd fallen asleep at his desk. *Again.* He hadn't been sleeping good since, well, forever.

A flashing red light suddenly illuminated their vision, pulsating, steady, begging for attention. It was a new soul bond notification. Fergie closed his eyes shut until the flashing light deactivated. All he saw now was a gulf of blackness, empty, dark, inviting.

Tired, disgruntled, he wasn't in the mood for another assignment. Not just yet.

Johnson screamed, "*Holy shit.*" His voice hit an octave that Fergie had never heard, not in the six months they'd been partners.

Intrigued, Fergie opened his eyes and said, "Who'd we get this time?" Forgetting his dreams has always been easy for him; it's been easy because he only dreamed one thing—every night, every nap, every day—always the same flack, the same crash, the same drowning death.

He lounged in an oblong chair the shape of a hollowed-out vertical pill, with a high back and nothing keeping it upright but for a small four-square inch slab of magnetite that was bolted to the ground. The pill-chair stood in place but was able to do endless circles with the slightest push. He stretched deeply, hurled his feet on the large mahogany desk, hands behind his head as if he were laying on a hammock under a canopy of coconut trees on a beach in some exotic country, counting the passing clouds.

Johnson, who answered the soul bond notification, blinked two times, which dimmed the briefing profile in his oculus so that it was superimposed under Fergie, a shit-eating grin branching off into an unapologetic smile. He waited, intentionally stretching his response, exasperating Fergie's childlike patience.

He sat back and swiveled in his chair, smiling, his feet dangling, twirling, meeting Fergie's eyes only when the chair faced him, twirling, smiling, twirling, smiling.

The entire time, the reward blinked dimly red in the background of his vision, faint, but noticeable, tugging at the strings of his greed.

"It's a little early in the week to get shot," Fergie said, unamused. "Ya keep playin' with me, I'll happily oblige." He balled a piece of paper and threw it at Johnson, who dodged the harmless projectile and laughed gleefully. Fergie picked up the stapler and made to throw that, too. He balked, but Johnson had no doubt in his mind that Fergie would throw the stapler. Just last week he'd caught an apple to the forehead for a side remark he made regarding Fergie's fiancé/ex-wife. He's married and divorced her twice already.

"Can't fix stupid," he'd said. The apple hit him perfectly between the eyes, exploding all over the desk.

"I'll give ya three guesses, yeah?" Johnson lived for moments like this—to torture his partner, whose well of patience ran dry many a year ago. It was almost *too* easy.

"Just *fuckin'* tell me, Johnny." Fergie closed his eyes again, being sure to keep them closed, not wanting to activate any modules, but to just savor the darkness; the beautiful, serene, darkness.

"You wanna hint?" Johnson said, interrupting the one thing his partner wanted.

Fergie opened his eyes to Johnson smiling in that goofy, childlike way he did sometimes, when he was pressing all the right buttons, then he started spinning in his chair again, whistling. With every turn, he could sense Fergie's anger rising by degrees.

Fergie wasn't in the mood for such cheeky games. He sighed heavily then blinked three times in rapid succession, activating his neuro-link interface with the oculus system—Johnson waited until the last second to tell him—and just as Fergie's eyes lit up with an incandescent milky white tinge, Johnson yelled, "*Ace of Spades.*"

Fergie wouldn't have believed him if not for the blinking red letters in his vision—the assignment bond for the Ace of Spades. Fergie blinked twice, dimming his oculus, mouth practically hitting the ground. *Ace of Spades?* The thought was exhilarating. A collar like that came along once in a lifetime. If ever. It was an RPCD bounty hunter's dream assignment. He could finally retire and perhaps find the peace that had evaded him most his life.

Perhaps.

They met eyes, smiling.

Johnson threw both hands in the air, rubbing the middle fingers and pointing fingers with his thumb—an old adage for counting the money.

Fergie whistled loudly then sat back, whittled his thumbs, and said, "Guess we're big game fishing, today, eh?"

"Fuckin' A. Right, we are." Johnson blinked twice, undimming his neuro-link interface. A screen popped up in his vision, translucent, malleable. It was the Reincarnation Pre-Crime Division's homepage—The Most Wanted List. The list was infinitely long and while in default mode, the names appeared in alphabetical order. The bounty hunter's guild had long been trying to convince the bigwigs in D.C. to make the default mode appear with the most wanted at the top, thus, the biggest rewards at the top. But the system was easy enough to navigate.

Simply by saying the words in his mind, Johnson typed into the search bar: *Ace of Spades*, and there, blinking at him like a winning slot machine at a Vegas casino, in big red letters, under REWARD, read: $200,000,000. Even split between Fergie and his ex-wife, whom Johnson still paid alimony, and with the firm taking their 25% finder's fee and processing fee, he'd still make enough to take his new wife and kids to the Lunar Disneyland. Maybe even get that 2030 Mustang GT classic he's wanted since he saw one in the museum when he was a kid. To hell with the hefty carbon tax he'd have to pay, which would be almost as much as the car.

You only live once.

They got a call on their eyephones, "Incoming Call: Boss Man" blinking in their eyes, their eardrums humming faintly. It was Lieutenant Jennings. His pudgy face popped up in their vision. "You guys get the alert?" His mouth was contorted in what Fergie thought to be a smile, but he couldn't be sure, because he couldn't recall ever seeing Jennings's smile.

"*Shit*, yeah, we got it, bro." Johnson was a little rough around the edges and was tact deficient when it came to talking to superiors, but he was a good enough bounty hunter, smart, eager.

"Is *it* real, sir," Fergie said. There was something in his voice that surprised him—hope, excitement—he couldn't quite source what it was, but it felt good, different.

"It's real," Jennings assured. "And it's time-sensitive."

"What's the window, sir?" Fergie blinked twice quickly, waited a beat, then blinked twice again, activating the split-screen module. Jennings's face slimmed and slid to the left of his vision. On the right, a word document popped up, the first line blinking, awaiting dictation.

"We have twenty-four hours before every agency from Boston to Bangkok scramble bounty hunters," Jennings said.

24-hour lead, Fergie thought before noting the time—*08:43.*

"Meet me in the easter egg in five minutes," Jennings said before disappearing.

Lieutenant Jennings was an obese man with an anger problem bigger than his waistline. Despite his doctor's prophetic warnings of excessively indulging in his beloved McDonald's 3D replicator machine, he continued to gorge himself on Big Macs and McNuggets five sometimes six times a week. Eating was how he dealt with the stresses of the job. His subordinates joked behind his back that he got that big by eating his anger.

"Did he already have his breakfast this morning?" they'd say, euphemistically questioning if he'd already chewed out someone's ass, for he seemed to have a finite amount of anger every day, and the sooner it was depleted, the better the day was in a manner of speaking.

From the look of his face, he not only had his breakfast, but was still digesting it.

Fergie walked into the conference room, a large circular area with no corners. They called it "The Easter Egg Room." The other thing the easter egg room lacked, aside from corners, and along with the rest of the world, was wires of any kind. After two-hundred-twenty years at the top of the energy pyramid, the alternating current was dethroned, ironically, by another one of Tesla's brainchildren—zero-point energy changed the world practically overnight.

Great big Tesla towers were strategically interspersed around the globe, running a steel rod deep under the earth, connecting tiller currents and underground rivers with the ionosphere, magnifying transmitters, turning the Schumann resonance into a beacon of unlimited energy.

"Nice of you to join us, Fergie." The vein in the middle of Jennings's forehead pulsated, his face the shade of a bad sunburn, his bulging shirt untucked in the front, swaying like a sheet door on a windy beach.

"Sorry, boss," Fergie offered. He settled in his chair next to a sneering Johnson.

The conference table was immense and oval. Jennings sat at the head while Fergie and Johnson sat at the opposite end, leaving eight empty chairs on either side. There were no light fixtures to be seen. The only light came from inside the walls, an ambient glow which lit the room in varying shades.

"Decrease lights," Jennings said to the voice-activated system. The mercury-like substance in the walls dimmed a shade at a time, with allotted intervals of two seconds between each shade for decision purposes. After five shades, Jennings said, "Stop." The lights stopped at level three, officially titled "Sensual Dusk."

"Projector," Jennings said lazily, his voice still crackling from the last ass-chewing he dished out.

A slit in the middle of the table opened and a small drone the size of a grapefruit ascended gracefully, noiselessly. The metallic-looking bird stopped a few inches away from the ceiling and projected onto the middle of the table a green, translucent globe the size of a Jeep Cherokee. The globe rotated slowly, billions of small, red dots scattered upon its face like a fierce case of chicken pox.

If you were to scroll in on an individual dot, you would find the name, location, and known past lives of the person attributed to the dot.

Beside the globe, in a joint program that complimented the globe, was a translucent copy of the RPD's most wanted list, a who's who of history's most nefarious adepts. The list was a living document that ebbed and flowed as individuals died and reincarnated. Even as they looked at the globe, dots disappeared from the ether, while other dots reappeared—the list changing in conjunction with the globe.

They called the globe program Lazarus—a government led endeavor assisted by quantum physicists who discovered that space wasn't empty, that there was an immense web of entanglement that connected the earth, and everyone on it, to the furthest planet in the furthest galaxy at the furthest corners of the universe. When they discovered how to tap into this web of entanglement, they started accumulating data, trillions upon trillions of bytes of data, enough to fill entire warehouses of towers and coolers. It cost the government hundreds of millions of dollars for the air condition bills alone. But it was worth it. Because the data collected was an incredible tool that registered and recorded the genetic makeup of all twelve billion souls on the planet, and, to everyone's surprise, trillions of other souls throughout the cosmos—irrefutable evidence of alien life.

The powers that be decided that humanity wasn't ready for such revelations, so they slapped a top-secret nomenclature to the project, made everyone sign NDAs, and denied all rumors as "unfounded conspiracy gibberish."

The few brave whistleblowers all met their untimely demise in some implausible accident—dissuading future whistleblowers from stepping forward.

Jennings married the mouse in his interface link to the most wanted list next to the rotating globe. He scrolled to reward and clicked on it, causing the letters to jumble and dance. When it settled, the list on the left was the highest reward starting at the top—The Ace of Spades—at $200,000,000. He clicked on it. The picture of an innocent, lovely looking girl appeared. Under the picture was her past life transgressions, a long list of debaucheries, which, since they were about to pick her up, had already been vetted by the DA and a judge said there was sufficient evidence to make the bond.

In bold letters under her picture was her name. Under that, it read—CHROMOSOME 23 DEFICIENT.

"Lena Paul," Jennings said, "five-years-old; flagged by an ocular scan yesterday morning at an oculus facility in South Philly—"

"They grow up so fast," Johnson said with a grimace.

"She's due to have the implant—" Jennings turned to the massive digital clock, opposite the rotating globe— "in one hour. DNA and fingerprint scan's pending—we don't need the dental scans because she's a juvie. I need you two to go to Pennsylvania and verify identity. Be quick but thorough. Check then double-check. I can't have another situation like last year." Nervously, he glanced at the clock again, then, "Your jump bags are already packed and loaded into the car, which is fully charged and just updated to the newest software system. You guys got an hour to grab chow and rollout."

"Why not fly, sir?" Johnson asked. "If it's time-sensitive, that is."

Jennings grimaced and shifted, but it was Fergie who answered, "We can't charter the company helicar without raising suspicions. And this all needs to be under the radar."

Jennings looked at Fergie, nodding. His eyes wandered to Johnson. He didn't say anything else. His eyes delivered the last message. "Don't fuck it up," they said.

When a person dies, their genetic sequence disappears from the ether, presumably—the scientists who were reading the data thought—forever. But then something happened that floored the scientist—the same genetic sequences started reappearing again following one's death. Sometimes it took only a couple of days, sometimes it took many years. But eventually, the dead rose again.

In this way, they discovered, unequivocally, that reincarnation was in fact real.

Unlike the lid of secrecy on alien life, the government announced to the world their findings in tandem with the scientific community.

First came the shock, then came the pushback, but the science was solid, empirical, undeniable.

They started exhuming graves, crypts, accumulating a comprehensive database of known DNA.

While conducting the studies, they discovered that bad souls are bad souls no matter what decade they lived. Consistently, without fail, despite a childhood showered with unconditional love, a murderer in one life, the numbers said, was 90% more likely to kill in the next.

Scientists were able to isolate a genetic defect in the Chromosome 23. They identified the defect as a marker for "the capacity of evil," said Dr. Cummings, lead scientist on the project.

They called it "the sociopath gene."

It took a few years before Congress started listening to the scientists who were calling to arrest people who were chromosome 23 deficient, arrest them before they broke any crimes—a direct violation of the United States Constitution. But every year when the crime demographics came out, and carriers with the sociopath gene proliferated representation, the decision was made to instate the Reincarnation Pre-Crime Division.

Their mission statement—to stop the spread of evil *before* they have another chance.

For lunch, they decided on a small corner café not far from HQ called Soup and Sammy. It was a new place; everyone was raving about their assortment of soups that boasted heavily guarded recipes from six of the seven continents. You could get borscht from Russia or caldo de frijoles from South America. Bacon and cabbage soup from Ireland had a cult following.

The only continent without a soup was Antarctica. "But we're working on a gourmet penguin soup," the advertisements joked.

Fergie and Johnson sat themselves at a booth that had a line of sight to both the front and back exits, something they learned in training.

The café smelled of fresh baked bread and strong coffee, dark roasted. There was a lovely elderly couple sitting at a table across the room and a family of four sat at the booth across from them. There were no waitresses, but four touchscreen tablets embedded inside the face of the table.

Johnson scrolled down the list, examining the soup selections while Fergie went straight to the burger section, adding bacon and condiments. He ordered quickly, leaned back, and observed the nice-looking family who were in the middle of eating their lunches. The two boys were young, between four and six, if he were to guess. The older one looked like a famished savage, licking and sucking sauce from his fingers while the younger one refused to eat. The mother was an attractive woman, early thirties, flaming red hair, throbbing breasts, beautiful face. The father was short and stocky with a square jaw and balding hair.

Fergie noticed all this in passing, for what truly caught his attention was the incandescent milky-white tinge emanating from their eyes like a family of lions on a nocturnal hunt.

They were so immersed in their oculi, they might as well have been alone. It was sad to witness the systematic disconnect, the dissociation of familiar bonds.

The father balled his hands into a fist and pumped victoriously. *He must be watching the game,* Fergie thought.

The mother smiling coyly. *Probably watching whatever new reality tv series popular among lonely housewives.*

Even the kids were laughing at different intervals—*which probably means they aren't even watching the same program.*

They sat together, they ate together, but they were not together.

Fergie remembered a time—long, long ago—when oculus implants were relegated to fanciful science fiction. He remembered a time when phones and computers were external devices, a time before the holy matrimony between man and machine. He wished he could say he missed "the good ol' days," if it could even be called that. But the truth was, it was just as bad when he was a kid—if not worse. Now people have their eyes buried behind a nano-lens instead of down at their hands.

He glanced over at the elderly couple, who were also immersed in whatever content was under the incandescent screen of white.

His heart wrenched. He wished it were different. He wished he were different. It takes a special kind of courage to ostracize yourself from the herd, to do what you think is right, proudly and unapologetically. Fergie was a courageous man in his own right, full of spit and vinegar, but in this one aspect, he was a coward through and through. He lacked the courage of his conviction to get the implant removed, because the truth of it was—it was pretty fucking sweet.

The technology was proceeding at an exponentially fast rate, and there were rumors that the next step was thought transference—a fanciful way of saying "Telepathy," the ultimate DM.

Guiltily, he sighed, blinked three times, and interfaced with his oculus.

Johnson decided on *sinigang*, a tangy Filipino soup with Chinese cabbage and beef ribs so tender, the flesh falls off the bone and the bone has the mushy density of a candy bar, with a lovely bone marrow nugget in the middle.

Something was bugging him, something Jennings said in the meeting earlier. "What happened last year?" he said. He only received the promotion to Headquarters six months prior. A year ago, he was lead Marshal at the RPCD in Dubai. He spent two years sweating in the sandbox because he knew that was the fastest track to get to HQ, thus, the fastest track to a lucrative career instead of fighting for scraps at the bottom.

Fergie didn't even bother dimming his oculus, he just looked at Johnson like he tried sleeping with his wife, then he remembered Johnson had only recently transferred. He sighed heavily. He was a simple man with simple pleasures. And silence was a luxury he rarely enjoyed with the chatty Johnson. He missed his old partner.

"You know Marshals Piper and Schafer?" Fergie said, blinking twice.

There was a moment of earnest searching projected on Johnson's face before he decided to use his interface, searching the names Piper and Schafer in his vast contacts list. "No Match" blinked in red letters across the space in his mind's eye. He shook his head.

"*Precisely.*" Fergie's eyes suddenly grew big. He threw his hands up and rubbed them together, licking his lips. An autoboot—that was essentially a small, knee-high table with wheels—strolled out with their orders. Everything looked hot, fresh, and delicious.

After they divvied up the food, Johnson said, "So, what happened to them?"

"They got shit-canned." Fergie woke the tablet and poked the "extra ketchup" tab. The table that was heading back to the kitchen stopped, went backwards, then a hole in the middle yawned open, producing a cold bottle of Heinz 57. Johnson took the bottle and handed it to Fergie.

"They were lazy, sloppy," Fergie said, lathering the top bun with a thick layer of ketchup. He bit into his bacon cheeseburger, grease and ketchup dripping down his chin. He blinked twice, his eyes distant, vacant, hiding behind a sheet of white.

Johnson knew that he was on his interface, checking the news, emails, sports, watching porn. "Speaking of lazy," he said.

Fergie looked up, annoyed. "What?" He spoke while chewing. Johnson was only a vague silhouette under the oculus screen.

"You can't get a girl all wet n'not finish." Johnson wiggled his eyebrows then winked flirtatiously. "It's unbecoming."

Fergie sighed, went distant and vacant; he finished the email he was writing to his daughter then blinked three times.

It always took a few seconds for your eyes to adjust to regular lighting when you got off your oculus. The flashing spots in his vision slowed before disintegrating completely.

He looked at Johnson. "They were on a routine call to pick up what they thought to be low-level collar. But when they did the ocular scan, they realized they'd collared the Ace of Hearts." While Fergie talked, Johnson entered the database to look up the Ace of Hearts—*Genghis Kahn.*

Immediately, Johnson knew the dilemma—ocular scans aren't verifiable for people who lived at a time when it was impossible to conduct an ocular scan. Only DNA can determine that, and you'd need to be able to verify the DNA was from a descendant. Luckily, Genghis Kahn had a million descendants, so that was simple enough.

But simple and easy aren't always mutually exclusive.

"They did everything but the DNA," Fergie said, staring at Johnson, nodding. "The only thing that mattered." Just when he was about to bite into his burger, Johnson said, "Why do you think they did it?"

Fergie talked with his eyes closed, rubbing the bridge of his nose with one hand, holding the burger in the other. Swaths of ketchup fell from the burger as he moved his hand, talking. "Marshal Schafer was an eager rookie with stars in his eyes and Piper was a long-timer, twenty-nine years in, a few years away from retirement."

Fergie pulled his lips back almost as if he were hurt, disappointed. And right away, Johnson knew that Fergie knew Marshal Piper. They came up together, went to each other's houses for barbecues, birthday parties.

Blankly staring at the table, Fergie said, "He got complacent, greedy. All they saw was the reward—I'll save you the search. It was a $100,000,000 reward. And it was still under the radar at the time, no one knew about it. So, rather than doing it by the book, they took a shot. The DA threw the book at them, citing negligence, tampering, conspiracy to commit a crime, and a slew of other charges."

Marshals Kevin Schafer and Lucas Piper were currently at California Federal penitentiary in Pasadena, California, where they would remain until their dying day.

A white flashing light covered Fergie's vision in pulsating sheets like a blanket of heavy snowfall—the alarm he'd set after the meeting with Jennings. It was time to leave and pick up the soul bond.

The five-year-old girl whose body housed the most notoriously evil spirit to ever incarnate on the earth plane lived on the top floor of an inner-city apartment complex in Philadelphia. From Virginia, it was a two-hour drive.

Fergie tried fruitlessly to catch up on sleep while Johnson watched an episode of the timeless classic, *The Office*—the episode where Michael Scott staunchly follows the GPS instructions despite there being a lake where the voice was directing him to turn, and he drives directly into the lake.

Johnson ate a laugh then almost choked on it; he blew steam from his nostrils in short, choppy spurts. The last thing he wanted to do was wake his boss. But it was too late.

Fergie stirred angrily. "What the hell's so *funny*," he said. They were at the cusp of returning a soul bond that was worth $200,000,000—*$200,000,000*. There was no sleeping, not even for the hardened Marshal Vincent Ferguson. He'd been laying there, eyes closed, oculus off, enjoying the stillness of the dark void behind his eyes, appreciating, yearning. He was old, old and tired. He used to be a devout atheist in the world before quantum physicists discovered the web of entanglement—before they discovered that souls reincarnate—something he knew on a visceral level to be true even before the announcement was made. He knew it was true because he remembered things from a past life that he had no business knowing—like the hauling capacity of a B-17, or how to crash land effectively on water.

Still, the news shattered everything he knew as a young man, seventeen, leaving home early not because he wanted to, but because his parents were murdered. He was one of the first bounty hunters, turning down promotion after promotion in a sick way, because he wanted to punish the bad ones returning, the murderers, the ones carrying the sociopath gene; he wanted to stop the collateral damage left in the wake of the evil souls.

The man that killed his parents died in the struggle; his father shot him. But he reincarnated not long after. Fergie'd been looking for him ever since as the Lazarus program could determine whether a soul is in the ether, but it could not locate a soul until they'd been vetted through DNA, dental and ocular scans, and fingerprints—each one unique to a soul, "God's snowflake" they were called in the department field manual, the one that all bounty hunters use as the bible.

But in the long search, he realized, quite adamantly, that he hated living on planet earth. He didn't understand human behaviors—their need for violence, their addiction to technology, their greed and senseless racism—every social construct was an enigma to him. He never understood why humans do what they do. He suspected his soul belonged somewhere else, an aquatic planet with talking dolphins, perhaps; a rocky planet with bird-like people; one-eyed cyborgs; ape men; tiny dwarfs.

Wherever his soul was originally from, and whatever he was, he didn't even want that anymore either. He wished he could just die and stay dead. How he craved the stillness of sublime nothingness.

"Sorry, boss." Johnson leaned his seat forward.

An alarm in the car dinged three times, signifying they were pulling up to the destination. "Damn it to hell," Fergie bellowed. He opened his eyes just as the front dash and side window's blackout mode faded out, slowly letting the light back in. They were a few blocks away from their destination, the urban streets lined with rotating holophoto advertisements of beautiful men and women selling something or another. He keyed on a particular hologram photo of a stunning, exotic woman. She looked so real, as if she were cat walking the Calvin Klein fall release right there in the middle of downtown Philadelphia. She looked physical. But he knew that if he tried to hug her, his arms would pass right through her.

Johnson was still watching the twenty-four-inch tablet that was the only thing on the dashboard, laughing unapologetically now.

"Isn't this show like fifty years old?" Fergie remembered a poll when he was just a kid after the death of Steve Carrol, how even thirty years after the show went off the air, it was still in the top three comedy sitcoms of all time, a feat lost on him. For whenever Fergie heard of *anyone* dying, he always got lost in thought on who they would reincarnate as next, on why they must come back at all, at the unfairness of the divine order that he had no say in.

"Fifty-two years old," said Johnson, a self-proclaimed movie/television nerd and a pop culture fanatic. He looked at Fergie with serious eyes. "Comedy is timeless, my friend."

Fergie ignored him. He blinked four times, connecting his oculus to the tablet on the dashboard, bringing up a picture of their soul bond. The little girl's hair was split into pink tails, her smile incomplete, missing three bottom teeth and one top. *They always look so innocent,* he thought, thinking back on his long career. Because he always refused promotions, he'd made the most collars of any bounty hunter. The closest one to him would have to work another twenty years to catch up, but they'd move up in rank before that ever happened.

Fergie scrolled down the list of past-life transgressions committed by the girl. In her very last life, she was a dirty politician—the dirtiest. She started a war under false pretenses, green-lighting the execution of a false flag attack upon the American people, killing thousands—a catalyst that spawned a fervor of patriotic duty and pulled America into a war that lasted over twenty years. Before that, she was a house-wife in the early 1900s, and she killed four husbands, six children, and fifteen grandchildren to keep her inheritance. She was an aristocrat that bathed in the blood of young, beautiful women. A tribal leader who traded his brethren into slavery. A savage Viking warlord that raped and pillaged his way across Europe. A Romanian prince, known to impale his enemies on the long winding road that led to his castle.

The list was endless.

"How you wanna play this?" Johnson was excited, but nervous. He'd never been on such a huge soul bond before.

The blinking light returned, but this time, it was blue. Red flash-ing lights were internal HQ soul bonds, blue lights were soul bonds released at the global level.

They both blinked three times, answering the bond. There, on the dashboard tablet, was the lovely, innocent smiling face of a cute little girl with pink tails and missing teeth. Blinking in red was the reward amount, and, below this, the location.

They were supposed to have another twenty hours before the siren call went out. Someone at HQ dropped the ball.

Since Fergie's oculus was connected to the car system, the kids' face on the screen was replaced with "Incoming Call: Boss Man" before they got the call on their eyephones.

Fergie answered immediately. "What happened?" he said.

"Dunno." Jennings was unusually calm for having just blown the element of surprise and potentially letting the biggest fish of his life off the line. "I suspect other agencies have moles on their payroll for moments like this."

Fergie and Johnson both turned off their oculus and used the dash.

"Where are you?"

"Outside the bond's home."

"That's good," Jennings said nodding with a smile. "That's very good."

"How much time you think we got before Philly RPCD sends their BH's?" Johnson asked.

"Well, they'll call first, of course, following procedure—making sure it's real," Jennings said. "I can buy you guys some time, but to be on the safe side, I'd say you have an hour max to make the bond."

With a sense of urgency, they got out of the car.

The sky was filled with delivery drones, zigging and zagging across the blue sky like a patched quilt.

Fergie always avoided looking at the sky, because the flying devices, the exhaust lines, would incite anxiety in him, deep and uncontrollable. No one knew about his past-life PTSD and he'd rather it that way. He always kept his eyes at ground level. He walked past the stunning, exotic Calvin Klein holophoto and very nearly tried putting his hand through her, she looked so real.

A drone the size of a basketball descended slowly, its familiar beeping a tribute to its cargo predecessor—the delivery truck. It carried a package in its mouth like a stork delivering a baby. It descended to the doorstep of the apartment building where the soul bond lived. When it was a few feet off the ground, it dropped the package perfectly at the doorstep, then shot vertically up at dizzying speed, stopped midway up the sky, the AI traffic control allowing for a series of other drones to pass, then it continued its silent ascent into the clouds. Soon it was out of sight.

They walked over the package into the front entrance. There hadn't been a homeless person in Philly—or the world for that matter—in many decades. The 3D printed filing cabinet apartment complexes were as close as you could get to being poor.

The hallway smelled of ammonia and rotting fruit.

"Meetcha at the top, brotha," Johnson said. He removed the small kinetic service weapon from the holster and started climbing the steps two at a time. Fergie waited at the bottom, babysitting the elevator, just in case.

Six minutes later, Fergie got a call on his eyephone. Johnson was breathing heavily, sweating. "C'mon up n'join the party," he says.

Fergie entered the elevator and ascended to the forty-fourth floor.

They met outside the soul bond's apartment, the air electric, filled with looming celebration—two-hundred-million dollars' worth of celebration.

A geriatric woman answered the door. She wore an old, loose, Amish-style dress that trickled down to her ankles, covering everything but her face and hands. Her snow-white hair was in a bun, her glasses perched on the bridge of her nose. Her head was tilted, looking at the men before her with her chin to her chest. Her eyes and nose were the bright red of frostbite. She clutched a wet handkerchief in her left hand, squeezing it so hard her fingers were white. Very clearly, she'd been crying.

Johnson looked to Fergie for guidance. He'd prepared himself for any number of resistances, mostly physical, but he never considered having to deal with a crying elderly woman who was a dead ringer for Tweety Bird's granny from the Looney Tunes, which he used to watch whenever he visited his grandparents in Wyoming. They never had cable, just an old relic called a DVD player, with a select few DVDs. The Looney Tunes collection being his favorite.

Fergie stepped forward. "I'm very sorry to bother you, ma'am," he said, "but does Lena Paul live here?"

The woman's wrinkled face contorted grotesquely, an utterly perfect mask of heartbreak. With wobbly knees, she lurched forward, grabbing her chest, and very nearly fell over. Fergie stepped forward and supported her inside. He set her on a recliner.

She lifted her arms to the sky and wailed, shaking her arms as if she were banging on a cellar door.

"Is there anything the matter, miss?" asked the young Johnson.

But Fergie sourced the look on the woman's face as grief, and he knew what the next words out of the woman's mouth would be—

But when did it happen? Fergie thought. *How did it happen?*

Just as Fergie was about to ask the particulars, a white flashing light obstructed his vision. He knew who was calling on his eyephone. He raised a finger and said, "One minute, ma'am." He turned around and answered.

"What's going on?" Lieutenant Jennings had a concerned look on his face, his brow furrowing like a pug. "The soul bond blipped off the screen for a few minutes, then reappeared. The techs say they've never seen anything like that happen to a living person."

Came back, Fergie thought. *That would mean that—*

Johnson was putting the pieces together, too—the heartbroken woman before them, the blip in the ether, the reappearance, Lena Paul—the soul bond of the Ace of Spades, had died and already, within a matter of minutes, reincarnated somewhere else in the ether.

Johnson's stomach turned cold; a stone formed in his throat. They were so close. He was so close—$54,000,000. He'd already done the math and after paying taxes and fees and alimony, that was his cut—$54,000,000. He wanted to scream. He wanted to—

The old woman hunched over and faceplanted with a loud thud.

"What was that?" Jennings asked.

"Huh," Fergie grunted.

Johnson bent over and checked the woman's pulse; she didn't have one. With malice in his heart, he flipped her over, preparing to initiate CPR. The woman had a picture frame clutched in one hand and a rolled-up piece of paper in the other.

Johnson snatched the paper and gaped at it—

It was a wrongful death form for Lena Paul, citing negligence by a drunken anesthesiologist, who blew a .40 at the time of his arrest. Contact information for lawyers, etc.

Somewhere in the back of the apartment a door opened and closed, then tiny feet scurrying across the hallway.

"What was that noise?" Jennings said impatiently.

Johnson peeled the woman's cold hands from the frame and gasped at what he saw. He lunged forward and handed Fergie the picture frame, then started for the hallway.

"Well, sir," Fergie said as he dropped the picture frame and bent over to pick it up, "Lena Paul and her guardian—"

Fergie fell silent. He couldn't believe his eyes. In the picture was Lena Paul smiling happily, with her arms wrapped around another little girl that looked *exactly* like Lena Paul—her twin sister.

Johnson bumped into a little girl where the hallways and the living room meet.

"I'll call you back, sir." Fergie blinked three times, his mouth practically on the ground, his mind racing.

Two of them?

"Granma?" The little girl started for the old woman. She fell on her, her ears on the woman's robust bosom. "She's not breathin', mista," she said, looking at Fergie, tears already starting to punch her eyes. "Help her!"

She prostrated herself on the woman and cried hysterically, her tiny shoulders shaking.

Johnson and Fergie looked at each other. Johnson blinked twice, waited a beat, then blinked once. His DM popped up in his vision. Simply by thinking, he wrote his partner who was standing three feet away.

Are you thinking what I'm thinking?

Fergie shrugged, annoyed. *We call the medics and hit the bar to drown our sorrows?* he thought.

We can still make the bond, Ferg, Johnson thought. *We pull a switch.*

Are you crazy? How the hell would we do that? Even as the words left his mind, Fergie realized, it was possible, even probable that they'd get away with it.

We make the arrest now. Put the crown on her, and that's that. She'd be comatose for eternity.

Or until—Fergie couldn't finish the thought. It was too dark to even conceive. He felt dirty to even consider it. But he did consider it.

When Congress adapted the laws for the sociopath gene, the decision was made to waive the criminal's right to a fair trial. After identification was made, the person would be immediately detained by a crown device, then shipped to California Federal Penitentiary where they were placed in a cryogenic tube, and from there, they would no longer be a problem for society, frozen in a cryogenic state, kept alive indefinitely, unable to die, and therefore, unable to reincarnate and spread their evil across the globe.

The more Fergie thought about it, the more he realized they could get away with it. No one would know until the new Lena Paul died again and blipped off the map, and, by then, Fergie and Johnson would be dead, reincarnated somewhere else, as someone else.

Lean Paul's twin threw her head up to the sky and started head-butting her grandmother's chest. Fergie's heart ached for her. Within a matter of hours, she'd lost a sister and her grandmother.

What if she's got parents, Johnny? Fergie thought.

"Hey, kid, do you have any other family?" Johnson said, bending over.

She looked up, her face covered in drool and snot, a confused look in her eyes.

"Parents, aunts, uncles—*anyone?*" Johnson said, beads of sweat forming on his brow.

She shook her head then laid it back down gently on her grandmother, her tiny arms wrapping around her, squeezing, holding on, not wanting to let go.

Johnson wasn't Chromosome 23 deficient, therefore he wasn't a sociopath, but he lacked a certain degree of integrity that a man in his position should value. Cunningly, he used her being an orphan as ammunition to serve his will. *No parents. No brothers. No sisters. No one will know the difference,* he thought.

Fergie shook his head. *What if HQ sees Lena Paul's death on the news?*

There's twelve billion people on the planet, Ferg. HQ doesn't give a flying fuck about some random girl dying. And thanks to the liberal's fear of backlash on families, Johnny Q public doesn't know the names of the soul bonds, only their rank. To us, the select few, she's Lena Paul, but to everyone else, we arrested the Ace of Spades. People that know them will just think the twin's the Ace of Spades.

What about the checks? Fergie thought. *Twins' DNA aren't exact, and the ocular scans, fingerprints, dental records. None of them. None of them would match up.*

"Hey, kid," Johnson said, "d'ya have a holophoto of your sister somewhere?"

Without looking up, the kid pointed to a 3D projector sitting on the middle table.

Johnson's eyes grew big, wicked. He licked his lips, nodding, thinking.

Okay, he thought. *We get the ocular scans from the holophoto, we get the DNA and prints from her toothbrush, we—*

We can't fake dental records, Johnny, Fergie thought, tugging at strings, fully aware of what the response would be.

—Cut the shit, Johnson thought. *She's a minor. Ipso facto, fuck a dental record.*

The little girl looked up, the heartbreak on her face punching holes in Johnson's plan.

"Aren't you gonna help my granma?" she asked. Then the heartbroken look transformed to one of sudden inspiration. She licked her lips then started blinking her eyes and it was obvious what she was doing—

Lena Paul's grandmother didn't play favorites, she sprung for both grandchildren to get their oculus systems put in today.

With the DNA, prints and ocular scan, we have enough to make the bond now, before anyone else can crown her.

"Hello," the little girl said, her eyes behind a milky-white incandescent glow. "Is this the am-boolince?"

Johnson sprang to action. He reached in his back pouch where most cops carry handcuffs, but where RPCD bounty hunters keep their crown—a metal device that almost looked like a queen's crown, slim, circular, shiny, with a light in the middle that would turn green when activated so that it looked like a shiny emerald. When applied and activated, an electrical current intercepted the synapses firing to the wearer's nervous system, inhibiting thought.

From there, they experienced nothing but darkness, forevermore.

Nothing but darkness—a thought that finally made Fergie get on board with the devious plot. It was a win-win situation, really. If they got away with it, they'd be able to retire. If they didn't—something Fergie secretly hoped happened—*then we'd get crowned and would spend the rest of our lives in still darkness.*

The thought was exhilarating.

Fergie had instinctively stepped forward to stop Johnson's advance. But now, he stepped aside and let Johnson creep up behind the girl and place the crown upon her head, the electrical pulse cutting the feed to her oculus.

Her eyes stayed white, and she stood straight, standing, waiting to be herded to her cryogenic cell.

They both blinked twice, waited a beat, then blinked once.

There was only one thing stopping Fergie from committing entirely.

"There's just one thing," Fergie said. "If we make the arrest, then that would mean—"

"Then that would mean the new Ace of Spades will be running out there freely, spreading their evilness across the globe." Johnson finished the thought for him.

Fergie nodded slowly, squinting his eyes, thinking, digging deep, wondering if he was capable of such a diabolical act.

"And even when the new Lena Paul gets her oculus and gets her adult teeth," Fergie said, thinking aloud, "there'd be no way to confirm their identity, because everyone will assume it's a glitch in the system."

"'That's not possible,' they'd say," Johnson said, his arms raised at his side, his head shaking, feigning worry. "'The Ace of Spades is already crowned in Cali.'"

Johnson lowered his arms, smile bigger than a full moon.

Wiggling his eyebrows, he said, "There must be something wrong with the system."

Fergie shook his head, tears forming in his eyes.

"We can do this," Johnson said. "This can be done." He nodded and started for the holophoto to secure the ocular scan. It turned on with a low hum. The screen saver was the same picture that was in the frame that the old woman clung to.

Johnson laughed, then, "Shit, she looks just like the picture, I betcha no one even looks at the checks."

Fergie stepped toward the holophoto. They looked so real, so happy.

Johnson reached in the inside pocket of his blazer, retrieving his standard issue scanner—a long, skinny, tubular device that could easily be confused for eyeliner or lipstick, if not for the small lens that covered the top inch.

Fergie watched with a detached sort of horror as Johnson took a guess and scanned the girl on the left, a red laser emanating from the end of the device, scanning left and right like a small spotlight. It blinked red. He shrugged and scanned the eyes of the girl on the right, scanning left and right, then, it blinked green.

Fergie was lost in abstraction. He thought of his old friend Lucas Piper, the poor fuck was crowned, standing in a cryogenic tube in California Penitentiary.

We'd be cellmates, old friend, he thought.

There was a hard knock at the door, then, shouts, "*RPCD, you have thirty seconds to answer the door, or we will utilize force.*"

Johnson turned off the holophoto and ran to grab two toothbrushes from the bathroom—one light pink and the other bright pink. He scanned the bright pink along the handle, and this time, he was a first-time go. He touched the bristles of the toothbrush to the edge of the device, and it confirmed that the saliva matched the DNA to the Ace of Spades.

He threw the toothbrushes down the hall and looked at the door that was knocking again, announcing, "*Ten seconds or we will be forced to use our kinetic weapons.*"

Johnson looked at Fergie. "$200,000,000," he said, his eyes big with excitement, and permission. He looked like how Fergie's daughter looked last summer when she was begging him to spend two weeks in Cancun.

"Lemme do the talking," Fergie said, nodding.

"Five, four ..."

"You're the greatest partner alive," Johnson said with a big smile.

The K-3 service revolver, or, the Kinetic Three, was a small weapon the size of a .45 pistol, with a muzzle that was an inch long and the girth of a four-inch pipe. It was the best non-lethal weapon used by police departments, and government agencies the world over. Created by a Black man from Chicago, who, as a kid, witnessed his father get shot twenty-three times, the kinetic weapon released a wave of energy that mimiced the force of a car slamming into a wall at forty-five miles an hour.

"Lest no child be orphaned."—was the mission statement for the man's company, making him richer than Winchester or Smith and Wesson.

The doorknob blew out, and two bounty hunters from the Philadelphia branch of the Reincarnation Pre-Crime Division burst into the room with smiles on their faces and dollar signs in their eyes, a short-lived sentiment as they stopped a foot in the house.

Fergie was walking hand and hand with the soul bond. With the other hand, he had his RPCD badge extended. "Sorry, boys," he said. "Maybe nex' time."

Johnson walked behind them, smiling.

The bigger of the two bounty hunters stepped forward and said, "Wait'a minute, now. Did you confirm the—"

"Checks?" Fergie said. "Show 'em, Johnny." He picked up the speed a gear.

Johnson showed the green-lit scanner, his face like a kid telling their parents, "See, I told ya so."

The man blocked the path anyway, not ready to let go of a $200,000,000 soul bond without a fight.

"D'you know who I am?" Fergie was staring the man down.

The man swallowed hard and nodded.

"It would behoove you to step aside, son," Fergie said. He pivoted and waved an open hand like a game show model showing off merchandise. "It is *very clearly* her."

Squinting hatred at Fergie, the man then stepped aside.

Marshals Ferguson and Johnson walked past them.

"Oh, and one more thing," Johnson said, nodding at the dead old woman. "Call the medics, yeah?"

———

Fergie looked down at his cuffed wrists, a coy smirk playing at his lips. He lifted his hands and tried rubbing the burning sensation from his eyes with the back of his hands. He hadn't slept in forty-eight hours.

He went through with the plan accordingly. And they pulled it off. They actually pulled it off. The poor girl was sent to California penitentiary twenty-four hours prior, and, at the same time, the money hit his account.

$60,000,000 was his cut—sixty million dollars.

He had stared at the balance in his account, his eyes glowing white, his heart growing cold. It was never about the money for him. And he never actually planned to go through with it. His plan, all along, was darkness—sweet, sweet, emancipating darkness.

He looked around the familiar interrogation room. How many times had he been at the opposite end? *Eighteen hundred? Two thousand?*

Jennings walks in, his face puckered and red like a bamboo's asshole, his lips pulled back. "Welp," he said, "it took us a while, but Johnny finally came clean." He set down a black coffee on the table before Fergie, who nodded politely. "You know I have no choice now but to arrest you two idiots, right?" Jennings looked hurt, apprehensive.

Fergie nodded slowly, his eyes dropping to the table.

The payoff of eternal nothingness outweighed taking Johnson down with him and he felt very little remorse.

He wouldn't miss anything in the world but his kids, even his ex-wife/fiancé could get fucked along with everyone else.

And he probably wouldn't have done it if not for the comatose state he'd be in for the rest of his life, reasoning that, "You can't miss something if you can't think."

His kids would be okay, though. Already the news had taken to calling him "the villain hero," saying that even though he took a bite out of temptation, he grew a conscience and came clean in the end, after the payment had been made, after Johnson already put in for retirement, after there was no way him or Johnson or even Jennings could do anything to stop him from being punished.

He closed his eyes, relishing the sweet nothingness behind his eyelids, giddy, yearning.

The Council

Nicaea, Turchia
June 3, 325
Scribe Adir Nahum

My dearest friend,

I do so pray this correspondence finds you and yours in abundance
of health and spirits. But I have not the time for cordial pleasantries,
for it is with great haste—under lantern and threat of life—that I
pen this. Please do forgive my bluntness, but perilous and urgent
this message is, to be handled with delicate care. The carrier is the
only person I urge you to trust regarding this matter. Do not be
bamboozled by his tender age. What he lacks in experience, he more
than makes up for with a pureness that is scarcely seen. His heart is
true, dear friend, as much you or me or anyone I've ever met. He lives
to spread the good word, and I am not fibbing in the least, when I
say he would die for the cause we are about to undertake; a cause of
which—upon reading this letter—has turned you into an accomplice,
I fear. For this, again, I must apologize, but as you shall soon realize,
it is not without reason.

   In his possession is a collection of clay pots, the contents of which
are more rare and more valuable than all the treasures in all the
kingdoms under God and those too whose bounties remain buried.
These manuscripts will someday soon be the last of their kind, I fear,
and, paradoxically, I also pray. For that would mean they survived

the long and arduous journey to you. If you are reading this, then my prayers have only been half answered. The last leg of the tumultuous journey is up to you, and you alone, dear friend. Cumbersome it must feel, this unsolicited burden of responsibility. For all hope will surely be lost if you fail in your task. But first, allow me a brief explanation, for it is impossible to understand the blasphemous task I ask of you, when lacking context.

As you well know, I am a scribe by trade, as was my father before me, and his father, going back eight generations. Hitherto my family has been tasked with what is perhaps the most important job in the kingdom of heaven: the passage of knowledge and information from one generation to the next, a meticulous process that will forever be unappreciated. 'Tis true, I have not received a lavish inheritance; I will never be made rich, nor do I wish so. For what I do have is more valuable than gold or silver: the means of time travel, in a sense, passing down the cumulative history and knowledge of our great forefathers, Abraham, Isaac, and Jacob.

Now, to the point: I received a summon a fortnight ago, to arrive at Nicaea, which I happily obliged through caravan from Egypt where I scribe at the great library. Though I was not made privy to the purpose of this summon, I was told that our great emperor, Constantine, would be present. Imagine such a humbling opportunity given to me, but a lowly scribe, though high-ranking a scribe I am. It made me feel infinitesimal. That is, until I discovered the purpose of the convening council and the method of which they declared to execute said purpose.

Emperor Constantine sought to unite all Christian tribes under one house, hundreds of sects bound by one book. The thought was exhilarating. I was truly honored to take part in such a just undertaking. With members from every tribe and sect, we were to sift through our ancient scrolls, dissecting each one, deciding which books would become canon law and which books would become heretical. To create a book that Jesus Christ himself would be proud of was our goal. Indeed, I can think of no other goal more desirable for a man with my pedigree. It was a dream come true.

The night of the banquet was two moons ago, and that is when I discovered the rumors to be true; our great emperor is not infallible; he falls prey to vanity and just like any other man, his competitive nature is embellished when taken to drink. Thus, they drank, and they ate and discussed which texts would survive the sacred purge to become the world's most important book.

From the start, people were disagreeable. Constantine was arguing the importance of the Book of Enoch, how it must be included. But Saint Nicholas disagreed vehemently. He threw a fig at our great emperor, and a curiously satisfying thing then occurred—even I must admit the vain pleasure—when the fig landed in the cup.

"Now you must drink," Saint Nicholas declared, a challenge our great warrior leader was all too happy to oblige, drinking the mug of wine in one gulp. He spit the fig out onto his hand, and then he himself threw it, too, not aimed at Saint Nicholas, but at his cup that was perched at the end of the table. He missed his mark. But the mood changed after that. The air wasn't so stuffy. Tempers weren't so flared. It'd become something of a contest, a game.

"I declare you shan't do it again," Constantine said, the embers of his competitive spirit stoked, eyes big with humor and determination in equal measure. There were hundreds of open scrolls scattered upon the table, the cumulative knowledge of our forefathers awaiting to be married. Constantine seemed to forget himself. He rolled the wet fig across the table, drips of red wine tainting the sacred text. This was the first of many transgressions, for only I and the other scribes seemed to care.

"Stop this at once," said Bartholomew, an elderly scribe representing the agnostic sect. There was much yelling and no less than twoscore figs thrown at him.

"Shut ye mouth and fetch more bales of wine," Constantine said. "And as many mugs as your feeble little arms can carry." He pointed at me. "You, there, go with him," he said.

We returned with five mugs each. We set the ten mugs up at the end of the table, in the shape of a triangle. "Do you not know that God's beauty lies in his symmetry, you fool," Constantine said. "Go fetch us ten more mugs posthaste." Thus, we endeavored to get ten more mugs. We then set them in a triangle at the opposite end of the table.

The table set up in a triangle of wine-filled cups on either side. Saint Nicholas closed one eye, aiming. God guided his hand and his eyes true, and he sank the fig into the middle mug with a pleasant bloop. Red wine splashed upon The Book of Adam. I could hardly believe my eyes. What then followed was what I perceive to be a game made for teenagers.

Instead of obliging the council's intended purpose, arguing a case for each book, they drank and discussed the rules of the new game they had just discovered, laughing and toasting and spilling upon the sacred texts.

"Please, sir," I begged. My voice was shaky but stern. I could scarcely believe that I vocalized my disdain. I dug deep for the strength of Samson. "If you must partake in childish games, may I put the documents in a safer place." Constantine's eyes conflagrated when he saw that The Book of Enoch had already been stained with red wine. He made to grab it, to save it, but Saint Nicholas screamed, "You scoundrel, how dare you."

There was a great fuss. Each member at the table tried grabbing their sect's text for protection of omission while simultaneously grabbing the other sect's text to hide forever.

It was a drunken Constantine, and this I swear upon our holy father to be true, dear friend; it was he who spoke the foulest and most vile words ever uttered. "Let God decide which text becomes canonical," he said. "Just as he guides the sword and the spear of warriors amidst a trial by combat, so too, let the alpha and omega guide our hands and our eyes." There was a gayness about the air, everyone knowing what he was to say next, everyone taken with spirits, thinking it to be the best idea ever conceived. "The sect that loses in wine fig shall lose in history, too."

"Wine fig?" Saint Nicholas said.

"You don't like it?" Constantine said.

"It's brilliant," Saint Nicholas admitted.

"Splendid idea, sir," said Marcus of Calabria. "Brilliant. *Just* brilliant."

They placed the text on five adjacent tables, laid them out by sect, and whomever lost the round would not only have to drink their fill, but they would also lose a text of the opposing sects' choosing. And this, old friend, I fear will be the reason Christianity will lose their text, lose their history, their identity: an unbecoming game suited for teenagers.

Constantine won the first round. He decided to rid the world of the Book of Noah. Forevermore. No longer shall it be part of canon. It is a disgrace, I declare, that any books be omitted. And suddenly the purpose of the council dawned on me as oppressive, as systematic censorship, an eradication of history, an intellectual purge. But, alas, I could not vocalize my disdain.

Our beloved emperor lost the next game whereupon he lost his beloved Book of Enoch. I wanted to shake him by the shoulders and scream, "Do not let them do it. Exert some authority, sire. You are the emperor, after all."

What then followed, in rapid succession, was the savage, spiteful discarding of the other parties' sacred text. Book of the Giants, Jubilees, Wisdom of Sirach, Gospel of Thomas, and so many more. All of them, discarded as if they were but a used xlospongium; they shall forever be relegated to the likes of heretical text. Second class. Illegal. How it breaks my heart so.

The other scribes and myself, we were made to take the losing text and "Burn them in the fire along with every copy in our stores." We regretfully burned many texts that tragic night, though we did not— we could not—burn them all.

The manuscripts within the clay pots before you are all that remains of a history that will soon be forgotten. I trust you understand the urgency now. I pray that you do, and I pray that you will be brave enough to do what is required next.

Every word I pen is truth, dear friend, and because it is true, I bid for you to burn this letter like the conflagration they wanted to do upon the very text that are in the pots before you. They could very well be the last of their kind. Treat them with the loving care they deserve. Ultimately, though, you must promise to hide them, hide these cherished texts like the hidden treasures of the copper scroll. Hide them where they will not see the light of day for many centuries, until man is ready to receive such knowledge and remember their true history, what we, the first Christians, understood as truth, for I fear, dear friend, it shall be forgotten to the stain of time, that the kingdom of heaven is not found outside, but that it lives in you and me and indeed, all that wish it so. And I fear that if these cherished texts were omitted from historical records, that the church of the future will look very different, that they would inflate their stations, insert themselves as necessary mediums to the almighty, outsourcing humanity's innate ability to commune with the creator, monopolizing salvation. We shan't let this come to pass.

I have arranged for two caravans to leave at first light. The young man before you shall take half the scrolls, and head to Egypt. You shall take the other half to Qumran. Please, please, search high and low, find suitable amenities—a dark, secluded cave perhaps—and turn it into a tomb for our beloved history.

Eternally grateful,
Adir Nahum

Discovery: July 7, 1945
Discovery Location: Qumarun
Discoverer: Teenage Goat Farmers
Authenticated By Vatican Librarian Giovanni
Mercatti On July 21, 1945
Catalogued By Vatican Librarian Giovanni
Mercatti On July 21,1945
Translated Aramaic

Betty woke up gradually, a slow drip of adrenaline jumpstarting her consciousness. She usually started her day off with gratitude, thanking the good Lord for seeing fit to give her another day above ground. But not today. She opened her eyes and was horrified. Though the nightmare wasn't nearly as bad as the previous few nights—there were no cannibals, or dead babies. But there was a simplistic horror at play, and she felt the dreadful sorrow of the early Christian, Adir Nahum, whose beliefs and sacred texts were butchered, one and all.

She was horrified how one man convening one council could have such a far-reaching influence upon the world. That's what she was thinking about when she entered REM, and the feelings of horror were replaced with giddy anticipation.

She could hardly wait for the event to take place.

Sunday Funday

"WE DON'T NEED ALL THAT, NOW, HON," said Sheriff Tyson. He tugged on the chain link that dangled across his chest and pulled out his pocket watch; he pressed the button and the gold face popped open to reveal the time: 11:45. He closed the face and placed it back in the inside pocket of his vest before reaching in his back pocket, producing a disgruntled handkerchief, blowing a stream of snot into the already moist cloth, then dabbing his forehead.

"Don't you rush me, mister," his wife, Tabatha, said with serious eyes, though she did speed up the process of cutting the watermelon into tiny triangles and placing them in the bowl. After that she started removing grapes from vines, washing them in the deep sink.

She placed the Tupperware bowls full of fruit in the bottom of the picnic basket, along with a head of cheddar cheese, and a bottle of *champagne* for the celebration.

A shrieking kid wailed in the background, the shriek seamlessly melting into a heavy sob. Tiny footsteps approach the kitchen.

"Colt hit me, Mama," said their youngest, Tyson Jr.

"Did not," said Colt from the other room.

"Did so."

"Did—"

"You boys need to stop this racket, at once," Tabatha said, wiping her hands on her blue and white apron. She walked over to her husband and ran her fingers across his chest, straightening his collar. "Yawl know how big today is for your father," she said, looking down at her kids with hurt eyes. She gasped, leaped forward, and said, "Tyson Jr., what in the *world* did you get into that made you so dirty?"

The filthy boy flinched and lifted his hands to his face as his mother stepped forward, thinking she was going to slap him on the back of his head as he was accustomed, but she only tried smacking the dirt off him. Swaths of dust fell to the ground about him. She stood straight, licked her fingers, and tried removing dried mud from his nose. He squirmed and leaned back.

"This simply will not do," she said, giving up on the allogrooming. "Upstairs at once, young man." She took a deep breath and leaned her head back, her face toward the ceiling as if she were about to howl at the moon. "*Geraldine*," she called out, making for the living room. "*Geraldine,* where in the—there you are. I need you to go upstairs and give Jr. a bath, ya hear?"

"Yes ma'am," Geraldine said with big eyes. "Right away, mam." Geraldine was a third-generation slave. She was quiet, hardworking, and not so pleasant on the eyes, which is why Mrs. Tabatha preferred her in the house as opposed to the *good-lookin' high-yella one with the robust bosom and wandering eyes*—her name was Chastity, but Mrs. Tabatha refused to dignify her with a name whenever she accused her husband of infidelity.

"Both her parents are darker than two lumps a'coal," she'd always say, "so don't chu think I don't know what *disgraceful* sins you men get up to—sins of the flesh. No, I don't care if it was your pops, I just better never ever catch ya even lookin' at her, ya hear?"

"There is no time for a bath, Tabby," Sheriff Tyson argued, pulling out his pocket watch again and gesturing at it with his eyes. The festivities were supposed to start in just ten minutes. *Ten minutes.* He should've already been down there, setting up, planning, schmoozing, networking. Elections were happening in a few weeks and a joyous day like today was always a good time to try and solicit votes—people are more approachable and amicable when they are in good spirits and having fun.

"You are no longer the deputy, Ty," Tabatha reminded her husband. "You are the *sheriff* of *Waco, Texas*, and, as an *absolute* requisite, nothing shall commence in your absence. We can afford to be a few minutes late." She turned and headed toward the boys' room. Over her shoulders, she said, "But I refuse to leave this house with my children lookin' like they bathed in a mud pile. Imagine what everyone would say. No. No, it simply will not do. You just be patient now. We'll be on our way soon enough."

Sheriff Tyson sighed and sat on the ottoman. He looked across the room to the calendar that was nailed above the fireplace. Today was Sunday, July 4, 1868. The date was circled in black ink, along with the words, *Sunday Funday.* It'd been there for a week, circled, screaming for attention.

You would think she would be on time, he thought. Just *this once.*

They left their house on Main Street at 12:20, Tabatha combing Ty Jr.'s wet hair as they walked off the porch into the dirt road.

The streets were flooded with citizens of not only Waco, but the surrounding towns and counties as well; everyone wanted to see the show up close, and a natural inclination to migrate toward the town center captivated all in attendance, everyone wishing desperately to be in the picture that the town photographer, Charles Landry, was planning on taking. He'd announced his intention of turning the picture into a collectible postcard at the town meeting a week prior. Everyone thought it was a grand idea, and the news spread among the good people of Waco, as news does in all small towns, gaining weight, notoriety, and a few embellishments along the way.

Mundane happenings in the burgeoning town were the norm, with intermittent spurts of excitement, few and far between; something of this magnitude only happened once every ten years. Therefore, anyone fortunate enough to be photographed on the postcard would become local celebrities if only for a short time. For many, it would be the defining moment of their lives, their most cherished memory, the one thing they'd want to be remembered for, tales passed down the family tree, an inheritance of repute.

"There you are," said Deputy Sheriff Klaus, who was tall and skinny, and his fair skin didn't fare so well in the blazing Texas sun. No matter the weather, Klaus always had on long-sleeve shirts and pants, with boots and a hat. His long skinny arms perfectly matched his long, skinny legs. Every time Mrs. Tabatha saw him, she always thought the same thing: *That poor man needs to find him a proper woman who'll feed him the way a man should be fed.*

He was too skinny for her liking, too scrawny, and if ever he needed to back up her husband, his presence would inspire fear in nobody. She had a few single women in mind she was resolute to introduce him to, starting with her sister, who was newly widowed. Her husband had died the previous spring in a legal duel with his business partner who accused him of stealing money from the cattle company they co-owned. He was shot at noon on a hot, windy Saturday in the middle of town square. Murdered, is the term Tabatha's sister preferred. But it was a fair duel, everything was above board, so her brother-in-law, the deputy sheriff at the time, didn't have cause to arrest the man.

"What'll you have me do?" he'd ask whenever she came crying to her sister and him. "Arrest the man for a legal duel? I'm sorry, hon, but he was within his rights."

"We were gettin' worried, Sheriff," Klaus said, pivoting and walking side by side with Sheriff Tyson down the dirt road, looking more like a pale, walking scarecrow than a man.

Mrs. Tabatha shook her head in disappointment.

"Don't be so melodramatic, Klaus," Sheriff Tyson said, though he detested having to justify his tardiness, as he himself, as a rule, detested tardiness; he believed tardiness was an indication of character, or the lack thereof.

But he knew his wife was listening and before they left the house, she'd pestered, "Now don't you take no back guff from nobody. You're the sheriff n'they can wait however damn long you want 'em to wait, ya hear."

A swarm of rambunctious kids came running out of Ace's Wild—the most popular saloon in town and "the best poker tables this side of the Mississippi." Or so said the saloon owner. The kids crashed through the batwing doors, hands raised, chasing each other with fake guns.

"Bang, bang, bang," Billy said. "I got you."

"Naha, I got you first," whined the cobbler's daughter.

The sheriff's two kids ran to join in the reindeer games, running, aiming their pointing fingers, pulling back their hammer thumbs. "Bang. Bang. *Bang*—"

It was hot, dry. There was a slight wind riding the air, carrying on it the lifeblood of the crowd, the jovial spirit seemingly infused in the sun's rays, infecting all with a giddy-like anticipation.

There were red, white, and blue banners and streamers and balloons and the smell of barbecued meat wafting, whetting everyone's appetites. Sheriff Tyson had to walk slowly because there was so many people in the streets. He weaved his way through the crowd. Every so often someone would stop him and shake his hand. "Great turn out," said one person. "We must do this more often," said another. "Indeed," Sheriff Tyson said. "*Indeed.*"

He hated mingling, but it was part of the job. These were all voters. And if he wanted reelection, he had to play the game.

Mayor Redding was sitting on the porch of the barber shop, his head tilted to the sky, his neck full of shaving cream, as Old man Sammons went about his employ meticulously.

Sheriff Tyson greeted a few more people, shaking their hands before clambering up the steps of the old barber shop. His boots hit the patio deck like a sack of rocks, shaking the porch something fierce. Old man Sammons put his chin to his chest and looked at Sheriff Tyson over his glasses. Had it been anyone else, he would've delivered a lashing, but, since it was the sheriff, he simply just pulled his lips back and shook his head.

"Sorry, Sammy," offered Sheriff Tyson, "ya want me to get these here boards looked at?"

"My bo-*rds* are jus' fine, *Sheriff*," Sammons said, stroking the razor on the mayor's neck. "It just ain't used ta peoples walkin' like they a *dyno*-so-*ris* or whatever they callin' 'em bones they keep findin' over yonder."

Sammons' uncle slammed down his cane and grunted from the corner. He was sixty years old, by all accounts an old man. He spent his days sitting on the porch of his nephew's barber shop, talking with the customers. "I keep tryna tell ya, them r'dragon *bo*-nes," he said, leaning on his cane, his long white hair waving as he moved his head and mouth. "Ain't no such thing as a *dyno*-so-*ris.*"

"I don't walk like I'm—" Sheriff Tyson was about to defend himself when Mayor Riley intervened.

"You are most assuredly heavy-footed, there, Sheriff," Mayor Riley said. "Nothing to be embarrassed about, son. We could all use to lose a few pounds. Now, ya tardiness is another matter entire-ly."

Sherriff Tyson winced and shifted. "I'm sorry, sir," he said. "My wife—"

"The fine folk of Waco, Texas have come out in record numbers to show their support," said Mayor Riley. Like a seasoned pro, Old man Sammons withdrew as Mayor Riley talked, then went back in during the silence between words. "Least we can do is be on time," Mayor Riley insisted.

"Yes sir," Sheriff Tyson said, nodding.

Sammons finished the last streak of shaving cream. He placed a hot towel around the mayor's face then applied some blue aftershave on his neck and cheeks, the air smelling of talc powder and antiseptic.

The mayor paid the man a quarter, and said, "Keep the change, Sammy."

Old man Sammons gaped upon the quarter as if it were buried treasure. The sign on the porch informed patrons that haircuts were only two cents. The quarter was a week's worth of labor. At least.

He nodded and thanked the mayor profusely. "Thank ya, sir," he said bowing like a Japanese pupil. "Thank ya. Thank ya, so much."

Mayor Riley walked to the edge of the porch and shook Sheriff Tyson's hand. Together they stood tall, proud leaders of Waco, Texas, looking upon their constituents with warm affection.

There was an electric feeling riding the air, pulsating, contagious. Everyone was laughing and enjoying themselves, not a sullen face in the crowd.

The kids scurried about, playing hopscotch in the sand, jacks on the boarded sidewalk, or they ran about playing tag and cops and robbers.

Deep in the background, the sound of the town band, playing upbeat music, low but perceptible.

Everyone in the town came together on such short notice and chipped in for the decorations. The red, white, and blue ribbons and banners were provided by the fine, hardworking men in the oil fields.

The town's butcher, Reggie Frier, was able to catch a wild boar that was five feet high and weighed in at a whopping four hundred pounds—enough meat to feed everyone in attendance their fill, plus seconds.

The Browns, who owned the deli and bakery at the end of Elm Street, already had a banner made a few years prior for when their son returned from the front line, but he never made it back. He died "a hero's death," they were told in a letter signed by their son's commanding officer, General Robert E. Lee. The banner had been sitting in their cellar for the past two years, collecting dust, as they were unable to discard it, sentimental values and such. Made of thick, white canvas, the banner was five feet wide and seventy-five feet long. And for two years it remained a blank canvas, awaiting to be used. A week prior, when the mayor and sheriff announced the joyous occasion, the Browns had volunteered the banner.

It currently hung over the good people of Waco, tied to a steel bar that hung from the roof of the bank, running across the street to *Colligan's Place*—a hodge-podge shop that consisted of the town doctor, dentist, and veterinarian, Dr. Jon Colligan.

The embroidery shop on Vine Street welcomed the banner, happy to do their part, and they stitched onto the thick canvas, *Nigger Lynching Barbecue Fourth of July Party.* The subtext informed the patrons that it was "*A potluck with fun and games for the kids. Bring one, bring all.*"

Sheriff Tyson and Mayor Riley descended the steps and made their way across town square to the gallows.

Charles Landry, the photographer, was speaking with Jasper Felix, the county hangman. When Jasper saw the sheriff and mayor walking up, he pulled out his pocket watch and shook his head.

"I know, *I know,*" said Sheriff Tyson. "Apologies on behalf of my kinfolk." He pulled his lips back then. "Tabatha is a dear soul, bless her heart, but she comes from money and hasn't the slightest inclination of the concept of *punctuality.*"

He shook Jasper's hand then stepped forward and gripped Charles's hand firmly. His attention was on the bulky contraption he'd only heard of but had yet to see in person.

"So, this is it, huh," Sheriff Tyson said, appraising the apparatus that looked like a big accordion with a lens at the end. It laid on a tripod with a black hood behind it.

"That's right," Charles said with a smirk. "Top of the line, she is." He patted it as if it were a cherished pet. "Only takes *five minutes* to take."

"*Five minutes?*" Mayor Riley was rather impressed. The few photos he'd taken all took more than fifteen minutes. "That's it, eh," he said.

"*That's it,*" Charles said, his face contorted in a way that Sheriff got the impression that Charles thought Mayor Riley was calling him a liar.

Jasper interrupted the small talk. "'Scuse me, gentlemen," he said, holding the pocket watch out for all to see. "I ain't neva been late to hang nota-*no*-body, and though I reckin we olready is late, howsabout we get started, fellas? How's that sound?"

Everyone agreed, nodding their heads.

They all made their way up the gallows where a poor Black man stood. His hands were tied down at his sides by a four-inch-thick leather strap. The man was naked, and there were fresh lashes on his back, torso, and legs. He was weak, dehydrated, sweating profusely. His eyes were bugging out of his head, and he was whispering something or another under his breath. Despite his predicament, he stood tall, proud.

Mayor Riley raised his arms and pumped them.

A wave of rolling shushes from the audience.

"They 'bout to start," said an eager kid in the front row.

"'Bout time," said the kid's mother.

Silence.

"Jeremiah Sanders, you stand *accused* of winkin' at a po-or White woman," said Sheriff Tyson. "And are hereby sentenced to death."

The crowd was drunk on violence. Everyone screamed obscenities—

"Die, nigger," said the Baptist pastor who stood tall in the middle of the crowd.

"Yeah, die, nigger." This from the sheriff's eldest son, Colt.

Sherriff Tyson pumped his arms, quieting the mob. "D'ya got any last words, nigger?"

The Black man straightened his back. He shook his head, still whispering, praying.

Sherriff Tyson nodded at Jasper, who pulled the Black man forward, setting his feet on the trapdoor. The rope was of the best hemp quality, silky, strong. Jasper had inspected it earlier, after he'd greased the bolt and hinges on the cellar-flap door of the scaffold. Jasper pulled from his black bag a black leather strap, much like the one that tied the man's hands to his side, and bounded the man's ankles together. Then he cinched the rope around the man's neck.

"*A long drop?*" screamed Baxter Getz, the town jailer and the husband of the woman who received the unsolicited wink by the accused. He raised his hands over his head and threw them down to his sides. "That nigger don't deserve no long drop," he said.

A sea of heads all nodded at the same time as if the murmurs were hopping from head-to-head. "Yeah," said some. "Short drop the nigger," said others. "Short drop."

A long drop was a hangman technique which ensured the person being hanged broke their neck and died of asphyxia while unconscious rather than the slow process of strangulation. It was a mercy that most hangmen favored. But it was a mercy that Baxter Getz declared the man didn't deserve.

Jasper looked at Sheriff Tyson, who shrugged and said, "Your rope, your call."

Jasper looked at the faces in the crowd; everyone seemed to be possessed with the spirit of the occasion, screaming, shaking their hands over their heads, screaming for a "short drop" "short drop" "SHORT DROP." Everyone but Beatrice Getz, the woman who had accused the Black man of winking at her. There was something playing in her face that seemed odd, out of place. Her eyes were glued to the ground, and she was trying desperately to hide the fact that she was crying.

Baxter turned his head and looked at her and what Jasper saw on the husband's face wasn't protection, it was shame—pure as the driven snow. He looked at his wife with disgust, and disdain, and revulsion—the way you look at an alley dog that was covered in scabs and fleas. That's how he was looking at his wife. And Jasper had a sneaking suspicion that *not only did the nigger wink at Mrs. Beatrice, but he probably bedded her, too.* And the thought of it, the unconscionable thought of *this* man sleeping with a white woman, swept over him. A wave of indignation possessed him. He grew angry, bitter.

And he adjusted his rope to the short drop method.

The crowd went wild save for Beatrice Getz, who put her head down and tried walking away from the spectacle, but her husband grabbed her by the arm and yanked her back. He grabbed her chin and lifted it up, then whispered something in her ear, and Jasper reckoned it was something like, "No. No, you ain't goin' nowheres. I want you to see what happens to niggers that fuck my dirty whore wife."

Jasper adjusted the rope to accommodate a short drop, then wrapped it around the man's neck. Being so close to the cuckold infuriated him, and he spat in the man's face.

Everyone screamed their approval.

The Black man didn't flinch. There was nothing they could do to him that would relinquish his dignity—the one thing he had left in this cold, hard world. They couldn't take that, though they could try. But it would be a vain attempt.

Jasper bent over and grabbed a white-hooded cap from his black bag. He placed it on the man's head and stepped aside.

Sheriff Tyson pulled out his pocket watch. The second hand was on the ten. He waited until it was on the eleven then threw five fingers up, four, three, two—

Jasper pulled the lever and the man fell six feet, dangling, coughing, choking; he thrashed his bound legs like a swimming mermaid.

Everyone was screaming and cheering.

Jasper looked at Beatrice, who was still crying.

The naked, hooded man, full of lashes and cuts, refused to give them a short death. He wiggled around, gasping for time, acutely aware that that's what they wanted—to prolong his death. With sheer will, he rolled around the guts of the gallows, thinking about his mother and father, about his brothers and sisters, nieces and nephews; about the unfairness of a world that said he was less than, about the law that forbade him to fall in love with a white woman, and she, him.

He could see kids eating watermelon, and the smoke drifting in the air from the grill. The faces, the decorations, the banner, the joyous occasion.

He thrashed about for *thirty-nine minutes* before dying.

"Closer," Charles said, bringing his hands to his chest as if he were manipulating a ball of *chi*. "*Closer.*" Hundreds of people squeezed in around the gallows, kids hanging from the wooden planks, smiling.

"Tha's it," Charles said. "Now no one move."

He hit the button and the short process of developing the photo commenced.

There was big money to be had from the hanging of a Black man in the south. Charles would profit from the picture that he was currently taking, turning it into a collectible postcard, coveted, rare, expensive.

The hangman Jasper would cut the rope he used to end the poor Black man's life into two-inch knots, cauterizing the ends so that it was like a rope-ball. The first one he'd give to Baxter Getz, as a talisman, and the other two hundred, he'd sell as good luck tokens at the market at the end of the month.

A bright flash exploded from the contraption, then a swath of smoke flew in the air.

Everyone couldn't wait to get a copy of the postcard, particularly the people closest to the hanging corpse—it was a sign of prestige the closer you were to the hanging corpse.

Everyone but Beatrice Getz looked as though they were taking a picture with their favorite hero.

Betty Hill started from the nightmare, gasping, crying. She could hardly understand why she would dream such a reprehensible event. It was untenable. She rolled over and snuggled up to her husband, an African American. She wanted to shake him awake and hug him and kiss him and apologize profusely for the sinful dream, for the potential of evil that lurked inside her; her and everyone else. But then she would be forced to explain in detail the depravity of her subconscious mind.

That simply will not do, she thought, thinking she sounded like Tabatha, the sheriff's wife. She cried silently, hugging her dearly beloved husband, the man of her dreams; hugging him, holding him, willing forgiveness for a crime she didn't commit.

The Five Hives

REENACTMENT
April 1, 2050
Little Rock, Minnesota

THREE STATE CHAMPIONSHIP BANNERS from the legendary women's volleyball team dynasty of the late 80s strung along the north side of the gym, accompanied by just as many conference championships from the same era. The only other banner—and the crown jewel of the town for the past twenty years—was the 1A Minnesota state football championship banner.

The local pizzeria delivered thirty large pies to feed the one-hundred-sixty-two students, who were being treated as if they were the business end of a hostage situation. Tensions were high, patience depleted. Like every other student body in every other school, the students were escorted into the quaint, small-town gym several hours prior without notice. They grew cagey, irritated; squirming in their seats as if the bleachers were a massive, twenty-tiered anthill that'd suddenly been stepped on, the tiny ferocious critters fanning out, accosting their bottoms in a synchronized attack, making every kid squirm in what seemed, from the teacher's perspective, like a choreographed dance— *the ant shuffle.*

The mood changed in stages. Going from morbid curiosity to annoyance after the first hour, palpable to the seasoned teachers who had a sixth sense about such things.

Now, after three more hours—the annoyance presently teetering on the edge of anger, mutiny—even the teachers grew cagey and irritated.

"Probably just *another* shooting," Billy said with heartbreaking casualness. He scanned his hive, the ones wearing cowboy hats, counting in threes: *twelve, fifteen*—including him, there were sixteen members of the hive known as Country Folk.

"Bet it was the Emos *again*. *Whatever it* is." Billy stretched his neck, craning over his hive, glaring at the Emo swarm with suspicious eyes. "You can never trust those dudes," he added.

"Naw, bruh," Scott said, "if there was an active shooter, they wouldn't just cram us altogether."

Stacy nodded thoughtfully then said, "Fish in a barrel."

"*Exactly,*" Scott agreed.

"Maybe a bomb threat, then?" Billy said this more to himself than to anyone else, his attention trapped on the middle of the court where the school's mascot—a smiling tiger in the likeness of Tony the Tiger—shimmered and shone in a series of pulsating red and green lights that bounced off the meticulously waxed floor, hypnotizing him as he went down the list, vetting the many morbid possibilities. He shook his head, perplexed, then shared a glance with his hive leader, Scott, who shrugged and said, "Maybe." Like any good leader, Scott ensured his people were always in the right place, at the right time, and wearing the right clothes.

"Everyone needs to be on point this week." That's what he told his hive at the weekly video conference that past Sunday night. His position as hive leader—like the leaders of the four other hives—afforded him a position that was typically in the know. He didn't like being left out of the loop.

It must be something serious, he thought.

"Whatever the reason, they didn't want us to have access to our phones," Stacy said with a notable degree of resentment in her voice. She dug in the kangaroo pocket of her OshKosh overalls and fumbled with her phone like a person tonguing the hole where a tooth used to reside, an absent-minded gesture she had no recollection doing.

At the mention of phones, the brothers and sisters within her orbit all looked at theirs compulsively, the compulsion giving way to obsession, activating synapses which create symptoms that mimic the effects of minor alcohol and drug withdrawal. Though, as any of the teenagers would attest, there was *nothing* minor about it.

"It's cruel," any one of them would argue, "this mad world that mandates kids to have phones, but then strips them of the one thing that give the phones any utility." The phones were all functional but none of them had any service at the moment. At the behest of the new government, every home, business, and school in America was outfitted with a signal jammer which came lock, stock, and barrel with modern routers. The signal jammer, dubbed "Project Blackout," was the byproduct of a government thinktank. The official goal of the committee was to replicate the blanket of censorship and secrecy draped across China and Russia. The unofficial goal was control, coercion, manipulation—but the best and brightest among them never considered it would spawn something so simplistically tragic and potentially dangerous.

The hive known—registered and legally binding—as the Hipsters looked up at the signal blocker, eternally festive, flashing in red and green lights. It was fifteen feet long and ten feet wide, rounder at the top and beveling at the bottom like a massive beehive, dangling over the Tony the Tiger emblem.

Bouncing off the gym walls, there was a constant low-grade electric hum that complemented the beehive contention.

The school bell wailed, signifying the time: 3:00. The students looked at each other, hesitant, hopeful. The leaders of the five hives all stood. They looked at each other, nodding in solidarity, getting on the same page, then they made to get off the bleachers. What followed was a great big perturbance as the rest of the students roused from their seats and followed their leaders, gathering their belongings in a simultaneous action, as if by some unseen force they were connected, one entity, a hive mind, each individual, a microcosm of the macrocosm; to Mrs. Robinson, the school principal, their in-sync movements reminded her of a massive flock of birds twisting and turning in synchronicity, beautiful, majestic, and—*what if the leader kamikazes head first into a tree and breaks its neck? Would the rest then not follow?*—dangerous.

Mrs. Robinson cleared her throat and spoke into the microphone: "I apologize for the delay," she said uneasily; everyone stopped moving and gawked at her. "I'm sorry, but no one can leave just yet."

"But we've got basketball practice." This from a Brain hive member at the front of the bleachers.

"Yeah," said John, a member of the Hip-Hoppers hive. "We've got mathlete team semi-finals coming up."

As if the decision had been unanimously made to veto Mrs. Robinson's position, everyone started moving again.

Mrs. Robinson pumped her arms and spoke more curtly. "All after-school activities have been canceled for the next week along with school," she said. "The buses are on standby." There was a tangible weight to the silence that followed, heavy and lengthy and worrisome. "Don-chu worry, now," she said, "we'll get you all out of here just as soon as all the parents of a hive arrive. Should be any minute now don-chu-know."

When she sat down, she realized she had given the kids too much information. She shouldn't have said anything about waiting for parents.

Now they know it's something bad, she thought.

"Who do you think did what?" This from the Whitney Henderson—female president of the Emo Hive. "Bet those damn Hip-Hoppers tried having another rap battle that ended in bloodshed." She itched the back of her left knee, which had become raw over the last few hours. She was allergic to something in the fishnet stockings she was made to wear, and the knee-high boots were a little too tight, digging the stockings in, causing an irritation.

"We should thank them," said Chris Bailey—the male president of the Emo hive. "'Specially if it gets us the rest of the week off." While the rest of the girls and boys in their hive had blue hair, Whitney and Chris had red hair, a sign of status they shared with every other Emo hive president in every other school across the country. But every hive president had something to set them apart from the hive. They followed blindly what their hive leaders, Madeline Yamar and Cody Baier, instructed.

Whitney laughed and raised an open hand. Chris smacked it.

At the opposite end of the bleachers sat the hive known as the Hip-Hoppers. Billy Stenton was their male president. "I'm going to pretend to use the bathroom and check the news feeds," Billy said. *And see what they don't want us to know,* he thought.

He got up and made his way through his hive. His clunky Timberland boots were too big, a hand-me-down from his older brother. He jumped from the third row over a wall of preppy-dressed kids, landing awkwardly, stumbling. He pulled up his pants, composed himself, and took a few steps to one of the three tables that sat directly in front of the bleachers. "I really gotta use the restroom, Mr. Johnson," Billy said as he squirmed with his hands over his groin.

Mr. Johnson finished chewing his pizza. He wiped his mouth and glared intensely at Billy. "Notta problem, William," he said. "Jus' lemme get your phone and I'll send ya on your merry way." Billy stopped squirming and stood straight. He no longer projected a kid about to lose control of his bladder, but a liar that'd just gotten a bucket of ice water poured down the front of his pants. "But … but … I *really* gotta pee," he stammered.

Mr. Johnson put his hand out then opened and closed it and not without a great deal of satisfaction, Billy noted. Mr. Johnson had the reputation of being a sadist among the students. There were always open spots in his classes and the students present were usually underclassmen. The savvy upperclassmen knew that he was a miserable prick who hated his life and the only thing that got his rocks off was picking on kids that shared a certain demographic, kids who would've been considered nerds back in his day.

Now, whether or not this was true didn't matter for Billy Stenton. Not at that moment. All that mattered to him was that he failed to think ahead. And without an appropriate recourse, Billy had no option but to give Johnson his phone, which he did, reluctantly, with hurt, puppy-dog eyes.

Damn crackheads can't go two minutes without their devices, thought Mr. Johnson.

The hives congregated in clusters, covering a patch of the bleachers that went up and down as well as left and right.

To the right were the Hip-Hoppers; the last consensus showed thirty-two students were members, the third highest demographic at the school, a high number for such a rural area. They filled a space five wide and six down.

The left consisted of the two smallest hives, the Emos (twenty deep) and the Country Folk (sixteen) with the Emos at the top left.

The Hipsters' hive was easily the biggest. They sat in the middle of the bleachers. At fifty-eight students, they sat eight long and seven wide with a few stragglers on either side.

The last hive—the Brains—were always different. They sat horizontally and were the only ones in the front two rows—forty of the best and brightest students at the school. Like the rest of the hives, they'd gotten their dressing assignments for the week on Sunday night. It was Wednesday. Per the dressing assignment, the boys wore khaki slacks with a white long-sleeve polo and polished Doc Martens. The girls wore a smart pinstriped blazer pantsuit, snug as to accentuate the firmness that comes with a young body, but classy as to instill in them, if only subconsciously, their status as a rising star.

"Future makers and shakers of the world always sit up front and center." That's what the Brains' hive leaders, Jerred Triston and Cindy Bello, said this week in their weekly vlog after disseminating the dressing schedule for the week.

Like soldiers in an elite army, the hive members always obeyed without question, never veering off course, never adding their own personal flair.

Never.

Pete, who was usually too smart for his own good, was sitting in the third-row center and noticed how the interaction between Billy and Mr. Johnson transpired. He concocted a plan.

"Gimme your phone," he said to his best friend, Sean, who scoffed and shrugged him off. "No way, dude." Sean's eyes grew big as a particularly juicy sequence of candies and chocolates lined up perfectly. He swiped left and right, up and down, licking his lips as a cascading mountain of fresh chocolates and hard candy replaced the section he'd just matched. "I'm almost to level *seven hundred fifty thousand*," he added with stars in his eyes.

Pete should've known better. A teenage boy would just as soon dip his testicles in a lagoon full of famished piranhas then surrender his phone willingly. He punched Sean on the arm and said, "You wanna know what's going on r'not?"

"'Course I do," Sean said, rubbing his arm.

"Well, then, gimme your phone, and I'll put mine in my pocket," Pete said. "Then when Johnson asks for my phone, I'll give him yours." There was a mischievous twinkle of pride emanating from Pete's eyes as he cocked his black trucker hat to the left. Everyone else in his hive, save for the female president, Sara Foxx, wore white hats. "I'll check out the feeds and see what they don't want us to know."

Sean's eyes lit up. "That's why you're our president, my dude," he said.

After the rigged presidential elections of 2028, there was a coup committed by the United States government against all social media platforms. They made away with the likes of TikTok, Facebook, Twitter, Snapchat—banned them outright, declaring them a threat to national security and an enemy of democracy itself. Then they planted their own social media platform. After the government-sanctioned social media took over, every school in America held elections where representatives of the five national hives were voted in as elected presidents to their respective hive. You could distinguish them from the crowd by the letterman jackets they wore, or, in cases such as the Emos, by their hair, or Pete's hat.

In many ways, the new system was preferable to the olden days when popularity was based solely on looks or athletic abilities and some kids were overly endowed with both, while the vast majority were perfectly basic. But none of that mattered in the new system. When everyone was a part of a hive, no one was ostracized; everyone was part of a family. Terms like ugly, nerdy, or gawky no longer held validity and the ugliest, nerdiest, and gawkiest were often the leaders of a hive, and therefore, the coolest kids in school.

Sean looked around, spying for onlookers. He slid his phone into

Pete's hand. Pete put his phone in his pocket, jumped over the first two rows with the dummy phone already extended. In the old system, Pete would've been considered a nerd, a leper, an outcast. He was a good kid, smart, polite, but unremarkable in terms of good looks, athletic abilities, presence, or anything else that used to matter.

Mr. Johnson looked up from his pizza and saw Pete's skinny, awkward gait. He used to torture kids like this. How he missed the good old days, when letterman jackets were reserved for athletes and the only leadership role a kid like Pete could aspire to was on the chess team or the debate team. What he wouldn't give to stick Pete's head in the toilet and flush it. *Just one time.* He relished the thought.

"Yo, Mr. J," Pete said, shimmying this way and that, "can I use the bathroom?" Green and red lights bounced off the black mirror screen and cut into Johnson's eyes. Johnson took another bite of his pizza and chewed slowly, deliberately. He disliked Pete on a deep and visceral level. It wasn't hate—but damn near close to it. He knew he shouldn't base his feelings on outdated concepts such as looks, but something in him deeply despised the young man before him. In his opinion, kids like Pete were permitted entry into an echelon of society they had no business being in. He often used the example of wasps allowing hobos into their country club. He felt like the world had been reversed, turned upside down, like he had awoken in a Twilight Zone episode that had lasted these last twenty years.

"My name is—" he said slowly, wiping his mouth, "—Mr. Johnson."

"I'm sorry," Pete offered. "May I please go to the bathroom, *sir?*"

Pete heard footsteps coming from behind him. He pivoted. Mr. Johnson threw up his right arm with his pointing finger extended as if to say one minute, then he grabbed a phone that sat on the table and handed it to Billy.

"Give me your phone and you're welcome to use the restroom." Mr. Johnson smirked and savored the prospect of breaking Pete's heart, but Pete tossed his phone and speedwalked out of sight, the awkwardness of his walk digging into Johnson's rigid susceptibilities, the way he walked without swinging his arms, the way he held his head high with the confidence of a boy who should be completely lacking.

What in the fuck has the world come to? Mr. Johnson thought. He was the school's PE teacher. He had also played quarterback on the 2030 Minnesota state Class A football championship team. He remembered a time when cool kids were cool and nerdy kids were nerdy—the natural balance in a delicate ecosystem that'd segregated high schools for decades, putting kids in their appointed places, casting indelible shadows on their probable futures, building confidences, shaping egos, solidifying futures. But somewhere around the time he was graduating high school, the world around him had begun to change at the base fundamental level, and he was incapable of changing with it. He lied to himself often with the running narrative of: "It's not personal. I don't like Pete for the same reason a lion doesn't rub elbows with antelope. It's unnatural." But he knew that was rubbish. He came from a long line of athletes; two uncles played college football and one even made it to the NFL. He disliked Pete for the same reason the Nazis hated the Jews, and with the same fervor—it was taught to him.

He scanned the sea of teenagers squirming in the bleachers and although there were nearly two hundred students crammed into the small gym, he could make out only five distinct styles, five distinct copies, five distinct hives.

He turned to Mrs. Glennon, the resident mental health and crisis counselor, and said, "What do high school students and birds have in common?" Mrs. Glennon, though usually chipper and amicable, was currently void of anything even remotely resembling a sense of humor. The nation was in mourning and the looming disaster was still on the wrong side of the hill, climbing, climbing, climbing to a dizzying precipice before a long, steep drop. The proverbial nuclear missile was still in the air and the hard part was still ahead of them.

"I don't know," Mrs. Glennon said, shrugging absently, trying to be polite. "What do high school students and birds have in common?" She was suddenly aware that she didn't want to know the punchline, because knowing Johnson, the answer would be in bad taste at best and morbidly inappropriate at worst.

Johnson nodded at the bleachers, a mischievous grin tugging at the corners of his mouth, reaching his eyes, ironing out the wrinkles that usually settled there making him look twenty years younger. "Birds of a feather flock together," he said, nodding, the smirk transforming into a Cheshire cat grin, ear to ear, teeth stained by tobacco smoke and coffee, wrinkles completely gone, hints of his good-looking, alpha male genes protruding from twenty years of living in a world that had broken his heart and lied to him with the constant reminder, *You peaked in high school.*

"You just watch and see," he added.

God, I hope not, Mrs. Glennon thought. Her hands shaking, she glanced at her note cards which were filled with inadequate notes to handle the nation's present crisis. Chase Young, lead administrator for FEMA, assembled the best crisis management team he could several hours prior when the disaster went public. He was the one who made the call for every school to initiate the blackout order, then, with what the news called the A-team (and later the L-team), they came up with the itinerary and guidelines that Mrs. Glennon currently fumbled nervously with. In her professional opinion, though, notes were not enough. When there was a nuclear missile already in the air, heading toward every home in America, notes just didn't seem the answer.

Like most mental health and crisis counselors, she lobbied to quarantine all students in the gym, which could double as a bunker for the night, or even the next couple of nights. But Chase Young didn't want to make a bad situation worse by overreacting.

A ringing cellphone disturbed the monotony like a boulder tossed into a still lake. Everyone fell silent. The kids all looked like dogs hearing a distant whistle, everyone stretching their necks to see whose phone it was. *Who had service? Would they be allowed to use it? Could they share? Could they check their feeds? Their likes? Comments? Tags? Who is it? For the love of God, who has service?*

Mrs. Robinson stood and answered her phone. It was bulky and had a long antenna protruding out of it—a blackout phone, the only capable means of communication within the beehives' range. The silence rang with acute awareness, everyone holding their breath, straining their necks, listening.

"Uhuh. Uhuh," she said, her turkey gobbler neck jiggling as she nodded. "Okay. Okay. Thank you." She hung up the phone, pulled her lips in a strange way, and glanced nervously at Mrs. Glennon, giving her a thumbs-up that looked odd and misplaced given the morose look on her face. Mrs. Glennon returned the thumbs up. But panic set in as she realized that she *wasn't* ready. She wasn't ready because she suspected that Mr. Johnson was right—he was despicable and completely inappropriate—but he was right: birds of a feather do flock together. She was terrified of what that meant for her students, for the country, for the world.

A team of police officers filed into the gym from the outer entrance with a swarm of concerned parents on their heels. They walked single file and staggered in ranks behind the microphone so that the parents were standing, facing the student body. There were eighty-five parents altogether. Of the eighty-five, fifty of them were single parents. The Hipsters hive at Donald J. Trump High made for the highest percentage of any hive. These were their parents.

"Sorry to keep you all waiting for so long," Mrs. Robinson said into the microphone. "Unfortunately, it was necessary." She cleared her throat, took a sip from the glass of water perched at the end of the podium. "I'm sure most of you know Mrs. Glennon"—she waved Mrs. Glennon over, the flaps under her arms jiggling in concert with her neck— "but if not, she is the school's mental health and crisis counselor. Please give her your undivided attention."

As Mrs. Glennon walked to the microphone, she felt naked, exposed, and worst of all, egregiously unprepared. It wasn't a big school. Most would even call it small. The graduating class was sitting at a meager fifty-three students—fifty-four if Casey Yates could close out the semester strong and string together two good quarters with at least a 3.75 GPA.

She observed the anxious faces staring back at her. Not for the first time, she was grateful that she didn't accept the job offer at Joe R. Biden High in Minneapolis, which had more than 1,500 students.

They're so young, she thought. *So young and impressionable—*

—Birds of a feather flock together.

She cleared her throat and spoke with a telling crack that shook her voice, inspiring confidence in no one. "My job is quite unique in that I both love and hate it in equal measures," she said. "I *love* helping people. But I *hate* that for me even to have a job, something so terrible must happen, something so unthinkable ..." Her voice tapered off as her mind followed the flow of thoughts, a catastrophizing wave that terrified her to her core. She glanced at the note cards and tapped them on the podium before pocketing them, deciding that no amount of preparation would be adequate, that this was a disaster that could potentially kill one thousand kids. At least those were the numbers that FEMA initially kicked out—the projected dead by the end of the week. But by the end of the year, that number would reach ten thousand—*ten thousand,* within a year.

"Which would be a win," said Dr. Gliotone, lead consulting psychiatrist working with FEMA. At the globally televised event, he explained the projections on a bar graph. Using a laser pointer, he swooped the far-left side, circling the highly coveted but equally doubtful number: 1,000. And on the opposite end of the board—the board that they picked to show the world the dreadful projections—one of those playful vanity boards that had Britney's bright smile staring back, in one of the greatest blunders in historical memory—the bar graph showed 10,000 in a year, 25,000 in 3 years, 50,000 in 5 years. The numbers went up exponentially every year.

"The over under is 10,000," Dr. Gliotone had said with a hopeful grimace, as if he had a gun to his head, forced to decide which testicle he favored more to keep. Then, with a look of utter finality, and regret, he dubbed it, aptly, "The slow drip suicide."

"There really is no easy way to say this ..." Mrs. Glennon paused and looked at Mr. Johnson, who smirked and put his thumbs together, flapping them as if he were making shadow puppets of a flying bird.

Mrs. Glennon scoffed in disgust then turned back to the kids. Looking into their faces, she struggled to say the words.

"Britney Sammons took her own life last night," she finally blurted out.

Gasps from the front two rows.

Murmurs from the bleachers on the left.

Giggles from the bleachers on the right.

Cries of agony from the middle.

"You fuckin' *liar*," Sean screamed from the third row. The students all checked their phones in a hurried frenzy, an action they knew was utterly worthless. Sara Foxx shook her phone then threw it at the podium. Mrs. Glennon dodged the projectile and a team of cops mobilized to restrain Sara.

Mrs. Glennon turned to face the approaching cops. She took a step forward, pumping her hands. "Stand down," she said, eyes bulging with fear, panic. The look in her eyes is what stopped the cops; the gut-wrenching look of disappointment; the scolding look that said, "Don't you dare punish a suffering child." She stared at the cops and nodded with unmistakable determination. All the adults had talked about this: emotions would be high, tempers flailing, children's lives at stake. She'd already briefed everyone. Briefed them after she received her brief by FEMA. Briefed them while the kids sat in the blackout gym for four hours. Briefed them as the nation went to Defcon 1.

Britney Sammons was the female leader of the Hipsters. Her hive consisted of 35% of the school. Of the five hives, it was the biggest at a national level, sitting snug at 33%. Like every other high school mental health and crisis counselor in the nation, Mrs. Glennon made sure the adults understood the precarious circumstances that lay ahead in the next twenty-four hours (and beyond) for the highest demographic of children.

She pivoted to face the student body.

"I know this is hard to hear," she said. "And I can only imagine what is going through your minds: to think that the leader of a hive would do something like this …" She paused, pulling her lips back, shaking her head. "But it's true."

"Prove it." Sean rose from his seat, prompting the rest of his hive to follow.

"Yeah, prove it," said Nick Learn, rising from his seat. Being the leader of the Brains garnered him a following of forty students. They all stood.

The embers of dissent had been stoked. Every student stood. They yelled and flailed their arms, the anger inside looking for an outlet, an escape.

Mrs. Glennon pumped her hands and spoke into the microphone: "We are going to turn off the beehive in just a few minutes. But not until we can ensure everyone's safety. However you are feeling is perfectly normal, but if any of you are having thoughts of hurting yourselves ..."

"*Oh shit.*" Sean jumped over the first two rows of the Brain hive. He tripped, veered, then sprinted toward the doors. He made it to half-court before a team of cops tackled him.

"Get off me," he screamed and squirmed. "Get the heck off me."

A middle-aged couple weaved their way around the cops and knelt before Sean. The woman was crying, clutching her purse, white knuckles accentuated on her red hand.

"It's okay, Seany," she said.

"*You don't get it, Ma,*" Sean screamed. "*It's Pete.*"

"What about him?" This from Sean's father; a tall, stern-looking man with bushy eyebrows. He would not give up his battle with baldness and the long hairs from the back combed over the front. Usually, it wasn't so obvious. But the flashing red and green lights bounced off his skull.

"He's in the bathroom." Sean's voice was low. He stopped fighting. He closed his eyes and let out a noise that sounded like an alley cat quartet.

Hushed murmurs.

A concerned woman walked through the crowd, parting it with respect. It was Pete's mother. She was alone. Like more than half of the kids in the nation and at the school, Pete was the product of a broken home. His mother was his everything, and he was hers. "So what if he is in the bathroom?" She couldn't connect the dots. She couldn't fathom why that would elicit such a response from Sean, whom she adored and who had been staying at her house for years. He was the captain of the football team and an all-state wrestler, which garnered him a full-ride scholarship to Minnesota—he was to be a Gopher next fall. A good-looking kid with a squared jaw and beautiful blue eyes, Sean was like a second son to Mrs. Sanchez. She knew him well. And she could tell when he was hiding something.

Sean opened his mouth to say something but hesitated, a terrified look permeating his eyes.

"What is it, Sean?" Pete's mom said. "It's okay, son. You can tell us."

Sean's father took a step forward and made like he was going to kick his son.

"He's *got a phone*," Sean blurted out. His face contorted in a grotesque exhibition of pain, anguish, regret.

"*Bullshit*," Mr. Johnson said. "I've got his phone right here." He raised the phone over his head and pumped it victoriously as if it were the game ball from his championship win. He looked around for validation. Nobody cared.

Sean lay on his back, breathing deeply, staring at the blinking beehive. He lurched over and started to cry.

Pete's mother bent over and shook him. "What aren't you telling us?"

Sean looked up but couldn't maintain eye contact with Mrs. Sanchez. He lowered his eyes, then: "I gave him my phone."

The gymnasium fell silent as everyone digested the inference. But the silence was misleading, for everyone felt a panic looming on the horizon, substantial, inevitable.

The adults had already been made privy to the mortal consequences of anyone in Britney's hive receiving the news without proper grief counseling. It's why they trapped the kids in the gymnasium like unwanted refugees, with no news of the outside world. The students were just then realizing the same thing that the adults feared: how dangerous this situation was for any member of Britney's hive, but especially for a president.

The air charged with a heavy weight that was tangible, stifling, coursing through everyone, the prospect of death connecting them in their shared horror.

"Not my Petey," his mother said shakily. She turned clumsily, tripping over her feet, looking for the entrance to the inner school. She stumbled like a drunken fawn, veering to the right, throwing her arms out for balance, then, with pronounced effort, she stood straight and took off in a dead sprint toward the doors. But she was an obese woman and she looked like she was swimming in a pool of Jell-O. She was already out of breath by the time she reached the door, hunched over, coughing, breathing laboriously.

The cops shot past her, teachers on the cops' heels, and parents, too. With no one left to keep the kids in check, they followed the crowd, checking their social media feeds when they hit the hallway. There was a symphony of beeps and bells and chirps and whistles as their phones all connected at once.

"Oh my god," Alex said. "They weren't lying." He laughed nervously then read aloud: "Britney Sammons, Queen of the Hipsters, posted a suicide note on her feed this morning. The government tracked her phone to her friend's house. The friend said that she planned to swim out to sea and never come back, that she was inconsolable, battling anxiety, depression, and the crushing weight of expectation to be perfect, fueled by the recent smear campaign by the Hip-Hoppers' hive leader, Jake Taint, who said, 'She's just a goody two shoes, mama's girl. She'll never be as cool as she thinks.'"

Pete's mother was the last to reach the bathroom. She turned a corner, panting, gasping for air. There was a line of kids leading to the boys' restroom. She pushed through the crowd, an odd mix of hopeful caution tugging at her heart. She turned the corner, sweat dripping down her body. Everyone's faces sullen. No one looked her in the eye. She walked slowly, almost gliding. Later she wouldn't be able to recall this part. She saw Sean, curled into a ball in the corner, crying. She closed her eyes, held her breath, stepped forward. She knew what she was going to see even before she opened her eyes—she could see it, see it seared on the canvas of her inner world, her lifeless son. With sheer will, she forced herself to open her eyes and saw her son lying on the ground, his skin already ash gray, his face up, eyes unblinking, with several welts and gashes on his forehead.

Mr. Johnson ran away from the scene, laughing hysterically.

The coroner's report would later read rather poetically, "He hit his head on the porcelain lip no less than six times (nine is my estimation), then, just before he lost consciousness, he placed his head in the toilet and waited to join Britney."

The Road to Recovery: Twenty Years Later
A Documentary
Written/Produced/Directed
By Shane Best
University of Minnesota Film School Final Project
Excerpt Transcript

Derrick Johnson and Debby Glennon-Johnson
Former Teachers at Donald J. Trump High
Little Rock, Minnesota

DJ: I did *not* run away laughing. I might've
           giggled a little. Then Mrs. Robinson shot
           daggers at me and pointed toward the door,
           essentially kicking me out. But I definitely
           didn't run away laughing. And you guys
           couldn't find someone better looking to play
           me in the reenactment? Yawl made me look
           like an asshole.

Best: Could you please just answer the question?

DJ: Sure, kid. Eh, what was the question again?

Best: Were you surprised that Pete Sanchez killed
           himself?

DJ: No. I wasn't surprised. Not in the least
           bit. Do I feel bad the kid died by what
           essentially amounted to a self-imposed
           swirly? Sure. It was tragic. But back in
           the day when I won the 2030 Minnesota state
           championship—

DGJ: Here we go.

DJ: What? It's a valid argument. I'm not just

	bringing it up just to "bring it up," (air quotes) now. Anyways … *shit*. See. You made me lose my chain of thought. She always does that. Where was I, kid?
Best:	Back in the day …
DJ:	That's right—back in the day, that kid would've gotten a swirly every day. I think this was the universe's way of balancing out. Ya know? Resetting. Equilibrium. I realize that makes me sound insensitive, but it was unnatural for kids like that to be the leaders of anything besides a Dungeons and Dragons committee.
Best:	What about you, Mrs. Glennon-Johnson? You were there, too. What do you make of the whole thing? Did the reenactment meet your expectations?
DGJ:	Yes, it did. Yawl did a wonderful job. Just wonderful. Don-chu listen to Derrick, he's just a miserable old man, always has been. Dunno why I put up with him all these years.
DJ:	I do. And it has something to do with you and me and a bottle of KY gel and—
DGJ:	You hush it now. Don-chu listen to him, sweetheart. Not 'bout nothin'. You guys did a brilliant job don-chu-know.
Best:	Thank you. Now, you've been quoted several times in several press releases saying, "You knew something like this was going to happen."
DGJ:	Surely did.
Best:	Could you elaborate on that please.
DGJ:	Well, lemme tell you, sonny, you don't gotta be a prophet to see what's right in front of your eyes. But it was like the whole world was blind to it.
Best:	To what? What were they blind to?
DGJ:	Just how impressionable kids truly are. When I was a youngin there were kids sniffin' laundry detergent on them silly TikTok thingamajiggers—
DJ:	Challenges.
DGJ:	Tha's it. Those *dogone* challenges. They knew it was dangerous, the kids. But

they did it anyway. Just to fit in. Just
to be cool. It didn't matter how dumb or
unsafe the challenge was because it was
an inclusion thing, see? Kids'll do just
about anything to fit in. It just didn't
matter. So, when the government took over
and decided to give that platform even more
power, I just … well … *yeah* … I just knew
nothing good could come of it.

DJ: Birds of a feather flock together.

DGJ: You behave now, Derrick. Don't pay him any
          mind, sweetheart.

Best: At least one good thing came from it all.
          You guys got married.

DJ: N'lemme tell you, boyo, did she earn that
          hyphen.

                    SNL Writer/Comedian
                        Josh Dylan
                    Chicago, Illinois

Best: The skits where you parody the Britney
          board were instant classics. Every single
          one of them was sheer comic genius.

Dylan: Thank you. Thank you.

Best: You did four or five of them, right?

Dylan: Seven, actually. I was kind of forced into
          the last two or three by my agent, who has
          since been fired. I didn't want to do 'em
          'cuz I felt like the novelty was played
          out. Ya dig? That vein had been all tapped
          out and I was working on new material, but
          he kept pulling me back to the Britney bit,
          saying, "We should do it this way," and "We
          haven't done it that way." I half did it
          just to shut him up. But the first four were
          well enough received.

Best: Well enough received? I think that's a bit
          of an understatement, no? The first one was
          watched 1,000,000,000 times in the first
          week alone. To this day, it's the most
          watched video. Ever.

Dylan:	Yeah, it was kinda nuts, the feedback. It for sure put me on the map. It was like … what the cowbell did for Ferrell and the van down by the river did for Farley, that's what the Britney board skit did for me. I wouldn't be who I am today without it.
Best:	It skyrocketed you to fame and fortune.
Dylan:	One hundred percent.
Best:	Why do you think they were so popular?
Dylan:	I've given this *a lot* of thought. And I think it was a threefold process. For one, after the mandate ended, so did the firewall. The wall of secrecy and censorship fell, and people got their freedoms back overnight. But more importantly, without the hive mandate, kids weren't being told what to do. They could watch whatever they wanted.
Best:	What was the last leg of the tripod?
Dylan:	The third leg, my astute friend, is perhaps the most important one—and I can't stress this enough—that is, laughing is nature's medicine. It brings people together. Ya know? The whole thing was such an uncomfortably dark moment in history, dark comedy seemed appropriate.
Best:	Have you ever sent Dr. Gliotone a thank-you letter for his oversight?
Dylan:	No. No. But that's a *great* idea.
Best:	I'm sure you know the story behind how so many intellectuals-doctors, teachers, lawyers, journalists, military officers, therapists—how so many people missed the board.
Dylan:	Can you blame 'em though? They were locked in, goal-oriented, blinder-visioned, all they cared about was the mission before them. I can totally understand the mishap.
Best:	For sure. For sure. But for anyone who's been living under a rock for the past twenty years, could you paint a picture for us, please? For the younger generation.
Dylan:	Sure. Well, the first thing you gotta

realize, is that it was a much different world from today. After the system failed the pendulum slingshot to the polar opposite and kids nowadays are so insanely independent, they can't even fathom doing something so dangerous just because someone else did it. But that was our society in a nutshell. And after they got the call that Britney took her own life, they went to Defcon I. I've been told by multiple insiders that they treated the incident on the same level as a nuclear attack because it had the same potential for damage. Especially the fallout.

Best: *Really*?

Dylan: I'm for serious, man. And if you think about it, I mean *really* think about it, break it down to its base level, the system was basically five cults with ten cult leaders. Britney's cult had hundreds of millions of kids. I say that again … *hundreds of millions of kids.* All of them conditioned to do what their hive leaders do. Dress how they dress. Think how they think. Do what they do. It was hella dangerous. So, when they got the call that she'd killed herself, with no time to waste, they set up shop at Calvin Coolidge middle school in D.C. where Dr. Gliotone's daughter attended, turning an eighth-grade English class into a makeshift headquarters and ground zero. FEMA put out the call that would later become the infamous A-team and—

Best: Now, are they still the A-team in your book? Or are they the L-team?

Dylan: A-team. All the way, babay. N'I'll tell you why in a few minutes.

Best: Fair enough.

Dylan: So, FEMA puts out a call to arms, right, for anyone in the mental health field that could help. They kept the radius small, from D.C. to Langley, or anyone that could get to Calvin Coolidge within a certain time period. I don't remember exactly how much time it was. But we were working against the clock. Which ... I will say this, though—we Americans, we are some tough bastards. In the face of crisis, we lean on each other, we care about each other. And in no time at all every social worker, sociologist, and therapist were fighting each other to be a part of the team. It was definitely a niche field, and everyone was vetted as much as they could in the amount of time they had. FEMA picked the top thirty candidates they thought were the best qualified to handle every aspect of the fallout. Meow, the way I understand it, as soon as a candidate was selected they went directly into the classroom and got to work on their area of expertise. There was no time to think about anything but the task at hand. Someone—it's not really clear who, as no one has admitted it—grabbed a board that was already in the room. They used the board to put their plans on.

Best: Unfortunately, it happened to be a Britney vanity board.

Dylan: Talk about shit luck, right? I mean ... how they didn't notice her big smiling face is beyond me. It was bright pink and had lips blowing kisses all over the border. Sheez. Anyways, halfway through the video, the camera goes to the audience, and right there in the front row were the joint chiefs of staff, staring and nodding obediently like the rest of the crowd. And then you see the "Oh shit" moment on General Good's face when he realizes the blunder. His eyes grew big, his face turned a shade of red I'll never forget. Then he turns to General Sing and whispers something. Sing looks at the board, his mouth drops, he says, "God damn motherfucking shit," very clearly, then he turns and whispers to Admiral Jones. If you ever want to see someone have a moment of dread and anger in real time, watch the message go down the line. It was like watching a macabre game of telephone unfold. When the message got to House Speaker, Cox, he leans forward, puts his elbows on his knees and his head in his hands, shaking his head. Some say he was crying. Others say he was laughing. Neither would surprise me.

Best: Why do you think they didn't stop it?

Dylan: If it wasn't live, that would've worked just fine. But it was live, and there was something like a few billion viewers worldwide watching. If they tried to correct it, erase it, transfer it, if they brought attention to it in *any way*, everyone would notice it for sure, but if they did nothing there was still a chance that no one would notice.

Best: But then you wouldn't be where you are today.

Dylan: No, I wouldn't. But a' least my father would still be talking to me. He's a die-hard patriot, served thirty years in the Space Force, fought in Russia and China, and he was *incensed* that I exploited the military, says, "It's cheap comedy" and that "I should be ashamed of myself."

Best: Which is why you still consider them the A-team, I take it.

Dylan: Precisely.

Random Kids
Carroll Middle School
Carroll, Iowa

Best: What are the kids saying these days about what happened?

Kid 1:   Well, I heard that the real Britney actually did kill herself, but they cloned her to make it look like it was a practical joke. Because the government was afraid that if she didn't pop up, there would've been a lot more kids killing themselves then in "The Dark Night."

Best:	And you believe that?
Kid 1:	I mean, if you compare before and after videos, it makes sense. Sure. Her nose is different and even her personality is different. She used to be all perky and bubbly. Lowkey, she seems like a robot now.
Kid 2:	A clone? That's so dumb, dude.
Kid 1:	Your mom's dumb.
Best:	What do you think happened?
Kid 2:	I'm pretty sure she's a double agent spy for China and they used her as a depopulation tool.
Best:	A depopulation tool?
Kid 2:	Everyone knows that the Illuminati wants to kill half the planet. There's a "conspiracy theory" (air quotes) that it was all a deep deep, I'm talkin' *deeeep deep*, like Cooper's mom's vagina—
Kid 3:	Hey, screw you, man.
Kid 2:	—*Bottomless* pit deep dark secret conducted by Chase Young, FEMA, and Britney. That they wanted to kill as many kids as possible and that's why they didn't keep the kids in the gyms.
Best:	What about you, kid? Do you think the same thing? That she's a Chinese spy? That it was an elaborate depopulation campaign?
Kid 4:	Sure. But only 'cuz it's all over YouTube.
Best:	That she's a double agent for China?
Kid 4:	Yeah, but I been watchin' this dude's podcast, his name's Alex Bones, right, and I'm startin' to think all that jazz is just misinformation, that she's really a spy for Russia, not China.

Random couple
New York City, New York
Times Square

Man:	Man, were people pissed when Britney posted "April Fools" the next morning. I mean … what the fuck … *April Fools?*

Woman:	Yeah, I 'member that like it was yesterday. It was hella *cra*-zy.
Man:	She said she was gonna come clean lata that night, but she smoked some grade-A medicinal and fell asleep; didn' wake up 'til the nex' mornin'. By then, shit had already hit the fan.
Woman:	Yeah. I mean, I'm all for laughin' n'havin' a good time with practical jokes n'all, but not irresponsible ones that create the biggest mass suicide in history. What was it? Somethin' like 6,000 kids?
Best:	87,359
Man:	Fuck you, 87,359. Gedafagouttahere.
Best:	I'm serious.
Man:	You sure 'bout that, bruh?
Woman:	Yeah, booboo. That seems a lil' high, no? I 'member 6,000.
Best:	That was the death toll from the first night. The rest happened later.
Woman:	N'you're for sure, for sure?
Best:	I'm certain. My brother was one of them.
Woman:	Oh, I'm so sorry, suga. Come here n'gimme a hug.
Man:	I'm sorry for ya loss. Hey, watch ya hands now, m'man. Watch ya hands.
Best:	No worries.
Man:	And that's jus'it, innit, the worst thing of it all: the families were the ones that really suffered. Could'ja imagine bein' the parent ta one of 'em kids. Po' bastads.
Best:	I don't have to imagine. I lived it.

Senator Wayne Boggs (New York)\
Retired Salem, Massachusetts

Best:	Thank you for meeting me on such short notice, sir. It really means a lot to me; and it'll give the film undeniable credibility.
Boggs:	I'm happy to help, son. So long as I don't miss my two o'clock tee time, that is.
Best:	This won't take long, sir. I promise.

Boggs: Okay.

Best: You were instrumental in bringing the
            five hives mandate down. Exposing it.
            Dismantling it. Would you like to tell the
            story of how you got so involved?

Boggs: Well, like any savvy parent of a kid who
            was in Britney's hive, my Bianca didn't
            leave our side that night. Which, in
            retrospect, I think we should've done more
            for the first twenty-four hours—for it all,
            but especially that first night, it kind of
            set the wrong tone. Chase Young didn't want
            to start a panic by keeping the kids in the
            containment gyms longer than they needed
            to. But that's what they were built for.

Best: So, you were personally vested?

Boggs: Yes. My daughter was president of the
            Britney hive at the high school she
            attended. She made it past "The Dark Night"
            but she didn't make it past the fallout.

Best: Could you tell us more about the fallout?

Boggs: Well, the next morning, after the biggest
            volunteer force ever assembled by the state
            of New York canvassed the forest and netted
            the river, Britney reappeared alive and
            well. She didn't even have the foresight
            to assess the damage she'd done. She just
            posted her morning video like she always
            did.

Best: Do you remember what she said?

Boggs: "April fools, bitches. Who's a mama's girl
            now, Jakey?" Then she took a shower and
            went about her morning routine. It wasn't
            until she sat down for breakfast, an hour
            after she'd posted the video, that she
            realized what she'd done.

Best: But the damage had already been done.

Boggs: That's right, son. The night before, when
            everyone thought she was dead, there was
            an ominous feeling in the air, stifling,
            ripe with inevitability. The media called
            it "The Dark Night." Which had a certain
            ring to it, so it stuck. All parents were
            supposed to be with their kids, supporting

	them, watching them. But let's face it: not every parent is a good parent, and even then, sometimes situations such as single-parent families, being there isn't always possible.
Best:	Single-parent families got hit the hardest that first night.
Boggs:	4,026 of the suicides from "The Dark Night" were from single-parent families. Then came the fallout from the parents' suicides when 2,989 of those parents couldn't fathom life without their kids, so they followed suit. Kids lost their best friends, so they decided to follow suit as well. Then the parents of those kids, and the best friends, all of them, like a stack of dominoes—it was a mess.
Best:	Yes sir. It was. My brother, Sean, he was a casualty, too. But not in "The Dark Night." My mom wouldn't let him out of her sight for months. It wasn't until five months later, in his first week away at college. I was six.
Boggs:	I'm very sorry to hear that, son.
Best:	Thank you, thank you. But, for "The Dark Night," why didn't they sign an emergency bill to allow parents to miss work that first night or something to that effect? Surely companies could've gone one night without operations.
Boggs:	Indeed. Capitalism at its finest. Furthermore, why didn't they just keep the students in the gyms where they were perfectly safe? Why didn't they—there was a litany of mistakes made. It wasn't the first blunder in FEMA history, and I venture to say it will not be the last. But it is why Chase Young lost his job.
Best:	The mass suicide?
Boggs:	Mass suicide? What a *joke*. That's what they called it: "Mass suicide." I wanted to have Britney charged with 6,000 counts of assisted suicide, third-degree murder, manslaughter, coercion, conspiracy to

commit murder. Something. *Anything*,
anything for her role in "The Dark Night."

Best: We'll circle back to that in a bit. First,
          could you tell us about the copycats?

Boggs: Ah, yes. Those *goddamn* copycats—what a
          stupid fucking problem to have.

Best: Agreed, sir. Could you say more about it?

Boggs: Well, the second night we lost something
          like 1300 kids; third night was just below
          1000. By Sunday night it seemed like any
          kid that was going to kill themselves had
          done so already. Then, the very next week,
          we had thousands upon thousands of these
          damn kids faking their suicides. They all
          wanted to "outdo" (air quotes) Britney.
          They disappeared for one day, two days—the
          new challenge, you see, seemed to be the
          kid who could stay disappeared the longest
          got the most popularity.

Best: And for our younger audience, could you
          explain a challenge?

Boggs: A challenge is a wave of conformity, and
          acceptance; it's like a fad, you see. When
          I was a kid, the challenges started out
          benign enough, things like the ice bucket
          challenge. But, as time went on, the
          challenges grew in danger and stupidity.
          It didn't matter how much parents and
          teachers begged kids not to do it if it had
          gone viral because when that happened, it
          grew wings and took off. Then there was no
          controlling it. You have a better chance at
          stopping a forest fire with a garden hose
          than stopping children from trying to fit
          in.

Best: But it wasn't just with Britney's hive. Was
          it?

Boggs: No. No, it wasn't. All five hives
          participated. And lemme tell you, son, it
          was a logistical fuckjob to fumble and
          unfuck. Police departments were stretched
          thin looking for "missing" (air quotes)
          children only for them to show up joking
          and laughing, sometimes weeks later.

Best: Which made it difficult to differentiate
           between kids who were legitimately missing
           and the fakers, right?

Boggs: That's right. A few weeks into this
           clusterfuck of a nightmare, my daughter
           went missing. Now, I'll be the first
           to admit it: my Bianca was just as
           impressionable as any other kid, but she
           wasn't dumb. She knew where to draw the
           line and torturing her mother and me with a
           fake suicide was that line.

Best: So, what happened?

Boggs: Well, days turned into a week which turned
           into two and then three and we didn't know
           what to do. Her friends were no help. They
           swore they didn't know where she was, and I
           believed them. Then, one cold Tuesday morning,
           they found her body buried in the woods.

Best: If you are willing, could you tell us about
           the circumstances?

Boggs: Right away, we knew whoever killed her was
           a novice. They only halfway buried her; it
           looked like they got scared halfway and
           took off. A hunter and his dog found her.
           She had been … she'd been (inaudible) …
           she'd been beaten pretty good, but she
           always had a fierce fire burning deep within
           her; a fire that would rather die for a
           cause than give up without a fight, and so,
           with a chest full of what I imagine tasted
           and smelled like fire, in her last moments,
           she put up a fight. She had the bastard's
           DNA under her fingernails.

Best: Whose DNA was it?

Boggs: Samuel Holmes, her piece of shit ex-
           boyfriend. She tried breaking up with him
           and he used the chaos of the missing kids
           as an opportunity to kill her.

Best: What's even more tragic is that this wasn't
           the only such case. Was it?

Boggs: No, it wasn't. As a nation, there were more
           kids' bodies found in the following months
           than in the previous five years combined.
           Not all of them were brought to justice
           like my Bianca, though.

Best: So, as a former district attorney, why

	didn't you try and prosecute Britney?
Boggs:	*I did!* The government, in their infinite wisdom, decided she was untouchable. We couldn't even file a civil suit against her. They treated her like how we treated informants or witness protection. They called her "an entity beyond reprisal." Beyond reprisal? You believe that shit? Like the too big to fail banks before her. She was a cash cow, a golden goose, and we couldn't touch her. It was a despicable exhibition of democracy and the judicial system.
Best:	You were unable to prosecute her, but you *were* able to spearhead the class action lawsuit to get the five hives mandate expunged. Now we're back to the old system.
Boggs:	Which many think is worse.
Best:	What do you have to say to those people?
Boggs:	I understand the appeal of the five hives, I really do. Parents don't want their kids to be ostracized. I get that. But what they fail to realize is that by allowing their kids to partake in the mob mentality, they were stripping their kids of independence and their ability to think for themselves. Peer pressure has been and always will be something concerned parents must deal with, but, when kids are being pressured to do something that is potentially dangerous, and they do it anyway, despite any common sense, the blame lies on the system whose power is able and responsible for such wanton death. Even just one death is one too many.
Best:	Well said, sir. Well said.

Yolanda Sanchez
(Pete Sanchez's mother)
Little Rock, Minnesota

Sanchez:	My, have you gotten big. Ya look more and more like your brotha every time I see you.

	Dead-ringer, ya are.
Best:	Thank you, Mrs. Sanchez,
Sanchez:	But you could use to gain a few pounds, sweetie, my lawd, what, they not feeding you in college? You're libel to get blown away by a gusta wind. Skin and bones. It's not right. Cute boy like yaself should have some meat on his bones.
Best:	I eat plenty, Mrs. Sanchez. Cursed with the metabolism of youth.
Sanchez:	Well, we'll jus' have ta see 'bout that, now, won't we. I'm gonna fix you up some proper Mexican food, not like that fake joint downtown—wassit called? The one on Main Street?
Best:	Señor Salsa?
Sanchez:	That's the one. It's a damn crime what masquerades as Mexican food now'a'days. But don-chu worry, doll. Mama Jolie's gonna hook ya right n'proper. You and that pretty little producer girl I seent you whisperin' all sweet like. Is that your lady?
Best:	Yes ma'am.
Sanchez:	Well, *alright*. A'least ya doin' somethin' right. She's a pretty little number, perky, and brown, *too*. She *Mexicana*?
Best:	Puerto Rican.
Sanchez:	Well, I won't hold that against her, ya hear. But she best be feeding you better, hon, 'cuz ya ain't nothin' but a twig.
Best:	Yes ma'am.
Sanchez:	I gotta nice big pot of yella rice on the stove as we speak. Soon as we got off the phone, I started whippin' it up. It'll be ready soon, but firs', you said you had some questions for me, 'bout Petey?
Best:	Yes ma'am. And I just wanna thank you for agreeing to meet with me. I know how hard it is to talk about him and how much you miss him.
Sanchez:	I'm happy to help, hon. Now, watcha got to ass me?
Best:	Are you glad they got rid of the five hives mandate?

Sanchez: Am I glad they got rid of the five hives
           mandate? R'ya kiddin' me? You're goddamn
           right I am. We shoulda been able to bring a
           civil suit against Britney and the goment,
           too. They always gotta try'n overstep their
           bounds—the goment; get their greedy hands
           into erything. Eryone knows that they got
           rid of the old social media outlets in
           Trump's third term because he didn' like
           China's and Russia's ability to sway our
           system—talkin' 'bout it was "a threat to
           democracy." Phhh. No sir. They just wanted
           that privilege all to themselves. 'Em
           bastads.
Best: So, you blame the government for what
           happened and not Britney?
Sanchez: Don't you go throwin' words in my mouf,
           mister. I didn't say that.
Besat: Apologies. So, who do you blame?
Sanchez: I blame 'em *both*. But Britney was jus' a
           kid herself, don-chu-know. She was fightin'
           with that dimwit, Jake Taint—my lawd whata
           name, am I right? Taint? Poor fellar.
           Anyways, she was fightin' with 'im n' she
           wanted to prove she was cool. I get that.
           What kid hasn't done somethin' stupid
           to prove they was cool? But it was the
           goment's idea to mandate the five hives in
           the firs' place. It was their idea to give
           children the power of gods. The fuck did
           they think was gonna happen?

                    Dr. Robert Gliotone
       (Former lead consulting Psychiatrist for FEMA)
                    Tacoma, Washington

Best: It's an honor to meet you, sir. Truly. You
           guys got a bad rap for how FEMA decided
           to handle the crisis. But you were right,
           the A-team was right, all along. Can you
           tell us a little about how you were able
           to foretell such a huge fallout with such
           uncanny accuracy?

```
Gliotone:   It was a matter of identity, really.
Best:       Identity?
Gliotone:   Precisely.
Best:       How do you mean?
Gliotone:   Well, our team was comprised of therapists,
            psychologists, sociologists, behavioral
            scientists and just about any profession
            dealing with human behavior and the mind.
            The consensus, right from the start, was
            that this incident would be the reason the
            five hives mandate got expunged and the
            reason was the utter shattering of one's
            identity—it would cause three generations
            of kids to go through a simultaneous
            identity crisis. They'd be lost, a lone
            duck with a broken inner compass pointing
            north instead of south. Notwithstanding
            accidents and natural causes, the
            projections said that this incident—
            long after it had passed, mind you—would
            grudgingly force itself in the top cause
            of death for *anyone* under twenty years
            old twenty years down the road. We knew
            that some kids would be able to adapt, the
            younger ones certainly, the good-looking
            ones, athletes, and the more headstrong
            older kids, but, according to the numbers,
            that made up less than half the kids—a
            shockingly low number. The other kids, the
            ones who would have problems integrating,
            many of them were projected to die for one
            reason or another, directly or indirectly,
            over this incident, be that suicide or
            later down the road from self-medicating
            with alcohol and drugs. Simply put, we knew
            many kids wouldn't be able to cope with the
            real world. Not when their identities had
            been stripped, the very essence of their
            being, ripped away from them. They didn't
            know who they were, they didn't know how
            to be autonomous. And their psychology
            mimicked that of escaped children from sex
            trafficking rings, or cults.
Best:       If it was that bad, why do you think Chase
```

Young handled it the way he did? Why didn't
he listen to you guys?

Gliotone: I won't presume to know what was going on
in Chase's head. We did the job we were
tasked to do in the time we were allotted
to do them in. It was his decision what
to do with the predictions we made.
But I suspect he thought we were being
melodramatic.

Best: Is it true that the A-team wanted to
quarantine for forty-eight hours?

Gliotone: That is erroneous. We advised to extend the
blackout for *at least* the initial twenty-
four hours. But it wasn't only just the
fallout from "The Dark Night" in which we,
as a government and as a nation, erred,
though; it certainly didn't help that our
projected number of one thousand kids, a
shockingly high number at first glance, had
been exceeded by six hundred percent that
first night. We should've done more after
that; we should've known it was going to
get exceedingly worse.

Best: But you did. I've seen the video a million
times, and every time I see it, what gets
me so angry is the blatant disregard to
what the professionals predicted. Chase
Young's premature—

Gliotone: You mustn't blame Mr. Young solely. There
were many factors at play. We shouldn't
have rushed the shift after the mandate
got expunged, it should've been gradual.
Because when things went back to the
old ways, overnight, where coolness and
sexiness was mostly a byproduct of sexy
genes and charm, half the kids grew up to
become adults without a tribe. By the time
the twenty-year-olds were thirty, they were
regularly communicating only with one or
two of their former hive members, brothers,
sisters, people they were once intimately
connected, people they could always depend
on, a fellowship, a family, a tribe,
their bonds transcending the superficial

paradigm that society once abandoned—the one of preferred treatment toward good-looking people—and the society they were now obliged to grovel back to like a man returning to an unfaithful wife. For if not, if someone decided to weaponize the system, it would be catastrophic, as we inadvertently had already experienced.

Best: The system had been exposed.

Gliotone: Precisely. It was too dangerous, too easily manipulated, too capable of destruction. When you create a world of stripped liberties—a fake world used by the government to create drones—you create a world of drones. Three billion children—the ones that were twenty and younger when it happened. The ones who grew up in a hive. They got their freedoms for the first time, their identities, the very essence of who they were, and it was too much for many of them, and they drowned under the weight of it all. Not being told what to wear, what to do, who to like—the complete and total gain of one's identity, slowly dismantling their former selves, giving them their autonomy back after not having it—it was disastrous. And we knew it.

Best: The slow drip suicide.

Pastor Tom Reynolds
Church of Jesus Christ of the Latter-day Saints
Salt Lake City, Utah

Best: Your congregation has been notoriously vocal on its stance concerning the fallout. Can you tell us a little bit about that?

Reynolds: I'd love to, son. Ya, see, we here at the ol' CJCLDS, well, we value three things above all else—God, family, and country. Now, of course, God is and always will be atop that list, but family is a close second. The family unit was *supposed* to be a sacred thing, cherished above all else, save for God as we've well established. The family unit was *supposed* to help guide children, give them love, direction; it's *supposed* to be the backbone of society, son; the family unit is … why, it's the bedrock to which every other foundation derives its pure and intentional uniformity, be that a good, solid foundation, or a shaky, flimsy one. A tight-knit family begets strong children, Mr. Best, resilient children. Kids who grow up in broken homes don't have that same strength, that same resilience. They become lost, ya see, oscilating shitstorms, rolling stones. They gotta bed here and they gotta bed there and they gotta bed at their *grayyyparents' houses.* They have beds everywhere, but they don't have a home, ya see, and they get confused, these poor children. Now I ain't sayin' it's their faults, they're just kids. I blame the parents—I blame the parents for living in sin.

Best: It's hard to argue with you on that, but I think a case could be made that kids from broken homes can be quite strong and resilient as a direct result of their upbringing. Hardship breeds resilience.

Reynolds: Now, I'm not gonna sit here and argue with you, son. You asked, and I told.

Best: My parents weren't divorced, and my brother still killed himself.

Reynolds: I'm sorry to hear that, son. And I shall pray that his soul is purged of the unforgivable sin he committed— 'cuz *it is a sin* to kill oneself. Just as it is a sin to divorce.

Best: And taking twenty wives is perfectly acceptable? I don't see how that's so.

Reynolds: You just need more Jesus Christ in your life, s'all, son.

Dr. Dani Sullivan
Head of Sociology Department
Stanford University

Best: How would you sum up the five hives mandate
            fiasco?
Sullivan: Well, I think the title of my book pretty
            much sums that up.
Best: "The Classic and Unfortunate Case of the
            Blind Leading the Blind."
Sullivan: Quite.
Best: And, in your professional opinion, through
            the eyes of a sociologist and the lens of
            time, why do you think the mandate failed?
Sullivan: To answer that question, we'd have to look
            at history and the echelons of society
            regarding adolescence. The two major cliques
            used to be jocks slash popular kids, and
            nerds slash unpopular kids. There were
            subcategories for style, sure; and confidence
            and personality were tremendous equalizers,
            evening the playing field for kids who didn't
            meet the traditional standard of beauty;
            but, essentially, there were cool kids and
            the rest. If you were to visit *any* middle
            school or high school cafeteria circa 2030,
            you would see this play out in real time,
            the separation of good-looking kids and the
            others—birds of a feather flock together,
            as it were. But the five hives mandate
            changed *everything*, it segregated schools
            by social media following, thus ending the
            "lone wolf syndrome." Every child had a
            pack. After that, jocks and nerds were in
            the same subclass and were equally cool.
            In fact, most hive presidents were what
            society would classify today as nerdy. The
            presidents were leaders of their group.
            They were consistently the most popular
            kids in schools. A leader of one of the five
            hives was always voted as homecoming king
            and queen, ditto for prom. Instead of nerds
            sucking up to jocks to try and fit in, it

was the opposite. It was a very interesting
twenty years to say the least. But, to
answer your question, Mr. Best, I believe
the mandate failed because the government
tried to weaponize human behavior, and
like a nuclear meltdown, the fallout was
catastrophic. In my research for writing my
book, I happened upon an interesting article
about a TikTok challenge popular among the
youth of 2021, it was called the "Forty-
Eight Hour Challenge." Stop me if this
sounds familiar—the premise of the challenge
was to go missing for forty-eight hours.

Best: *Really*?
Sullivan: Indeed. You could say it was a precursor
             to the copycat prankers. But the five
             hives mandate wasn't going to be around
             forever. It's a wonder how we allowed it to
             happen in the first place. But, eventually,
             something like this was bound to happen.
             And we damn well should've known better
             than to give that platform more power.
             History repeats itself, and the history
             of social media spawned events such as
             the boiling water challenge, the choking
             challenge, Benadryl challenge, running in
             traffic challenge—that last one killed a
             poor kid from Asia.
Best: That's tragic.
Sullivan   Agreed.
Best: Are you of the opinion that Britney
             should've been brought up on charges?
Sullivan: I think that she should've at the very
             least stayed out of the spotlight, met
             a nice man, retired to the mountains,
             somewhere peaceful, somewhere where she
             could repair her conscience, atone for her
             mistakes. However, in order to atone, an
             absolute requisite of guilt is required,
             a sentiment I believe she is completely
             lacking. I don't think she feels guilty in
             the least, because if she did, she wouldn't
             be doing what she's doing today. The true
             irony, of course, is that she is still the

most popular woman on the planet—to this day. Because a year after the April fool's day fiasco, when congress decided to disband the five hives mandate, Jake "accidentally" (air quotes) released a sex tape he'd made with her to the public.

Best: Why do you use air quotes with accidentally? Do you believe it was intentional?

Sullivan: I believe he was so mad at her for being the reason he no longer had a hive that he wanted her to *really* kill herself. But the joke was on him. Because at the same time, virtual reality companies were developing interactive porn software and Britney, being the adorable, albeit attention-craving beauty that she is, capitalized on the leak, turning an otherwise embarrassing moment into a thriving career in the interactive porn industry where she exploited being the most recognized female on the planet. Everyone loved her. She grew up in homes the world over and became a multi-generational talent with her first few films.

Best: You're talking about *My Stepdad Abused Me, A Boner of a Foster Home*, and her first trilogy saga, *Home Inv-ass-ions*.

Sullivan: Disturbing, to say the least. I urge your viewers to research the most viewed videos on their preferred porn site. I guarantee it'll have either incest or rape or forced sex in a kidnapping slash home invasion scenario. Porn is a business, and like all businesses, they cater to their customers, their biggest customers being males fifteen to forty. And the fantasies men have, by and large, are quite disturbing. Depraved, even. Her first film, *My Stepdad Abused Me*, was released fifteen years ago. Seventy-six pornos later, she is still the most popular woman on the planet. Which tells you really all you need to know about the society we live in.

Best: You make a valid argument.

Sullivan: Thank you.

```
Best:      In your professional opinion, why do you
           think so many kids copycatted? Why did so
           many kids—at the risk of putting their
           parents through hell—why did so many fake
           their suicides? Or, better yet, why did so
           many go through with it?
Sullivan:  The new social media system was a great
           tool for kids in high school who otherwise
           would've had no tribe. There were no longer
           kids sitting alone at the lunch tables and
           everyone was included. But it was also a
           perfect tool of control for the governments
           and businesses. It used to be companies
           lobbied politicians, but for that twenty-
           year period—that tiny, terrifying twenty-
           year period—they need only lobby the hive
           leaders, for it was the hive leaders that
           swayed entire GOP's. It erased the need to
           think for yourself. If they wanted to sway
           popular opinion, all they had to do was get
           one of the hive leaders to cosign, then, by
           weaponizing psychology, their hives would
           follow suit. That's why so many copycatted or
           pulled the trigger, pun intended—systematic
           coercion. Buy this phone. Watch this movie.
           Vote this way. Kill yourself. No one thought
           for themselves anymore, a carbon-copy society
           where everyone was just a copy of a copy of
           a copy. A world of puppets with hive leaders
           pulling the strings on the surface, but big
           business and government covertly with their
           hands up the hive leaders' bums.
```

Britney Sammons
(Former queen of the Hipsters Hive)
Houston, Texas

```
Best:      Why'd you do it?
Britney:   I obviously didn't think it through. *Duh.* I
           was young and dumb and just … yeah. I just
           didn't think it through.
Best:      Do you regret it?
```

Britney: What the fuck kinda question is that?
           Didn't my producers vet your questions?
           Do I regret it? What the hell, you lil'
           fuckin' nerd. What you getting at?

Best: It's a simple question, Britney. And might
           I add, one that you owe many, many people.

Britney: *Of course I regret it.* Jeez. It nearly
           ruined my life. And it definitely ruined the
           five hives system.

Best: Maybe the system needed to be ruined, no?

Britney: I liked the old system.

Best: But you guys had entirely way too much
           power. You must see that now? You guys were
           trendsetters, influencers, moguls. You were
           gods for all intents and purposes.

Britney: Exactly. Who wouldn't love having that much
           power?

Best: Okay, but with that much power, don't you
           think you had a moral obligation to behave
           rationally?

Britney: How do you mean?

Best: *How do I mean?* After all these years, you
           still don't get it, do you?

Britney: Get what?

Best: You were in control of the biggest hive
           in the world with arguably one of the
           biggest secular gatherings of like-minded
           individuals the world had ever seen. Three
           billion people worldwide followed you,
           worshipped you, emulated you. Kids had
           dolls of you for chris' sake. Merchandise
           with your face on it. You were a brand.
           There's a moral responsibility that comes
           with that much power.

Britney : Like I said—I didn't think it would be that
           big of a deal.

Best: *Of course* you didn't. How's your acting
           career?

Britney: I'm glad you asked. It's going really
           great. *Gang Bang Britney Three: Return of
           the Glory Hole* will be available for stream
           soon. And if you buy it through the VR
           Mattel network, you're going to get a very
           special treat in there from me.

Best: What's the surprise?
Britney: If I told you then it wouldn't be a
          surprise, now, would it?
Best: Fair n'ough. Okay, so, what—
Britney: Okay, you twisted my arm. I'll tell ya;
          I'll tell ya—they're gonna kick off the
          release with a huge sale. For those of you
          who don't already have a sex doll of me—
          with a mold of my vajayjay so that it's
          like you're actually inside me—it's gonna
          be *half off*. For a limited time, only,
          though. And for those that do already
          have one, there'll be different-sized
          attachments for sale that you can switch
          out with *any* of the holes on the doll.
          The biggest complaint—the only complaint
          really—has been that the holes are too
          loose. "It's like throwing a hotdog down a
          hallway," one man moaned in an email. So,
          we took molds of my pretty, tight-tight
          vagina and all is right back in the world.
          The attachments are the resolution to the
          "size" problem. I'm pretty stoked.
Best: I bet you are.

                    Jake Taint
        (Former king of the Hip-Hopper hive)
              Los Angeles, California

Best: Thank you for meeting with me.
Taint: I'm happy too. It gives me a chance to
          clear the air and set the record straight.
Best: In regards to?
Taint: Don't play coy with me, man. I know why
          you're here—you want to know if I leaked
          the sex tape on purpose.
Best: We'll get to that. First, can you paint a
          picture of the events that happened before,
          please? This documentary is tailored more
          toward a younger audience, kids who only
          know what happened by what the history
          books say.

Taint: Sure. Sure. So, where should I begin?

Best: Well, what was the whole deal with your
            post about Britney? Saying she was, "A
            momma's girl, goody two shoes?"

Taint: Ironically enough, and you're probably *not*
            gonna believe this, but that was about her
            refusing to make a sex tape with me.

Best: You're kidding.

Taint: I shit you *not,* my dude.

Best: Wait, then that would mean—just so I'm
            clear, you're saying that the sex tape was
            made *after* the April Fools deal?

Taint: I am. *Everyone* thinks it was made before
            and that I got mad at her and leaked it.
            But we didn't even film our first film 'til
            a few months later. Britney calls me one
            night, right, drunker than a skunk, cryin'.
            She'd been gettin' death threats, and she
            was scared. I came over, and one thing led
            to another. When we got to her bedroom,
            everything was already set up, the camera,
            the candles—*everything.*

Best: So, it was her idea? "Goody two shoes,
            Britney" (air quotes)? That's what you're
            sayin'?

Taint: One hundred percent.

Best: Okay. So, you guys record yourselves having
            sex. Walk me through what happens next.

Taint: This was during the class action lawsuit
            trial to get the mandate expunged. And
            we all knew they were going to win, we,
            meaning me and the eight other hive
            leaders. And everyone was furious with
            Britney. I was the only one that was
            talkin' to her. She was lonely, and I kinda
            felt mildly responsible. Had I not called
            her out in public, she wouldn't have done
            something so stupid.

Best: How does the tape get out, though? You said
            you lost your phone, and someone hacked
            into it? Was that true?

Taint: No. The bitch was so paranoid about a sex

	tape being leaked that she didn't even gimme a fuckin' copy of the tapes—none of them.
Best:	There was more than one?
Taint:	Boy, was there. We probably made fifty tapes. A'least.
Best:	I see.
Taint:	Like I said, she was lonely, and I was horny. She said we could make as many as I wanted, but she had two requirements. One—that no copies ever left her house, and two—that I never tell anyone about it. Which was cool with me. I was nineteen, basically a walking boner, and she was super—hot. So, I slid through a few days a week and we'd watch old sex tapes and make new ones.
Best:	So, who leaked the tape then?
Taint:	I don't know who leaked it. Truly. I don't. But I know Britney was the only one with a copy. And like I said—by the time the trial was over, we'd made maybe fifty videos, and she *really* took to it. I mean, like, really, *really* took to it. You watch the first video, she's all timid and scared, and by the last tape, she's deep throating me and doing anal and all kindsa shit like a pro. We used to watch 'em after we made 'em and she used to say jokingly that if the mandate ended, she was going to become the biggest porn star on the planet. A year later, it actually happened.
Best:	Are you saying that Britney leaked the tape herself?
Taint:	I'm saying that I didn't, and that she was the only one with a copy.
Best:	Why are you just now saying this? Twenty years later? Why didn't you come clean back then, just say that it wasn't you? Why lie about your phone being stolen?
Taint:	*Honestly*? I'd fallen in love with her. And I think I didn't want to know the truth—that she did it on purpose to skyrocket a new career getting plowed by other dudes.
Best:	Fair n'ough.

                       Chase Young
            (Former FEMA lead administrator)
                  Sonata Senior Living
                   Orlando, Florida

Best: Thank you for meeting me, sir. It's an
           honor.
Young: No, thank you, son. I haven't had a visitor
           in some time.
Best: I'm happy to visit.
Young: What did you say this video was about,
           again?
Best: It's a documentary about the five hives
           fiasco.
Young: What's that now? You gotta speak up, kiddo.
           M'ears ain't what they used to be.
Best: I said— *"It's a documentary about the five
           hives fiasco."*
Young: That's not what you said before on the
           phone. I have nothing to say on the matter.
Best: Yes, it is, sir. We talked on the phone.
           Don't you remember? You said it was okay
           that me and my girlfriend stopped by for a
           few questions.
Young: You calling me a liar, son?
Best: Not at all, sir. I'm simply saying that
           we called you two days ago from New York,
           asking if we could visit, explicitly
           stating the reason was to ask questions for
           a college documentary about your role in
           the five hives fiasco. You said, "I'd love
           the company."
Young: My memory isn't what it used to be, kid. I
           don't even remember talking to ya.
Best: Well, you didn't speak with me personally,
           sir. You spoke with the producer, my
           girlfriend—the cutie behind the camera.
Lisa: He's not lying, Mr. Young. We had a very
           nice conversation that ended with you
           agreeing to meet us. We drove for two days
           to get here. Won't you please just answer
           some questions?
Young: Questions? Questions 'bout what?

```
Best:     The five hives.
Young:    Oh, well … go on ahead with your questions,
          then, son.
Best:     Thank you, sir. I appreciate the
          opportunity. You've been notoriously quiet
          on the topic, and I think now's a good time
          to tell the world your side of the story. I
          mean, what happened that day?
Young:    It ruined me, is what happened. My wife
          left me. My kids stopped talking to me. I
          lost my job. I lost my marriage; my home,
          my dog, my friends—everything. I lost
          everything.
Best:     I'm sorry to hear it, sir. But don't you
          think this all coulda been avoided if you'd
          just kept the kids in the gyms? That's what
          they were made for and—
Young:    Get the fuck outta here—right now. I'm not
          kidding. Go on. Git.
```

Chase Young refused to answer any more questions.

Inmate 38454763
Samuel Holmes
New York Federal Corrections
Syracuse, New York

```
Best:     Why'd you do it?
Holmes:   I don't know man. It was an accident—a
          dumb, dumb accident. Really dumb. But,
          like, she was cheatin' on me. Did you know
          that? I keep tellin' people that and no one
          believes me, everyone thinks she was just
          this perfect angel. But she wahent.
Best:     Even if she was cheating on you, why not
          just break up with her? Why kill her?
Holmes:   Like I said a million times before—it was
          an accident. But she broke my heart. Tore
          it to pieces. And what's worse—she didn't
          even care that she'd hurt me so badly.
Best:     So, you killed her?
Holmes:   I didn't mean to kill her. I followed her
          one day after she left her new boyfriend's
```

house. She was jogging. I'd been following
her for a week or so, so I knew her route
and I hid in the woods, far away from
prying ears. I just wanted to talk with
her. I just wanted to know how she could be
so cruel. I just wanted to hold her.

Best: Then what happened.

Holmes: She flipped shit s'what happened. Started
callin' me all kindsa names, sayin' I was
a loser and that she couldn't believe that
she ever loved someone like me and how I was
a stalker and—just shit like that, right.
Real mean, venomous like. And I was jus' so
mad at her, but I still loved her, too, and
I jus', I jus' wanted a hug, jus' one small
hug. Tha's it. Tha's all I wanted. But she
pushed me away and tried runnin'. I tackled
her and tried to get her to calm down, but
she started hittin' me and scratchin' me and
started screamin'. I'd seen a car on the
way in, and I knew it was a popular hunting
spot, so I puts my hands around her neck
to get her to stop screamin'. But I guess
I jus', I jus' squeezed too hard. I jus'
wanted her to stop screaming s'all.

Best: So, it was an accident? You're still
sticking to that story, eh?

Holmes: I'm stickin' to it 'cuz it's true. Aight.
N'you keep paytonizing me n'I'll jus' end
this interview. Right here n'right now. I
don't need this.

Best: And I'll forget to bring you that
cotton candy and put that money in your
commissary.

Holmes: Fine. Jus' stop paytonizin' me, that's all
I'm sayin'—stop paytonizin' me.

Best: Okay. I'll stop patronizing you. But I
gotta ask—you didn't intentionally use the
confusion of the missing copycat prankers
to your advantage?

Holmes: Like I said—it was an accident.

Best: How much time do you have left before your
execution?

Holmes: Eighteen months, three days.

```
Best:      And the Lullaby—is it as vivid as they say?
Holmes:    Sure is. Every night I gotsta relive
           killin' the woman I loved. Shit ain't
           right. You would think that'd be punishment
           n'ough. But *noooo*. Mr. Fred Fuckin'
           Fitzgerald says at the end of my suffering
           is the electric chair. That dude has way
           too much power.


                    Shane Best
               (Brother of Sean Best)
              University of Minnesota


Lisa:      Can you tell us why you decided to make
           this film, baby?
Best:      Of course, baby. I made it because I
           couldn't *not* make it. When I saw the
           syllabus and saw what the final project
           was gonna be—to make a documentary about
           something that you cared about, something
           that you were personally vested in—well, I
           knew then exactly what my documentary was
           gonna be about. Because, though this all
           happened twenty years ago, when I was just
           six, it had a huge impact on my life, on
           the world.
Lisa:      That it did. Can you tell us how it
           affected you, personally?
Best:      The most obvious answer is that I lost my
           older brother. My only brother, Sean Best.
           "I'm the *Best* brother ever," he used to say
           with that goofy look on his face.
Lisa:      Can you tell us more about him. I know it's
           getting harder to remember him, but what do
           you remember?
Best:      He was cool and funny and just *so* full
           of life. And he was kind and loving. Most
           siblings that are twelve years apart
           usually aren't very close, ya know. But not
           me and Sean. He made it a point to make me
           feel loved, he went out of his way to let
```

	me know that he was always there for me. He
	used to take me everywhere he went. I was
	his little shadow.
Lisa:	That sounds nice.
Best:	It was.
Lisa:	Can you tell us about what happened after
	April 1, 2030?
Best:	Well, after Pete killed himself,
	everything changed. Sean changed. The
	world changed. And I remember thinking on
	"The Dark Night," even then, being that
	young, knowing that a paradigm shift had
	occurred, and that the world was gonna be
	significantly different. My mom and dad made
	us sleep in the same bed as them on "The
	Dark Night" and the day after, and the day
	after that. It wasn't until like a month
	later, when Sean started smiling again,
	that my mom let up. She thought the worst
	was behind us—we all did.
Lisa:	How long did he last until he decided he
	didn't want to live anymore?
Best:	Honestly, I think he'd always known. But
	officially, it was five months—the first week
	of September.
Lisa:	Did he leave a note or anything?
Best:	Nope. No note. No goodbye. Nothing like
	that. But the weekend before, when he was
	clearing out his room to move to the dorm
	at state, he trashed a lot of important
	things, special things, and gave away the
	rest of his stuff, saying he was too old
	for some of them. Which should've raised
	some red flags. And my mom, bless her broken
	heart, I think she blamed herself. Because
	she should've known that was why he was
	giving away everything—that he was planning
	on taking his life. Especially his—he
	had a huge comic collection, we'd been
	collecting since, well, forever. It was
	kind of our thing. But he gave them *all* to
	me, which was—it was a big deal because we
	had a pretty sweet, pretty rare collection.
	It's how I funded this film—how we got to

	travel across America—I sold a few of the comics. But I should've known back then that something was wrong, that he wasn't planning on coming back.
Lisa:	Don't do that, baby. There's no way you could've known. You were only six.
Best:	I know, hon. I just wish things were different.
Lisa:	Me too, my love. Me too. Can you tell us about your mom and dad? How did the loss of their oldest child affect them?
Best:	Well, like I said, my mother blamed herself for not seeing the signs, and she spiraled pretty quickly, into a deep, *deep*, dark depression. She didn't eat, she didn't shower, she didn't get out of bed for weeks. My father finally got sick of her behavior and called a shrink who prescribed her Valium and Xanax. She was better able to cope with life with the chemical facilitator. But she'd developed an addiction to benzos. From when I was six to sixteen, those ten years, she was practically a zombie, always with one foot out of reality, halfway present, that lost look in her eyes. She died of an accidental overdose a few days after my sixteenth birthday.
Lisa:	I'm so sorry, baby.
Best:	It's okay. This is important, what we're doing is important. We gotta let the world know, so that it never happens again.
Lisa:	I love you so much.
Best:	Me, too, I love you, too. And, to finish the question, my father left when I was nine years old. He couldn't take my mom's inability to deal with life on life's terms and he couldn't—he never said it, but I could see it in his eyes—he couldn't look at me without seeing Sean. I think he blamed himself and every time he looked at me, he was reminded of his biggest failure in life. He's got a new family in St. Cloud, two kids, a boy and a girl, ten and

six. He seems happy and I'm happy for him,
too, ya know. I'd have to be the biggest,
most miserable, petty prick alive to not
wish my father happiness. So, I love him
from afar.

Lisa: If he were to see this, d'ya think he'd
approve?

Best: Sure. He's the one that got me into filming
to begin with. Gave me my first camera when
I was five years old, along with one of
those Hollywood director chairs. I still
have it, the chair. Man, I used to think
I was so cool sitting in it, filming my
stuffed animals, telling them, "I need more
passion from you, Teddy. You're not giving
me *enough* passion." Sean was in a few of my
movies too. He was a good brother. He made
time for me.

Lisa: If you could tell your father one thing,
what would it be?

Best: *Really*? You're going to sneak in an
unvetted question on me, baby?

Lisa: I think it's important to be assertive, and
what better way?

Best: I guess you're right, but, if I don't dig
it, I'm eighty-sixing it.

Lisa: We'll just see 'bout that, mister.

Best: Let's see—if I could tell my father one
thing, what would it be? I'd tell him
that I love him, that I love him and that
I forgive him and that I'm sorry, I'm
sorry about Sean and Mom and the endless,
irreconcilable space between us, like
two opposites of a magnet. I'm sorry for
being so distant, and I wished things were
different between us. And that I'm not mad
at him for leaving me with my depressed
mom, leaving me to clean up after her and
cook for her and make up excuses for her
whenever she did something embarrassing or
forgot something—which happened all the
time, 'specially toward the end. I'd tell
him that I'm not mad at him for starting a
whole new life, a whole new family. But I

wished that he would call more than just
on Christmases and birthdays. I'd tell him
that I miss Sean, too. I miss him so much.
But he's dead and that sucks, but I'm still
alive, I'm right here and I wish he would
just be a dad, s'all. I just wish he would
acknowledge me, that he remembers he has
another son, instead of hiding me from his
new life as if I were the worst mistake
he'd ever made. I'm sorry, hon. I guess
that was more than one thing, huh?

Lisa: Come here, you.

A SHANE BEST JOINT
Director
Shane Best
Executive Producer
Lisa Joules
Editor
Shane Best

Forgive Me, Father, For I Have Sinned

Their footsteps were faint at first, whispers of mortality bouncing off the narrow corridor walls—becoming more pronounced as they marched ever slowly, closer, closer.

"The footsteps feel like the last force of a dying heart beating." That's what one of the other prisoners said a few years back. Jim was his name. Or was it Gerry? Their names and faces sort of melted together after a while, their memories diluted with time.

Every so often—when it was someone's time—Jack would remember the conversation with Jim or Gerry. He would remember Lansky and Smitty, Peterson and Johnson. He would remember all the friends he'd made over the years. All of them, dead and gone. Now, when it was his turn, he thought the uncanny comparison mightily appropriate as the footsteps of death had finally arrived at his doorstep.

Finally.

But the weight of fear no longer sat on his chest, for he was no longer host to fear. No. Not after the last few hours—after the last few hours, his world had been turned upside down, flipped on its head, granting him a luxury that most condemned men never get. That is, namely, *closure.*

Aside from the constant dribble of dropping footsteps, there was utter silence. Every prisoner in the death row block at New York Federal Corrections knew who the footsteps belonged to—the prison warden, Fred Fitzgerald, and his goon entourage of Android Correctional Officers. Typically speaking, a visit of this magnitude would result in a coordinated upheaval that would endure until the vents in the cells hatched open and released a noxious gas which would strip the prisoners of their energies and their consciousness.

Without exception, all the prisoners at NYFC hated their trailblazing warden, but none more so than the residents of death row. He was something of a celebrity, Fred Fitzgerald. A celebrity with polarizing allegiances. People either loved him or loved to hate him. There was no middle ground. When he rubbed elbows at parties reserved for the upper echelons of society, he had an air of divinity about him. Everyone wanted to shake his hand, listen to his inspiring vision for the future, let him kiss their baby. He was well received with the upper class and perhaps more importantly, he was trusted—a conflicting disparity from his image with the lower and middle classes, who wanted to have him arrested, locked in a cell, and forced to watch memories of his gentrification programs, which, like its preceding programs, targeted predominantly minority and low-income demographics.

Religious Republicans loved him, while religious Democrats thought him to be the antichrist.

No middle ground.

Nevertheless, this was the new system passed by Congress, spearheaded by the warden, who, forty years prior, was the brains behind the inception of realer than life VR simulations. His disdain for murderers and rapists had been ingrained in him at the tender age of six, when his mother was raped and murdered as he watched through the cracked door of a closet, searing the memory into his mind. Then, twenty years later, when DNA matched his mother's killer to a new victim, he bought the prison the man was sent to, tweaked his VR technology, and forced every prisoner to relive their worst crimes as they slept. He called the technology the Lullaby, a fitting if not misleading name. But he was a gifted orator, and he was able to convince Congress to install the new system at the federal level, installing the devices in every cell in every prison across the country, making him one of the richest men on the planet.

"The Lullaby is such an effective tool to dissuade repeat offenders from a continued career in criminal activity, recidivism is at an all-time high," Congresswomen (New Jersey) Jackson said.

The more liberal communities especially despised him. Their argument being that death row prisoners should be exempt from the new prison modality. That to relive the moment of their violent crimes on a loop in a virtual reality should suffice as punishment enough, but to execute them after their long suffering was double jeopardy of the worst kind.

—

Over the years it had become something of a tradition that whenever the warden came to escort a condemned prisoner to the chair, their fellow prisoners would show their respect with a vow of silence for the day, a Sabbath of solidarity. One might have to watch their back on any other day. But on execution days, it was unwritten custom that everyone was family—a universal truce. It was the only way they could pay their respect. For today was for Jack what tomorrow was for them: the chair.

The faint footsteps grew more pronounced. Jack could make out the hissing hydraulic hoses releasing air from the Android's piston legs as they crept closer. The footsteps and the hissing stopped just outside his cell. The door was made of reinforced plexiglass and when Jack looked up from the ground, he beheld a squad of four androids. They stood ominously erect, surrounding the small pudgy warden like a team of famished sharks. Made of a sleek carbon-titanium alloy that was midnight-black and as beautiful as it was strong, the androids were six feet in stature and carried stun guns strapped across their bulging chests.

The warden waved his hand in front of the door and the microchip in his wedding ring married its counterpart in the door and a slot in the middle yawned open with mechanical precision.

"Prisoner 748543, turn around, put your hands behind your back, and take four steps back." This from the lead android. "Acknowledge compliance."

A mechanical buzzing bounced off the small cell walls as the android's lenses zoomed in and out, its state-of-the-art system of cameras changing from infrared to X-ray to normal, its full spectrum system scanning Jack's heartbeat, body temperature, facial expressions, posture, and demeanor, prepared for any fight that he might make. But Jack had accepted his death willingly and with great excitement upon the visit of Father Rodgers.

"I comply," Jack said in a low voice.

The liberals lost the injunction that would've prohibited the double jeopardy policy, but they were able to keep the federal law that mandates prisons to offer a last rites confession for anyone scheduled to be executed. Anyone could refuse their given rights to this accommodation, but Jack had never heard of such an event occurring.

Although he had never given much thought to or put much faith in religion, he welcomed the young *padre* as if he were an old friend. Jack had always admired the pious their faith despite the lack of proof, but he could never wrap his mind around their forgiveness policy: how someone could commit all manner of sin and yet, after confessing and accepting Jesus Christ as their lord and savior, their sins would be absolved, and their souls treated the same as a lifelong believer. It just didn't sit well with him. He felt anger and bitterness on behalf of those lifelong believers, the ones who dedicated their life to the good book while others found a way to cheat the system, a back door into heaven.

But, when someone is facing imminent death, they invariably find God and Jack wasn't any different. Like a soldier in a foxhole dodging mortars and bullets and malaria, he got on board the faith train and played the game, and what's more, he was sincere about it, too.

Jack put his hands behind his back and walked backwards slowly. He placed his hands through the slit and as the lead ACO placed him in restraints, he and the *padre* shared a conversation with their eyes, tethered at the heart of their long-shared torment and severed by the one thing man can buy no more of: time.

The warden interrupted their moment of reconciliation. "Let's get this show going," he said, looking at his watch then smacking his lips in disdain. "I've got a round of golf scheduled with the governor."

Golf? Jack thought. *What an asshole.*

"Take two steps and face forward," the ACO said, its eyes zooming out. "Comply."

Jack took two steps, staring into Father Rodgers's eyes, which were bloodshot and shrink-wrapped in a haze of tears, his face frozen in a perfect depiction of anguish and regret.

"Face forward." The mechanical twirling slapped against the walls as the camera lens zoomed in and out, making appropriate readings. When Jack did not comply after three seconds, then came the noise all prisoners feared: the loud, resonating charge of the small particle accelerator stored inside all ACOs' chests. It started with a high-pitched charging tone, then plateaued quickly before stopping abruptly. From beginning to end, the charge only took three seconds. The Androids were programed to give the prisoners another three-second allotment before they took the full brunt of the charge: 4444 volts, delivering just enough pain that you'll be in the infirmary for a few weeks, relearning basic functions such as walking, brushing your teeth. But you'll survive. It was the best means of nonlethal combatants. More of a deterrent than anything else.

The prisoners called it "The Bolt of Zeus," as in "Yo, get ya ass down before you get The Bolt of Zeus all up in that ass."

Fear is a healthy motivator and in the twenty years since androids became correctional officers, it had only been used twice. The charging sound sends a bolt of fear down the body of anyone in its vicinity, and like a choreographed prank on some Japanese television show, everyone hits the deck.

Despite the certainty of death in his immediate future, Jack was no different. He turned slowly but his head remained fixed. He looked funny as his body turned against the neck like an owl, big wet eyes locked on Father Rodgers.

The lead ACO extended its hand and the pointing finger opened, swirling in a small, pinpoint vortex. Then a spring-loaded key popped out. He stuck the key in a slit on the wall and the door opened.

The silence was unnerving as Jack walked into the hallway and took his appropriate place in the middle of the ACOs, which used their survey technology to calculate distance and form a perfect four-foot square around Jack. The warden checked his watch again and then started down the hall toward the chair that would soon end Jack's life. The convoy of hissing machines followed, Jack in the middle.

Suddenly aware that this was the last walk he'd ever take, Jack decided to practice the advice his wife was always going on about. "It's such a beautiful world," she would always say. "Don't take it for granted, ya hear."

He felt nostalgic as he thought, *I won't, my love.*

Jack closed his eyes and took a deep breath. He noticed the odd no-fragrance smell of the prison, neither liking it nor disliking it—just noticing it. His mouth was dry, his throat sore. He opened his eyes. The lights seemed unusually bright, forcing him to squint through the thick blanket of tears that refused to drip. They just congealed there, wet, blurry. He took another deep breath, this time appreciating the no fragrance. *Don't take it for granted.* His neck was tight, his stomach grumbling. He noted that his legs seemed heavier than usual and that his mind had to override the body's typically autonomous act of walking, for the body seemed to know where it was walking and Jack had the feeling if he didn't consciously move his legs, they would plant themselves and grow roots and there he would remain until his dying day, right there in the middle of the hallway, vegetation growing around him, death springing forth life. *Janey would've loved that.* Jack smiled at the thought.

He started thinking of his life: a dizzying kaleidoscope panorama of images. He thought of the wins, the losses, the good times and the bad. He thought of barbecues and picnics, anthills and clouds. But mostly, he thought of his family. *I'll be joining you guys soon enough.* The thought was like a cup of hot cocoa for his soul, warm, inviting.

Halfway down the corridor, Father Rodgers interrupted their journey, delaying Jack's death for thirty seconds more. Deep down, he was grateful.

The *padre* had an awkward limp to his walk, favoring the right side more than the left. Jack imagined the man of cloth as a renegade pirate with a splintered wooden stub for a leg, heroically coming to aid in his rescue. Except, of course, Father Rodgers was sniffling like a child, and renegade pirates with splintered wooden stubs for a leg were of a different breed than most, tough as nails and full of piss and vinegar, as they say.

Father Rodgers stopped, his face glowing like a small puddle on a moonlit night as he attempted to free his face of tears and snot, but only served to spread it.

"I'm so sorry, Jack," Father Rodgers cried. "Please forgive me."

Jack scoffed and bit his lip, agitating a recently opened scab. He felt the heat rise in his chest and was certain if the ACOs scanned him right then, they'd think him to be hostile and he'd get the bolt of Zeus all up in that ass.

"What're you going on about, now?" the warden said.

Unless you were a politician, a booster, or an eighteen-year-old blonde with throbbing breasts, it was hard to catch and keep Warden Fitzgerald's attention. Jack saw the moment when the warden looked at the *padre* for the first time—*really* looked at him—and he knew what he was thinking because he had thought the same thing: that *padre* is a fucking child.

There is no programing in the ACOs hardware that dictates how to handle civilians, so they let Father Rodgers enter the forbidden area between them and their con.

Jack and the *padre* locked eyes and for an instant they were one person, connected at the roots of their tragic lives, bound together for the remainder of their lives, however long that may be.

Father Rodgers threw his cane aside then prostrated himself at Jack's feet and begged for forgiveness. Jack could have refused. He could have told him to get fucked and rot in hell, and perhaps he should have, but Jack had just recently found God. And with his newfound faith, he accepted the apology, forcing a smile, nodding.

"Good grief, Father, compose yourself." The warden looked at his watch again, annoyed. He nodded at Jack and the ACOs split them up. Father Rodgers clung to Jack's leg, pulling, hugging, crying. After a brief struggle, the ACOs finally succeeded at their task of separation, then they continued the walk toward the chair.

One could relive their entire life in the three-minute walk from their lonely cell to the electric chair. As for Jack, he relived the last two hours of his life. For in that span of time was his absolute salvation.

Two hours ago

Anyone slated to die by lethal methods doesn't have to die on an empty stomach, but "It'll make my job a hellava lot easier," the city coroner argued, "and cleaner." Prior to the scheduled death, the prison offered an accommodation the prisoners dubbed "the last supper." It was a much-appreciated amends for the subpar meals the prisoners had to endure over the years. The AI replicator machines made anything a prisoner desired. Although it was 3D printed food it looked, tasted, and even smelled like the real deal. Jack's best friend, Samuel Holmes, picked cotton candy as his last meal. The other prisoners poked and made fun, but he did not waver. No. Not Sam. He stuck to his conviction to the moment they pulled the switch, arguing that it reminded him of the happiest moments of his childhood. He was executed a few months prior. Jack missed him dearly.

Unlike Sam, Jack opted to die on a full stomach. For his last meal he ordered a nice, hearty T-bone steak, medium rare, of course, with a side of sunny-side-up eggs and fried hashbrowns "crispier than a thirteen-year-old's nut rag," he instructed the ACO that took his order. Rounding out the plate was two slices of buttered wheat toast. Jack laughed at himself as he bit into a corner, realizing the indoctrination into a healthy lifestyle instilled by his wife had been rooted deeply. *I'll be dead in a few hours,* he thought, *and I'm worried about my cholesterol?* He acknowledged the irony, shrugged, then mopped up a swath of steak sauce and threw the slice in his mouth.

He was licking what remained on the plate—a delightful concoction of steak sauce mixed with egg yolk—when the *padre* entered his cell. He was so preoccupied with the task he didn't even hear the door open. What first caught his attention was the song the man of cloth was humming: *You are my sunshine.* It was the same song his wife used to hum to their daughter whenever she was scared or sick. The same song, the same tone and tempo, soft, majestic, beautiful.

The man cleared his throat. Jack looked up, embarrassed. The stranger introduced himself as Father Rodgers, extending his hand, waiting to be reciprocated. Jack unpacked the man before him. *If you can even call him a man,* he thought.

Father Rodgers didn't carry himself with much authority, he lacked that innate confidence and glowing aura about him that most believers harbored. Timid and frail, was Jack's first impression. *A fraud.* He had the wan, tired face of a holocaust survivor. His cheeks sucked in. And his shifty eyes didn't instill much faith or trust in Jack.

His hand stood suspended in the air, shaking nervously, seemingly afraid of the embarrassment if Jack did not take it.

Jack smirked and used the palm of his hand to wipe his mouth free of dinner. Then he stood and mirrored the awkward pose: hand suspended in midair, solid, unshaking, looking into Father Rodgers's eyes—which shifted from Jack's eyes to his hand full of steak sauce and yolk—genuinely curious what a man of faith would do when presented with such blatant disrespect. *Turn the other cheek?* Jack thought. He wasn't a cruel man by nature. It was prison that'd turned him that way.

After having his fun, he wiped his hand on his pants, stepped forward, grabbed Father Rodgers's hand firmly then shook his hand with the respect a man of position deserves.

"Jack the Ripper," he said, giving the name his fellow prisoners had taken to calling him. "It's a pleasure to meet you, *Padre.*" Father retracted his arm as soon as was appropriately possible, seemingly afraid that murder was contagious and that touching the hand of a convicted murderer for more than three seconds was how it spread, a number that was as arbitrary as twenty seconds to wash hands or six feet to stop the spread of germs.

In a past life, Jack would've felt snubbed, offended. But that was long ago. His uptight personality had been reshaped, molded by the dark happenings of prison life. Now instead of being offended, he rather enjoyed making people feel uncomfortable, their reactions, the way they cowered into themselves absently. He laughed and leapt onto the magnetic levitating bedframe. It hovered over the ground forty-two inches precisely, with nothing under it but light and shadows. The mattress itself was only an inch thick, made of a metamaterial that absorbed the contact of his falling body perfectly. The material had since been used to create military and police grade Kevlar. It was lighter, stronger, and there was a massive gulf between it and its competitors in terms of efficiency. NASA and car manufacturers used it as the inner lining of insulation, the latter also using it for air bags, too.

Warden Fitzgerald's research laboratory was at the forefront of the burgeoning interstellar mining industry. While androids policed convicts down on earth, he had several teams on the moon, mining

Helium3, and they had just started their second colony on Mars. Every nine months, a shuttle full of precious metals and ores was shipped back to earth for the inventive genius to tinker with.

Father Rodgers examined the room. Jack enjoyed watching him make for the bed, think better of it, look around the room, contemplate sitting on the ground, then make for the bed again only to stop short.

Within the wall, like every cell in the nation, hid the typical furnishings.

Jack laughed lightly and said to the ceiling, "Can a *brotha* getta *chair?*"

A mechanical ticking within the walls startled Father Rodgers as unseen wheels and gears grinded and shifted. He went about in circles, searching for the source, when a retractable arm attached to the wall that was adjacent to the bed extended and a foldable chair was presented to him. Jack motioned for him to sit, and he obliged. He settled in the chair and with steady eyes, he looked at Jack, suddenly carrying himself with more confidence than before. There was a tenderness to his eyes, an apologetic sincerity cultivated by years of practice that Jack imagined every veterinarian has prior to euthanizing a family pet. He didn't say it, but then, he didn't have to. Jack could tell he felt bad for him.

Jack studied the young *padre*, who stood his ground.

It was Jack who finally looked away.

Father Rodgers's gaze crawled up the floor to the walls. He wondered what secret technology laid hidden within.

His eyes gravitated to the only other mass in the room save for the levitating bed—on the ceiling was a mechanical device with two arms and layered extensions that were retracted. On the end of the two arms was a netted device in the shape of a skull and dangling from the net was a breathing apparatus used to deliver sleeping gas. It looked like a cross between dentist equipment and a pilot's breathing apparatus. Jack followed Father Rodgers's bewildered stare.

"Is that it?" Father Rodgers asked, gesturing toward the hanging contraption.

Warden Fitzgerald's metamaterials paved the road into a new age, "an upgrade into the world of tomorrow" as it was advertised, far exceeding the industrial revolution or the information wave. Flying cars, drone delivery systems, 3D printed homes, Warden Fitzgerald's company had a hand in them all, pushing the envelope, leading the changing future by making the change.

"Sure is," Jack said, enjoying the novelty of someone new to play with. A new toy.

"So, every night when you go to sleep, you relive your crimes?"

Jack nodded and glared at Father Rodgers, who seemed extremely young to be a priest. Jack was clueless on the process it took to become ordained, but from the looks of it, all you needed was a high school diploma.

"How old are you?" Jack asked, shifting on the maglift bed. He was suddenly intrigued by the young man before him. *Who was this young man?* he thought. *And what gives him the authority to forgive me? Even when I can't forgive myself?*

"Twenty-five." Father Rodgers seemed a little too proud of his tender age.

"Huh," was all Jack could think of saying. He racked his memory, filtering through the mess of useless knowledge he'd accumulated over a lifetime of scholarly interest, trying to recollect something he'd read in a *National Geographic* article years prior about the reason most men of the cloth were old, and most women of the cloth were much younger. But his memory failed him.

And as he would soon discover, *not* for the first time.

"How old is the average priest?"

"I don't know," Father Rodgers said in earnest. He shrugged, then guessed, "Thirty-five?"

With the weight of certain death crushing down on him, guilt squeezing his chest into fearsome knots, Jack let out a loud rambunctious laugh. It was a nervous laugh, timid, like when the dentist tells you he ran out of Novocain just moments prior to digging in for a root canal. Jack was suddenly mad. Irate, even. Not for the young father before him, but for how his life turned out, for how his life would end. He projected that anger on Father Rodgers.

"What in the fuck could you possibly know about life, about death?" he said. "You're a goddamn child." The words felt like hot venom coming out of his mouth. He instantly regretted them.

Father Rodgers twitched suddenly and without cause. It was more of a jerk than a twitch. A violent jerk. Unordinary. Ominous. His slouched posture straightened, shoulders back, head held high as if he had a book perched on it, a malevolent grin tugging at the corner of his lips. But it was his eyes that worried Jack the most, for something had changed in his eyes, something subtle, but equally profound. Whereas before his eyes shifted timidly about the room like a nervous teenager about to steal a CD, now he projected utter confidence, pure and untapped.

Jack was mighty curious. He had met his wife at Stanford his senior year. She was a sophomore and an esteemed member of the drama club. He fell in love with her the moment he saw her, that day, so long ago, reading the horror classic *The Outsider* by Stephen King under the weeping willow in the middle of campus square. It would take him years to admit that he did in fact stalk her to the drama building, running, crawling, hiding behind trees and garbage cans. So smitten was he that he forgot his aversion to sweat, and as he lay between two bags of trash, breathing laboriously, sweating admirably, he vowed to produce the bravery to speak with her. He scarcely slept that night. The next morning, he signed up to be stagehand even though he had a massive workload writing his dissertation. He watched from the shadows her ritual preparation, memorizing every curve of her face, the way the skylights accentuated her high cheekbones and made the blue in her eyes pop. She did this funny thing right before she went on stage: she closed her eyes and shook her body (the same way Rodgers did just then) and when she opened her eyes, they seemed different, as if she were shedding her identity and assuming another. "It's how I get in character," she'd always say.

That's the impression Jack got just then—that Father Rodgers was shedding his identity and assuming another, switching roles, getting into character.

"I was an orphan, but I grew up in the church," Father Rodgers said. "In many ways, I have been training for this my whole life. I can assure you with the utmost of sentiment that I am more than enough qualified for the task at hand." He paused, squinted, then smirked slyly. "In fact, I may be the *only* person on this blessed planet that can forgive you of your crimes."

"*Crimes?*" Jack never attended church but for the two big holidays (Easter and Christmas) when his wife dragged him along like a captured slave. And even when he did attend, he surely didn't pay attention to the sermon. But he was quite certain that sins were forgiven by the church and crimes were forgiven by the state.

Father Rodgers seemed to catch onto this. "*Sins.*" He corrected himself. "I'm the only person on the planet that can forgive you of your *sins.*"

With the twitching attack that seemingly shed his meek skin, the inorganic bravado Father Rodgers tried to project earlier melted into the real deal, as if another person had shot down from the heavens and entered his body at freefall speed.

The Holy Spirit maybe? Jack thought.

It didn't matter. Jack was very pleased with the answer.

"If you wouldn't mind, I would like to begin at once." Father Rodgers looked at his watch. "We haven't much time left."

"Swell." Jack slapped the bed and sat upright before swinging his legs over the edge, his feet dangling a few inches from the ground, swinging back and forth.

"So, how does this work exactly?" he said. "I give you money and you pay Saint Patrick or what?"

"Saint Peter."

"Huh?"

"Saint Peter mans heaven's gate," Father Rodgers said. "Not Saint Patrick."

Jack twisted his face and said, "Then there's a drunken midget somewhere in Chicago that owes me alotta money."

Father Rodgers sighed the embellished sigh of one who wasn't entertained. He leaned back, clasped his hands on his stomach, twiddled his thumbs. His demeanor suggested annoyance but a well full of patience. Jack was impressed with his maturity, most twenty-five-year-olds aren't so serious. "Sorry," he said.

"I take it you don't trust the church?" Father Rodgers said.

"I've never given the church much thought one way or another," Jack admitted. "What I *don't trust* is man."

"Fair enough." Rodgers smacked his hands together then put his elbows on his knees, leaning forward. "I can leave you to your own devices if you'd prefer." He stood and made for the door.

"No, wait. *Wait.*" Jack grabbed the *padre's* arm. He noticed blood stains on the right cuff of the inner shirt sleeve, splotches like red ink soaking into a napkin. Jack lifted the shirt ever slightly, exposing more blood. Father Rodgers followed Jack's concerned eyes to his cuff then ripped his arm away.

"Are you okay?" Jack asked.

"I'm fine," he said. "I've a proclivity for nosebleeds."

He sat back down and waited for Jack to speak. They stared at each other for a long moment. The air buzzed with electricity.

"I just don't know how to start, s'all," Jack lied. He knew because his wife knew. They shared everything.

"Well, have you ever sinned, my child?"

Jack scoffed, winced, then stared bitingly at Father Rodgers who stood his ground, shaking his head, gesturing that he didn't understand the source of Jack's sudden anger.

"Please don't call me child," Jack said. "I'm twice your age."

"As you wish." Father Rodgers nodded respectfully. "Have you ever sinned, Jack?"

"Me, sin?" Jack lifted his arms as if he wanted to hug a massive bear. "Never. I'm just quite fond of my stripped liberties. But mostly—" he said looking at the walls, nodding, "—I really dig the state-of-the-art voice-activated latrine module."

The wall across from the bed lit green and an automated voice said, "Activating latrine module." The seamless wall yawned open, and a commode crawled out. Rodgers seemed stunned.

"Not now, Lucy," Jack said.

"Who's Lucy?"

"That's what I call the toilet voice."

Father Rodgers thought hard as he stared at the toilet. He re-phrased the question. "Is there something you would like to confess?" he said.

This struck a somber chord in Jack. He *did* have something he wanted to confess, something that had been weighing on him for years. He cleared his throat and began his confession.

"Forgive me, Father, for I have sinned," Jack whispered. "This is my first confession." His eyes were distant, obscure, locked on the cold concrete floor. Father Rodgers leaned against his cane. He attempted to make eye contact, but his efforts were futile as Jack's eyes remained staunchly on the ground. After a pronounced silence, he straightened his back and urged Jack to press forward.

"I'm afraid this is a time-sensitive matter," he said. "As you well know."

"I don't know where to begin."

"The beginning is usually a good start."

Jack smiled and nodded. He licked his lips, then: "It was a special day for my wife and I. But not special in a good kinda way. It was special in a bad kinda way. You see, it was the anniversary of a horrible accident we had eight years prior. As was our tradition, we went to the cemetery where the family was buried—to pay our respects."

Jack finally looked up. His eyes were full of tears, puddles that re-fused to drip. "It was the *least* we could do." His voice crackled with unseen pain.

Father Rodgers nodded solemnly. After a few short moments of continued silence, he motioned for Jack to continue.

Jack sniffled, wiped his nose, and complied.

"It's funny, most days of the year, I was on autopilot. Going through the motions of life but never really present. Which is how most people live their lives, I suspect. Day in and day out. But every year on August 8th, my wife and I, we would have an annual reprieve. It was the one day of the year we were able to take a step back and count our bless-ings. It may sound weird, and perhaps even a little fucked up to admit it: but it was hands down my favorite day of the year. It was the only day for certain when I was aware of every breath I took."

Jack inhaled deeply, his breath shallow, shaky. He heard his wife's voice. "Don't take it for granted, love." But he did take it for granted. Every breath, every moment, every experience. He took it all for granted. Everything. And now, with death at his doorstep, he wished he could have the time back. What he wouldn't give for just a little bit of time. But it was too late.

"You will feel better after you let it all out," Father Rodgers said. "Let it all out. Purify your soul."

Jack looked up, small beads of sweat dripping down his nose, connecting with the strings of snot dangling from his nostrils.

"On any other day, I would just wash the dishes or drive the car but on August 8th, I felt the texture of the bubbles as waves of a pleasant lemon-scented aroma ignited my sense of smell with every inhalation."

Jack got lost in the memory, experiencing a knowing nostalgia by the remnants of such a feeling. He could almost feel the bubbles now. Smell them. He stared at the ground with lost eyes. Father Rodgers knew his mind's eye saw something deeply profound: a nugget of wisdom about life that comes only with the promise of death.

Don't take it for granted.

Father Rodgers cleared his throat, beguiling Jack from his trance-like state.

"Then what happened?" he said.

Jack returned from whatever internal memory he had been lost in and continued.

"Jane and I were rolling high on the euphoria of just simply being alive. Ya know? That inner joy that just springs forth from your chest. It was the one night a year when we put down the electronics and played board games with our daughter, Layla."

Father Rodgers smiled and nodded. "What game did you play?"

"We played Monopoly." Jack laughed loudly, putting his hand to his lips, shaking his head, returning to the land of abstraction.

"God, did I *hate* playing Monopoly," he said to the memory playing on the ground. "It's such an insufferably boring game. But Layla loved it. So, we played. Now on any other day, my mind woulda been elsewhere—patients I'd seen that week, articles I'd read, planning our next vacation. My mind woulda been *anywhere* but there—but on that day, I was utterly immersed in it. We played for hours and ... and ..."

Jack's breathing became erratic. He swallowed huge swaths of air as if he had just resurfaced from an undertow that'd nearly ended him. He fell to the ground, pulled his knees to his chest. Then, hugging his knees, he swayed back and forth, crying.

Father Rodgers rested his hand on Jack's head. "What happened next, Jack?"

It was odd to Jack, this compulsive pushing of the story.

Didn't they teach students at the clergy some fucking tact? he thought. *Some bedside manner?*

He didn't want Father Rodgers's pity. *But you gotta warm a lady up before you try and stick the tip in*, he thought.

Father Rodgers had no warmup in him. He was all go. His complete lack of etiquette, though surprising, was also a blessing for Jack, a marvelous distraction allowing him to compose himself more readily. He took several deep breaths, searching the depths of his intellect to bring the memory forth. *There it is.*

"I read a bedtime story to Layla and then made love to my wife," he said. "I don't know why I did it. Maybe I snapped because of the anniversary or—" His eyes dropped, following the descent of his speech. He looked at the ground for several moments before speaking again.

"—Maybe deep down, on a visceral level, I felt guilty and undeserving of the perfect day I just had—that I deserved penance for depriving another family of such immense joy."

Father Rodgers kneeled beside Jack and embraced him. He whispered in Jack's ear, not words of comfort or solace, but words of encouragement to continue with the confession.

"You will not attain absolution unless you say the words, Jack," he said. "You will not be allowed entry into heaven unless your spirit is completely purged of sin."

Jack reined in tears and continued.

"I took a long shower, and we made love, my wife and I. Then I checked the appointments I had the following day; it was a light load. Only two clients. I brushed my teeth and read *Man's Search for Meaning* by Viktor Frankl. By the time I finished my nightly routine, my wife was sound asleep. I inched into bed beside her and stared at her until I finally dozed off, counting my lucky stars. She was so beautiful. The kind of woman you would have to look at twice, just to make sure she wasn't a figment of your imagination."

He straightened his back and met Father Rodgers's eyes. His brow furrowed and he shook his head, confused. "But this is where things get all wonky and confusing," he said. "That night, ya see, I dreamt that I woke up at precisely 2 a.m. I went downstairs to the kitchen and grabbed a glass of water. As I placed the cup in the sink, a butcher knife caught my attention. I picked it up, completely unambiguous in my intentions. As soon as my fingers touched the cold wooden handle, I was filled with a murderous impulse that never faded. It consumed me, entirely. I tiptoed back upstairs, crept into my daughter's room, and started stabbing her."

Jack was bone dry of tears. The moment of intense emotion drifted away like a storm passing in the distance. He recalled the event with utter detachment. It was as if he were remembering a grocery list, he'd written a week ago.

"I killed her dog after that—the fucking dog?" He shook his head in disgust. "Then dropped the knife on the blood-soaked carpet and went to the bedroom where my wife was sound asleep. I grabbed the sound pillow she got me for our anniversary and suffocated her. The casual demeanor which possessed me while doing all of this is staggering—like I was conducting another one of life's mundane task—washing the dishes, mowing the grass, folding the laundry. I fucking killed her on autopilot. I killed them both. When she stopped struggling, I laid beside her and drifted to sleep. I was tired. I remember that. But how I was able to fall asleep, to this day, it astounds me. I had not a care in the world. Not a *fucking* care in the world.

"The next morning, I realized my dream was actually a memory. I stabbed my baby girl twenty-three times. There is no place in heaven for me."

Father Rodgers placed his hand on Jack's head and recited a prayer in a language that was foreign to Jack. Even though he didn't understand the words, the incantation was oddly comforting. Liberating, even. It was rare for him, experiencing such a freeing feeling. He opened his heart up, surrendered his life, gave it to a higher power whom he chose to call Jesus Christ. He'd never felt so free in his entire life. It was like he was soaring in the clouds. His stomach filled with an intoxicating sereneness that was majestic, empowering. Father Rodgers continued speaking in whispers. As the words washed over Jack, something within him awoke. He began to weep, not tears of anguish or regret or pain, but tears of forgiveness, reconciliation. Tears of salvation—in fact, letting go of his past. Father Rodgers grabbed him firmly by the shoulders and stood him erect. He looked Jack in the eyes and told him that he would be allowed entry into heaven if only he said ten "Our Fathers."

Jack was astonished by the meager fee for atonement dished out by one of God's homies. But he most definitely was not disappointed.

He recited the given punishment on his knees, rocking humbly back and forth, the freeing love of God coursing through him. He laid there in the child's pose for a few seconds more then he stood and lunged at Father Rodgers, swallowing him in his arms, squeezing him, holding him until Father Rodgers cleared his throat.

"Sorry." Jack laughed. "Didn't mean to make it weird."

"No worries."

They took their seats, Jack on the maglev bed and Father on the chair. Each were lost in thought, Jack brimming with a freedom and inner joy he'd never experienced before and Father Rodgers seemingly brooding over something or another. He was clearly upset about something. Jack was perplexed.

"Are you okay, *Padre?*" he asked.

"You mentioned a tragic accident earlier," Father Rodgers said. "Something about a family."

All at once the bubble of serenity Jack had been in, popped, dissipated. The faucet in his tear ducts turned on. He began to cry. He fell to his knees and begged Father Rodgers to listen to one more confession. "*Please*," he said. "Just one more."

Father Rodgers glanced at his watch and nodded.

Confession 2

"My wife and I were heading home from her parents' house in Boston. It was their fortieth anniversary and a rare treat for Janey, who hadn't seen her siblings together at the same time in something like twenty years. Jane's parents were Irish immigrants, from the motherland itself, Dublin. As you can imagine, the occasion turned into a drinking affair. My wife was seven months pregnant with my daughter, so she only had a few glasses of wine. Whenever I objected, she pulled the doctor card. 'You worry about shrinking people's heads, my pretty 'lil darling,' she said. 'I'll worry about the medicinal side.'

"She had her own practice, ya know?"

Jack smiled, the memory of her face, her hair, potent and fading in equal measures. The sadistic ritual of seeing her every night, of murdering her every night, didn't help him remember her face as one would think. Her memory was fading from him at the same rate it would without the nightly visits provided by the Lullaby.

"Now, I'm not one to back down from a challenge," Jack said, "so when my five brothers-in-law challenged me to some beer bongs, I answered the call and drank more than I care to remember."

Jack stopped and smiled, remembering how after his fifth consecutive beer bong, he vomited back into the translucent tube, but he refused to let his mouth break the seal. The vomit mixed with the golden lager. He took a few moments to compose himself, looking at chunks of cabbage and corned beef floating, spinning. He had a determined look in his eyes, a look his wife knew well. "Don't you dare do it," she said. He wanted to laugh but that would've broken the seal, spilling the contents and every Irish man worth their salt lived by the golden rule: You never spill liquor.

To combat the urge to laugh, he parachuted the rest—vomit and all—quickly and efficiently. He remembered jumping up and down, his belly a tumbling mass of liquid swishing and mixing with the remnants of his last meal.

He doesn't remember much after that.

"Yeah, I was in no condition to drive," Jack admitted. He paused, biting his bottom lip, a compulsive habit his wife abhorred. He nibbled at an old scab, opening the wound. He stopped himself after the coppery taste of blood touched the tip of his tongue.

"That's disgusting, Jack," his wife used to say. He would chase her around, pinching her butt, blowing raspberries at her, tackling her, tickling her, kissing her. He could almost feel her lips as the memory swept him away to better times.

Rodgers interrupted the buzzing silence. "So, it was your *wife* that drove home?"

Jack was the lead psychologist and scientist of a crack-shot team in the behavioral health science department at Columbia University in New York City. In another life he was the world's foremost authority on schizophrenia, his paper, titled "Schizophrenia: The Hidden Battle," garnered him a cult following in the mental health community. His specialty was schizophrenia, but the study he worked on for ten years concerned patients with chronic mental illnesses. After countless hours observing patients, he quickly noticed Rodgers's peculiar idiosyncrasies.

Involuntary spasm of the shoulder and neck, he thought. *Recurring twitch. Mannerisms inconsistent. Maybe schizophrenia, possibly personality disorder.*

He fed the insatiable curiosity he'd had since he was six and his grandfather, who was also a scientist (aeronautical engineering), showed him how to build a rocket. Like Rodgers's spasm and twitch, this thought process was entirely involuntary, something Jack had no control over.

He caught himself, bringing his mind back to the matter at hand.

Once upon a time, he would've wanted nothing more than to have Rodgers lie down, close his eyes, and spill his guts out, peeling back the onion of his mind. The scientist in him begged for answers. But the man in him wanted only one thing: he wanted to feel the brief but potent feeling he'd felt a few minutes prior, the liberating feeling that comes only after cleansing one's soul.

He wanted to finish the confession.

He needed to finish the confession.

"It was snowing quite a bit when we left," he said. "Visibility was only a few feet. I fell into a liquid coma before we even left Boston. I probably would've slept until we made it back to New York, but my wife woke me with a godawful scream. My mind started spinning in a whirlwind and I couldn't tell whether it was the alcohol or the world that was spinning.

"Then came the screeching slide, and the hard smack." Jack smacked his hands together, startling Rodgers who nearly fell out of his chair. Jack smirked but kept his eyes on the ground where he knew hid the pop-out dinner table waiting to be activated when he said "Dinner."

"It was dark. The only thing we could see was what the headlights lit up. We were at a four-way stop on a dark country road. We hit a small car in the cross traffic. After making sure my wife was okay, I got out of the van and saw that the other car had been flipped upside down. I saw a spark then everything started glowing orange from the fire."

Jack's eyes grew big as he imagined the fire. He was so immersed in the thought that Rodgers could almost see the dancing flames, too.

"It spread quickly." Jack raised his arms as he spoke, waving them above his head. "Growing bigger. *Bigger.* When the car caught fire, I noticed a woman had been ejected twenty yards or so. She was clearly dead. The man in the driver side had a piece of our bumper lodged in his neck. I'll never forget the look in his eyes. They won't *lemme* forget the look in his eyes," Jack said, pointing toward the Lullaby.

He put his face in his hands. But he didn't cry. He just saw the dead look in the man's eyes, the same dead look that'd haunted his sleep for fifteen years. The memory of his wife was fading fast, but the dead man was seared into his vision. Guilt is funny that way.

"What about the kid?" Rodgers's tone sounded accusatory.

"What happened to the kid?" he said.

Did I mention the kid? Jack looked up, confused. Father Rodgers's face was flat, hardened. *I must've said something about the kid. But then ...*

Through all the long years, Jack had never spoken about the kid. Yet he had to have said something. But how? Why? Was it because of his impending death? Like his departed wife and daughter, anytime he thought of the kid, a sickening feeling sank to the pit of his stomach and rose to his chest. Guilt. Shame. Regret. Remorse. All mixed together like ingredients, using his stomach as a kettle, then lodging in his chest where it would remain for some time, rotting.

I must've, he thought, knowing full well he didn't.

"I heard faint screams layered under that goddamn alarm," Jack continued. "High-pitched screams. A child's scream. He may have been crying the entire time and I just then heard it. Maybe not. All I knew was that I didn't have much time before the fire got too big for me to help him.

"I struggled with the car seat but was able to pull him out just in time. The explosion was not like what you see in the movies. But for sure it would've barbecued the poor kid."

Jack laughed and felt bad that he didn't feel bad about laughing. He was never into dark humor, despised it in fact. But after a few years in the clink, every con develops sadistic personalities.

He remembered a particularly gratuitous joke Samuel had told him the first night they met, something about a Holocaust survivor, an oven, and dead babies. He was appalled at first. Now, fifteen years later, he wished to God he could remember the punchline.

"What happened next?" Father Rodgers was growing impatient.

Jack's scientific brain analyzed Rodgers's body language—the way he stared at him like a child asking their parents to open their Christmas presents early. *Please,* his eyes said. *Only one.*

"I took the boy to the van and told my wife to move to the passenger side. 'Don't get out of the car,' I said. 'Slide over the center console.' She tried arguing but I shut that shit down lickity split. She could see in my eyes I was about to do something stupid. She could always see in my eyes when I was going to do something stupid."—*Chug. Chug. Chug. Don't you dare drink that—*

"And she said, 'What are you going to do?' Her voice was shaky.

"But I didn't answer. I ran outside and made the snow tracks tell the story I needed it to tell. Jane only had a few drinks and was probably sober, but I couldn't take that chance. I just couldn't. She tried objecting but all I needed to say was, 'D'you want to have our baby in prison?'

"We got the story straight then called 911."

Rodgers shifted in his seat uneasily, his eyes bulging, unblinking, wrinkles burrowing into his forehead, etching deep crevices like the rolling dunes of an ancient desert. He took a deep breath, exhaled with force. Another deep breath. Long, steady exhalation.

Patient has General Anxiety Disorder. Presumably Panic Disorder? Patient appears to—

"*Finish the story,*" Father Rodgers demanded, interrupting Jack's thought process. "What happened next."

Father Rodgers seemed to be teetering on the ledge of some unseen cliff. The twitch from before returned and he jerked his head and limbs like a stringed puppet dancing vivaciously.

Maybe he's a sociopathic killer here to beat the chair and murder me—Jack thought, growing wary—*a crazed fan perhaps?*

Jack had gotten plenty of fan mail and hate mail in equal measure. He'd get panties smelling of roses, lavender, tuna. He'd get totes of boxes sent with chocolates, poems, homemade cards—and death threats, mostly in the form of either a drawing of a guillotine or a man hanging from a tree.

He peered deeper into Rodgers's eyes, the way he cowered like a scared child. Something about him looked mighty familiar.

Then it hit Jack and hit him hard.

His stomach rose to his chest, his heart thumping like a washer with an oversized load.

It couldn't be. Could it—

He did some calculations in his head. Counting years, trying to estimate how old the kid would be today.

Rodgers threw his hands up, apparently annoyed by Jack's silence.

Jack talked slowly—

"Because the roads were so bad, and the fact that we had no idea where we were at, the ambulance took over an hour to get to us." *He's about the right age,* Jack thought, *but it can't be him. He's walking.*

How about the boy? I must've mentioned him first. But—

Jack spent a few years as head liaison during a joint operation between Columbia University and the FBI, overseeing the psychological profile curriculum taught to cadets at the academy and training the counterintelligence investigators how to bait a perp into giving themselves away.

He knew Rodgers was horny for the child, prying, desperate.

He dangled the bait, watching Rodgers's reaction intently.

"You know what," he said. "I don't need to confess anymore."

"You did *nothing* wrong?" Rodgers's voice was filled with shock, venom, his face a mask commensurate with his voice.

Jack shrugged indifferently, further baiting him.

Rodgers clenched his jaw. "What about the boy?" His voice was low, shaky.

"They could smell alcohol on my breath and asked how many drinks I'd had, and I knew it would *behoove* me to not lie. So, I said, 'Too many.'" Jack intentionally left the kid out, acting as if he didn't hear the question.

"*WHAT ABOUT THE BOY?*"

Jack shrunk at the loud and unsuspecting scream. Rodgers was inching forward, his eyes full of rage, the thirst to inflict harm. The room filled with the dreadful weight of impending violence.

Okay, Jack thought, *the game's over.*

"The whole time the kid was screaming hysterically." Jack proceeded cautiously. He dug deep, finding that soft, gentle voice he'd cultivated after many years and many patients. "Jane held the kid tight, rocking him, humming to him the same song you were humming earlier. Same song, same tone, same tempo."

They locked eyes. Jack nodded, squinted at him, peering deeper, deeper.

"The kid was paralyzed," he said, "and I got five years for involuntary manslaughter."

"Why'd you take the fault?" Rodgers stared intently.

Jack laughed and shook his head. He couldn't fathom how Rodgers didn't know why he would do such a thing. "To protect my family," he said sharply. "Two people died. *Someone* was going to jail. I couldn't let that be my wife." He shook his head. "I just couldn't."

Jack felt great. His conscience was clean, the blessed feeling of liberation emanating from his chest made him feel fifty pounds lighter. *I should've gotten on the Jesus train years ago,* he thought.

His heart was light, and he felt the need to lighten the mood.

"So, what'll it be this time, *Padre*? Twenty bloody Marys and ten Our Fathers?"

Father Rodgers threw his hands over his eyes, desperately trying to hide his tears. Jack tried comforting him, but Rodgers withdrew from the contact, standing up and pacing the small cell.

Jack clenched his fist, ready to put up a fight.

Father Rodgers stopped in the far corner, his back toward Jack, his head and arms moving back and forth, speaking to himself in hissing whispers. His body shook violently for a few seconds before his posture loosened. He brought his hands to his ears and turned abruptly to the left, cracking his neck—*crack*—then to the right—*crack*.

He started jumping and rolling his shoulders like a boxer during prefight introductions.

Jack observed the mannerisms, the shifting personalities, the different look in the eye. Now he knew for sure Father Rodgers had a serious medical condition—dissociative identity disorder.

Or, more commonly known as multiple personality disorder.

Jack was perfectly satisfied with the conclusion. He knew Rodgers would have a different look in his eyes when he turned around, and somehow, he knew that he would also be smirking.

He was not disappointed.

Rodgers turned slowly, the smirk even more disturbing than anything Jack could ever imagine. "Remove chair," Rodgers said. The chair disappeared in an impressive display of ingenuity. Rodgers walked slowly to the levitating bed, his limp seemingly gone.

He sat on the bed a few feet away from Jack.

"I'm not a priest, Jack." Father Rodgers kept his threatening squint on Jack, nodding slowly. "Shit, I don't even believe in God." He rubbed his chin, revealing the blood-sprinkled cuff again, the blood-sprinkled cuff that Jack had forgotten about.

A sudden convulsion shook Rodgers out of nowhere and everything about his expression and demeanor changed. He looked at Jack, then started pacing. Every so often he stopped, whispering to himself, swatting at the air as if he disapproved of what was being offered, shooing it away.

More incoherent whispers.

Then, clear as day, "I'm not doing it," he said. "*You do it.*"

Dissociative patients don't have conversations with their alters, Jack thought. *Schizophrenia accompanied with dissociation, perhaps.*

Jack's mind salivated with the possibility. A combination such as that was academic gold. The prospect titillated his ego, launching his mind into abstraction—award-winning papers, fame, and, what most intellects crave more than anything, recognition.

"He should do it." The voice was distinct from the last one, smaller, anxious. Rodgers was pointing and looking to his left, shoulders slumped forward, an awkward air about him.

His knees buckled with a small convulsion, and it reminded Jack of videos of Elvis dancing.

"Get fucked," said another voice, higher, older—the baritone of the group.

The guardian perhaps?

Rodgers's posture straightened, he looked before him and stabbed the air with his pointing finger. "You're the reason we're in this fucking garbage of a mess," he hissed vehemently at unseen enemies.

Wheels, gears, and springs clicked and clanked in concert with each other. On the wall left of the door, a small square materialized and broke away, tilting at a 45-degree angle with its mouth open, waiting to eat the presumed garbage and fulfill its sole reason for existence.

"I'll *fucking* do it," Rodgers said. There was no convulsion this time, only a quick and violent shock to the torso. Rodgers turned and strolled toward Jack, kneeling before him. "I too have a confession to make Jack: My name ... is Jeff Roberts."

Jack stood quickly.

Jack's eyes were brimming with tears, years of pent-up guilt and anguish melting away. "I thought you were paralyzed?" he said.

Jeff smiled, rapped his knuckles on his right leg, then lifted his pants revealing a black titanium alloy, the same that the ACOs were made of, the same new cars were made of, jets, planes, trains, rockets. The metamaterial was created in a lab by a company owned by Warden Fitzgerald.

Jack had spent many sleepless nights thinking of Jeff Roberts—the poor child his wife had orphaned, confined to a chair for the remainder of his life. "I can't tell you how guilty I've felt over the years," Jack said.

He lurched at Jeff and held him tight, letting go after a few seconds with his arms on his shoulders, eyes glistening with tears of gratitude flowing through him in sputtering waves.

Jeff could sense by Jack's demeanor and tone that he meant every single word but, unfortunately, that could not negate fifteen years of stored hatred.

"He's not done with his confession," Jeff said coldly.

His confession? Jack thought ominously.

Jeff's Confession

"I grew up in an orphanage run by the church where pedo-priests traded children like livestock." Beads of sweat started to form on his forehead, nose. "I was so young. Most of us were. They liked us young.

"My first memories—"

"I'm so sorry that happened to you, Jeff. If I'd known …"

"—*Shut your fucking mouth and listen.*"

Jack nodded, his analytical mind noting the defensive and aggressive behavior. He motioned for Jeff to continue, gauging his demeanor and body language, anything to better understand the root and severity of his ailment.

In Jack's mind, he wasn't in prison anymore, he was in his old office, sitting on his two-thousand-dollar leather recliner with the matching ottoman, the one that his wife got for him when he started his own practice.

He crossed his legs, and took a quick glance above Jeff's head, looking for a clock that wasn't there. *Old habits die hard,* he thought.

"My first memories are of being mouthfucked by my monsignor," Jeff said. "D'you know what that does to a boy's psyche? The memory of it? The shame of it? The recurring dreams? It destroys them is what it does. Turns them into something they don't want to be. Makes them question their own sexuality."

Jack wanted to stop him and hold him and spend the rest of his short life whispering apologies into his ear, but he knew Jeff didn't come there for an apology, he came to be heard, to be validated. Jack sat in silence, maintaining staunch eye contact, nodding when appropriate, every so often pressing his thumb down as if he were holding an invisible click pen.

He looked just above Jeff's head again, searching for a clock that wasn't there.

"When I was six, Warden Fitzgerald's company made a sizeable donation to my church and started doing medical experiments on us orphans with the first models of technology that'd soon envelop the world. They fitted me with my first set of titanium legs."

The smile on Jeff's face looked wrong, misplaced. He was looking Jack in the eyes, but, it seemed, right through him, too, seeing something that wasn't there, a memory that wasn't there. He laughed lightly.

"They were large and clunky," he said. "Walking proved difficult. But I persisted, training by day, getting raped by night. When I turned seven, I hit a growth spurt and grew into the legs and as soon as I could, I tried running away from the orphanage, but I didn't even make it a block before those goddamn ocular scanners identified me and the android PD brought me back. That mother fucker tortured me endlessly for a week." The smile looked evil now. "But monsignor got his in the end."

Jeff tugged at his clergy collar, removing it, and for the first time, Jack realized there was splashes of blood on the neck and torso as well.

"What did you do, Jeff?"

Jeff answered the question out of context—

"I tried killing myself and thereby was excommunicated by the church, sent to live in the state-run psychiatric hospital. Most of my time there was spent in a chemical lobotomy. The little I can remember, I wish I could forget—like the doctors and orderlies sneaking into my room late at night, laughing, taking turns.

"But Warden Fitzgerald had a dream, a dream that begot others to dream, literally, using us as guinea pigs to test the prototypes that would soon become what you and every other prisoner sleep with every night."

For the first time, Jeff broke eye contact, gazing up at the innocent-looking contraption—the Lullaby.

"Very quickly, those sick fucks learned that they could tweak and perfect the virtual reality system by wiping their nightly visits. So, while I was being raped, I dreamt dreams of the false reality they wanted me to believe. But the technology was in its infancy and defective and I knew reality from a goddamn screen memory. You want to know the difference?"

Jeff didn't wait for an answer. "Pain," he said, shaking his head. "And lots of it. They could figure out how to manipulate all the senses but pain. And there is no greater pain than the pleasure of being sodomized. I didn't want to like it. I hated myself for liking it. But I did.

"They gave me the boot when I turned eighteen. I had nowhere to go. No proper education. No marketable skills. I linked up with others like me—there were many—and picked up a few bad habits along the way.

"We pimped ourselves out to pay for drugs and one day, a man I had only seen in my dreams stopped on my corner, rolled down his window, and said, 'How much?' His voice, the way the streetlight lit his familiar face, the strands of white ear hairs protruding from his lobe, dancing in the wind like a sea urchin's tentacles—I knew that man as Dr. Valent. He was a scientist at the hospital.

"I said, 'Free if you feed me and get me off the streets for a night.' I thought he'd just take me to some cheap hotel, but we ended up in a high-end condo instead, one of many if I were to guess, one he used especially for his vices.

"After I killed him, I found a first-generation Lullaby stashed in his closet. He'd stolen it from the hospital and when I searched the hard drive, I figured out why his condo was practically unfurnished—it was his jerk-off cave. The sick fuck had all kindsa videos saved to the Lullaby, a virtual reality Disneyland where the sick and depraved could live out all manner of sin in the sanctity of their own living rooms.

"This was my introduction to the underground world of virtual pleasures."

Jack recalled rumors surrounding the evil underground virtual reality scene. How could he not? There was an endless news blitz for several years, an aggressive attempt to identify, stigmatize, and locate what the news called, "The crack house of the future."

The stolen Lullaby that was subsequently stolen by Jeff was only one of hundreds that disappeared from research facilities. Not all the simulations were of child porn and rape videos, though. The spectrum of fabricated realities was far and wide, feeding off humanity's most guarded proclivities and primal desires, ranging from scuba diving in the Great Barrier Reef to making love to Halle Berry under a waterfall in Puerto Rico and sky diving at freefall speed from the moon.

Some people wanted to relive family vacations, while others wanted to fuck their wife's sister. If you had the money, and a savvy practitioner, they could create a tailored experience to your liking. But humans are predictable creatures, and on the flip side of sex and adventure was murder, which is what many of the Lullaby modalities portrayed—unfaithful partners, obnoxious neighbors, your daughter's boyfriend, that jerk off who cut you off in traffic, ungrateful bosses, inept political leaders.

You could murder anyone you wanted. Jack always thought the proliferation of which the news went on about the stolen Lullaby technology, "that criminal masterminds reverse engineer and use as a method to deliver sin," was misleading and furthered an agenda paid for by Fitzgerald's company to deter people from using their stolen technology.

But looking into Jeff's eyes, he no longer believed that.

"I brought the prototype to some tech savvy addicts, and they taught me how to tweak it. We started charging people for their heart's desire by the hour. We ran several VR houses, whole warehouses with rooms separated by blankets on a wire, rooms with nothing but a cot and a Lullaby. I felt good about myself, proud. I didn't think I was doing anything wrong. Some people sell drugs, other people sell cheeseburgers, smokes, liquor, guns. We were selling dreams."

Jack could see in Jeff's eyes the utter conviction in which he believed this. And, in a strange, paternal sort of way, he found himself proud of Jeff, too. He'd weathered a shitstorm of a life and came out a champion, not a victim.

Not only did he corner a niche market, but he also practically created it, supplying a demand that was unending. And what's more, his product didn't create diabetes, high cholesterol, heart disease, war, cirrhosis, or lung cancer.

"I was visiting my parents' grave one year to tell them about their orphaned son who beat the odds to become a successful businessman when I saw you and your wife visit. I followed you home and was furious when I saw how happy you were—the big house, the white picket fence, the beautiful daughter, the professions that brought you both fame and fortune. And that fucking golden retriever. Where the fuck was my golden retriever?

"I wanted to kill you but that wasn't enough. Not even close. I wanted you to suffer as I had over the years. I needed you to suffer."

Jack's stomach dropped, and he felt as if he were at the tail end of a long climb up a steep mountain ten-thousand feet above sea level. The air seemed thicker, his legs, heavier. He could hardly breathe. His muscles felt weak, fatigued.

Seared memories flashed before his eyes. His wife. His daughter. His dog. All of them. Killed. Killed by his hand. But—

—was it really my hand?

"I watched your family play Monopoly through your picturesque front window, the epitome of a perfect family. That was it, I think, that was what made me do it—the charm of a family game night that I was deprived of."

The room started spinning as Jack took shallow breaths.

"I went home and tweaked a modality I'd programed just a few weeks prior—some miserable fuck who hated his life commissioned me to simulate a man killing his family at the dinner table with a butcher knife. All I had to do was reprogram it so that you murdered them while they slept. Easy peasy."

Their footsteps were faint at first; whispers of mortality bouncing off the narrow corridor walls—becoming more pronounced as they marched ever closer, closer.

"I watched from a window as you read a story to your daughter, then made love to your wife. A few hours after you turned your bedroom light off, I walked in the front door—you should really lock your door. The world's full of crazies.

"I grabbed the butcher knife and went to your daughter's room. I killed your little girl, Jack. *Me*. Not *you*."

They were both in tears now. One racked with guilt. The other with absolution.

"I crept into your room, injected you with ketamine, and suffocated your wife. After that, I slipped the Lullaby on you and waited. A few hours later, you started talking in your sleep.

"'Good bye, Jane,' you said, 'I love you.'"

—

"I thought you were the cause of my suffering, the cause of my empty life. I wanted to get even, kill those closest to you—as I thought you had done to me. Had I known that your wife was the cause of my sorrow, it would be her in a jail cell, waiting to be executed with the memory of killing her family instead of you. I'm sorry, Jack.

"Please forgive me."

As Jack walked to the chair that would soon end his life, he could hear Jeff sobbing in the distance. He glanced back and saw that he was curled in the fetal position, shaking, crying. Jack felt bad for him, he must live racked with guilt for the remainder of his life, whereas the rest of Jack's life would be over in a matter of minutes—and he couldn't be happier.

He was at peace with the world, the air in his lungs had never felt sweeter.

Today was August 8, 2095, and he wasn't going to take what little time he had left for granted.

I won't, baby, he thought. *I promise. I won't.*

For so long Jack had lived with the memory of killing his family. The internal anguish this caused, the shame, there are no words in all the languages in all the lands combined that can express a feeling like that. The thought sounded familiar, and he sourced it to something Jeff had said earlier—

"Do you know what that does to a boy's psyche? The memory of it? The shame of it? The recurring dreams? It destroys them is what it does. Turns them into something they don't want to be."

Jack could relate.

Now my conscience is free, and I am ready to die, to reunite with my family. Make no mistake, there is a heaven and now that I know where I'm going, I can't wait. I imagine you think me crazy for not being mad. And perhaps I should be. I imagine anyone else would at least attempt to clear their name, force a retrial—hell, Jeff is so distraught, he'd probably admit to the whole thing. But why try. I can see it now, begging the warden for a last-minute pardon because I was innocent, and it was the handicapped padre who was the culprit. He would've enjoyed a good laugh at my expense and continued with the show—he had a goddamn tee-time. Did he not?

In any event, I am not mad, I am not sad. I am genuinely grateful for the visit. My sins have been washed away, absolved, liberated. And as they strap me to the chair, I am not only ready for death, but I am actually looking forward to it.

I would pull the switch myself if I—

New York Federal Corrections
Execution of Jack Kline
August 8, 2095
Time of death: 1432 C.T.
Witnessed by Warden Fred Fitzgerald
and Father Jeff Rodgers

The Moth King

"C AN YOU TELL IT ONE MORE TIME, MAMA?" the baby moth begged. "*Please.* Just one more time."

"Oh, my. But I've already told it twice, tonight."

"I know." The baby moth pulled at his mother's long, spindly limbs. "But it's my *absolute* favoritists story," he said, chin to his chest, furrow in his brow, eyes like two big ponds of desperation.

The mother moth laughed at her son's innocence. "Well, okay," she said. "But this is the absolute last time. You must promise to sleep after this."

"Yay! I promise! I *promise!*" exclaimed the baby moth. He shifted his weight about and slid down his canopy hammock before wrapping his leaf blanket snuggly, waiting. His mother tucked at the veins that ran along the edges of the leaf next to his collar bone and patted his head warmly. She cleared her throat and begun:

"Long, *long ago,* in the time before time, when the sun was all alone and patiently awaiting the planets to form in the bosom of the great spiral, the sun was so *very lonely.* To appease this unending loneliness, it decided to create *millions* of children. And it was so. For eons they danced around the sun, frolicking about, enjoying each other's company, brothers and sisters of the high mighty sun.

"In orbiting the sun so closely, they retained its marvelous glow and exquisite warmth. Indeed, save for the sun's massive size, the sun's children were indistinguishable from the sun itself, for they were brilliantly bright.

"But as is often the case with children, they eventually grew up. And as the children matured so too did the planets and the moons of the Milky Way galaxy. The sun's children saw the planetary bodies form from afar and a burning desire developed in their very core. They wished to go out into the world, to find their own purpose and make their own way. The sun gathered them all together and told them they were created for reasons beyond mere companionship. She told them they were to go to the earth and with the power of the sun harnessed within their essence, they were to restore the balance of the universe. Because you see, the earth was in perpetual darkness for half its days.

"'Tis' true. The moon does provide light on some nights. But her children's lights were immutable and as eternal as the sun itself. As such, they were to be the light at night when there otherwise was only darkness. 'You were created to restore the balance of the planet,' she told them and when the bugs of the world entered their force field, they would be sacrificed. In so doing, these brave bugs were creating a world of abundance for those still living and the sacrifice would purify the souls of those willing to make the ultimate sacrifice. Theirs was the only clean death. And any bug that died by the hand or foot, or were eaten by prey, or succumbed to old age, they will repeatedly reincarnate until they finally obliged the contract of their souls' purpose and found a great zapping light.

"The sun held her children tight, and then from her heart chakra, sent out a massive Corona flare that was so hot, it glowed blue and white. The blast pushed her children off to their corresponding positions on the earth and lives in the hearts of the little orbs.

"There are many beliefs in the world today. But most will keep you stuck in a perpetual state of reincarnation. Our goal, as nocturnal bugs, is to find one of these children of the sun and die a clean death. Which is why a moth's life is by and large spent lurking about the shadows of darkness, looking for one of the sun's elusive children. The end."

"What a great story," the young moth proclaimed. "Have you seen one yet, Mama? Have you? *Have you?*"

"Not yet, my love," said mother moth. "I have, however, been acquainted with many of the false prophets. Remember always to find the white and blue lights and not orange or yellow ones. I'm told to follow the loud buzzing sound associated with it. For just as mother earth has its own resonance, so too does the sun and its children. They are elusive buggers, and they test our faith. But we are a relentless lot."

"Aww, man." The baby moth was clearly disheartened. The mother moth shared her son's disappointment. Wishing to put his little moth mind at ease, she consoled him with hope. "Not to worry little one," she said. "You mustn't lose faith. In fact, there have been credible reports of an orb child not too far from here. Which reminds me. Tomorrow I will be leaving with others from the colony to see if the rumors are true. Your uncle is passing through town and has volunteered to babysit you for free. I do not subscribe to his methods and ideology as he is a tad bit eccentric and a true outcast. But we can use the extra leaf rations that would otherwise be spent on childcare. So, I agreed to let him watch you until my return.

"He has forsaken the way of our great ancestors, choosing to live a nomadic lifestyle—traveling the world and obtaining blasphemous beliefs along the way. His faith in the moth prophecies have been compromised. So please, take what he has to say with a grain of salt. And no matter what he says, you must promise to complete your daily sacraments."

"Yes, mother dear."

When the moon's rays penetrated the thick canopy of leaves, the baby moth sprang to life with a series of rituals meant to commemorate the life-giving properties of the sun. But his diligence was interrupted by a voice, a voice he didn't recognize.

"Hello, little man," the strange man said. "I'm your uncle, Manny."

"Hello," said the baby moth. "I'm Marco."

"It's an absolute pleasure to meet you, Marco," said Uncle Manny. Marco nodded curtly then went back to his duties. He knelt and faced the east where the sun would be returning in a few hours, just as it returned every day. "Watcha doing there, little man?"

"I'm giving thanks and showing my undying gratitude for the sun." Marco said this in a scolding manner, as if he were annoyed that he needed to explain that which was abundantly clear.

"Of course," Uncle Manny said. "Do you enjoy spending your mornings doing these rituals?"

The baby moth examined his uncle's demeanor. There was something emanating from his eyes which was absent from any other moth Marco had ever encountered. There was no judgment residing within them. No strict adherence to false proclivities. Only a well of acceptance. The baby moth trusted him instantly and felt as if he could speak candidly.

"Not particularly," Marco admitted, "if I am being honest. But mother says I must continue to conduct my rituals so that on the day we find the great zapper, my soul will be purged, and I will be allowed entry into the great shining one."

"That great shining one sure is picky," Manny said. "Can I tell you a little secret?" Uncle Manny looked around, playfully spying for onlookers that he knew he would not find. He bent over and whispered, "Your mother is quite pious in her elder years. But when she was your age, she had a real rebel streak."

"I don't believe you," Marco said. He put his hands on his hips and as he shook his head. His wings vibrated in a low hum.

"What reason have I to lie about such things? She used to fly about the dark night, skirting her rituals. And I'll tell you what." Uncle Manny stood straight, shaking his head. "Oh, never mind," he said. "You're too young anyways."

"Am not," Marco declared. "What is it," he said, "what will you tell me?"

"You can spend your morning conducting these rituals. Or, if you'd like, you can come with me on an expedition of self-discovery. And I'll show you a world of possibilities that were previously inconceivable."

Uncle Manny saw that his nephew was flirting with the proposition. He enticed further. "Your mother won't be back for a few days," he said. "If ya come with me, we can do the rituals and chores tomorrow night. Together."

"But what if we stumble upon the great light and my soul isn't pure?"

"I don't know," Uncle Manny said. "What says you? Is your god so wrathful and unforgiving that he wouldn't accept you into the great shining hall just for missing one day of rituals? After a lifetime of devotion? Doesn't seem fair. Does it?"

"I guess not," Marco agreed. "Okay, let's go."

"Atta boy."

Uncle Manny rummaged through his sack and pulled out a large white clump that was brittle to the touch. He delicately wrapped the clump in a leaf and placed it inside a carrying bag that he slung across his shoulder and they set off into the great unknown—the forest. Marco stopped short. Only heretics and blasphemers lived in the forest.

"We're not supposed to go into the land of nod," he said.

"I won't tell if you won't."

Baby Marco had never been this far without his mother or an elder. But like all sentient creatures, the little moth was in a constant battle of duality between good and bad, dark and light. He rather enjoyed how good it felt being so bad. And he entered the only place he was restricted to enter.

As they walked, Uncle Manny spoke of his many travels. "You know, I've probably traveled more than any other moth in history," he said. "Yep, I've been all over this great continent and have seen every insect crawling or flying under the great shining one. And do you know what I've come away with?"

The baby moth thought long and hard. But he was confounded by the question. Finally, he shrugged his shoulders in defeat.

"I've found that you can't trust anyone who presumes to know the unknowable." Uncle Manny looked at Marco from the side, then nodded with absolute conviction.

Marco muttered to himself, ensuring that he understood what he had just heard. "Know the unknowable? Know the unknowable?" he said, shaking his head. "What does that mean?"

"Well, take moths for example. They spend the entirety of their lives looking for the great zapper and presume to know that their way is the only way for the salvation of their eternal soul. But how do they know?"

The baby moth was so transfixed by the new level of thinking that he hadn't noticed they had stopped walking in a field of dandelions. He watched intently as his uncle rummaged through his pack and pulled out the grainy white lump. He set it on the ground. Then plumped down on a small pebble that was nestled between a family of small pebbles. He patted the rock next to him and the baby moth sat down.

After a moment of pronounced silence, Marco said, "Well, *of course everyone* knows that the bright light is the only way to salvation."

"You must be careful, using such words, my young nephew. *Everyone* is so ... *absolute*, and deceivingly presumes that no one is left outside its all-encompassing grasps. Not to mention, it's a false claim."

"Is not?"

"It most certainly is," Manny said. "Do you suppose the birds in the sky spend their lives looking for the bright white light when they can simply fly to the sun itself?"

Marco had never thought of it in these terms and the thought snowballed in his tiny little moth brain into an avalanche of uncertainty. "What about the fish in the sea," he said. "There's no way they can even reach the bright light."

His uncle smirked, and said, "That's right. They *can't*. And if they can't, what do you suppose happens to them when they die?"

"What do you mean?"

"Well, if amphibious creatures cannot survive out of water, does it make sense that they could leave to find one of the sun's children? And if they can't find a great shining one, do you think God would condemn them by default?"

"What does by default mean?"

"Through no fault of their own."

"Oh," said Baby Marco. He thought hard and admitted to himself that it didn't make much sense.

"Doesn't seem fair," Uncle Manny said. "Does it?"

Marco conceded. It did not seem fair.

The baby moth racked his little moth brain trying to understand the unfair dilemma and his uncle pressed further. "Surely God wouldn't create a creature just to condemn them. Would he?" he said.

Just then the ground began to shake as a line of red ants marched toward the lump of sugar that was just a few feet away.

"And what of the lowly ants?" said Uncle Manny.

Marco had never seen such a display of unity before. They marched in a single file toward their mutual goal. He noticed how the tail end of the line was children and he became lost in thought.

The two of them sat quietly as chunks of sugar were ripped off and taken back to a towering mound in the distance.

When the last child climbed the cascading dunes and vanished within a cavity of the earth, Marco turned to his uncle, and said, "What do ants believe in?"

His uncle smirked slyly. "Welp, that is an outstanding question," he said. "Ants don't believe in an afterlife. They do however worship glucose and the queen ant."

"What's glucose?"

"It's sugar."

Marco gasped in horror. "Blasphemers," he exclaimed.

"They aren't wired like us and it's what their worlds revolve around. It's what gives their lives meaning and sustenance. Do you understand?"

"And why do they worship the queen ant?"

"Because she is their mother. She gives birth to the entire colony. And in return, they become her slaves, getting her food, worshipping her."

The lingering battle of duality within the baby moth grew increasingly dark as he became jealous of the queen ant. *Why should she have slaves and not me?* he thought.

Just then the air palpably changed and the dust on the ground began swooping about.

They looked up to see a swarm of bees jumping from one dandelion to the next. Marco could hardly believe his eyes. Trailing the tail end of the swarm was a handful of baby bees. They flew away into the backdrop of the bright moon.

Manny watched the excitement of the event turn to pure anguish on the face of his nephew. "Uncle Manny," he said, "what do bees believe in?"

"Aha, a lifetime of shelter has made your mind quite inquisitive. Well, bees, like ants, do not believe in an afterlife. And they worship honey and their queen."

Again, Marco gasped in horror and again, he proclaimed, "Blasphemers."

"They aren't wired like us and it's what their worlds revolve around. It's what gives their lives meaning and sustenance. Moreover, bees pollinate the world, and their hives produce honey, which is glucose. They feed scores of animals. So, you see, we live in a delicate eco system. A perpetual cycle of death and creation. But no one set of ideas is better than the next. We are all equal. Do you understand what I'm trying to tell you?"

Uncle Manny could tell that his words were falling on deaf ears as Marco was muttering the same phrase under his breath. "Those poor children's souls are damned," he kept saying.

"Damned is a tad bit harsh, no?"

"*No*," Marco yelled.

"How do you figure they are damned?"

"Because they will never enter the great light."

"Yes, but how do you know the great light is the only way to salvation?" Manny said. "Or that it even exists?"

"Because that's what God said." But even as the baby moth spoke, he knew. He knew he was lying. Deep down, he knew the dark side was winning the battle and that he grew increasingly jealous of the queen bee and her band of slaves.

"Let us be clear about one thing, buddy. God did not say any of this—moth did. The entire dogmatic foundation was conjured up by moth. How else would God leave the rest of his creation out of the loop? The birds in the air and the fish in the sea? According to moth scripture, only moths, lightning bugs, mosquitos and other nocturnal flying bugs who find the bright light can enter heaven."

Uncle Manny looked at his nephew, who had a disturbing look plastered on his little moth face. Manny wanted to free Marco's mind. But perhaps Marco's mind wasn't ready to be free. He felt bad and contemplated a different route to drive his point home. What he didn't realize was that all the baby moth could think of was how unfair it was that others should have slaves. And not himself.

"What about the kid that got squashed not too long ago," said Uncle Manny, pivoting.

"Max?"

"Yes. Max. He was your friend, yes?"

"Yes."

"Okay, perfect," Manny said. "So, your poor friend, Max, he died by the foot, right? Some giant demon squashed him like the bug that he was. Do you suppose he isn't allowed entry into the great shining one? Or is he fated to be reborn with another opportunity?"

Marco thought of the good times he had with Max. Manny was right. It did seem unfair. Max never had the chance to even meet the great zapping light. How could he not be allowed entry into the great shining one if he was never even given the opportunity?

Just then, a few mosquitos came buzzing about. Uncle Manny watched the curiosity form on his nephew's face. The mosquitos flew away in an instant. After a few moments, Manny broke the silence. "In all my travels," he said thoughtfully, "mosquitos are by far the smartest of all of earth's creatures and they don't even subscribe to the dogmatic scripture of the moth prophecies."

"They don't?"

"Nope. Their brilliance is commensurate only with their addiction for blood. Which is what they worship. It's true, they do getta bit belligerent when they've had too much of the sauce. But if ya ever have the chance to talk with one, they are extremely wise and enlightened creatures."

Marco looked scared and confused. Uncle Manny felt bad. His purpose was to expand Marco's horizons, not frighten him. "The fact is every creature on earth has their own set of beliefs and no one species is inherently correct," he said. "Because there's no way of knowing for sure, one way or another."

Marco contemplated this very hard and then he looked at his uncle with a smirk and said, "You can't trust anyone who presumes to know the unknowable."

Manny was elated and patted his nephew on the head. "That's right," he said. "You cannot trust 'em, I declare. But that's not to say you treat them any less. Live and let live, I say. If it tickles your fancy to worship balls of feces as the dung beetle does, then that's their prerogative. Bats worship the moon. Lightning bugs each other's lights."

"That seems a bit vain."

"Yes, well, no other insect is vainer than a butterfly," Manny said. "They emerge from the cocoon and worship themselves. There are hundreds of variations of dog religions. But they all spawned from the same one—the mighty bone."

Marco sat looking at the stampede trail left behind by the ants.

"What's wrong?" asked Manny.

"I didn't realize there were so many beliefs," Marco said. "And if there's so many different beliefs, that means a majority are wrong."

"Ah yes, but who's right and who's wrong?"

"Why isn't there just one belief?"

"I don't know."

"How did they all come about?"

"Welp, insects are innately wired to want and seek a purpose to life. Long, *long* ago, the first of us wished to make sense of it all. I mean the thought is confounding; it can drive one mad, ya know. What is the point of this racket called life?"

Marco didn't answer and Manny continued.

"I cannot tell you all the answers because I do not presume to have all of them," he said. "I figure it out as I go. But I can tell you what I believe: I believe the scriptures were created thousands of years ago to give insects morals. Otherwise, admittedly, it would be anarchy. But they were also created to scare moths into salvation. Insects can get crazy when it comes to their ideas. In that sense, an idea is dangerous. You must be weary of such an ideology, Marco. Most ideas are harmless. But ideas of religion can be very dangerous."

Manny looked at Marco who was hopelessly staring at the ground. He felt bad so he added, "But it was also created as a sense of love. I can see it in you and other devotees. It's like you guys know something that the others don't. And I must confess at times I envy insects like your mother because she full-heartedly believes in something that can't be proven and it gives her a sense of comfort that I'll never know. But to that end—is it a gift or a curse?"

"But who wrote our scriptures?"

"Moths did."

"But mother says it was God."

"Ah, yes. I always have trouble understanding how others understood this."

"What do you mean?"

"What if I told you a burning bush told me something? You'd think me mad. No?"

"Probably," Marco admitted. "But that's different."

"Is it though? All the commandments and belief systems from every religion stem from ancients professing to have been given instruction by the otherworldly. So, yes, in that sense the belief is that God told it to certain moths, and they wrote it down. Therefore, it is the word of God. But do you not see the problem with believing this?"

Marco thought long and hard before answering. "They could make stuff up?" he said.

"Precisely. And in the olden days, the scriptures were written only in Latin and were translated exclusively by priests. So, ya see, it gave the priests all the power which they often abused." Marco's jealousy of the queen insects transcended to the priest powers now, too.

"No one is born into a belief," Manny said. "If you take a moth at their birth and put them in a bee colony, he will undoubtedly worship the queen bee as everyone else does. So, you see, a belief is not inherently true. To the contrary. We are, all of us, a byproduct of our environment. We are raised into a certain belief, and we perpetuate that belief by enlisting our children into the same belief. So, beliefs aren't inherent. They are inherited."

"If that's true, then why don't you believe, Uncle Manny?"

"I am different, Marco," Manny said. "It's not that I don't believe in the great shining one or that I don't love him. It's that they don't believe in me. That they don't love me."

"What do you mean?"

"I'm homosexual," Uncle Manny said.

"Blasphemer," said the baby moth. But he instantly regretted it. "I'm sorry, Uncle Manny," he said.

"It's quite okay, little man. I understand how you feel. For a long time, I hated myself as well. But then I realized God made me this way. I didn't choose this. And so, the hate I had for myself, well, it kinda just went away." Marco could relate. It seemed unfair to create a creature a certain way that has been deemed unworthy. In his little moth brain, he imagined a day when he had his own slaves, and he could create his own laws.

"Uncle Manny."

"Yes."

"Why aren't homosexuals allowed into the great shining one?"

"Another excellent question," Manny said. "I can't tell you for sure. But I can tell you what I think."

Marco nodded.

"Remember when I said we inherit our beliefs from our parents?"

"Yes."

"Well, many of those beliefs are created to further the reach of the religion."

"What do you mean?" Marco said.

"Take for example the ants. They don't allow contraception because the more babies the queen has, the more slaves she has."

Baby Marco hated the queen's ability to create slaves. But he was confused about one thing. "What does that have to do with being gay?" he said.

"Homosexuals don't procreate," Uncle Manny said, bluntly. "There would be no more flock if there were no more babies. Do you understand."

Marco did understand. He understood more now than ever before. He looked at his uncle in a new light. He almost admired his bravery for not following the herd and being true to himself. "How'd you get so smart, Uncle Manny?" he said.

Uncle Manny laughed loudly and patted his nephew's head. "I've lived many, many moons. I have traveled about the world with an open mind. And without the blinders of the moth way, I was able to take in much more."

"I wish I was as smart as you," Marco said. "I'd do so many things."

"Like what?"

"I'd make a colony of slaves."

"That's an awful thing to say, Marco."

"I'm sorry," said Marco. And he was sorry. But he couldn't help the way he felt, and, in that respect, he felt like he was fighting his true self.

He thought if anyone would understand that feeling, it would be his uncle Manny.

"You are a very smart moth," Manny said. "You can be a great leader one day because you are not rigid in your beliefs. But you must be careful to not use your smarts for bad."

"What do you mean?"

"Well, take for example the eclipse that's going to happen tonight," Manny said.

"There's going to be an eclipse tonight?" Marco's mouth was on the ground.

"Yep."

"Nuh-uh."

"Is so."

"How do you know that?"

"I became quite chummy with a bat from a cave in West Virginia," Manny said. "He confided in me the ways of their people and taught me the cycles of the moon."

"I don't believe you," Marco said, his arms crossed, his head shaking.

"Be that as it may, if I knew something like the moon cycles, which I do, I could create my own religion and have scores of insects worshiping me." Baby Marco's mind drooled with the possibilities. "Now to the bats, knowing the predictable does not make you a profit. But with insects, who don't know these things, knowing the unknowable is indistinguishable from the otherworldly. And that's how the priest of old kept their power."

"Imagine what you could do with so much power," said the baby moth with big eyes. He imagined a world where other moths bowed in his presence of greatness. The thought alone made Marco feel guilty of self-idolization and brought the poor kid to tears.

"What's wrong?" asked Uncle Manny.

"I don't know who I am anymore."

"Sure, you do. You're the same kid. You are just free now."

"I don't feel free."

"Trust me," Manny said. "You are. The seed has been planted, and you will forever remember this conversation."

"But I don't want to," Marco said. "I wanna go back to not knowing."

"Cognitive dissonance is a foe to freedom."

"What's that?"

"Nothing. Look, I didn't bring you here and didn't tell you all this for you to have an identity crisis. I just wanted you to think for yourself. Okay? Because one day you lot will find the bright white light and I fear you will follow the crowd and march to your death."

"Yes, but that is our purpose," Marco said.

"I refuse to believe that God would create anything just to see that it has a premature death," Manny said.

"What happens when you die?"

"I don't know. No one does. That's what I've been trying to explain to you."

"Yes, but Mother says..."

"Stop it. Please just stop it," Manny said, his eyes closed. "Listen to me. Okay? No one knows what happens when you die. Because no one can possibly know. Don't you see? The great shining one is an insect construct created by ancient insects who were looking for a meaning to life and has since been used to conquer the minds of those who subscribe to it. If history has taught us anything, it's that controlling the mind is a prerequisite to controlling the body and has been at the root cause for many of our wars."

This made Marco very upset. "Can we go home now?" he said.

On their way back, Marco was completely silent. The baby moth was daydreaming about having the power of the priests of old. He was almost intoxicated by it.

When they got back home, his mother and several elders were waiting eagerly. "We have found one of the great orbs, my love," she said. "Can you hardly believe it? We must go at once lest we lose it forever."

"But Mama, I haven't done any of my daily rituals," argued Marco.

"Don't worry about that stuff," she said, dismissively. "We must go at once." She grabbed his hand and headed out of the tree.

Uncle Manny argued on behalf of sanity. But his logic fell on deaf ears. When he said his goodbyes, he whispered into his nephew's ear.

"Please don't go into the zapper," he said. "You will die." And he flew away.

On the way to the great light, Marco felt a wave of panic nestle into his being. He asked his mother how it was that he would enter the great light if he hadn't done his rituals. She told him, "Most of that stuff was rubbish anyway."

This floored him. He had spent his entire life dedicated to the rituals and lifestyle of the moth prophecies. And for his mother to admit it was rubbish was a direct assault on his life, an affront to everything he'd been told. He was overcome by rage and spite.

Marco heard the buzzing noise riding the moist air and he knew they were getting closer. Soon, above the buzzing noise, were zapping sounds.

There was a line when they arrived at the great shining one. Hundreds of thousands of bugs were flying about saying their goodbyes with giddy anticipation.

A group of mosquitos were huddled next to a small cavity full of water. Marco snuck away from his mother and started asking the mosquito questions.

"Hello, sir," he said.

"Wadaya want, kid?"

"Answers."

"What's the question?"

"Is the moth way the right way?" Marco said.

"What do you mean?"

"I mean, when we walk into the light, will my soul be purged? Thus, ending the perpetual cycle of reincarnation? Or are we just committing mass suicide?"

The mosquito laughed under his breath. "Oh that," he said. "What do you think?"

"I don't know," Marco admitted. "That's why I'm asking you."

"Look it, kid, I don't wanna step on any toes and ruin your belief," said the mosquito. "But if I were you, I'd escape at once."

The mosquito pulled his lips back and flew away. Marco looked past the mosquito. The orb of light was hanging from a gazebo in a picnic area on the lake. Directly above the gazebo was a brilliant full moon. Marco remembered what his uncle had told him earlier and just then he concocted a brilliant plan that would save everyone and improve his lot in life.

He started shaking vigorously and rolled his eyes in the back of his head while speaking gibberish. He could hear the excitement change and when he was certain he had enough attention, he stopped abruptly, opened his eyes, and screamed loudly, "Stop! Don't go into the light."

"What's wrong, honey?" Mother Moth said. "What happened to you?"

"The sun just spoke to me," Marco said. "She said she no longer wished for her children to worship her children. She said she wants you all to worship me."

Roaring laughter shook the gazebo, but Marco was steadfast. "I can prove it," he exclaimed. "There will be a full eclipse tonight!" There was a wave of gasps. "Blasphemer," said some. "There's no way you could know that," said others.

"What is this about?" one of the elders asked. "Do you believe him?"

The mother moth was a well-respected member of the community. But she refused to vouch for her son's insolence. "No," she said, shaking her head vehemently. "His crazy uncle has polluted his faith."

The line of insects continued into the zapping light. But it wasn't moving so quickly. The seed of doubt had been planted and everyone questioned, *What if he's right?*

Before long, only the hum emanating from the sun's child could be heard as no more insects went into the great big ball of light. They stared at the moon in wonder. *What if?* they thought.

A few seconds later, a shadow started overwhelming the moon.

Marco's heart leapt into his throat. His prayers had been answered. He will have the power of a god. "Hear me now," he said. "The moon aligns with the sun tonight, just as she sought fit for me to prophesize. Now, bow and worship me, slaves."

There was a great perturbance among the moths. Their hearts rattled and their wings vibrated with fear. There were hushed whispers, silent conversations conveyed by wandering eyes. Eventually, everyone looked to Methuselah, the oldest and wisest of all moths. His eyes dropped to the ground, vacant. He nodded his head subtly as if to answer an internal question that'd been weighing on him for some time, ceding to an outcome he was at first reluctant to accept. His weary knees bent ever so slightly before plummeting to the earth, prostrating himself before his new god. Half the moths followed within a second and the rest were bowing dutifully only a second more. Everyone but his mother, who stood staunchly, shaking her head, her face a perfect depiction of maternal discipline. Marco had seen it many times before.

She started for Marco, preparing to unleash the fury of a mother scorned, but when she was only five feet away, two of the prostrating moths stood and grabbed her by the arms. Her feet feathered the ground as she thrashed and swayed. She stopped fighting and locked eyes with her son. "You are no god," she said.

The sea of moths let out a loud gasp in unison. Already their collective indoctrination had transferred vessels, instantly elevating Marco to a status that was infallible. Marco acknowledged the reaction and smiled internally. Then, as he looked into his mother's eyes, contemplating what her fate was to be, memories of false rituals which had dictated his entire life flooded his vision.

His mother's voice echoed in a hidden cavity of his mind: "Don't worry about that stuff."

His whole life he'd been told no one would be allowed into the great shining ball unless they performed daily sacraments. And for her to disregard it right before entering a great zapper, well, it could mean only one thing: it was all a lie.

How many hours did I dedicate my life to these sacraments, he thought bitterly. *What percentage of my life has been wasted?*

He gazed upon his army of followers. Most of them looked at him with utter awe and respect. The others were looking at his mother with murderous hate. He knew what must be done.

"You leave me no choice, Mother," he said, stepping forward. He stopped a few feet away, his eyes squinting. "The mother sun has declared the great zapper to no longer be the way to her, but the conduit to eternal reincarnation." He smiled and exclaimed, "Into the zapper she goes."

The moths let out rambunctious roars.

They dragged the screaming mother toward the great zapper, blindly following their newly appointed prophet, intent on committing murder.

And it was so.

Vicarious Intruders

Part 1

JEROME MENGELE COULDN'T ESCAPE THE DREADFUL FEELING that someone else had commandeered the vessel that was his body. For despite a vague recollection, the man returning his dazed gaze in the rearview mirror seemed foreign to him. Like a bewildered Alzheimer's patient in the bowels of an episode of amnesia-induced paranoia, he found that riding the wave of panic was less rigorous than swimming against the current.

He surrendered and stared back—acknowledging the physical attributes as his own, sure enough. It was his face, of that there was no doubt, but it was not him. The conflicting evidence prompted a more thorough examination, upon which, he determined, it was the eyes that were the imposter, or, more aptly, the person inside them.

He opened his eyes as wide as his face would permit, desperately searching for some semblance of his former self in the foreboding vacancy where the eyes laid and lied. The exaggerated gesture made them bulge out of their cozy sockets, seemingly engulfing half the landmass of his face.

Yes, he was certain of it now, with unwavering conviction—it wasn't him.

The concept of gravity is often reserved, and exclusively so, for falling objects and large celestial bodies. However, its fidelity in that arranged marriage should be called into question, particularly when bearing in mind the predicament we find our mystified protagonist in. Indeed, there was no better word to articulate his circumstance without gravity's promiscuity in the erroneous matrimony. For the eyes held its gaze, captivated by an invisible force, infused with magnetic properties he was obligated to obey.

The wave of panic he rode heightened when he realized he could not escape the boundaries of the rearview mirror—gravity be damned.

A thick jacket of goosebumps enveloped Jerry like a layer of armor before suddenly, and quite inexplicably, the mirror fractured into three separate partitions. He thought it odd how no noise echoed the manifestation of the cracks—lightning without the thunder. Although he was looking into the left partition, the evidence refused to corroborate this, opting instead to divulge that the now pseudo-familiar stranger was still its sole occupant.

His focus shifted to the middle crack where yet another set of eyes, separate from the first but still not his own, stared back.

Distraught but not discouraged, Jerry noticed a familiar spark in the eyes residing in the far-right crack. It was, however, a reprehensible reunion that made him pregnant with disgust at the very sight of himself, and he yearned for the ability to forget yet again.

The silent wish was quickly granted as the cracks dissolved and absorbed into one another, becoming whole again, and he found himself right back where he started, gawking into the eyes of a stranger, utterly lost.

Before he could comprehend the event, he catapulted high into the sky and remained there, caught in the transparent canopy of clouds above and looking down on the world below. He saw two tiny black rafts afloat in a placid sea of milk-colored water—two rafts but only one survivor.

A large commercial freighter aflame and capsized, culminating its descent into the eternal abyss nearby as the howling winds carried whispers in the distance, coming closer and closer yet.

"This is your destiny," they whispered.

That was all Jerry could make out above the sound of the whispering gales and his rapidly thumping heartbeat. A small voice in his head concurred with the whispers. This *was* his destiny—to drift aimlessly alone for all eternity—a lost soul in the sea of humanity.

The whispers began screaming Jerry's name as he slowly descended from the clouds onto one of the tiny black rafts. Heat radiated off the slick layer of oil that rose to the top of the flowing waves and burned like liquid fire.

Suddenly, something like a robust piece of unchewed meat lodged in his throat. Jerry gasped for air and hunched over to begin the painful process of regurgitating the foreign body from his own.

A translucent tail squirmed out of his mouth. He took a deep breath, and the body followed. He took one more breath, and a massive maggot came sliding out like a newborn baby. The maggot crawled to Jerry, rubbing up against his leg, warm, familiar. He felt deeply connected to the creature, tethered by a long-ago encounter like a childhood dog had just returned from the grave.

Jerry belched loudly, and the afterbirth of a bloody finger and toe fell to the bed of the raft.

The distant winds picked up once more, carrying thousands of incoherent murmurs, which progressed louder the closer they got until they crawled atop of him like a heavy blanket. Jerry could make out only one distinction—they were all children's voices.

"Welcome home, Jerry," whispered the kid's choir in a staggered manner. "Jerry! Jerry! JERRY!"

There seemed to be an echo as the furthest winds caught up.

A familiar burning sensation originating at his fingers and toes sparked to life, and Jerry blacked out in anticipation of what typically succeeded such a feeling in his past.

He found himself back in the car. His intellect returned slowly at first; he struggled to remember even the most innocuous bit of information. *Where am I?* he thought. *Who am I?*

But the harder he tried to remember, the deeper into abstraction he slipped, sliding slowly, surely, from the grip of his mind. He certainly had no recollection of the bizarre experience he just had. It was nothing more than a collection of buried memories he was restricted to access now, a dream of which he was unaware—time lost.

Beep. Beep. Beep.

The watch his daughter bought him for his fortieth birthday beguiled him from the trance-like state. He remembered pulling into the driveway at 7:20 p.m. and nothing more. It was now 8:00 p.m.

Not again, Jerry thought, *not tonight.*

Although his nagging blackout episodes had increased of late, the missing forty minutes were the least of his worries.

He added the odd occurrence to a rapidly growing list of odd occurrences and made a mental note to schedule an appointment with Dr. Caulfield all the same.

Presently, he focused on the task at hand and reluctantly snubbed the voice in his head, the one screaming for him to tuck tail and drive away before exiting the vehicle. When he got to the front door, in one swooping moment, he conceded to desire over reason. He simply couldn't face his wife. Not tonight.

Just as Jerry turned to escape, an angry hand violently slung the door open. He cringed and turned slowly.

His wife greeted him with a familiar, condescending glare that penetrated the exterior of his manhood and imploded upon impact like a beau-bunker-buster designed to decimate a male's ego. The stare alluded to the probability that she was privy to him losing his job. Jerry knew before she even told him that Sal had called to see how he was doing, inadvertently sparing him from delivering the bad news himself—a bittersweet moment, indeed.

Jerry said a silent prayer as he bravely entered the house. He was terrified, and rightfully so, for there is no foe to man more cunning and capable of bringing him to his knees than a pissed-off housewife primed for combat.

What sets domestic warfare apart from its psychological (warfare) predecessor is that the former is predominantly one-sided, and there should be no riddle as to which side tips the scales.

The power residing in the missing Y chromosome is without parallel. Ergo, the tables of love are unequivocally tilted in favor of the species which is the fairest of them all. Indeed, a woman can be a man's most profound source of strength and inspiration and help usher him to inconceivable heights where dreams reside. Conversely, they can also be a soul-sucking succubus and the chained weight that drowns him in a dead sea of inadequacy.

She was the latter, and he was under her spell.

Oscillating screams ebbed and flowed across the house as Mary chased Jerry from one room to the next—an odd-enough occurrence at the

Mengele residence, where the illusion of happiness was more important than happiness itself. Although their portrayal of a perfect marriage was spot on, sadly, it was but a sham. The household seemingly fed off their negative energy and emitted a sinister ambiance, leaving the bright-white paint just a few shades darker.

As is often the case—in matters of domestic warfare—the fight was over money, or the lack thereof. Their daughter had just received an acceptance letter into Harvard, followed promptly by an admission bill. But Jerry could not fully appreciate the accomplishment due to incessant worry.

He could barely afford to support his wife's lavish lifestyle while employed and without a college education to boot. Drowning in debt, he was already working north of eighty hours a week just to stay ahead of the piling bills, but it was never enough for the insatiable Mary.

Jerry had promised her a world he could never deliver, an observation she routinely delighted in reminding him. However, divorce was not a viable option as he was still smitten with her, and she preferred misery with all his money over happiness with just half. A financial hostage was what she fancied herself, owed restitution for promises of a lavish dowry not obliged.

The steady stream of income was the glue holding their sham marriage together. With no money coming in, he was now expendable. Right on cue and with a twinkle in her eyes, Mary handed him the divorce papers. To have them this quickly, she must have been sitting on them for some time, just waiting on a reason to serve him.

How long ago did she have them drawn up? Jerry wondered.

A glance revealed she had filed a year ago to the day.

Upon seeing the date, his broken heart was liberated by a calloused contempt, and Jerry let loose, spewing a slew of demeaning insults aimed at cutting and cutting deep. He wanted to hurt her the way she had hurt him but realized from the apathetic look in her eyes, she cared not. His newly calloused heart was broken once more.

A strong woman in her own right, Mary countered with a venomous assault of her own with the revelation of the affair she was having with his best friend, Sal. She continued the verbal onslaught until an unknown force possessed Jerry to strike her. She collapsed to her knees and looked up in disbelief.

The maddening anger Jerry had felt just seconds before was replaced with a growing disdain for himself and the situation in its entirety. She started crying, and he despised himself for being the reason behind the tears. Even then, he still loved her.

But when he went to console her, she scurried away like a frightened animal and, once in the safety of a buffer zone provided by a corner of the room, she finally looked at him with disgust that was deep and pure. The vile look shattered his newly broken heart into eternal oblivion.

The void between them filled with a ringing phone; the contemptuous look of disgust transformed into one of high anxiety. Mary had dropped it when he hit her, and it was now closer to Jerry than it was to her. He took a few steps and picked it up. It was Sal.

Terrified of the irrational anger careening through every cell of his being screaming for him to hit her again, he tossed her the phone and stormed out of the house to lose himself on the beach.

Jerry had never felt more ashamed or alone in his entire life.

The full moon illuminated the night sky magnificently, but the light obstructed somewhere in the canopy above. He thought it odd how dark the surface was, given the moon's brightness which he marveled at, noticing how the distant craters resembled giant footprints.

Jerry listened to the hypnotic rhythm of the ocean as it ebbed and flowed, obeying the orders silently spoken by the moon.

"God's in the small things," he whispered to himself—a mantra instilled in him by someone long gone but never forgotten and then reaffirmed by his psychiatrist, Dr. Caulfield. Heeding their words, Jerry coerced himself to be more conscious of his environment.

He noticed how the cold sand seeped between the cracks of his toes like a blanket of ooze as the warm breeze gently caressed his body, unseen fingers giving a divine massage. He closed his eyes, and a band of seagulls sang their organic melody gaily to him.

It was far too dark to see more than a few feet, but he knew this beach well, and in his mind's eye was the layout—straight ahead was a commercial fishing dock; behind and to his left was an abandoned air force base; opposite of that, an Eskimo reservation. The two separated by a vast sea of bright green pine trees.

He had been escaping to this secluded nirvana for as long as he could remember. Walking it was his meditation, a transcendental pilgrimage that nourished his soul the way nutrients do the body—it was a magnificent gem tucked away in a small corner of his world.

Shifting lights from the Aurora Borealis danced quaintly in the night sky as if on a beat to the serene symphony provided by the surf that was gently crashing on the shore. He heard a familiar crashing in the distance, and although he couldn't see the source, he knew it to be a massive glacier, breaking off into chunks of ice and falling into the otherwise calm waters, reminiscent of his own life falling to pieces.

He decided to take one last walk in this paradise lost before taking his own life.

As he moseyed along, his thoughts drifted to the distant past and the nefarious environment in which he was reared. The residual abandonment issues that haunted every facet of his life stemmed from losing both parents before he was old enough to retain memory. His only inheritance was a subsequent attachment disorder that forced him to cling to people for fear of losing them, a character defect that made it near impossible for him to develop any meaningful relationships to note.

As Jerry reflected on his past, he realized the predominant emotion of his life was pain—*so much* pain.

If not for his best friend Sal, he surely would've killed himself long ago. Their friendship kept him alive long enough to meet the succubus named Mary, which bridged the gap to the only good thing left in his miserable existence—his daughter Mikayla.

A loving family was what Jerry wanted more than anything. Growing up without one of his own, he would daydream endlessly what it'd be like to be loved unconditionally and to love unequivocally. But when one doesn't love oneself, partaking in a reciprocated love is a futile endeavor, and the persistent insecurities were a constant nuisance in his failing marriage.

However, to be fair, for Mary, happiness was irrevocably synonymous with money. The former was directly correlated with how much of the latter was in their bank account at any given time. Her moods fluctuated as the amounts peaked and dipped, and if Jerry were to be perfectly candid with himself, there would've been much more dipping than peaking of late.

He knew his inability to deliver this material happiness was the driving force that drove his wife into the arms of his best friend.

At the very least, he wished he could say he was a good father, but deep down, Jerry knew this to be bullshit as well. He had spent most of his daughter's childhood immersed in work, discovering too late that the only commodity that mattered was time.

The ever-abstract concept of time was such that in the moment, it seemed eternal—a bottomless pit easily tapped into, until one day, and rather abruptly, it was all tapped out, escaping him entirely, and he found that instead of memories holding his past together, there was a cohesive string of endless excuses: *I'll catch the next ballet recital. It's just one piano rehearsal. She'll have other soccer games*—more excuses than there were stars in the sky.

Before long, her childhood was all but gone, and now his validation for missing it was gone as well. Jerry had always told her that he worked so many hours so he could afford to send her to a good college, a belief she nursed that slowly turned into her dream—a dream now destroyed, not for lack of intellectual capability on her end, mind you, but for financial incompetence on her father's behalf.

Jerry was never one to measure success in life with money. He even mocked the exodus to suburban utopia conducted by herds of the middle class in their absurd pursuit to attain happiness by way of material appropriation. But he was quickly learning just how easy it was to mock someone from a bubble of comfort. For without the safety net of financial stability, he could never be the man he wanted to be. His only wish now was that he would have enough courage to take his own life.

—

An hour had passed since he embarked on the path to nowhere in particular. *Nothing more than an hour closer to death,* Jerry thought, as the omnipresent memory of promises made and promises broken that had infiltrated every facet of his life and connected his dreams with his nightmares, and waking life, weighed heavily on him with the suffocation begotten by regret.

He had been living on borrowed time for longer than he cared to remember, because to remember was to acknowledge he had squandered the opportunity.

He planned to paddle out to the open sea in one of the tiny black rafts tied to the dock and drift aimlessly alone, dying the way he should've—once upon a time—before the squandered reprieve.

There's poetic justice in that, Jerry thought, *an honorable gesture to the universe for disrespecting its decision to keep me alive.*

With the welcoming certainty of death in his immediate future, an uncanny clarity formed fully developed within his intellect, and Jerry suddenly became overwhelmed with a childlike giddiness that spawned from a childlike anticipation, as if his death shared in the majestic and endearing qualities of a Christmas morning.

He was suddenly a man on a mission—his last mission.

But when Jerry turned, he was shocked to find himself standing in the same footprints he had made an hour before with his house only a hundred feet away. *How did I manage to end where I started when I walked only in a straight line?* he thought.

A sudden and severe drop in temperature made it so his breath was perceptible, which was peculiar because at the same time warm steam splashed off the crashing waves, filling the cold void with an inviting warmth that smelled of sea salt. It was like he was in a vortex of ocean currents of varying degrees.

He dwelled in the dichotomy for a spell, contemplating.

The warm water seemed to call his name, beckoning him to return to the womb from which he was born. He rolled up his pants leg and dipped his feet in the tepid water. The big toe of his left foot was missing. He quickly pivoted his thoughts to keep the painful memory marooned on whatever island of misery it had been for these past thirty-five years.

Although the full moon illuminated the sky in a marvelous display, the surface was still very much dark, yet there was not a cloud in the sky. Jerry wondered why the moon's rays couldn't penetrate the vast nothingness hovering above.

All the same, something made him pretend to bask in the nonexistent moonlight like a sea lion basking in the sun on an island of rocks. Again, Jerry recalled his childhood and begged a god he had never seen to see him through these tumultuous times.

Just then, at his most desperate moment, something brushed against his foot from the blackness of the vast ocean.

It was a glass bottle.

Then, as if God had spoken the infamous words of his first day's labor, the moment his fingers touched its smooth surface, the invisible barrier that prevented the moon's rays from penetrating the stratosphere instantly vanished—and then there was light.

The light bounced off the globetrotting glass and glistened like a diamond in a field of snow. However, the sudden divine illumination escaped Jerry entirely as he became transfixed by the faded wrapper on the bottle that spelled out MK ULTRA. Paralyzing anxiety burrowed in deep and evicted the suppressed memories which had previously resided there, forcing them to bubble to the surface like pools of oil.

He cocked his hand back, intent on tossing the bottle back into the sea from whence it came, until he felt something within it. Interest piqued, Jerry removed the cork and relieved the bottle of its contents with a quick shake. It was a scroll, brittle and yellowed with age. He took care of unrolling it, as to not further damage the delicate parchment.

The first few paragraphs tugged at the strings of Jerry's soul, and a foreign feeling of hope manifested within him like a sanctioned reprieve just moments before execution. So captivated by its grandiose candor, he forgot the losing battle with his wife, along with every other aspect of his unfulfilled life. Its relevance to his dilemma convinced Jerry that he alone was meant to find this message in a bottle.

He reread the first page once, twice, three times over.

Yes, he was certain of it now, with absolute conviction; it was his fate.

Using our lunar neighbor as a lamp, he read on.

Part 2

The Letter

To whom it may concern,

I will be dead before this manuscript reaches its intended beneficiary, which fate has vetted thoroughly and deemed worthy to receive. However, do not fret, for it is not your pity I seek, only your understanding.

In many ways, I am dying so that you may not only live but also thrive in every aspect of your life. Make no mistake about it, dear friend, this crude nautical vessel escaped a plethora of potentially disastrous fates to reach you, and you alone. As if by divine winds and a conduit of whimsical currents, it has reached the proverbial finish line in its epic odyssey when you, whoever you are, resuscitated its vitality and solidified your destiny with the very words you breathe life into, like an enchanted spell unleashed upon its utterance.

The laws of attraction, or synchronicity, to those savvy few, dictate divine intervention at integral epochs in an individual's life as to satisfy a copacetic course, consistent with the most favorable timeline for humanity at large. Indeed, the apple didn't just fall upon Newton's head. It was strategically situated there to inspire the desired consequence, which consequently conceived the complex concept known thereafter as gravity.

Instilling credence into its creation, the universe utilized said gravity by defying all probability of time and space and acquainting us precisely at a period in your life in which you most desperately desire direction—consider this correspondence the apple to your Newton.

Presumably, since you're reading this now, it most certainly means you're suffering from rampant emotional pain. You feel hopelessly alone in this endeavor and, indeed, those that have not yet come to pass; deprived of an intrinsic joy that most, nay, that all save you are born with, utterly convinced that your defective DNA is missing the prerequisite chromosome necessary to achieve said happiness.

I know this because I, too, share such an affliction.

As a matter of perspective, it just so happens, some say, the key to happiness is a matter of perspective. And what is perspective, if not a choice? This realization is paramount in the understanding that so too is happiness. For the choices we make about the events that take place directly affect the outcome of the event itself—rose-colored glasses to the initiated.

Too many of us walk around, cups half-empty, going through the motions of life but failing to live it, stuck in our heads in a perpetual daydream of the life we want when the life we have passes us by. And it isn't hard to understand why.

We, humans, are a dramatic and attention-crazed species, emotional masochists, and eternal slaves to the intricate idiosyncrasies of the human psyche and its endless array of manufactured crises conjured up by our primordial addiction to feed the egotistical beast within.

That vulgar voice in your head whose imperishable diet of victimized drama serves but as an appetizer to a gluttony of self-loathing paradigms and all its glory—an insatiable tapeworm which would cease to exist if only deprived of its self-sabotaging fuel source. And this holds true for ninety-nine percent of the populace.

For the remaining one percent—those unfortunates who've procured a surplus of unspeakable pain and anguish—happiness is an elusive sentiment; an unattainable fairytale, simply extinct in their repertoire of emotions.

The average person has no inkling of what I speak, but I'm certain you do.

I speak, of course, of how morgues would go out of business if not kept stocked with a fresh supply of unidentified bodies. Missing corpses with an attached Doe nomenclature, taken against their will and sold into a macabre underground railroad, meant not to free slaves but to keep them in bondage, disgracing and indeed mocking the famous enterprise with which it stole its namesake.

We seldom hear the bittersweet stories of brave men, women, and children held captive for years, decades even, before finally evading their captors. But when we do, it inspires something profoundly majestic within the human soul, tugging at the strings of our collective conscience and uniting us as one as we absorb a share of their pain in solidarity.

As if by grand design, an inconspicuous occurrence unfolds upon hearing the morbid news—the same sky becomes bluer and the same grass greener. You savor your next meal as a man on death row might savor his last. You can hear the birds chirping and smell the roses from which they feast. By grand design, indeed. Can something so conspicuously inconspicuous be anything but?

The tiding of misfortune instigates an involuntary inventory of our own lives, and the perspective allows us to take a step back and count our blessings, if only briefly. And sadly, it usually is, only briefly.

Not long after, we again become wage slaves in the cog that is the fast-paced rat race of today's society, letting this precious perspective slip through our very fingers as we embark on the never-ending pursuit to attain happiness by way of material appropriation, not knowing, we had it all along. For true happiness can only come from within.

You won't find it for sale at your local shop, nor will you discover it in an empty bottle of spirits, for many a man has drowned trying. Another may blossom this happiness, but the seeds must be sown from within first, as a seed cannot grow until planted.

This, dear reader, my dying wish, is that you stop wasting your life with the trivially mundane and choose happiness.

Perhaps some perspective can assist in this endeavor, so without further ado, here is my tragedy.

—

As the story goes, I was born in Green Mental Institution in Quebec, Canada, on the twenty-first day of the tenth month in the year 1953. My mother was a failed actress turned high-end escort and employed by the U.S. government. They used her as a pawn to monitor potential enemies of the state. My father fit such a profile.

Toward the tail end of WWII, shadow elements within the U.S. government foresaw the inevitable future of a juggernaut Soviet Union being their most significant threat and, wanting an advantage over their former allies, enemies of the state with expertise in specific disciplines were highly coveted and poached outright from the Nazi regime in a quick and concise operation, dubbed Project Paperclip.

My father abdicated and was granted asylum in lieu of a judge and jury at Nuremberg. They pardoned him and his band of criminal scientists for their heinous war crimes in exchange for their wits and services.

Theirs was an arranged marriage, my parents, as the newly acquired Nazi was issued a wife as part of his terms of surrender to keep him honest. The arrangement proved detrimental to my mother as the good doctor was all too happy to share in the bottomless supply of morphine at his disposal. As these things typically go, soon the morphine did not suffice, instigating her graduation to heroin.

When she was six months pregnant, she visited my father at work and ransacked his medicine cabinet. My father found her unresponsive with a needle still in her arm and performed an emergency C-section on my mother's dead body. I gasped my first breaths at 11:11 a.m. "An enchanted moment," I was told.

Due to my premature birth and addiction to heroin, I was only four pounds and relied on a respirator to breathe in my stead. "As fitting a way as any to enter the world"—again, I was told.

I spent my first few months in the hospital receiving daily doses of methadone to tolerate gradual weaning off the opiates entirely. Because babies in my condition often developed disorders that prove difficult to endure, even for the most seasoned of couples, the doctors urged my newly widowed father to place me in a care facility. He adamantly, and admirably, refused.

We moved to a small farm in Montauk, New York, where my father was encouraged to perfect the unorthodox brainchild he had birthed with the SS—the overtly occult organization funded his research in creating biological replicas—clones to you, along with the paranormal studies of remote viewing, astral projection, telekinesis, and the like. But the reason he was given a new face and identity, along with a highly coveted position within the U.S. government, was his trailblazing advancement in the novel study of Gedankenkontrolle—mind control in English.

He headed a top-secret program called MK ULTRA and used the patients at the mental institution as unwitting test subjects.

He quite literally wrote the book on trauma-based dissociation and fragmented compartmentalization of the mind. This highly controversial science requires its subjects to endure unspeakable procedures (in a hospital setting, it's called a procedure, but a worthy synonym would be torture), which overwhelms the patient's capacity to process the unfounded reasons behind their torture.

Contemporary science contends the blueprint that creates humans, and indeed, all living organisms, namely DNA, is the deciding factor for the tangible characteristics exhibited by any one entity. DNA determines eye and hair color, blood type, and even something as innocuous as the amount and locale of freckles. What's more, intangible characteristics such as athletic abilities and intelligence are also embedded in the double helix structure.

Like a recipe for ingredients to bake a cake, every attribute, no matter how minute, is mixed in the ovaries and placed in the slow-cooking womb for nine months at 98.6 degrees—a metaphorical bun in the old proverbial oven.

Without the assistance of an artificial facilitator (i.e., hair dye, colored contacts) these characteristics remain absolute and therefore are not subject to change. A cupcake cannot transform into a muffin despite any ambitious desire to do so, and just the same, blue eyes cannot turn brown nor brown eyes blue—or so said conventional science.

My father's Frankensteinian research empirically repudiated this long-held belief.

Before the war, he studied the metamorphosis a caterpillar endures to become a monarch butterfly—how they incubated in the cocoon and emerged a seemingly different species, yet the same on a molecular level, absolutely fascinated him. How could such an awe-inspiring change in nature occur without even the slightest deviation to its DNA?

He set out to familiarize himself with the intricacies of the transformation and found that although the DNA never physically changed, its expression varied in one profound aspect—environmental and hormonal influences during puberty (cocoon) forced the caterpillar to create different protein enzymes that targeted dormant genes, thus activating mass physiological changes.

In layman's terms, the production of the new proteins granted the caterpillar access to the full potential of its DNA—it was the manipulation of junk DNA to create something new out of something old. Since over ninety-five percent of our own DNA is considered junk, the potential for practical application in humans was infinite.

By locating where specific attributes resided on the double helix and finding a method to activate or alter it, you could theoretically play God (brown eyes to blue). But all hope was seemingly lost, as his thesis, although academically sound, didn't inspire inspiration from timid sponsors unwilling to fund an experiment that had no known methods of testing its hypothesis in a clinical setting.

How does one activate junk DNA?

It was an enigma wrapped in a conundrum.

Distraught over his inability to control nature, he wallowed in self-pity until Hitler invaded Poland. Then he became a high-ranking physician within the ranks of the SS. His obsession with manipulating the human genome proved especially intriguing to Heinrich Himmler and his never-ending quest to usurp the world with a master race of Aryans. Superhumans with Germanic blood and extraordinary powers whose dominion would reach every corner of the globe was the end game.

Himmler rewarded my father's ingenuity with Auschwitz, or,

more aptly, he was afforded unlimited resources and, perhaps more importantly, unlimited prisoners who were to be used as guinea pigs.

The process of trial and error is exponentially boundless when an experiment committee governs itself independent and, therefore, exempt from any regulations imposed by the state—the ends justify the means as they say. The freedom to produce by all means possible gave rise to his nickname—The Angel of Death.

To make a tall Aryan, he practiced tying a rope around opposite ends of prisoners and had horses stretch them until their arms and legs dislocated from the shoulders and hips and dangled by tendons alone.

Aside from being strikingly tall, the archetypal Aryan also possessed a set of gorgeous blue eyes. To satisfy this requisite, he conducted experiments that called for injecting blue dye into irises and even transplanted entire eyes from one prisoner to the next.

He was obsessed with twin children and terrorized them, gratuitously. It was like a game to him, the torture. First, he disarmed their guard with artificial kindness, he'd shower them with keen attention their own parents failed to exhibit. He would bring them treats to eat and trinkets to play with before physically mutilating and psychologically condemning them. The Jekyll-and-Hyde approach caused some children to display peculiar mannerisms which were previously absent.

Most died, but those who survived were so traumatized by the experience that they seemed like completely different people. This intrigued the ever-diligent doctor, prompting him to further explore the new development with psychoanalysis. That's when he discovered they genuinely believed they were someone other than themselves, and often, multiple people.

With an unlimited supply of test subjects at his disposal, the man known to his victims as the Angel of Death made his mark on history by delving deep into the dark abyss that is the human psyche.

Despite what you may think of him, you must admire what he did with the opportunity. By capitalizing on the ripe conditions provided by the Holocaust and exploiting a naturally occurring chain reaction that serves as a defense mechanism to survivors of severe emotional and or physical trauma, he accidentally discovered the new science of biogenetic manipulation; in trying to alter the physical appearance of prisoners, he unwittingly stumbled upon the key to unlock the full potential of their minds—essentially, Frankenstein had discovered the human equivalent of turning a caterpillar into a butterfly.

Using the scientific method as a model, he developed concise methods to alter the brain's molecular structure, creating entirely new pathways which activated dormant areas of the DNA once considered junk. The formula was quite elementary in its approach.

By subjecting susceptible subjects (children due to their still-developing brain) to a series of successively sinister stressors (torture, but particularly the emotional anguish created when an otherwise loving and compassionate parent figure suddenly becomes the source of their malady), the subject's psyche would fragment into an unpredictable number of compartments or partitions, each one housing a new personality, separate from that of the host.

My father quickly discovered a common denominator shared by all the new personalities—the sole purpose of creation for any alter was that of protector. The lot of them intended to protect the host body from future pain, be that physical or otherwise. Anytime the subject was introduced to new stressors, an alter would commandeer the body and absorb the pain in the subject's stead. He found that when the host's reclaimed their bodies, they were oblivious to the pain their bodies endured.

Also, by switching between alters, the body was able to remain awake for periods once considered impossible and although the subject was aware of their new friend, they were unaware they were one and the same person—compartmentalizing in the literal sense.

However, with subjects who harbored more than one alter, the relay between them was far too erratic and incredulous to analyze thoroughly due to its inconsistent nature. And surely, he would not have earned the title of Angel of Death if he didn't set out to control this as well.

To serve this purpose, he utilized a well-known hypnotherapy tidbit known as a trigger phrase where he could summon any alter on command by simply uttering a designated phrase designed to bring them forward. The words could be something as innocuous as lyrics from a song or a passage from a book, but once heard, whoever was at the helm of the host body capitulated to the desired alter.

After you've fragmented the mind and developed the necessary phrases to conjure an alter, the next phase was indoctrination. It was around this time in my father's research when the allied powers began divvying up POW scientists, and he became a ward of the state for the U.S. government. But the only thing that really changed was the name of the agenda.

Instead of superhuman Nazis, he used the trauma-based dissociation technique to create American superspies, each spy indoctrinated with a specific agenda or skillset reserved for a particular class of agent. Due to their expendable nature, patsies were the most common, but there were countless others, to include Manchurian candidates.

By switching between alters, the rest didn't feel pain; others could run like the wind, and others still were strong as an ox. The power of the mind is so unfathomably and incomprehensibly extraordinary, that if they believed it to be true, their bodies would literally transform to comply with that belief.

One alter could be deathly allergic to peanuts while another considered it a healthy part of their diet—and all in the same body.

Suppose the host was exposed to a foreign language before the "procedure" but unable to speak it fluently. In that case, they could somehow access recall memories and implement a Rosetta stone of sorts that dissected the language's dialectics in their memory banks. And just like that, they became bilingual—*voila.*

My father may have been a monster to most, but I was never exposed to such atrocities. However, to be fair, I don't remember much about those early days, only that he loved reading to me every day from his favorite book, *The Catcher in the Rye* by J.D. Salinger. I was even named in the author's honor, Jerome Mengele.

I also remember the unconditional love and undying affection I felt for him. Unfortunately, the stress the doctors warned of proved stronger than his love for me, and when I was four years old, he committed suicide.

My uncle Henry and his wife Mary took me in after his death. They had a son my age named David, who would become a fantastic source of strength for me and taught me how to find God in the small things.

We lived outside an air force base on an Eskimo reservation in Alaska, where my uncle owned a large commercial fishing company. He would spend the summer months at sea while David and I kept busy, playing with Eskimos from the reservation and the children of my uncle's crew. Mary homeschooled us warmly and showed me what unconditional love looked like.

Our charmingly minuscule county boasted the highest rate for missing children in America per capita, as evidenced by thousands of laminated missing person pictures which had accumulated over the years. The pictures were nailed to a sea of bright-green pine trees in the forest, sandwiched between the reservation and air force base.

It would've been a serene scene if not for the gloomy aura that radiated from the massive shrine-like locale which created an ominous atmosphere typically reserved for graveyards and other sites where the prevalence of human suffering was still very much palpable (Auschwitz and Gettysburg come to mind). To make matters worse, the anguish created by the loss of a child was powerful enough to make even the most rational mind, hopelessly irrational. So much so, in fact, mourning mothers often confused the ambiguity of the howling wind for their child's hopeless cries, and like a mother penguin, who can tune out the obnoxious chorus of tens of thousands of other penguins, and home in on their child's cries alone, once a mother believed she'd heard her child within the forest, there was no force on earth strong enough to protect her from herself.

The thought would consume her entirely, until the day came, as it so often did, when she conceded to the howling cries, and then the forest consumed her entirely, lending credence to the Eskimo nickname—The Forest of Lost Souls.

The Eskimos were a highly superstitious lot. They believed the forest to be an active realm where spirits of the missing children congregated. And every year, without fail, mourning mothers made a one-way pilgrimage into the forest. As was customary, they would later be found, still clinging to the tree that donned their child's picture, reinforcing the credence to the nickname entirely.

After the sheriff's wife heard witnesses reporting they had seen the ghosts of mothers walking hand-in-hand with their missing children, she became stubbornly possessed with the idea and yearned for the happiness in death that was lacking in life. She had already expired to exposure by the time the search party found her—still hugging the tree and looking up at the picture of her son. A deluge of icy tears trickled down her cheeks to her resting chin, where nature froze it to the bark of the massive roots. The unbearable agony she felt in her last minutes, frozen in time and on exhibition for the world to see as her corpse howled at the moon like some ghastly creation of a deranged taxidermist.

To spare the sheriff the grief of having to pry his wife's body from the tree that served as his son's grave, the team that found her attempted to detach her from the organic shrine but, ever stubborn in death, just as in life, when the men liberated her head, her bottom jaw refused to corroborate and remained attached to the root. The tears acted as vines and fused the two, refusing to let go of her son.

Depending on who tells the story, her bottom jaw might remain there, perfectly indistinguishable from the bark of the tree.

The day after her funeral, the sheriff made it mandatory to register each poster posting along with the tree's location at the county office.

We spent the winter months shacked up like a family of bears, squirreling away our dry food during the warm season, supplemented with game from our traps and fish from our holes. A wolf den within the forest prompted a running territorial battle as they preferred the idle meals our traps were often chock-full of.

Every year, they'd kill a few unwitting pedestrians who were insufficiently equipped to fend them off while fetching their traps. It was a debt we were all too happy to repay with a declaration of war.

In the winter of my sixth year, we trapped and killed the mother of a fresh litter. Uncle loathed the idea of them growing up together as they would undoubtedly form a hive mentality with an alpha male pecking order, so David and I were made to kill all but the smallest female. She was pure white, and if not for a set of devastatingly piercing blue eyes, she was barely discernible in her natural habitat of the snow-covered landscape. We named her Alice in homage to *Alice in Wonderland*. David and I became her alpha, and we, all three of us, imprinted on each other's souls.

Notwithstanding the potentiality of wolf attacks, and the ubiquitous fear of being the next picture that went up, winters in Alaska were rather enjoyable. I loved spending time with my adopted family, as a family was genuinely all I have ever wanted since I was old enough to want anything genuinely.

We kept to a tight regimen and rarely deviated from it. Uncle trained David and me in various disciplines while Mary was charged with the task of stimulating us intellectually. We learned to skin the game and fish we caught and cook it with a fire built by our hands. We burned through books the way most burn through newspapers. Uncle, like Father, had an affinity for *Catcher in the Rye*, but we read everything.

I was partial to American literature: Poe, Hemingway, and Bradbury were my favorites, but I read anything that fancied my interest, as I had developed an insatiable thirst for knowledge that was unquenchable with an idle mind. By the age of eight, I was reading at a level akin to a high school senior. Because of my precociousness, I have been told that I come off as pretentious in how I converse with others. To wit, my rebuttal is always, "I couldn't help my pedigree any more than the next person. One brought up reading classic literature speaks with a classic tongue."

On weekends, we were allowed to watch films on an ancient projector. However, we only owned *Alice in Wonderland* and *Pinocchio*. So, Saturdays were spent exploring the rabbit hole with Alice, and on Sundays, we lived vicariously through the puppet known to the world as Pinocchio.

Mary was a world-class marionette, and on special occasions, or when the mood struck her, she treated us to puppet renditions of classical plays.

This was my life for six years, and I cherished every waking moment of it. Ours was a simple life, but a fulfilling one, pregnant with reciprocated love and affection—until one miserable day turned into a cohesive string of miserable days and, thus, a miserable life.

Not many people can remember, with great certainty anyway, the day that will ultimately define their lives. The day that every other day uses as a reference point and is known thereafter, for better or worse, as either before or after said day.

I only remember because that day for me just so happened to be my tenth birthday.

Every year since my adoption, they would wake me on my birthday with breakfast in bed and a serene shower of presents and love that could make a king cringe with warranted envy. Every year up until my tenth birthday, that is.

Upon awakening that day, I was overcome with an irrational contempt for their inability to keep up with tradition. *Surely, they must be dead,* I thought. *What other reason could there possibly be?*

I climbed out of bed and opened the door, fully expecting to smell and hear the distinct crackling and aroma of bacon and eggs—an expectation met with disappointment as there was no fragrance to smell nor noise to hear. I stood at the top of the steps and called out to no one in particular. Deafening silence echoed back.

I guess here is as good a time as any to confess that since I've been a wee lad, not yet old enough to remember, I've been vexed with a debilitating fear of abandonment which prevents my inclusion (by default, mind you) in hide-and-seek or any other reindeer games that call for the absurd requirement of voluntary isolation. The silent revelry of the house exacerbated this fear and abetted a frantic search of the dwelling in its entirety.

The quietness progressively increased in volume by degrees with each passing room until there were no rooms left to check, and I realized the ringing silence was the only other occupant.

Because the cellar was off-limits to David and me, I overlooked it in my initial sweep. But when I opened the door, a distinct scent hit me as if the particles took form and smacked me on the nose. The light refused to submit to the switch's command, and I dared not investigate why.

From my purview, I saw the silhouette of a man outside, just beyond the patio deck. He was on all fours, akin to some class of large canine. His back was toward me, and his head was buried, shaking haphazardly about. Instead of clothes, he appeared to be wearing an eccentric costume of sorts. Nothing about this seemed appropriate, but when one has a debilitating fear of abandonment, *anybody* is better than nobody.

I ran to the sliding door and slammed it theatrically to ensure the world heard the accentuated feelings of despair behind the click itself. *Click.*

His posture straightened upright like a dog upon hearing something in the distance. What came next was so incomprehensibly surreal that for a fleeting moment, I was certain that I was the unwitting subject of a terrible folly—I was not.

He turned ever so slowly, still on all fours and growling something fierce, until finally, we locked eyes. It was my uncle. He was bursting out of an ill-fitting Pinocchio costume. But what caught my attention wasn't his attire, but the steaming innards dangling from his mouth. I followed the entrails to a set of devastatingly piercing blue eyes encompassed within a motionless silhouette that was clearly discernible in the pool of blood in which it bathed.

It was Alice.

He sprang from his stance like an Olympic sprinter unleashed from the block that held him captive and closed the distance in one blink, halting abruptly a half-inch from my face with a menacing, primal look emanating from his cold, dead eyes. The entirety of his face was smothered in fresh blood, still warm from its short expiration and radiating steam in the otherwise frigid weather. Strings of chewed meat dangled from his chin; his breath smelled of coffee, and death.

When one's blood becomes frozen, the ice in their veins anchors each extremity where they lay and arrests their ability to either fight or flight.

Yes, dear reader, I wish I could say I was brave, that I fought, that I ran, but the truth of the matter is that I froze.

Opportunistically, he grabbed my shoulders and thrust me against the sliding door. My head whipped back and made a muffled cracking sound as it acquainted itself with the surface of the cold glass.

As if it were a dance, he pulled me in again, this time almost coddling me in his bosom, before rocking back and launching me through the glass door. I hit the ground and hydroplaned on the broken glass. He let out a terrifying laugh, his chest bounced as he roared, drunk on malice alone.

Hopelessly frozen, I had no recourse but to gawk in horror as he grabbed my hair and dragged me to the cellar door. The foul smell residing in the basement had escaped my intellect. Uncle savored it, taking in embellished breaths of the seemingly divine fragrance.

It became apparent he meant to throw me down the steps.

I tried pleading with him, but as I soon discovered, there is no rationalizing with a madman.

Only my grip on the door frame prevented him from disposing of me immediately, and scarcely so. He grabbed my legs and shook vigorously. I used the momentum of the wavy motion to kick him in the nose, momentarily stunning him. For a moment, I thought I'd be free, alas.

The thought of freedom was followed shortly with a shooting pain that burned through my foot and up my leg like lava spewing through my veins instead of blood.

Uncle let out a guttural roar.

He took a heaving inhale and spit, blood and saliva spraying everywhere.

An object fell upon my stomach.

It was a bloody toe—my bloody toe.

I assure you, dear reader, I have neither the gumption nor the inclination to fib about such trivial matters—he bit my big toe clean off and spit it out as if it were a piece of unsavory taffy.

I began screaming and crying, although no noise corroborated this as I was unable to fetch breath. Despite the pain, I didn't relinquish my locked grip on the door frame. To remedy this, he tried peeling my fingers off one by one.

Suddenly, something warm and wet dripped on my hand, trickled down my arm, and rested on my chest.

I opened my eyes to see David, a bloody finger with hairy knuckles dangled from his mouth.

David winked at me and then nothing. Darkness.

When I awoke, I found myself in a dog kennel. It took a few seconds to realize I wasn't in a coffin and a few more before the terror of thinking I was in a coffin finally subsided.

A fucking dog kennel.

It was darker than the darkest of darks. The only light came from a swinging, low-watt bulb in the far corner, illuminating just enough to cast a shadowy world that nightmares are made of.

The dreadful smell continued to boast its talents and triggered the memory of a decaying buck, left from a wolf attack. Thousands of maggots slithered inside its eye sockets and outside its mouth, up inside the nasal cavity and down outside the decomposing esophagus. The ground danced in the shape of a buck as they feasted. The rotting corpse emitted a horrid smell that seeped into your pores and shrink-wrapped your eyes in a steady flow of stinging tears.

It's not a fragrance one could forget and was the same smell present. Thus, if logic were to prevail, a rotting corpse would be its source.

Thoughts can manifest physical ailments just as well as physical objects. Take, for example, the epiphany that the source of the offensive smell, disrespecting my senses, was likely that of a dead body—I remember wishing I could go back to a simpler time, just seconds before when only a missing toe and throbbing body were cause for concern. Times were easier than.

Composing myself, I tried, at length, to assess the situation and recognized the steady sound of an oscillating fan which was surely obliging Newton's first law of gravity. For if not, the dim light dangling from the flimsy string would have remained stationary, but as it were, to and fro it went—

—and to and fro it went——and to and fro it went—

Time ceased to exist.

I busied myself doing the only activity there was to do—gaze upon the swinging bulb. It became my new sun, my new god, a secular savior that required nothing of me save for eternal salvation, which it got in spades from its only, and dare I say its most devout, disciple.

I watched it circling about like a planetary body for an undisclosed amount of time. Indeed, trying to ascertain the time, when you have no means to measure it, is like trying to escape from a pond of quicksand; it only gets harder the more time and energy exerted, and I realized then how Edmond Dantès must've felt in *The Count of Monte Cristo*. For seconds feel like hours and minutes like days in an environment where time rescinds time.

I appeased my new god's prerequisite for salvation by counting the rotations of the orbiting ball. The hypnotic rhythm of the light lulled me into a deep sleep, and the acidic smell awoke me until the silent lullaby of the rotating ball transfixed me into slumber once more.

Suddenly, it started raining piss and shit from atop the kennel.

Now, dear reader, I assure you, this is not some euphemism for my circumstances (although that would also be applicable), but literal excrement and urine rained down until finally, God said, "Let there be hail," and there was.

Loud thuds started hitting the roof of the kennel, and with it came storms of maggots, slipping through the cracks and dropping on my person. I know what you're thinking, and I agree; just recalling the experience makes my psyche dwell in madness as if it was presently occurring.

I once read an article in a survival guide which endorsed the utilization of maggots when in a jam for nutrients and/or antiseptic purposes. Revolted, but exceedingly more famished, I shoveled the squirmy critters into my mouth by the handful and regurgitated them back into my hands before reinserting them back into my mouth.

We don't waste food in The Church of Holy Fluorescents, I remember thinking. *Waste not want not.*

The Israelites had to trek the rolling dunes of the Sinai desert for forty years for Yahweh to rain down manna from the sky. I'm unsure how long I had to wait, but it was significantly less time. I daydreamed of a time when I could be a missionary to faraway and exotic lands and enlist converts as a show of my appreciation.

After my meal, I begrudgingly submerged my foot into a slithering pile of larva to eat the bacteria and stave off the otherwise inevitable gangrene. They congregated to the gaping hole, and images of the buck covered in maggots manifested on the screen of my mind's eye. Before long, the buck was replaced with Alice, and my heart ached with acute sorrow as I felt her presence there with me, her warm coat, the sandpaper texture of her tongue as she licked my face. I got lost in the memory until I heard and felt the familiar thuds.

Another storm of maggots. Hundreds of them graciously fell from the sky.

Strange enough, the thought of them crawling on me was more appalling than the thought of them crawling inside me, so I shamelessly ate until I had a stomach full of a lot of larvae.

The key to a good maggot, like any piece of prime meat, is in its preparation. I found that marinating them in urine for approximately 150-200 bulb cycles provided the juiciest and, therefore, most robust meal.

—

I was enjoying my breakfast when, alas, the basement door swung open. There was a struggle on the landing and a loud crash down the stairs. Whoever it was grunted as they landed hard.

Uncle took the steps with the frivolous gait of a person on a leisurely walk whilst whistling a familiar tune. He dragged something across the floor toward the kennel.

It was far too dark to discern anything absolutely until Uncle lit a match which sputtered to life, illuminating just enough to see his face. He transferred the energy from the match to a small black candle that sparkled erratically upon ignition. He placed the candle on the ground, and just outside the kennel, I saw David's unconscious body.

Uncle went back upstairs without saying a word, and on the floor, I beheld in white chalk, three triangles connected at the tips with one directly in front, and one on either side, giving the dreadful impression we were encompassed within a pentagram.

Uncle moseyed along down the steps again, still whistling. I was able to recognize the tune. It was the song Pinocchio sang to celebrate his liberation from the invisible strings that oppressed his desired claim as a real boy.

Uncle's hand was wrapped in a fresh bandage with blood soaking through where a finger should've resided. I wiggled my phantom toe in solidarity. He carried a silver serving tray with food and water. He set the tray down before kneeling and marveling at me as he had done so many times in the past. The crazed eyes were no more, my uncle was back, and all would be well—or so I initially thought.

I noticed he had a tape recorder clutched in his hand, and then his paternal demeanor changed. He suddenly became giddy with anticipation as he raised his free hand above his head and came down slowly with his pointing finger extended. The dreadful feeling of sheer terror promptly resurrected from its short expiration as he hit play.

It was my aunt's voice in a suicide recording, naming me solely as the reason behind the act. It would appear my presence suffocated her. She felt trapped and could pretend to love me no longer than it took to end her life—just to be rid of me.

"I'm gonna open the door so you can eat," my uncle said. "Be good, or I'll unload this can of pepper spray into your eyeballs." He pulled out a can from his cargo pocket.

I nodded slowly and he handed me a plate of fresh-caught salmon, smothered in my aunt's gourmet almond sauce.

"What's dinner without a little entertainment?" Uncle Henry asked. Then he replayed the diabolical recording—

This is no way to live. He is despicable. Now I know why his father killed himself, and I'm certain his mother's death wasn't an accidental overdose, but a suicide to spare herself from ever seeing that ugly face ...

As I listened, I was bombarded with memories of game nights, and tickle fights, bedtime stories, and puppet shows. Despite what I heard, I yearned for her embrace. If I could summon all the physical pain I have ever experienced simultaneously, it would be trivial to how I felt at that moment. It was irrefutable confirmation of what I had always suspected: I was, indeed, unlovable.

The predominant feelings of inadequacy and unworthiness that had haunted my entire life intensified until my uncle embraced me with a loving hug.

Forgetting everything, I cherished that hug as if I were terminally ill, and it was to be the last contact in which I would ever partake. To this day, I can still feel the warmth created by the love behind the hug itself and mixed in with the sheer terror that promptly followed when he whispered into my ear, "An occupational hazard of being your guardian seems to be suicide."

He enunciated each word slowly. His lips and tongue wrestled with dry saliva that made a vile sound and sent shivers throughout my entire being, with every syllable seemingly glued to his lips.

He slammed the kennel door and cackled maniacally. Light from the candle bounced off his face and revealed empty, calculating eyes. The madman had returned.

He handed me a set of Polaroids, and laughed a laugh that resonated within my bone marrow and violently convulsed my body as it desperately attempted to escape itself.

He hit play again on a separate recorder.

Click.

The puppet song from *Pinocchio* filled the otherwise somber atmosphere with a welcomingly joyous vibe.

I have no strings, so you can see, there are no strings on me.

I was surrounded by the quaint chorus and realized there were speakers embedded within the structure of the kennel. He had somehow rigged it, so the song played loudly. My heart sank into my stomach and then launched back up into my throat.

Against my better judgment, I peeked at the photos.

The Polaroids were of a time sequence which, when flipped through quickly, simulated an illusion of an action, like a rudimentary movie. We made them often in the long winter months as it was a fabulously productive method to combat boredom. I only made it halfway through before I dropped them as if they had spontaneously combusted.

Uncle Henry's laughter intensified, by degrees, in volume and horror. Surely, it couldn't be. I picked them up again to ensure it was indeed what I thought it to be—it was.

The pictures revealed his meal preparation, and what I thought was an almond sauce wasn't nuts at all but our missing appendages in a blender mixed into a pre-existing sauce. My intestines twisted and turned and rumbled and grumbled before I ejaculated the contents of my stomach. I noticed, riddled within the vomit, tiny pieces of nail and bone—finger food in the literal sense.

Uncle reveled in it like some crazed character from an Edgar Allen Poe epic.

"How many people can say they ate their own toe?" he asked mockingly. Then he chimed in on the song's chorus still playing in the background. "There are no strings on me."

He blew out the candle and my god did nothing to save me but dance in the corner, methodically swinging on a beat to what was now my most loathed song.

Click.

The sound of the first tape recorder replayed my aunt's suicide-note recording.

Click.

A third recording joined in the festivities, and I was suddenly surrounded by ceremonial chanting in Latin.

Not to be outdone, my uncle was still reeling in his demented, cannibalistic prank, wailing loudly as if being burned alive.

Eventually, he obliged my frantic screams with dead silence.

Complete silence can be the scariest thing in the boundless imagination of a terrified ten-year-old, where ghouls, goblins, and all things that go bump in the night reside. The unnerving silence usurped any rational thought that perhaps nothing happening was preferable to what may come next. But the fear was far too strong to combat, and I pleaded for proof of life from the vast darkness.

My cries were answered by a blinding strobe.

The wall behind him was outfitted in a mirror that stretched the entire surface and presented a dreadful reflection of the scenario in its entirety. For the first time, I was able to see the source of the foul smell and the reason behind my maggot buffet. Dangling just a few feet above the kettle was my aunt's half-decayed body. She hung naked from a rope, tied to a beam. Maggots had already eaten most of her face off as the bulk of them congregated within the cavity of her open stomach.

The delayed effect made by the strobe light was akin to a tangible time sequence, and I watched, seemingly in slow motion, as a handful of maggots fell from the gaping hole in her stomach before hearing the familiar thud that I was already conditioned to associate with food.

Uncle was elated; he danced frantically to the music, mimicking the awkward dance Pinocchio does in the movie.

When I closed my eyes, my imagination ran rampant with the raunchy ridiculousness of my aunt singing and dancing along, her emaciated jaw moved up and down, causing a waterfall of maggots to involuntarily salivate my glands with every imaginary thud.

I opened my eyes. A slow-forming evil smirk tugged at the left corner of my uncle's mouth like an invisible fishhook snagging a demonic spirit, then he let loose with the pepper spray, emptying the contents of the can into my eye sockets.

"Who should I kill?" he asked. "Who's it gonna be, boy? You or David. Eeny, meeny, miny, moe."

I couldn't see, but I could hear the crackling of a plastic bag along with the stretching sound duct tape makes when a long strip is procured from its home.

"Catch a tiger by its toe," he continued.

I tried reasoning with him, but as we've established, there is no negotiating with a madman.

"If he hollers, let him go."

I screamed so loud it felt as if a plunger made of molten iron was rapping my throat.

"Eeny, meeny, miny—"

"*David*," I screamed, "kill David. Please don't kill me." The words stung like a hive of hornets attacking my throat and heart.

"Moe."

The sound of duct tape being applied to something saturated the air. I forced my eyes open long enough to see the bag over David's head. He had regained consciousness, and he struggled to draw breath. The tears felt like fire as they poured out of my burning eyes. Before long, he stopped moving. David was dead.

Uncle rewound all the tapes and set them to repeat on a loop.

"I'll be back in a few days," he said. "Don't go anywhere." Insert evil laugh here. "Look at the bright side," he paused, "you're the only person in the world who can say they ate their own toe." *Click. Click. Click.* "*There are no strings on me*," he said singsong.

He threw a bottle of eye drops at me, then I heard him struggling with David's body before casually heading back upstairs, whistling all the while as if he were hauling a stack of hay and not the corpse of his only child.

Not long after applying the eye drops, I began to question my senses. Everything became fractal patterns and a kaleidoscope of utter madness. There was a deafening thump on the kennel roof, but I more than heard it. Oh no, I do not spin a web of lies when I assure you, with the greatest of integrity, that I saw the vibrations it created and was certain, in my heart of hearts, that a massive, malignant maggot had landed there.

It took me some time to summon the courage, but ever so slowly, incrementally, I looked up and beheld a maggot the size of a fucking sea lion. It seemed to be basking in the orbiting sun in the same fashion a sea lion might on an island of rocks. Its mouth was the size of a great white shark and with teeth to boot—what a terrifyingly beautiful spectacle it was.

Its face was void of eyes, but all the same, I knew it could see me.

No ears graced the sides of its head, and yet, somehow, I knew it could hear my thoughts.

Just then, it shifted its attention toward the mirror, and as if to oblige my suspicions, it shook its head up and down in the universal sign for yes. The unexpected gesture forced a screech out of me, and I saw the sound slowly leave my mouth. The maggot chased the letters about and started devouring the seemingly delicious snack. It was then that I realized my sight of sound was better than that of physical objects, and I tried focusing my attention on the cacophony of noises.

There are no strings on me.

More drops.

Individual strings from the suspended rope attached to Mary's neck broke free from the noose and mimicked the erratic nature of vines, slowly growing down into my kennel before painlessly burrowing into my arms, legs, and head. Ever the marionette, her motionless body started contorting and gyrating with the mannerisms of a bull rider having a seizure.

More curious than scared, I observed the occurrence as the wave of energy made its way toward my end of the rope, and then involuntary spasms forced me to dance to the music.

More drops.

The room rotated and shook vigorously. The walls became malleable, pixelated, and then disappeared entirely. To my utter horror, I realized we were in a graveyard. Gravity defied logic as Mary floated in the air, and I became upturned in a fresh grave, riddled with snakes, skeletons, and the undead. As I hung upside down in the fresh cavity, tethered to Mary as her unwitting puppet, I reasoned that her death had become my own, and I was reminded of a passage from *The Emerald Tablet of Hermes Trismegistus.* "Tis true without lying, certain and most true. That which is below is like that which is above, and that which is above is like that which is below."

As above so below.

More drops.

My aunt rode the maggot like a wild mustang. They stumbled upon a dead body that had appeared out of thin air. Half the head was gone, and a baby who looked as if he were Achilles (if Achilles had been dipped in a pool of blood instead of the River Styx) was crawling in the blood from a massive exit wound in the man's head. The baby's cries rang in my ears like a gruesome gong, and when the vibrations reached me, I felt my skin and bones melt like ice on a mid-summer's eve. I bade the thought for the maggot to eat the sound before I turned into a puddle of mush entirely. There never was a more obedient giant maggot, for she did as I bid.

With my guard dog maggot fending off any potential sonar attacks, I fumbled for the drops, sloppily squirted, and a generous amount got into my mouth as well. Soon thereafter, my aunt sang along to the words still playing in the background.

"There are no strings on me."

Diabolical Latin chanting layered underneath.

My aunt's recording under that.

The words were in the shape of colorful maggots, slowly dropping on me like a rainbow waterfall. I dubbed the massive maggot Maggie and ordered her to eat her brethren so as to deprive me of the colorful shower bestowed upon my person. The magnificent creature turned to cannibalism in my stead.

The thought of cannibalism prompted a curious hypothesis. *Experts say eating human flesh will inevitably make one go mad,* I thought.

At least you can say you're the only person to eat their own toe, a voice in my head said before the thought of becoming a zombie became my mind's dictator of dictation.

Mary's demeanor changed to that of a brain-famished zombie. She held her arms out like Frankenstein and groaned mockingly.

My eyes burned.

More drops.

The putrid smell protruding from my aunt launched an attack against the blinking rays of light provided by the strobe. The pungent odor transformed into the shadow of a bipedal rat before my very eyes. It wore an orange tuxedo, with a matching bowtie, top hat, and monocle. The vogue vermin continued chomping the rays, which made a thunderous crashing noise that took the form of vibrations.

Vibrations vary in shape and complexity, but the vibrations created by a chic rodent, chewing on strobes of light, resemble tiny black clouds in the shape of a lone wolf.

Every bite spawned a new wolf, and before long, an impressive pride of howling canines engulfed the basement. One turned into thousands in no time, for the rabid rat was ravenous. Their howling looked like blood vomit, which my glutton Maggie gorged herself in. It didn't take long before the wolves became territorial, split into factions, and started fighting and killing each other.

The noise made from thousands of yelping wolves reminded me too much of Alice. I demanded the sound to cease at once—tens of thousands of wolves turned their attention on me, uniting as one as I was now their common enemy. They stacked onto each other and slowly took the form of a wolf titan until they were all connected like a demonic Lego set, tethered by hatred alone. The alpha male.

As it closed the gap between us, the saliva that poured from its mouth transformed into tiny wolves, independent from the alpha but still very much connected to the hive mentality. They hit the ground running wildly, but Maggie blocked their path and dug in for a historic defense that could only be rivaled by the last stand of the Spartans. The whiskers of Maggie's beard broke off into baby maggots and battled the wolf drones provided by the alpha's drool. It was a beautiful massacre.

The slaughtering of thousands of wolves is the most beautiful sound ever conceived. It was so divine that it neglected to even manifest in form. I believe if it had, my brain would have imploded trying to comprehend its exquisite essence.

However, the damn rat continued eating the rays, which kept the assembly line of nefarious wolves trying to eat me afloat.

"Eat anything but the light," I begged.

Shocked by the sudden scolding, but seemingly intent on eating its way out of its attire, the rat started eating the dead wolves, which my gentle Maggie neglected because, well, because giant maggots aren't carnivorous, only cannibals.

More drops.

I catapulted to a serene scene of fresh snow garnishing a vast forest of bright-green pine trees. I recognized it instantly as the Forest of Lost Souls. Uncle was busy posting missing person's pictures of David and me on neighboring trees. The kid in the picture next to my tree winked at me, and at that moment, our fates fused forever. Although, I must confess, this was lost on me in the moment.

Suddenly, the pictures became animated, and thousands of children sang in unison the chorus to the song playing in the background.

"There are no strings on me."

Hell's choir.

Like a man adrift at sea amid a hurricane, the recordings and hallucinations became nothing more than white noise, and despite the chaos, I managed to slip into slumber.

The dream world was like watching a gritty film on an old projector. The dingy-looking film projected a clip of me on my ninth birthday with my aunt and uncle looking on so happy and proud. David was helping me blow out the candles as was our tradition. But the harder we blew, the bigger the fire grew, eventually engulfing the entire screen, which served as a backdrop to the rest of the movie.

Memories from the deepest cavities of my intellect conjured forth and projected onto the inferno of the screen until the very fire that brought it to life consumed it.

A scene of Uncle Henry, teaching me to ride a bike, went up in smoke. Poof.

The scene melted seamlessly into one of David and me playing King Arthur's court. Poof.

Another birthday scene. Poof.

I had just recently finished *The Curious Case of Benjamin Button* by F. Scott Fitzgerald. Presumably, my subconscious had borrowed the flow of the dry ink to weave its own tale and as the movie progressed, my age regressed.

A man I recognized from pictures as my father kissed a baby before placing it on his lap and blowing his brains out with a double-barrel shotgun. I felt the baby's shock and watched in horror as the poor lad retrieved a slippery handful of brains and tried putting it back inside the massive exit wound. Poof.

Then there was a beautiful scene between my father and me at the park. Poof. We built a couch fort and made flashlight shadows. Poof. Poof. Trick or treating, Christmas morning, and learning to walk. Poof. Poof. Poof.

The love was beautiful and palpable and then gone as fire inhaled the memory.

I suddenly became intolerably squeamish. My stomach was in terrible knots and ejaculating liquid from both ends. My bones ached, and a nagging migraine left me without sleep as I desperately craved whatever life-giving sustenance was in the bottle the nurse used to feed me.

It felt as if a colony of fire ants were congregating just under my skin, crawling, scratching, gnawing, in some coordinated escape as they tried burrowing out; I scratched and squirmed from the withdraw until, alas, I heard the nurse come into the room.

The ritual of her getting me ready to nurse was enough to curb the craving, although I was still itching with anticipation like an eager kid on Christmas morning. My heart rate slowed down, and the elastic nature of my skin wasn't so taut. I suddenly had an appetite again, but it was not for food that I craved.

Until finally, I was sucking at its sweet nectar.

In the off chance that you, dear reader, have never experienced the same ordeal, I find it pertinent to illustrate the dichotomy—whereas just seconds before I felt as if I were to suddenly drop dead, a slow blanket of blissful ecstasy hugged my body before submerging me entirely, utterly, and unequivocally, completing me. Nothing else mattered save the contents of that bottle. It was the only companionship I was ever to need.

Poof.

A dead woman appeared on the screen. Her stomach was sliced open with surgical precision, and the deafening screams of a baby saturated everything. I could feel the cortisol pumping through its teensy veins at maximum capacity as it seemed to be aware that the fire on the screen was burning it alive.

Poof.

Deprived of its fuel source the memories provided, the fire self-extinguished, and then nothing. Darkness. But a different class of darkness. I no longer feared it, nay, I embraced its stillness. It was so simplistically serene, like a motionless lake that cast a reflection of what I felt inside—nothing.

The void was filled with vibrations of the same song but, at the same time, inextricably different. I no longer loathed the familiarity of the high-pitched voice and delighted in its utterance as if it were a completely different person singing it, and I heard it, I mean really heard it, for the first time.

There are no strings on me. But of course, there aren't!

The vibrations were intoxicatingly beautiful. Pure love looked like a bright-pinkish glow in the shape and fashion of Pinocchio. The glow pulsated in waves that exuded some form of a neurotoxic compound that closely resembled the effects of the bottle of methadone. The light lent me its hand, and as I took it, the love increased exponentially.

The strings attached to its body each detached in their turn, and when the last string disconnected from his body, all at once, he became a real boy.

I tried hugging him, but my insolent body disobeyed my mind's command. My feet rooted where I stood, my arms unable to move, and my head felt as if it had swelled to the size of a beach ball. Only my eyes had the facility of mobility.

An array of strings dropped from the sky and attached to joint and pivot points on my arms, legs, and head. I shot Pinocchio a suspicious glance, but the love auspiciously increased. He hugged me, and it increased evermore. He then held me at arm's length, and in the plastic of his eyes, like a rearview mirror, I beheld my entire being.

His left eye suddenly and inexplicably shattered into two partitions, but no noise echoed the manifestation of the cracks—lighting without the thunder.

The smell of singed hair rode the air like a passenger, and the feeling of unconditional love was promptly replaced with a fierce burning sensation. Presently, I struggle to find words adequate to convey what I felt then, dear reader. As best as I can describe, it felt as if I were being baptized in a cesspool of molten lava, filled with famished piranha whose razor-sharp teeth ripped off chunks of flesh just as easily as they would a wet banana.

Pinocchio never said anything. Although, he never had to. I could sense he was there to protect me, that he would even take my pain away if it were at all possible. Like a concerned parent having to watch their child undergo a painful procedure without the use of anesthetics, I knew he wanted to shield me from such pain.

I know it hurts, his eyes said to me, *but we must destroy the old to make room for the new.*

In the mirror provided by his eyes, the invisible flames that were the source of my torment spontaneously combusted, starting from the tips of my fingers and toes and spreading rapidly before drowning the entire landscape of my body in flames like a wildfire as seen from space, incinerating a continent from coast to coast.

Although the fire didn't increase in temperature, upon its physical manifestation, the pain did so as a child who's sustained a painless, mundane injury, until they see the gushing of bright-red blood, and then the pain is miraculously conceived.

From the ashes, the burned skin coagulated into a shiny oak rash that took the path of least resistance and followed the footprints already paved by the wildfire. The wooden cocoon spread rapidly, covering every square inch of my body, filling every orifice, completing the momentous metamorphosis—I was the puppet now, and he was the boy.

The Eskimos believe the universe communicates to us through our dreams. Some messages are clear and concise, while others remain a mystery, hidden in the haiku of subliminal messaging created by our subconscious trying to convey something or another. I had always fancied them a crazy lot, but after the dream, I knew my old life was gone, and something new was on the horizon for me. Something special.

When I awoke, the recordings and strobe light had ceased. As far as I could ascertain, the fat rat ate his fill of wolves before waddling off to a place yet unknown, yet a place known to suffice a heavy diet. Maggie had also migrated. I missed her instantly and was again left with nothing but the rotting smell and rotating bulb as companions.

"You're the only person who can say they ate their own toe," my uncle's voice said from the shadows. "There are no strings on me."

The room suddenly funneled and vortexed in on itself. I felt dizzy, and a numb, tingly sensation enveloped me like when your leg falls asleep, but my entire body—like a phantom body. Through the lens of time, it's easy to see how naïve I was back then, for I never considered that I had just been through the "procedure," and he had just activated my trigger phrase.

The kennel door swung open; I waited for the worst to happen. Nothing. I cowered out and noticed Uncle had what I initially thought to be a ghost with him. It was the boy that had winked at me from the missing person's picture in what I thought was a dream.

"Jer, I'd like for you to meet Sal. Sal, this is Jerry," Uncle Henry said. "Let's get this place tiptop. We've a lotta work to do in the next seven months."

From the storage space under the stairs, we dug up exercise equipment, boxing gloves, and protective gear. We put them in a corner and found books on various subjects: *Bomb Making for Beginners, Intermediate Code-Breaking Strategies, Counter-intelligence Methods of The Cold War, Emergency Medical Procedures Volume II.*

We set the books aside and drudged up weapons of every kind: ninja stars, nunchuks, daggers, swords, knives big and small, rifles, shotguns, and even heavy explosives.

"Welp, I'll let you two get acquainted," Uncle Henry said. "Sal, you're in charge. Tell Jerry everything he needs to know."

Sal was a lot like David, only stronger, smarter, and even more resilient. We had much in common. He had also lost his parents when he was too young to understand the significance but old enough to have been affected by the circumstances. He had just undergone the same procedure in his uncle's basement.

He then informed me that the fishing company was but a front that made millions of dollars in only a few months. But more importantly, it allowed my uncle's armada to travel under the guise of an enterprise while conducting clandestine operations for the CIA. Sal countered my hysterical laughing with stern discipline.

"You mean a spy," I said incredulously. "You're telling me my uncle's a spy?"

He nodded slowly.

"So, what's our part in all of this?" I asked.

I wasn't ready for his rebuttal.

"I'm to be an assassin," he said with a certain cocksureness. "You're gonna be a parrot or carrier."

I remained silent but knew he was telling the truth. It wasn't necessarily what he said that was so convincing, but how he said it. He had this organic confidence about him that was enviable, and I quickly resented him.

"What the heck is a parrot?"

My insecurity made the words come out ruder than I initially intended. But I could tell Sal didn't mind. His maturity in the face of everything we had been through was also an admirable characteristic. I changed my perception and silently gave thanks for his presence, laid to bed any jealous sentiments regarding his confidence, and vowed to become like brothers.

"A parrot or carrier is someone with a photographic memory. They can also repeat verbatim anything they hear," Sal said. "They're used as a tape recorder of sorts to relay top-secret messages without the possibility of interception."

I would soon realize that everything he said was not only true, but it was just the tip of the iceberg.

I didn't know it at the time, but I'd been training for this my entire life. The survival skills instilled in me, and the endless readings, were easily tapped into.

We trained rigorously for the long seven-month winter, Sal to be an intrepid spy while I read and looked at number sequences and codes all day just to regurgitate what I saw later. Sal was right; because the subconscious mind is a repository of everything a person sees and hears, it can act as a recorder if it's brought forward. I can remember every page of a phone book in the same manner ordinary people remember phone numbers.

It boggles the mind of the average person that one ten-year-old has the visual acuity of forty times that of twenty-twenty and can shoot a quarter at four hundred yards while another is capable of quite literally recording everything they see and hear.

But then, we weren't your average ten-year-olds.

When old man winter was subdued, we embarked on our vessels with the kidnapped Eskimos from the reservation in tow (I didn't believe it until I saw the kids myself, chained below deck), fishing for crab, tuna, sardines, and everything in between. We hit the Hawaiian and Pacific islands first and then made our way back to the west coast of the United States, Canada, and South America, carrying drugs, arms, and human cargo.

No, my astute friend, your eyes do not deceive you. Although the fishing business was plenty profitable, it was but a money-laundering scheme for our true trade of arms dealing, murder for hire, and human and drug trafficking.

We flooded the western United States with an inordinate sum of heroin, cocaine, marijuana, and sex slaves, with our biggest export being semi-automatic weapons.

The global black market does not recognize the FDA's authority in business matters, and as such, it doesn't adhere to the regulations set forth by them. They have their own monetary system with an implemented currency exchange that resembles something like the following:

American machine guns for South American cocaine

South American cocaine for Pacific Island heroin

Pacific island heroin for kidnapped children from Mexico

Kidnapped children from Mexico for kidnapped children from America.

I have often wondered why the *pinche gringos* (as the Mexicans called us) didn't just rape the *pinche gringos* we were trading. Surely, it would be wiser, economically speaking. But I came to realize the driving force governing the laws of any commerce is subservient to supply and demand. After all, the only thing that gives a diamond or a pearl its value is its rare availability.

People always desire that which isn't regularly abundant. Which in the *pinche gringo's* case happened to be unaccountable, dark-skinned slaves.

The last thing command wanted was a mission gone awry because someone recognized our Manchurian candidate from the back of a milk carton. To avoid this logistical nightmare, we imported most of our assassins and went domestic for our patsies.

Our jurisdiction was vaster and wider than any other cartel or organized crime syndicate because we were the United States government and could call the Coast Guard to escort us if it tickled our fancy.

The unabated freedom to operate without checks and balances created a perfect storm of opportunity that rendered people (primarily children) vulnerable to an insidious endeavor of preposterous proportions and serves as a testament to the monetary value created by the scandalous side of humanity and their ugly addictions. For without demand, there would be no supply, and thus, no business—and boy, was business good.

Uncle liked to brag and say, "We're bigger than Disney and more subtle than a herpes outbreak, hiding in plain sight on government institutions the world over."

I will urge you, dear reader, to refrain from judging the likes of Sal or myself for the fact that we were happy to be a part of this business and perhaps even a little proud. Although we had no choice but to follow orders, we knew we were contributing to an evil enterprise and despite ourselves.

When brainwashed, you become but a mere passenger in the vehicle that is your body, and like a hermit crab commandeering an empty shell that belongs to you, the recluse bandit was now at the helm. Once there, the vicarious intruder refused to relinquish its command and strings you along for the ride, for better or worse.

We did the jobs we were trained to do in the bodies we were trained to do them in, but it wasn't us doing it. Not really.

While at sea, that job was primarily as prison guard to the children being trafficked below deck. Uncle's fleet was thirty-three boats strong. Ours was the Odysseus—a tribute to one of Uncle's favorite books. But all the ships had names of seafaring characters from books of antiquity, men of renown such as Poseidon, Atlas, Gilgamesh, and Noah.

Each ship carried one child assassin and one child parrot, reborn in the basement of one of Uncle's crew members just as we were—a crew of adults who had undergone the same procedure as children manned each station.

Ozzy, Ray, Chap, and Hany were all on the Odysseus with Sal and me at one point or another, but you know them as Lee Harvey Oswald, James Earl Ray, Mark David Chapman, and Sirhan Sirhan.

We were the world's foremost authority on murder for hire and often won uncontested bids for the kind of special missions that allow for these patsies to be household names. Although there were thirty-two other child assassins in our outfit, Sal always received assignments that harbored zero tolerance for failure. He was our poster boy—Uncle Sam's nephew, Sal.

He'd embark on his missions with one of the adult crew members, as they were always dispatched two at a time, one sniper and one spotter, or, more aptly, one sniper and one patsy. While anxiously awaiting his return, we'd hear on the radio how authorities had arrested a lone gunman—it was always a lone gunman.

We would then put (IT) our pawns in the media to work, and they'd flood the radio waves with a deceitful web of perception management and subliminal (WAS) messaging that nudged popular opinion and manipulated circumstances so that people believed their convictions were their own. The CIA called this effective tool of subtle manipulation Operation (A) Mockingbird. They knew better than most that if you (LONE) inundate the media with the same rubbish on repeat (GUNMAN), you can get the masses to believe just about anything, all but crucifying the alleged (LONE GUNMAN) before lady liberty ever had an opportunity at due process.

Sal would board the ship alone and ease my worries. "By the time the shots are even heard," he'd say, "it's already too late."

And, of course, I knew he was right. I knew because he knew.

In the aftermath of the manufactured chaos, with endless check zones and bag checks, the last person who raised suspicion in the eyes of authorities conducting a manhunt was a child. He often told the story of the events following his JFK assignment and how he was escorted outside the search zone in a cop car because, and fancy this, "it was too dangerous to be alone with a killer at large."

The cocksure way he told it was infectious. Ironically, it made me want to be him. It just goes to show how little I knew then.

But Lee, Ray, Chap, Hany, and countless others were not like us. Their sole purpose for creation was to throw the cops, and the public at large, off the CIA's scent, while Sal and I were part of a small, select group being groomed to be the next generation of handlers.

Every year, on October 1st, we'd drop off the remaining slaves at a privately owned island called Little St. James, located in the U.S.

Virgin Islands. From there, they would be distributed accordingly in our sex-trafficking ring. After that, we'd make our last trip to the Pearl Harbor naval base, where we'd drop off the remaining commodities (weapons and drugs) before heading back to Alaska.

Each ship kept one child, and we'd do to them what was done to us. We tortured them with sleep deprivation, hypnosis, starvation, satanic rituals, and other psychological methods to fragment their minds—such as unloading a can of pepper spray into their eyeballs and then giving them eye drops laden with LSD to alleviate the pain and augment their imagination with a mindfuck of a grand time.

I sympathized, of course, but we had a mission to do, and needed bodies to execute said mission, and with said bodies, we infiltrated Hollywood with sleeper agents in the guise of child actors. We created sex slaves with zero inhibitions and world-class assassins, devoid of even the slightest semblance of humanity. We could make anyone who had been through the procedure do anything we'd like. For example, I had long suspected (or hoped) that Mary had undergone the procedure and was made to make the suicide recording and take her own life.

Really, any form of specialized training could be learned with us in just seven short months. I once taught an eight-year-old how to perform a heart transplant using only an out-of-date medical book, dull scalpel, set of tongs, and sodding iron. Which he completed on two kidnapped Eskimos.

The milieu of the world began changing drastically toward the end of the 1960s and adhering to the laws of natural selection; our enterprise adapted with it. Assassinations were considered too erratic, too many loose ends left untied, least of which was a patsy becoming self-aware and remembering he was a patsy—such was the case with Ray and Hany.

So, from the top down, we shifted gears and accumulated power from various angles while simultaneously implementing a social engineering campaign to reopen Greek and Romanesque colosseums to keep the masses distracted. But instead of gladiators battling lions, we had humans tackling each other and promoting daytime television programs that sucked everyone into *The Days of Their Lives*.

Then we flooded the streets with drugs to further pollute their moral compasses.

The new agenda—in conjunction with the sex, drugs, and rock and roll theme that so easily manipulated the masses and created a docile populace who cared not what their governing rulers did, as they were too busy to care—was the collection of information.

Information was the new arms race, and evidence, the new nuclear bomb.

All over the planet, there are highly guarded vaults and personal safes filled with evidence of the despicable habits of elected officials, clergymen, and figureheads, which, for a small fee, we provided the apparatus (children and drugs) necessary to procure said information and, thus, leverage.

While Republican senators blackmailed Democratic congressmen and Democratic congressmen blackmailed civil rights leaders, we blackmailed the lot of them. It was rather easy to control both parties, and therefore, the country, when you have incriminating pictures of the bipartisan gang rape of a four-year-old Ecuadorian boy.

This was our life for ten years—winter months training new slaves on the farm (basements) and summers spent as proprietors of all things naughty, which brings us to my current predicament, unfortunate as it is.

An unusually early winter system was brewing, and since Odysseus was the only ship whose cargo was nil, save for the one recruit, Uncle ordered the other thirty-two ships to stay the course and unload at Pearl Harbor. The decision set into motion a chain of events that freed me from my mental bondage.

The storm was much fiercer than initially anticipated, and the water froze weeks earlier than was customary. Without the assistance of our point ship—the icebreaker—to pave the way, we became marooned on a thick layer of ice. It wouldn't have been a problem if we weren't already running dangerously low on rations.

The whispers of mutiny carry a different weight than other mutterings and can be heard just as loud as an opera singer at Carnegie Hall. Grumblings of poor captaining coupled with insufficient provisions made for a tremendously tense situation as it were, but once the yelling whispers of a coup are heard, they cannot be unheard.

Uncle dealt with it swiftly, slitting the throat of the man who dared oppose his authority. To my uncle's credit, he did thank him for volunteering as we sliced off pieces of him to eat.

We accumulated snow from the deck and refrigerated the dead body. The makeshift fridge was below deck next to our new recruit—a young Filipino girl with almond-shaped eyes, high cheekbones, and caramel skin—a *pinche gringo's* wet dream. The fact she had been dead for days wouldn't have stopped some of them.

I was sent to the captain's cabin to fetch "something that complements dark meat well." While exploring the foreign territory, I stumbled upon my uncle's journal. Within its macabre pages was my genesis, along with other tidbits such as how my father, the great and noble Dr. Josef Mengele, never actually died.

The body I saw as a child was a biological replica—that is, a clone.

My father underwent another round of plastic surgery and assumed a new position as lead handler in the Alaskan branch of the MK ULTRA program. They gave him a large enterprising fleet that allowed him to travel about inconspicuously. But more importantly, he was charged to see if he could create the perfect assassin. As such, my life was an experiment from its very inception. I was nothing more than a lab rat with a set of deadly skills and identity issues.

Laughing from below deck pulled me from abstraction. They were joking about drawing straws to determine who would eat their dead comrade's toes. The words reverberated in my head as flashbacks of pureed finger and toe assaulted the screen of my mind's eye.

Approaching footsteps saved me from the invasive memory; I returned the journal to its original home, pretending to search for the bottle of spirits. Father pushed the door open and then me aside before reaching into a drawer and pulling out a dusty bottle of unopened rum. He left the room without saying a word.

In the distance, I heard the rolling echoes of thunder but thought nothing of it. I was confused, lost even. I wanted to be mad, nay, furious, but I couldn't bring myself to partake in the warranted emotion. Mad over my inability to get mad, I went to join the rest of the crew below deck, but when I opened the door, a distinct scent hit me as if the particles took form and smacked me on the nose. It was the familiar stench of death.

I had more flashbacks of Father attempting to throw me down the steps. Still yet, I couldn't summon madness, and I wallowed down the mold-burdened steps that swelled and contracted with rheumatism from its eternal bath.

The drunken crew were in high spirits. All but Sal was singing gaily; he was horrifyingly transfixed on the dead Filipino girl as one of her arms dangled from a chain (that just as well could've been a rope) attached to a steel beam that met with the top of the cage (that just as well could've been a kennel). The flesh of her free hand was bare to the bone, allowing for gravity to slide it out of the shackles.

All I saw were galloping memories of Mary, suspended from a rope, inches above my kennel.

A steady drip of maggots made a drip-drip sound like raisins hitting the ground in a drip-drip beat as hundreds of them carpeted the dirty floor.

Drip-drip.

A massive rat gorged itself in the buffet before standing on its hind legs and nipping at the toes of the dead girl—more flashbacks of his bipedal brethren, capitalizing on a similar situation—as the storm moved directly overhead, the flashes resembling the effects of a strobe light. I could hear the song, which was my trigger phrase, pouring out of the drunken sailors, mixed in with laughter.

"There are no strings on me. Hahaha."

They were playing hot potato with a severed toe. The loser had to eat it.

The boat danced with the wind, the hanging light swung about in a steady, circular orbit, which was all too familiar, as vicious gales burst through the cracks of the ship, sounding eerily like an oscillating fan.

The singing stopped on the words, "There are no strings on me," followed by a burst of roaring laughter and yelling. Words were said, then a response to the words, followed by a response to the response. Which was, "You're the only person who can say they ate a toe."

The room suddenly funneled and vortexed in on itself. I felt dizzy, and a numb, tingly sensation enveloped me like when your leg falls asleep, but my entire body—like a phantom body.

I grabbed the knife with murderous intent but was ushered up the steps by Sal before I could jam it into my father's jugular. Sal understood just as well as I did; we were free.

I was already retrieving the dynamite before Sal could articulate the command and something urged me to grab my father's journal as well. We chucked several sticks of dynamite down the steps and then cut loose two tiny black rafts and threw them overboard.

The water from the storm and the increased temperature from the fire has started cracking the ice into patches, and the slushy water looks more like spoiled milk. It's night now, and I write this by the light of the burning ship as I fear Sal and I won't survive to tell the tale.

However, I have accepted the singularity of my fate, and so long as the recipient of this message retains the essence behind it, my life will have had value.

Upon breathing life into these words, you are hereby resurrected. No longer shall you waste your life with the trivially mundane, going through the motions of life, but failing to live it.

But above all else, *love*. Not only others but yourself.

To quote one of Sal's victims—John Lennon—"All you need is love." Sow more of it than you harvest, and everything else will work itself out.

I was used as a puppet to conduct unspeakable crimes against my fellow man, and for this, I will be eternally sorry. But my only real regret is that I was robbed of the opportunity to create my own happiness—a loving family was all I've ever wanted. A wife and kids whom I'd love unconditionally until I could no longer draw breath.

Although my life is ending, I shall live vicariously through you as yours has only just begun.

I'm confident this manuscript has put things into perspective for you—it would be criminal otherwise. But really, that's your choice, because make no mistake about it, dear friend, happiness is a choice.

I love you, as I love myself, and I pray that you reach your full potential and find that inner joy you so desperately seek.

With love,

Jerome Mengele

Part 3

The Reckoning

Jerome let the implications of the manuscript marinate as his thoughts whisked him back to that fateful day when his father's trailing armada found him unconscious. And with the blueprint to trigger obedience found within his father's journal, his freedom was again revoked. However, without his father there to protect his interests, the powers that be decided someone with Jerry's temperament possessed zero potential for practical application toward their agenda.

As such, ever since that day, Sal had been in control of Jerome's body.

Meanwhile, Jerry had been hibernating in the enchanted land of his subconscious, which came fully equipped with a manufactured fantasy world to live out his childhood dream.

Suddenly, an uncanny clarity Jerry had never known escaped the confines from which it was trapped, as if the keystone of the dam that housed his memories had finally eroded, and the pressure created by a lifetime of memories trying to escape at once caused a domino effect that sent spider-webbed cracks disseminating throughout the entire structure.

The foggy memories came to him slowly at first, leaking like a faulty pipe before erratically bursting through the cracks, then the foreboding flashes became more apparent. But the disarray of waves flooding the banks of his memory were foreign to Jerry, and he wrestled with himself trying to comprehend the incomprehensible.

He acknowledged the physical attributes as his own, sure enough. It was his face, of that, there was no doubt, but it wasn't him. For how could he have a memory of which he did not live?

And then an eruption burst through the cracks, pulverizing the concrete structure of his brain into dust, mixing with the water that carried his intellect into a cognitive concoction that made him perfectly drunk, with a sobering conviction. He saw himself lying prone on a grassy knoll, looking through a high-powered rifle scope aimed at a moving car. Amid the anarchy created by his hand, a concerned cop offered to escort him to safety.

The wind grew erratic, blowing and swooping down on Jerome with the velocity of an ethereal hurricane, conveying a collage of memories attributed to Sal.

All at once, Jerome realized Sal was his alter.

Jerry had always wondered what happened to an alter or subject when they didn't have the "light". Where did they go when they were on break? What did they do? Well, he was starting to realize that his entire world was a lie, that he had been hibernating in his subconscious for the past twenty years. He was becoming aware that he was in a dream world, an imaginary world, a constructed matrix of the real world—which is not impervious to the natural laws of the real world—that is, until the host becomes self-aware. Then it crashes like a house of cards, and all manner of chaos ensues.

As the ethereal winds brought Jerry this epiphany, it blew away the pages of the manuscript. They flew away like a fleet of paper airplanes equipped with jet engines and coasted over the endless waves until they were no longer visible in the bright light provided by the full moon, which was far too low and should not have been able to serve as a backdrop to the fleeing planes.

Jerry's subconscious deciphered the discrepancy, and within an instant, the moon migrated to its correct position—directly overhead and just as enormous as it was on the horizon. Jerry knew something was off and a sudden panic nestled in his chest.

The moon spun on its axis like a basketball on a globetrotter's extended finger. As it transitioned from the illuminated side to the dark side, it resembled the class of illumination that comes only from a rotating lighthouse. It continued spinning until a strong gust detached it from the invisible hook that ostensibly held it in place, causing it to fall a few inches from Jerry's vantage point before a phantom rope tugged at it and deprived it of an innate desire of adherence to the laws of gravity.

The whiplash and subsequent bouncing begotten by the rash inertia caused the moon to sway back and forth like a planetary pendulum. Before long, it was swinging in small circles—a yoyo wrapped around one of God's mighty fingers.

The earth cracked and roared in agony as a juggernaut of a tsunami rapidly approached the shore. The forthcoming stampede of water raped its way toward Jerry, who braced for impact, intent on getting into a shoving match with one of Mother Earth's most fierce and unforgiving children. But like Moses parting the Red Sea, Jerry was resistant to the bone-crushing entity—it split in half and neglected to recede from whence it came.

All Jerry could fathom in either direction was a straight line of jagged ocean floor and malleable walls of water five feet wide and as high as the eye could see.

A battle-scarred orca pursued a baby seal in the aquarium to his left. The hunt brought them to just a few feet above him, and as they jumped from one wall to the next, they splashed water on Jerry's head. Before he recovered from the unexpected shower, the orca had already inhaled the top half of the mammal and was nosediving to reacquaint itself with the remainder of its meal.

Jerry heard a familiar voice and tripped over himself as he turned to determine its location. The walls of water were no longer erect when he became so.

He found himself back on the shore with the naïve moon still swinging innocently about, oblivious to the repercussions of its quaint dance.

"Do you remember writing that?" a disembodied voice inquired.

Although Jerry couldn't see anyone, he instantly recognized it as the voice of Dr. Caulfield. But what's more, and for the first time ever, he knew it was also David.

Reading the constellation of questions rummaging through Jerry's mind, David answered: "Yes, it's really me," he said. "You're not doing so well, I gather." He paused, listening to Jerry's thoughts. "No, you're *not* Jerry. Otherwise, you would've never read that letter, and I wouldn't be seeing you until our next visit."

"What's happening to me?" Jerry asked, confounded. "Are you real or in my head?"

"Welp, technically both," David said. "I'm sorry, but this is what's best for Jerry. He's endured too much pain as it is, and your delicate ego has already begun the process of being absorbed into my own."

Jerry lost his composure. *"I am Jerry, goddamnit,"* he growled.

The wind picked up once more, this time coming in from the direction of the open sea. It carried on it what appeared to be an enormous flock of white birds that glided toward them in formation. It wasn't until Jerry heard the roaring of jet engines that he realized it was the flock of pages coming home to nest. They slowly landed, each in their turn, one by one, and in sequential order, perfectly at Jerry's feet.

The letter's opening dissolved before changing entirely from "To whom it may concern" to "To Jerry" and resting on "To David."

A conspicuous sensation enveloped Jerry's being the way a warm blanket does on a frigid winter morning. He embraced the familiar feelings before remembering the dream he had so long ago, and then panic set in with the memory of what succeeded the feelings of blissful ecstasy.

But it was already too late.

Not that he could've stopped the occurrence from happening of his own accord as it was long overdue; the invisible cocoon had already begun percolating one of nature's most momentous metamorphoses— the caterpillar into the butterfly.

A fierce burning sensation, originating at the tips of Jerry's fingers and toes, sparked to life. He raised his hands to his face, fully expecting his flesh to convert into a wooden rash. The fingers of his left hand began dissolving into sand-like particles and whirling in a vortex. The flesh-colored tornado slowly transferred Jerry's sustenance to the forming silhouette of a head where the disembodied voice of David was located.

The moon swung faster and broader until an unknown force cut the invisible string, causing its abrupt descent to earth, alas—gravity be damned.

Hurricane winds ripped trees from their roots and tossed them just as easily as if they were toothpicks. Thousands of children screamed Jerry's name and time slowed down as Jerry followed a tree with his picture on it. The image faded to Sal, and then to David, before disappearing into the night sky, reinforcing the credence to the nickname, The Forest of Lost Souls, and for the last time.

Jerry took the madness in and noticed a curious occurrence when he looked up—the closer the moon got, the smaller it appeared.

"*What the fuck is happening, David?*" Jerry screamed.

Jerry's left arm dissolved entirely as the vortex of energy transferred his essence to the face and head of his first best friend. Disembodied voice no more, David answered:

"This is all at your behest, don't you recall? You gave the instructions that if ever you were to read that letter," he paused, "a letter which by the way doesn't even exist, it meant Jerry no longer needed you as a passenger."

Jerry attempted to pick up the stack of papers with his remaining arm but try as he may, they remained stationary. The snubbed gesture reminded him of his favorite childhood story, King Arthur, and how the great and noble king was the only suitor pure enough to emancipate Excalibur from the stone, its prison for eons. The predominant feelings of inadequacy and failure that Jerry had felt his entire life intensified as his delicate ego sparred with the probability of his unworthiness.

The beach-ball-sized moon disrupted their argument when it

entered the stratosphere with an oscillating concussion. It shrank to the size of a baseball by the time it touched the water, and as they marveled at the paradoxical vision, a tide so high—if the builders of the Tower of Babel were on its surf, they'd be utterly content in any language—*voila!*

An invisible dome protected the shore like a fortified snow globe, and the water became their sky. The flowing currents adopted the dancing colors of the Aurora Borealis, and they watched in awe as the serene waves pulsated with unrivaled beauty.

Still, Jerry couldn't shake the burning sensation, and his attention went back to the vortex that was distributing his essence to David, who now had only a face and hand connected by the whirling dust—the rest of his body, a diffused appearance like a nebula.

"You mean this letter?" David said as he effortlessly picked them up. "Actually, I'd prefer not to be associated with such a miserable story."

The stack of papers disappeared from his clutch before reappearing in Jerome's remaining arm for a split second before they dropped to the sand with meteoritic force, like opposite charges on a powerful magnet; it nearly ripped Jerry's arm off, as he had been vetted thoroughly and deemed unworthy to receive.

How'd you do that? Jerry thought.

"You still don't get it, do you?" David said, shaking his head. "Sal isn't the only one you created," he said. "I was the first."

A phantom object began materializing within Jerry's mouth, but he was too distracted with childhood memories to fully notice. In his mind's eye, he saw himself playing chess alone, blowing out his birthday candles alone, playing King Arthur's court alone. He recalled every cherished memory he'd ever shared with David, alone.

Sticking with the morbid motif of the mood, the last memory Jerry had was of killing Alice's sibling alone.

The object in his mouth was now flamboyantly distinct, and all at once, Jerry had the memory of biting his father's finger clean off. Jerry spit out a bloody finger with hairy knuckles, and David winked at him.

"You created me when you were crawling around in what you thought was your father's brains. Then you created Sal after you thought I was killed. But I never actually died. It was more like purgatory. Nothing. Darkness. Until that day on the raft when you were convinced you would die, and something happened. I don't know what, and I don't know how, but it went from darkness to this world, which is just as bad if not worse than the darkness if you ask me."

David had been stuck sitting in a raft on a sea of ice for twenty years, waiting to see if Jerry would need him again. If that weren't bad enough, every week, he'd have to pretend to be Jerome's shrink just to protect his feeble mind. If not for watching Jerome and Sal living out their lives in the split screen television projected in the sky, he'd have gone mad long ago.

"I've been watching your pathetic dreamworld unfold like a Shakespearean tragedy," David continued, "Sal, on the other hand, is crushing it in the real world. While you're off playing house in la-la-land, Sal's just sold your armada for two hundred million dollars."

The flowing currents in the domed sky split in half and projected a first-person perspective on the right screen, which was the real world, and a third-person perspective view from Jerome's fantasy world on the left, as was evidenced by the screen which projected a live scene of his current predicament. Jerome looked around for the invisible cameras that were filming his life.

"Sal's done so well masquerading as Jerry," David said, "the new agenda calls for Jerry to go into politics. Unbeknownst to the naïve voters of the great state of Alaska, the upcoming elections are already bought and paid for—governor of Alaska by day, Manchurian candidate handler by night. It really is the perfect front. But Sal wants to spend more time in the imaginary world with your family and seeing as how we can't trust you to be out in the real world, I'm being tagged in essentially. I'm sorry, but that letter was intended for me. Not you."

Bullshit, Jerry thought, *this is a dream, a very bad, very vivid dream.*

David sensed Jerry's apprehension and pivoted.

"I can sense you're in denial," he said, "but do you fancy it a coincidence that when you put all our names together, it equates to Jerome David Salinger—J.D. fucking Salinger, esteemed writer of your favorite book. You've known all along, and this," David looked around at the awe-inspiring inner workings of Jerome's subconscious, "is all a figment of your imagination. I mean, look around you; nothing about this scene makes sense, even down to the most innocuous detail."

Jerry looked at the domed sky filled with pulsating waves of varying colors and although he acknowledged the absurdity of everything that had occurred, it was the most insignificant detail that finally convinced him, as his thoughts went back to the footprints in the sand. *How could he have ended up where he started when he walked only in a straight line and what's more, how can they be on a warm beach in Alaska?* He knew David was telling the truth, and the realization that he was in a dream world sped up the transformation.

The swirling vortex of sandy flesh increased and as Jerome lost more of his body, David's body filled in.

"Your inability to find happiness, even in your own fantasy, is truly an astounding feat," David said. "You couldn't even be the hero to your imaginary family. Shit, the only reason I'm even here now is that you were about to kill yourself. But where you're going, you won't have the power to do anything but watch our lives play out, and I'll show you what a real man is capable of with the amount of time you wasted."

The particles whirled in a vortex from Jerry's left side to David's right side, and everything the vortex didn't touch looked as if their arms, legs, and body had been cut from a black hole. As if half their bodies were obstructed behind an invisible wall.

"I tried giving you glimpses of what lay in wait," David said, "to veer you from the road you were going down. But instead of heeding my warnings, you suppressed them, and they became nothing more than a collection of buried memories you were restricted to access, a dream of which you were unaware. Time lost." David shook his head. "You never listened, and now, it's too late. We have a fiduciary duty to do what's best for Jerome. We're wired to protect you, even against yourself."

Only the right half of Jerry remained as the vortex pulled its vitality from one and gave to the other.

"I don't believe you," Jerry screamed, "this is a dream. I fucking exist, David. My world is real. I married my college sweetheart. I have a daughter who's going to Harvard in the fall. Her name is … *her name is* … why can't I *remember* her fucking name?"

Like an Alzheimer's patient in the bowels of an episode of amnesia-induced paranoia, Jerry struggled maddingly and pulled and tugged at the deepest recesses of his memory, trying to remember the name of his only child, but the harder he tried, the further away she slipped.

"You're erasing her from your memory to lessen the pain," David said. "If it's any consolation, Sal simply adores them and he will take good care of them both, and you'll be none the wiser once the process is complete."

Cherished memories from Jerry's dream world projected onto the plasma-looking screen in the sky. And like the film in his dream so long ago, the memories became engulfed in aquatic flames, only this time, when the fire self-extinguished, he would have no recollection they ever even occurred.

Poof.

The feeling you get when you're at the apex of a rollercoaster abruptly invaded Jerry's vertigo. He was catapulted high into the sky and remained there, caught in the transparent canopy of clouds above and looking down on the world below. He saw two tiny black rafts afloat in a placid sea of milk-colored water, two rafts but only one survivor. A large commercial freighter aflame and capsized was culminating its descent into the eternal abyss as the howling winds carried whispers in the distance, coming closer and closer yet.

"This is your destiny," the children's voices whispered loudly.

Jerry had always known deep down this was his destiny, to drift aimlessly alone for all eternity—a lost soul in the sea of humanity.

Smoke from the burned memories trickled down from the domed ceiling and wrapped Jerry's floating body in a familiar sensation. With each passing memory he lost, more smoke fell to submerge him in blissful ecstasy, like a baby bottle full of methadone, completing him, utterly and unequivocally. Despite his despair, Jerry had felt this class of euphoria only once before, in his dream when he became the puppet and Sal, the boy. That's when Jerry knew how this would play out, and, indicative of his draining spirits, he slowly descended from the sky.

"Please don't do this, David! I'm begging you! I can't be alone!

Please! I love you, David! Sal, can you hear me? I never wanted to kill you, David!" Jerry struggled to remember the names of his wife and daughter.

"Daughter, wife," he cried, "please don't leave me! *Everyone* leaves me. I'll do anything, *please!* I *tried* to be happy, but it's *impossible* for me. I'm *broken!*"

The last words coincided with his descent, and his feet were back on solid ground. The baseball-sized moon crashed through the wavy sky from directly above, it fell slowly, until it was a few feet above the ground, and then it hovered gingerly, glowing, a luminescent ball of white.

With the inferno of currents systematically burning memories in the domed sky, a thick layer of liquid smoke trickled down in waves and enveloped Jerry like a layer of armor. The feelings were so incomprehensibly exquisite, he could no longer resist; he rode the waves to a paradise lost.

Only the upper right quarter of Jerry's body remained as David filled all but his left hip and leg. Jerry grabbed the moon ball. His ring, middle, and index fingers wrapped around the dark side and disappeared somewhere within it. The other half was covered with craters shaped like footprints and riddled with structures from an advanced civilization long dead.

David shook his head and thought hard before he spoke.

"You've the audacity to claim that happiness is unattainable to you," he said, "when there are *footprints* on the fucking moon." He paused. "You truly are your worst enemy. Thinking happiness is inaccessible makes you find ways to reinforce that absurd belief."

David's voice was soft, kind. Although he despised spending his time watching Sal and Jerome live their lives, he was rooting for Jerry and wanted him to find happiness.

"You've played the victim your whole life," David said, "but you erred on one pivotal matter—the day that defined your life was the day on the raft, not the day in the basement. You could've been a survivor or a victim. You chose the wrong path, buddy."

As the vortex wrapped around Jerome's ears, swooshing like an unidentified vacuum, he knew it was the bottle that delivered the message, sucking him in—abducting him.

The smoke from a final blitz of burned memories filled him with bittersweet nostalgia. He was losing the memory of the only thing he cared about—his daughter, Mikayla.

He wanted to cry. He wanted to fight. But the more memories he lost, the more intoxicated he felt and the less he cared.

He embraced the feelings and watched on the domed television as his subconscious pixelated out the faces of his wife and daughter. Soon the pixels faded, and they turned into faceless beings. Jerry watched a young woman with no face at her high school prom, going on her first date, learning to drive. The memories came and went in rapid succession.

Midnight walks on the beach—Christmas mornings—giving birth—the lot of them—poof.

His psyche worked to eradicate his wife next. He saw himself being married to a woman with no face, buying a new house, first date, all of them, gone.

Jerry had forgotten them both.

All he could fathom now was that something supremely precious had been ripped from him, and despite the intoxicating wave he rode, he felt just as hollow as a gutted doll. The injustice was compounded by the lingering knowledge that he would be eternally alone.

"Please don't do this," Jerry screamed. "I'm begging you, David. Why are you doing this to me?"

The setting of his imagination faded rapidly. The beach he was on disappeared along with the domed sky, everything whirling in a vortex, sucking into the bottle, until the momentous metamorphosis was complete—Jerome was now the puppet and David the boy.

Jerry found himself marooned in a black raft on a sea of ice.

"If only you learned to find God in the small things, you would've been worthy to receive," David's voice boomed from the sky. "Such a pity. Welp, I gotta run; we've got a new generation of killers to train, but here's some company for you, buddy."

Just then, Maggie started licking Jerry's face.

—

Lights from the Aurora Borealis served as plasma pixels and projected onto the night sky a split screen. There were two shows on the left screen as David and Sal split time in the enchanted land, and Jerome spent half his time watching a family show about a man and his loving family. The other half of his time, he watched a show about an eligible bachelor living the kind of life others only dream of.

The right screen was always a first-person projection of the real world. The show was about the governor of Alaska running a massive underground farm. He was excited to get started with their new mission—project disarmament—which called for them to create a new generation of brainwashed patsies that would conduct mass shootings and help usher in legislation that would render the second amendment obsolete. Along with the shooters, they trained scores of crisis actors to help lubricate the bill into existence.

The first class looked mighty promising—three guys that would later become infamous for their acts of terror the world over and help pave the way for the disarmament of the American populace. Their names were Stephen Paddock, James Holmes, and Adam Lanza. But you know them as the Las Vegas Shooter, Theater Shooter, and Sandy Hook Shooter, respectively.

Betty Hill spent the following day hopelessly torn. She was perfectly adamant that the nightmare was actually a future memory. She struggled between reason and desire. She believed it to be her patriotic duty to warn President Kennedy of the assassination. But reason prevailed.

She dwelled in depression throughout the day, and that night, she found herself once again on the porch swing, staring at the moon. I'll never look at you the same, *she thought.*

The hypnotic rhythm rocked her into REM, and she found herself a passenger on a massive spaceship.

Legion: God's Last Cycle

This story is dedicated with love and admiration to fellow dreamer
JOHN LENNON—you're still not the only one.

God is dead, God remains dead, and we have killed him.
—FRIEDRICH NIETZSCHE

A PERVASIVE *THUMP, THUMP, THUMP* ECHOED FROM THE SOUL regeneration chamber like a band of pneumatic tubes at a busy bank. Its cargo, not money—*thump*—but the shining essence of angels—*thump*—returning from their incarnations on earth—*thump*. But there was only one *thump* that the gatekeeper, Azrael, cared of. He waited patiently, welcoming back the other angels with only passing interest. The floor was glass and Azrael looked down the window where the earth sat, big and round; it had thousands of ethereal slides protruding from its rugged face, all of them, thousands of miles high, connecting to the main slide that connected to the soul regeneration chamber like veins feeding into a main artery. Azrael watched as the tubular slides ebbed and flowed in an endless dance, disappearing in Africa then repapering to transit a soul that had just expired in Turkey. There was no rhyme or reason to the madness, but there was a sereness to it all the same, a poetic majesty more brilliant than a thousand sun rises.

A slide flickered then disappeared over New York City before reappearing over Ontario, Canada. He followed the glowing essence as it climbed the slide at supersonic speeds. When it reached the bottle neck where all slides converged, it slowed, steadily creeping forward as the line of souls entered the machine which translates their essence and returns them to their physical being; it turns them back into angels.

Finally, the angel he was waiting on arrived. Azrael unlocked the hatch and greeted him.

"Welcome back, sir," he said joyously.

The returning angel skipped the formalities and went right to work.

"How's it looking?" he asked. There was just a faint trace of hope in his voice, which was mostly filled with expectant failure.

"We didn't make the quota, sir." Azrael hung his head in disappointment.

The returning angel nodded curtly then muttered, "What a *fabulous* waste of time that was." He took a deep breath and blew steam from his nostrils. He looked at the ground and then back at Azrael. "How's he doing?" He didn't realize it, and if you asked him, he'd deny it, but the returning angel winced as he asked the question. He knew the answer. He knew the old man wasn't doing so well. *It's always the same,* he thought.

Shifting nervously, Azrael confirmed his suspicions when he said, "Teetering, sir."

"Is he coherent?" The angel's eyes were filled with heartbreak. The old man didn't have much time remaining, and the returning angel wanted to spend as much time with the old man as he could. He argued against going on this last mission, but the old man insisted. "We mustn't quit," the old man had said, his eyes twinkling with an inner fire that refused to extinguish. Even in his last days, even when he knew all was lost, he remained positive. "We mustn't forget our purpose," he'd said.

"He's been in pretty bad shape since you last left, sir," Azrael said, sullen, distraught. He, too, would miss the old man terribly. His only hope was that the old man remained lucid enough to spend more time with. It was a selfish hope. Azrael knew that. He knew that and didn't care. "But now that you're back," he said, "he'll be able to discern the singularity of his fate, sir."

"Take me to him," the other angel said. "And what's with all this sir business, Az? You are my equal."

Like all souls born as twins, the two angels were born at the same time and of the same breath. They were twin flames. And, despite rank, their relationship was such that they never recognized one as superior to the next.

Azrael smirked and motioned for the other angel to follow him.

They walked through an enormous corridor that commanded an awe-inspiring view of planet earth. From their perspective, the way it floated gingerly in isolation, amid the black backdrop of space, it looked like a massive blue marble, sprinkled sporadically with specks of brown and green and nestled snugly in a stupendous pond of black water. So black. Blacker than black, even.

"Boy, that view never gets old," the returning angel said. The previous incarnation was his seventeenth in this cycle alone, and though the view still took his breath away, he resented the devastating feelings of failure that quickly followed.

"No, it doesn't, sir," Azrael said. "Forgive me, sir, I forgot to ask ..." He paused for a second, wondering if he should even bring it up but he was committed now. "How was this last mission?"

A cascading flow of lights flickered on and off as sensors detected their presences and adjusted accordingly so that in each wing they entered, it was like the breaking of a thousand dawns, and in each wing they exited, it was like midnight on a moonless and lifeless land.

"Eh," the other angel said indifferently, "the same as every other mission in this cycle—irrelevant." If ever there was an overworked and underappreciated employee, it was the returning angel. He often joked with Azrael and the other angels about unionizing and though he was mostly joking, there was a part of him that thought they really should.

His motivation had long been depleted, and he was just going through the motions at this point.

"I'm sorry, sir," Azrael offered.

"Fucking humans," the other angel said with a heavy sigh.

Azrael was inclined to agree. "Fucking humans," he said, nodding.

A barely audible hiss indicated they had finally reached their destination as a seamless wall silently slid open, exposing an empty room with translucent walls that shared the same awe-inspiring view of earth as the corridor. An old man sat in the middle of the room with his legs crossed, floating up and down, staring out into the vastness of space. He had a distinct glow about him, an internal luminescence that bounced off him like rays of sun casting off a shimmering lake. The radiance was birthed by the immense knowledge residing within and emanating from the ascended master. Even in this, his last cycle, the esteemed glow was quite pronounced and warranted a level of respect of the highest measure.

"Would you like for me to stay, sir?" Azrael whispered nervously.

The other angel winced. "Seriously, Az," he said, "please stop with the sirs; it's unsettling."

Azrael nodded respectfully. "Would you like for me to stay, Michael?"

Michael the archangel just then realized the implication of the question and paused to think about it. "Why would I want you to stay?"

"He's been rather," Azrael searched for the appropriate word, "*violent* of late, and we wouldn't want to cause another premature pandemic. Would we, sss—Michael?"

"Was Covid him?"

Azrael nodded solemnly and cautioned further. "As I said, sir, he's been rather violent of late."

Michael shuffled over to the old man and greeted him. "Hello, sir. Sir, can you hear me?" But the old man was deep in mediation and unaware of his guests. Michael watched as the old man bobbed up a few inches, then descended a few.

He hovered over the old man just so and lightly touched his shoulder.

The old man fell suddenly, startled. There was a deep void in his eyes when he opened them, a gulf of emptiness; the spark that Michael had come to know and love was gone, extinguished. *Extinguished by humanity,* Michael thought.

The old man looked around the room and when he landed on Michael, the spark returned, burning fiercely, so full of life. His lips broke off at the corners and his smile lit up the room, literally. "Michael, my boy," the old man said excitedly, "where have you been, son?"

Michael turned and nodded at Azrael, who nodded back before walking toward the wall that hissed and opened as he approached it.

The old man uncrossed his legs and attempted to stand, but this, being the dwindling years of his last cycle, meant he was no longer sprightly, and Michael had to catch him from falling over. Michael stood him upright. They looked into each other's eyes, and a mutual adoration that tethered the two souls together made them feel at home in each other's company. It was rare, this level of shared affection, reciprocated by both, cherished, nurtured.

The old man had a luscious head of bright white hair that trickled down to his hips like the foaming white streak of a stupendous waterfall. Based on his lethargic reflexes and unconventional appearance, Michael suspected the old man had been sitting there, floating in the lotus since Michael last incarnated, twenty-five years prior. According to Legion regulations, the SOP for all ascended masters regarding hair length was baldness—for their connection to source was immense and the presence of hair acted as a buffer, hindering the cord to source. Michael had never seen him to the contrary.

The old man saw Michael staring sheepishly at his rolling mane and, as if to oblige Michael's proclivity for tradition, the old man did a quick shake with his head, and the hair slowly disintegrated like a phantom swept away by a gust of wind. His newly bald, glistening head was commensurate with the sparkling twinkle emanating from his deep blue eyes, which slowly melted into green eyes. Brown. Hazel. Being an ascended master for humanity, the color of his eyes changed as his consciousness interfaced with the eight and a half billion souls he was tethered to, and like a snowflake, you only saw him with the same set a few times spanning decades.

He embraced Michael warmly, then held him at arm's length and lightly squeezed his shoulders before walking over to the adjacent corner of the room. A minibar manifested out of thin air as the old man moseyed along.

"How was your mission, old friend?" the old man asked as he rummaged for ingredients.

"Well, sir," Michael said, a degree of hesitation in his voice, "unfortunately, it was curtailed due to a novel disease."

The old man stood straight, his anemic shoulders slumped forward, his brow furrowed with concern. He pivoted then, looking into Michael's eyes with deep concern. "How massive?"

"Deceivingly so, sir," Michael said, scratching his head. "It really wasn't so bad. The whole thing was blown out of proportion."

"Oh?" the old man said. "I didn't realize we had any novel diseases scheduled for some time now."

"It was an unscheduled event, sir; it appears you had an episode, and in your delirium, you incidentally caused it."

"Oh, me oh my," the old man said solemnly, "not again." In his mind's eye, he envisioned such events as Hurricane Katrina and the Taiwanese tsunami that killed 230,000 people. In fact, every major killer in the last five hundred years was indirectly caused by the old man's deteriorating state. Bubonic plague. Spanish flu. Influenza outbreaks. Covid. All of them were a direct correlation to him losing his powers.

"Yes sir," Michael said just as solemnly. "I'm sorry, sir."

The old man shook his head. "Don't be silly," he said with a sunny disposition, "you're not to blame, son. I'm simply too old, and my time has come." He paused, nodded, then whispered: "I just wish I had more time."

The lament broke Michael's heart. "*Fucking humans*," he said through gritted teeth. Over the eons, Michael had developed an immense resentment and everlasting hatred toward humanity, and with each failed cycle, the hate increased exponentially.

"You shan't blame them, Michael."

"If not them, then who, sir? You're certainly not responsible. Nor am I. We've given them every opportunity."

The old man went back to making drinks. He took an empty bottle out of the minibar and threw it over his shoulders where a garbage can appeared out of thin air, and the bottle landed perfectly in the basket. "Ahah," the old man said, finally finding his heart's desire. "Throughout these many cycles," the old man continued, "how many rise and falls have we witnessed, son?"

Michael did the math quickly in his head—one precession of the equinox cycle is 25,920 years. An ascended master of Legion has five cycles of 5,184 years to achieve their mission, and this current ascended master only had 210 years remaining of his last cycle.

"I've had the distinguished honor of serving under your brilliant guidance for almost a full precession cycle now, sir. 25,710 years. To be exact." Michael hoped the old man would calculate the not-so-subtle hint—his reign was all but over.

"Has it *really* been that long?" The old man's back was toward Michael, who was grateful he could not see the hurt in the old man's eyes. "I can barely remember the past century." He opened a dusty bottle, took a whiff, and a playful, sliding shuffle went down his shoulders, shaking his hips. He corked the bottle and then went back on the hunt.

"Precisely, sir, and your failing memory is directly correlated with humanity's inability to ascend. They're egregiously infantile and superbly inadequate."

The old man stopped what he was doing. He turned. His demeanor changed. He looked at Michael with the regretful eyes of a five-year-old that had just spilled grape juice all over their mother's white couch.

"Michael, my boy, I have decided," he said, eyes shrinking into little beads, head nodding with utter conviction, "that *you* are to be humanity's next ascended master."

Michael was genuinely shocked by the revelation, if not confused. He thought about it for a second and argued the decision's logistical probability. "But, sir," he said, thinking aloud, "an angel has never run a planet. It's unprecedented."

"Ah, yes," the old man said, "that is the natural order—*ttyyppiicaallyy.*"

The old man said typically slowly and with a distinct, upward inflection that hung in the air, as if it were a question. Michael knew the old man better than most, and he was confident a lecture was to follow.

As if to validate Michael's suspicion, the old man said, "How many times have you incarnated for me and done remarkable things, Michael?"

An ascended master of Legion is, for all intents and purposes, considered their respective planet's God. They are responsible for many of society's beliefs as they recruit a vanguard of old souls (star seeds and lightworkers) who sign contracts to incarnate on the planet with the design to raise vibrations and oblige the mission's purpose of achieving ascension.

A hierarchy of angels are assigned to each species in tandem with the volunteer souls. On earth, they are known as the biblical watchers. They incarnate into augmented avatars or split their essence and attach to several bodies in a parallel timeline. Though they don't remember their mission while alive, there is a definite code sequence imbedded into the fabric of their DNA, and, eventually, at preplanned intervals, the DNA will activate a burning desire in them and they will be driven to champion a cause that will utterly consume them, body, mind, and soul. It is written in their DNA, so shall it be done. These special souls are responsible for many of their respective planet's spiritual and scientific innovations, pushing forward the bounds of various disciplines and the consciousness of their planet.

On earth, there was no other angel that had more of a lasting effect than the archangel known as Michael.

"I don't know, sir," Michael said cynically, "too many times," he paused, "and yet," pause, "not enough, equally, sir."

The old man was hunched over the minibar with his back toward Michael. He turned and gave Michael his full attention. "Well, let's see—you incarnated as Jesus, two Dali Lamas, Da Vinci; you attached to Gandhi, Martin Luther King, and even Albert Einstein," the old man said, counting the fingers of his right hand. When he said Martin Luther King and Albert Einstein, a sixth and seventh finger sprouted on the outside edge of his hand. They were, however, the size of a baby's pinky. Indicating that although the old man's powers had faded with each failed cycle, his personality was still very much intact. He winked at Michael with smiling eyes as he wiggled the two deformed appendages. "Shall I continue?"

Michael wasn't in the mood for such cheeky theatrics as he was still coming to terms with yet another failed mission under yet another failed ascended master. He could no longer bite his tongue. "So many attempts and yet, I didn't even make a dent in the ascension." His voice was low, grave. He rubbed the bridge of his nose, then: "I'm tired, sir. I'm tired of trying in vain."

"Oh, but you did make a difference, son. A profound difference, in fact," the old man said. "The problem wasn't with our message."

"Then what was the problem, sir?" Michael's voice was harsh, acidic. He apologized with his eyes.

"Ah, yes," the old man said, "that is the ever-elusive answer to the most paramount of questions, now, is it not?" His head bobbled as he thought aloud. "And, as perplexing a question it is, the answer is invariably the same—*something*. But what is that something? Where did we go so terribly wrong, Michael?"

Michael didn't answer the question; he just watched as the old man went back to rummaging through the bar aimlessly. *What's the point? Michael thought. Humanity is a lost cause. Legion should just terminate their existence once and for all.*

"Did you know I'm the one-thousandth ascended master to champion humanity, Michael?" the old man asked over his shoulder. He combined two different drinks, tasted them, and poured it out. "Now, what was that recipe," he said to himself.

"You're the eleven hundredth ascended master to champion humanity, sir," Michael corrected with as much respect as he could muster.

"Yes, of course," the old man said. "So, then you are aware of their historically bad track record. Yes?"

"I am," Michael said with a sort of prideful misery, "I've been assigned to humanity since the committee's inception, sir. Back when humanity was on their home planet, Mars."

"Oh? I wasn't aware of that." The old man turned, projecting genuine confusion. When in fact, he was privy to this information. It was just suppressed somewhere deep within his intellect, buried under 25,710 sum years of heartbreak. Michael had seen this happen 1,099 other times. The gradual decline of an ascended master's powers accelerates drastically at the end of their last cycle. Michael knew the old man's mind would be unsalvageable, sooner rather than later.

But despite the heartbreak from anticipating the inevitable occurrence, deep down, Michael was almost relieved. For the old man had watched his most beloved children try and fail so many times, and although Michael was going to miss him dearly, he was glad the old man would no longer have to endure the immense burden of the broken-hearted loop he was otherwise doomed to repeat.

In time, Michael thought, desperately wishing to spend as much time with the old man as was possible, even if that time was spent watching him slowly disintegrate into a shadow of his former self. Love is selfish in that way.

But Michael knew the old man would choose the same itinerary as most other ascended masters and opt to self-destruct prematurely. The decision would be made to minimize his own suffering, certainly, but more so to spare humanity from an extended period of turmoil. For the closer an ascended master reaches the end of their last cycle, the more they have a penchant for violent dementia, which creates waves of cataclysm on their corresponding planet and resets the planet anew.

The perpetual cycles of creation, destruction, and renewal that have become the norm for humanity isn't how the divine script was originally written. It has only transpired that way due to humankind's eternal inability to achieve enlightenment. They have failed time and again, reaching levels of high technology, before crumbling to dust and starting anew. This is the core of truth behind the ubiquitous legends of ancient peoples, and the cyclical rise and fall of civilizations as humanity goes from age to age and sun to sun.

The Mayans believed humanity was in the fifth and final world, or sun. And in a way, they were right. For this is the last cycle under the current master as the energy from the population acts as beacons to the universe, letting it know what age to usher in next, for better or worse.

The intermittent periods between lucidity and dementia become fewer and further the closer an ascended master reaches their last failed cycle. Eventually, inevitably, all ascended masters who do not complete their missions in time enter a state of delirium, inadvertently wreaking havoc on the species that has broken their heart, which, coming full circle, is the root cause of the destruction itself in a superb exhibition of bittersweet irony. The last one hundred years of their fifth cycle are always the worst. As such, most ascended masters decide to self-destruct at the onset of the worst of times.

In his time serving as humanity's head archangel, Michael had encountered only one ascended master stubborn enough to endure until the contemptuous end. The subsequent destruction was so immense that Mars (where humanity was at the time) collided with another planet that previously orbited between Mars and Jupiter. And like so many other time-old stories, the enduring lore of the incident survived in the collective consciousness of humanity, passed down by the oral traditions of the ancients. The planet was called Tiamat, and the debris of evidence is commonly referred to on earth as the asteroid belt.

"What I can remember," the old man said, "is when I stepped forward, most thought I had either lost a bet or had gone stark raving mad." He shook his head, a small smile tugging at the corner of his lips, his eyes shifting colors. "The prevailing school of thought was then as it is now—that humanity shall forever remain cursed and any master who champions them is doomed to fail."

There was a loving twinkle in the old man's eyes as elusive memories returned.

Michael allowed the old man his fading memories, for he knew it would be a rare occurrence in the immediate future.

As predicted, after only a few short moments, the sparkling fire that the memory had given life to extinguished, and Michael knew the old man had lost it. It broke his heart to see the old man just so, and to nudge him back on course, he queried, innocently enough, "So, why did you take it then, sir?"

The old man looked at Michael with lost eyes. There was a second when no light emanated from them like a drunkard who gazes upon a mate but seemingly looks right through them. The occurrence was brief but pronounced, and Michael's heart was submerged with warranted spite for humanity's inability to reach ascension. *They are outright murderers,* he thought.

Meanwhile, the old man had recovered well enough as he finally found the ingredients, and he gave Michael his full attention.

"Why did I take what, son?" he asked.

"The mission to run earth," Michael said, "if it was said to be cursed, that is."

"Well," the old man said softly, "I imagine I took it for the same reason I don't regret taking it—I thought I could make a difference, son."

The old man shook what he thought to be two martinis and gave one to Michael, who reluctantly took it, despite the undeniable fact that angels don't drink alcohol. But in the declining years of their last cycle, and with their waning minds rapidly deceiving them, ascended masters often performed peculiar and irrational acts.

Michael had once been acquainted with an ascended master who became incurably enamored with carriers of the MC1R gene. Their fire hair and the polka-dotted blemishes that ran the length of their skin convinced her that they were somehow good luck and the missing link in saving humanity. The infatuation bordered on pathological, and in a desperate effort to save humanity, she recruited a slew of fifth-density souls whose DNA harbored this very chromosome. It wasn't a bad idea, in theory. However, her execution was flawed.

In her ailing state, she ignored Michael's counsel and refused to send them through the soul regenerator machines, opting instead to send them down in their natural form. Their descendants are commonly referred to today as gingers, but in their inaugural cycle, they were revered as gods as they were of giant proportions and possessed such knowledge, they seemed divine, indeed.

The old man held his drink at arm's length. Wishing to put his failing mind at ease, Michael partook in the toast. It was, however, noticeably pungent, and possibly even poisonous, Michael suspected. And when he glanced at the minibar, his suspicions were confirmed— instead of alcoholic beverages donning the ledges, there were several cleaning products, and Michael noticed the minibar wasn't a minibar at all—but a cleaning caddy.

The old man's dementia was making him a danger even to himself. He had been tiptoeing that invisible line of no return for some time and had just officially crossed it. He only had about another hundred years of a semi-lucid state remaining. *That's not long enough*, Michael thought.

The old man motioned Michael back to the translucent wall. After the gesturing nod, a fluffy cloud in the shape of a couch slowly manifested. By the time they reached it, it was finally a physical object. Michael noted the gradual progression of manifestation as an irrefutable indication that the old man was due presently to die.

The old man plumped down ever so slowly and patted the rolling mist of the cloudy cushion next to his own. Michael sat next to him. They sat silently for a spell, looking out of the translucent wall at the massive blue marble. "So, Michael, my boy," the old man said unsurely, "how was your last mission?"

"We've already broached that topic, sir," Michael said respectfully.

"Have we now?"

"Yes sir."

The old man nodded in defeat. "What was it we were talking about then, son? I have a sneaking suspicion; it was of paramount significance."

"We were discussing where we erred with humanity, why we were unable to achieve our objective, sir."

"Ah, yes," the old man said. "That is the question, now, isn't it?" He overcompensated for his disorientation with an exaggerated nod that swiftly bobbed up and down. "What indeed?"

Michael's heart ached for the old man. He had served under many other ascended masters, but with this one, he genuinely believed they had a chance at completing their mission the moment the tenth billion soul was born. He was certain, in fact, under this ascended master's guidance, they'd finally get humanity to the fifth density and end their suffering.

"So, then," the old man said, "where would you say we went wrong?"

"I don't know, sir," Michael said, trying to hide his annoyance.

"Oh, but you must have some inclination, son. After all," he lightly touched Michael's knee, "and feel free to correct me if I misspeak, but have you not incarnated on earth more than any other angel?"

Michael nodded in agreement, but the old man was waiting on a verbal cue.

"There's so much, sir," Michael said. "I wouldn't even know where to start."

"Start where you must, but it is *imperative* we speak on these matters directly. For I fear I will be unable to articulate my message in the very near future, and we have yet to have our after-action review, and transfer briefing. As I suspect, I've already informed you that you are to be my replacement—"

Michael opened his mouth to object, but the old man raised his hand and voice.

"—And as reluctant as you may be to accept the dubious honors," he continued, "the bylaws on this matter are very clear, son—if a volunteer does not step forward, the outgoing ascended master has full autonomy and shall pick their successor, and although there's never been an angel successor, I care not for tradition and only for the salvation of humanity."

The old man's eyes went blank again. Michael knew the expression wasn't spawned by amnesia but heartbreak and regret. For he had seen it many other times on many other ascended masters.

They sat in silence. The old man's eyes melted into brown eyes and then into hazel with specks of green; albino eyes; baby blue.

Aside from the changing colors, they remained blank and expressionless.

"I believe you're Legion's best chance at accomplishing the mission," the old man said, "but if by some chance you can't, then you terminate and are released from your torment." He looked at Michael warmly. "Either way, this is a win-win situation for you, Michael."

Michael realized he was right.

The old man gazed upon his favorite angel and closest confidant, and Michael was unable to refuse any longer.

"Well, sir," he said, "I guess we can start with my last incarnation."

"Yes, let's," the old man said with giddy anticipation. "Activate after-action review modality." The translucent walls blinked in a mercury-like substance and went back to the translucent walls.

"After-action review modality activated, sir," said the ship's AI system. "Will there be anything else?"

"That will be all for now," the old man said.

There was a long pause as Michael secretly hoped the old man's memory evaded him, but no such thing occurred. "Well," the old man said impatiently.

Michael dug deep for motivation to have what was, in his opinion, the most meaningless conversation. "As you well know, sir," he paused, looking for the best words, and decided on a direct approach, "due to your lingering dementia, my last incarnation was terminated prematurely."

"My word," the old man said, "what happened now?"

Michael let out a slightly perturbed sigh. "I was afflicted with an ailment from an untested vaccine, and like so many others, I was unable to shake the long-term effects, sir." The old man nodded as if he remembered, but Michael knew this was only a charade. "But even if my mission wasn't curtailed," Michael said, "I wouldn't have made much of a difference, regardless, sir."

"Uh-huh," the old man said, "and why do you suppose that is, Michael?"

Just then, the after-action review modality activated. The ship interfaced with Michael's consciousness, and the translucent walls became malleable, as ripples of a mercury-like substance began oscillating and transforming into checkered graphs. The squares were twelve inches by twelve inches, and they slowly covered the walls, ceiling, and floor.

Michael heard what they were before they fully manifested in form. They were television sets depicting live scenes from earth—social unrest, circus governments, banks, and corporations breaking laws with impunity, and wars aplenty.

Michael acknowledged the ship's interfacing and continued: "Well, it's 2026, sir."

He said this as if it were the be all end all of answers, but the old man couldn't fathom the significance of the date, and Michael sensed he wasn't satisfied with the answer. "Humanity is beyond salvation, sir," he added begrudgingly. A burning resentment was percolating toward the old man for making him state the obvious.

The old man shifted on the cloud couch. The rolling plumes gently massaged his aging body. "Specifics, Michael," he said.

Michael considered the myriad of problems facing humanity and decided to start at the source. "I guess we can start with the disconnect, sir."

The old man nodded with a smile on his face.

"Humanity is, and has been for some time now, estranged from source, sir. Their infantile manner of discerning the purpose of their lives has yet to evolve and most of them have failed to realize they're not even really humans, but spirits, having a human experience for the purpose of ascension. They identify with their physical bodies and never consider that perhaps it's only a vessel for their true being."

As Michael's thoughts pivoted, the screens projected the many failed cycles by humanity's previous ascended masters.

They always make the same mistakes, Michael thought.

"The divine script dictates that when our star seeds and lightworkers awaken and make the shift in consciousness, they are supposed to help guide others to find the same path and then reach critical mass (square root of one percent of the population). This paradigm shift in thinking, which was to be the catalyst and elevate humanity to the fifth density, was never a question of if, only when. But humanity has faltered time and again, sir."

They'll never make the shift because in every cycle—but especially in this last one—they're stuck in the material world, Michael thought.

The failed cycles on the screens gave way to commercials from across the planet. Car ads and retail stores boasted of their newest products. On the screen in front of Michael, an advertisement for the new iPhone 18 enticed him to make the trade from Android to iPhone because "once you go iPhone," the commercial said, "you never go back."

"Televisions, guns," Michael continued, "clothes and jewels—the shopping list is seemingly endless, until one day, they wake up and realize the only aspect of their lives, commensurate with their greed, is their emptiness."

Michael paused and observed a Mattel commercial placating sensory developing toddlers, subtly programming them to beg their parents for the new talking Elmo. He scoffed and continued:

"And like a mad dog chasing its tail," he said, "they teach their children this despicable paradigm, and their children teach theirs, and so the cycle continues unabated. Which leads to the current state of global affairs, sir." He nodded at the commercials surrounding them. "Consumerism," he said in disgust, "it's intrinsic in their system and embedded in their very psyches."

"School, *work*, death," the old man interrupted.

Michael nodded in agreement. "A contemptuous model they'll be slaves to—by design—for the duration of their sad, empty lives."

Like an enormous stack of dominos, the channels changed in rapid succession. One by one, the advertisements capitulated to news broadcasts from across America. Cameras followed looters destroying their own neighborhoods while stampedes of wild Americans trampled each other on a black Friday news segment. Michael singled out one news report on a robbery where a twelve-year-old kid was shot dead because he refused to relinquish his Air Jordans.

"And of course," Michael said, "they aren't satisfied with this absurdly inadequate existence—half of their waking life is spent working, and when an overwhelming majority of the planet despises their jobs, then an overwhelming majority of the planet despises their lives and becomes the walking dead. For this is how your soul dies before your physical being does."

The twelve-inch screens melted into each other and implemented the six-screen format where the four individual walls, along with the floor and ceiling, became one immersive 4D experience. They could suddenly smell sea salt as a warm beach invited them in with the surf crashing on the shore. The wavy motion of their cloud couch ceased as they found themselves on two lawn chairs buried peacefully in the sand, not a care in the world. CORONA in blue letters melted into the walls of their subconscious.

"They try different remedies to appease this festering disconnect, sure," Michael said. "They switch jobs and even partners; they pick up liquor and drugs, they play fantasy football and create avatars in their likeness of which they vicariously live in some fantasy land where high ratings stroke their delicate egos. But these superficial outlets are insufficiently equipped to melt the stress away, prompting them to find another, and so continues the cycle, extending their inheritance of depression to the next generation."

The walls rippled in gray liquid and returned to the twelve-inch screen format and projected live feeds of planet earth—a depressed man sat in his coffin cubicle, flipping aimlessly through portfolios and contemplating suicide, while a husband and wife passionately argued over bills in front of their children. On the screen in front of Michael, a middle school in Illinois conducted an active shooter drill, desensitizing them to such horrific realities.

Thousands of screens displayed varying degrees of the depression and disconnect prevalent on earth.

"They're majestic and eternal beings, sir," Michael said. "They weren't meant to work all day," he laughed lightly. "The human spirit cares not for a job, the economy, the absurd unnecessities they've been led to consider necessary." Michael paused and nodded to himself. "Slowly, inevitably, their souls suffocate, and then it happens." He looked at the old man whose brown eyes melted into milky gray cataracts. "They accept their miserable existence and become settlers. Settlers in love. Settlers in jobs. Settlers in life."

Michael stood up and walked to the wall. He placed his fingers on the screen and slid them diagonally a foot apart. The depressed lives disappeared on the televisions encompassed within the diagonal. He could see that beautiful blue ball, and he wondered how so many people could be so lost. He stood immersed in thought until the old man cleared his throat. Michael went back to the fluffy cloud and sat down.

"And amid this survival dance of carnal needs, they've forgotten all the ancient wisdom we bestowed upon them. The esoteric beliefs that once held sway are now suppressed by those in power, keeping the masses vibrating low and dependent upon the fiat system."

As Michael remembered times of old, ripples in the mercury substance transformed the walls to scenes of ancient peoples of earth. Yogis, deep in mediation, hovered over the ground like hummingbirds while a Tibetan monk's inanimate body became incandescent; he willingly shrank and atrophied as he attained *Jalu* or rainbow body.

The old man had been an instructor on achieving *Jalu* at the Legion academy before he took the assignment to champion humanity. He smiled as he remembered the good times and then frowned as he realized he would soon be unable to recall such events.

"That's precisely why I had you attach to Albert Einstein, Michael," the old man said softly. "To reintroduce the world to quantum physics with ambitious hopes that humanity would realize the universe is intrinsically participatory, that the outer is a manifestation of the inner."

The old man stopped talking. The twelve-inch screens shrunk down to one-inch screens, which depicted live feeds of people living their everyday lives. Michael noticed that most were either in school, working, or sleeping.

School, work, death, he thought, as a transparent web of a matrix tethered all the screens together before a holographic web stretched from the screens to Michael and the old man, tethering them to all of humanity.

"I wanted to remind them," the old man said, "that metaphysics and alchemy were indeed real, and that everything in the universe is energy, vibration, and frequency, so their thoughts create their reality. I wanted them to realize the connectedness we all share because everything," he raised his arms, "from the stars to the lowliest of insects—everything is connected in the web of the matrix."

The holographic web weaved through the old man's raised arms and branched out like tiny roots, connecting everyone. He closed his eyes, and the holographic web disappeared.

He opened his eyes and patted Michael's hands warmly. "You did a brilliant job at reintroducing this to humanity, son," he said, with a distinct glow of admiration emanating from his puppy-dog eyes.

The compliment felt backhanded to Michael and made him uneasy because he felt humanity had taken his gift and turned it into a curse. "Thank you, sir," he said, "but in their infinite wisdom, they used the knowledge to split the atom and created nuclear warfare."

The old man threw his hands up as if to catch Michael's persistent pessimism. "Which I suppose was inevitable. No?" the old man said. "Don't you recall the Vimanas from the last procession cycle?" But the Vimanas were from the first precession, and Michael didn't have the heart to correct him.

A deluge of liquid mercury engulfed the screens and ripples transformed the walls back into the six-screen 4D format; suddenly, massive flying ships maneuvered around destructive weapons in the skies of ancient India. A sleek cigar-shaped Vimana chased one in the shape of a bell, and as they progressed in distance, they went from wall to wall before a Vimana the size of a city shot a nuke that disintegrated huge swaths of Mohenjo Daro. Michael and the old man felt the concussion and immense heat that vitrified miles of sand into glass.

With unabated freedom, the old man continued to speak out of turn: "They also had this ancient wisdom and stumbled upon nuclear warfare. This last cycle alone, we had the Celtics, Olmecs, Lemurians, we were so close, and then they destroyed themselves."

Michael wanted to oblige the old man, but he instinctually disagreed. "No sir," he said.

"What's that?"

He was committed now. "That timeline's incorrect, sir. We destroyed the last cycle with the flood." Michael paused and hoped the old man would remember the rest of his own accord, but the old man's lost eyes suggested this was news to him, so Michael continued, in desperation.

"Because Lucifer helped the dark ones infiltrate our soul regeneration system and some of the ascended souls we recruited were nefarious entities and mutinied, and if we didn't remedy the situation, they were going to move the entire planet down in vibration. Don't you recall, sir?"

Michael knew that if the old man had forgotten this—his most regretful of moments—then he was simply a figurehead at this point, holding the position for the next ascended master anew. Michael remembered the instance very vividly as it was the first and last case of mutiny in the Legion's long history. The old man had spearheaded the tribunal and as punishment, Legion stripped the dark ones of their souls so they would remain trapped in the material world and could never again infiltrate the soul regeneration machines.

"Ah, yes, of course, I remember, Michael," the old man said, shaking his head emphatically, "but let us focus on the task at hand, lest we forget our intended purpose."

Michael knew the old man was lying but matched his deceit with ignorance, nevertheless. "And just so we're clear," he said, "what exactly is our intended purpose, sir?"

"Well, to learn, of course," the old man said bluntly. "Before I am to become an incurable amnesiac—which is very soon, I fear—I must know you won't commit the same errors, Michael. The madness stops with you, son. You must get humanity out of this doomed cycle they're stuck in."

Michael winced at the idea of running a fool's task. The old man saw the blatant gesture and looked at the ground, lost in regretful thought. Before long, the old man's gaze methodically rose from the floor, and his tear-filled eyes locked with Michael's. They glistened in a blue haze before changing to green.

A cold knot turned Michael's stomach. He knew better than most, that when an ascended master was in the last moments of their lucidity, just before they forget everything and wreak havoc on what they love so dearly, they're subdued by so many regrets. He would take the pain in the old man's stead if it were at all possible, and in a very tangible way, it was, if only he went all-in on what the old man was selling.

"I picked you," the old man said, "because there is no one else I trust more, and I'm certain another ascended master will only make the same mistakes the proceeding thousand ascended masters have made."

"One thousand ninety-nine, sir."

"Huh," the old man grunted.

"There have been one thousand ninety-nine previous ascended masters, sir."

The old man thought about it and raised his eyebrows. "That is precisely my point, Michael," the old man said. Shifting gears, he added, "You know, a very wise and enlightened soul once said: 'Insanity is doing the same thing over and over again and expecting a different result.'"

The old man thought that quoting Einstein would perhaps instigate hubris and passion in Michael and light a fire fueled by prideful determination.

Michael looked at the old man sideways. "Flattery is unbecoming, sir," he said.

The old man rose from the cloudy cushion and paced about, his hands behind his back. "Is there not logic in that? Indeed, to continue and try to fix the problem of humanity in the same tired fashion is utter insanity. We must think outside the box if they are to vibrate to the fifth density," the old man said. "Won't you oblige an old man's dying wish?"

He plumped down. The cloudy edges broke away and dissipated entirely.

Wanting to put the old man at ease, Michael nodded in solidarity.

"Splendid," the old man said, "what else is there then, son? Besides the disconnect consumerism breeds?"

Just as the old man said breeds, he dropped his martini glass accidentally on purpose. It shattered into several pieces and a well-to-do shard cut the old man's shin. The gash opened and bled profusely before coagulating whole again.

"What of medicine?" the old man asked with smiling eyes.

Michael knew the old man had his wits about him and made the occurrence happen on purpose, to spark an instance for a teaching moment. He had done it often and some of Michael's fondest memories regarding the old man were of watching him drop knowledge and life lessons on his fellow angels. The way he weaved "accidental" events together with the conversation was almost poetic.

"What of it, sir?" Michael said.

"How does humanity fare in this regard?"

A mechanism in the walls activated, and the liquid turned crimson red as blood vessels pumped from capillaries and veins and fed into every area of a massive brain like the inner workings of a clock on the 4D format. A titan of a tumor nestled in an inoperable area of the frontal lobe, laid dormant until brain synapses fired and sparked about. The tumor vibrated vigorously and then began disintegrating like Alka-Seltzer in a cup of water before it disappeared entirely. The imaging zoomed out through the person's skull and face to just a few feet before a man meditating in times of old. He had just healed the tumor using the power of thought alone.

"In this last cycle, sir?" Michael asked.

"If it pleases you."

"Well, that's one aspect of society they got correct in previous cycles," Michael said, "and some of the knowledge trickled down to this iteration, but its relevance has gotten lost to the stain of time, at least for the masses, sir."

"How so?"

Michael answered quickly: "A society that keeps the cures for diseases a secret so that a select few can profit isn't a society at all, but a piggy bank for the rich and depraved."

Oscillating ripples drowned the meditating man and the walls transformed into the twelve-inch screen format. Infomercials surrounded Michael and the old man from across the planet as approachable actors promoted pills for all manner of ailments. "Depressed? Take this pill," one commercial said. "Anxious? Take that pill," said another.

"Big pharma has created diseases out of everyday ailments," Michael said. "They take normal, everyday happenings, slap a haughty designation on it, and wouldn't you know it, sir, they have the cure wrapped in a chemical concoction in the form of a little pill."

One by one, the optimistic voices that had found their miracle drug changed to a more serious tone as commercials of class action lawsuits surrounded Michael and the old man. "Did you trust Johnson and Johnson enough to get their Covid vaccine?" the lawyer said seriously. "Are you now sterile for that dire mistake? If so, call us—"

"They've created a pill for every manufactured illness, sir," Michael continued. "But don't forget to read the fine print, for their bipolar pills create cancer and their cancer pills create diabetes. The masses are undereducated and overprescribed, and the pharmaceutical companies are left to run amuck, leaving people to wonder—what's wrong with their depressed and anxious lives? They can't quite put a finger on the source of their malady, but they're certain something is afoot. For the lot of them are afflicted with a bout of melancholy which seems contagious as it swoops through the masses like the plague galloping through Europe."

Michael and the old man were verbally assaulted by an alphabetical onslaught of class action lawsuits. Lawsuits for Accutane, Actemra, Actos, Ambien, Aredia, Avandia; then Bair, Baycol—Michael was disgusted and tuned out as the rest of the alphabet was represented each in their turn.

"Their souls are bereft," Michael said, "and missing that pivotal something at its very core, and like a joke they don't understand, they laugh anyway, but hidden in the forced laughter is their inner voice wondering if they're alone in their insanity."

The commercials stopped altogether, and the mercury vibrated as if droplets of rain interrupted its semi-solid state. Then a live feed of planet earth—as seen from space—was displayed on every screen. From different angles, the massive blue marble zoomed in rapidly to various areas of earth and revealed the diverse scope of humanity's nasty habits.

One man applied a tourniquet and tapped at his arm, feverishly searching for a vein. Michael's eyes scanned the screens and locked upon a three-hundred-pound woman impatiently awaiting her ten-thousand calorie lunch at McDonald's while a bored child squirmed in a doctor's office, waiting on his refill of amphetamines after receiving an unnecessary vaccination.

It's their lifestyles making them sick, Michael thought, *both physically and mentally, respectively.*

"They haven't yet realized that *they* are the placebo, that they harness the power of source within their very DNA," Michael said. "As such, they are gods in their own right, if only they stopped putting poison into their bodies and weren't ravaged by the plague of the new century—the stress of survival—which equates to the stress of money, sir."

The old man squinted at Michael. "So, if these are the problems," he said, "what then are the solutions?"

Michael answered without having to contemplate his answer. "A natural and holistic lifestyle, sir. An embargo on genetically modified foods and away with the Monsanto's of the world. Those disgraceful companies have bogarted the food industry and seized control of the people's inalienable rights to produce non-GMO foods."

An invisible remote changed the channels one by one in a cascading avalanche of debauchery as one news report exposed Subway's eat fresh campaign and their fake tuna, which "you should eat less," said the reporter, mocking their "eat fresh" slogan. While the report in front of Michael bragged of a new development—

"In today's news," the news anchor said, "scientists have successfully created lab-grown oranges which yield no seeds." He bit into the orange. "They taste pretty good too, John," he said as juices ran down his second chin.

Michael—who among other talents was an enormously powerful empath—was suddenly nauseated as he contemplated the dire conditions on earth. The old man knew Michael's predicament. He placed his hand an inch away from Michael's sternum. A vortex of dark energy funneled from Michael's heart chakra and into the old man's aura. Ripples of the dark energy distributed evenly across the old man's *chi* like a stone tossed into a still lake and then dissipated entirely. Michael's chest pulsated in a vibrant green and then went back to normal.

"No one should ever have to feel this level of injustice," the old man said. "After all, 'injustice anywhere is a threat to justice everywhere.'"

He thought perhaps by quoting Martin Luther King Jr.—another of Michael's attachments—he'd embrace the vile feelings and vow to banish it from existence.

"And yet," the old man continued, "eight and a half billion souls are suffering from rampant injustice." He patted Michael's hand warmly. "How else shall you remedy this epidemic?"

The old man knew what made Michael tick, and he pushed through. "I'll champion a holistic society, sir, one that recognizes they must feed their mind, body, and spirit, equally and respectively, sir."

The old man looked very pleased with this answer. "What about an economy, son," he said, moving on. "Will they have commerce? Careers?"

Michael looked at the old man like he was mad. *Haven't you been listening?* he thought but dared not say. "If I am to do the job entrusted of me to the best of my ability, then there can be no economy, sir," Michael said. "The world governments have agreed that corporations should have more rights than human beings. But if it were an organic entity, it would undoubtedly be an insatiable cancer, sir. For the economies of earth run on big oil, big pharma, and the military-industrial complex."

The individual screens melted into each other, and the mercury vibrated gray and then turned green and blue and red and pink and all manner of colors with faces in the middle and numbers on the corners.

American dollar bills attached to Pesos and Lei and Euro and every denomination from every country represented and covered all the screens save for a small twelve-inch spot directly in front of the cloud couch where static danced and then—breaking news: "Who needs accountability when you've got cold hard cash?" the broadcaster said as she reported on Purdue Pharma and the Sackler family's disgraceful evasion of justice. Heavy drops of a red liquid trickled onto the currency. Before long, the walls were covered in blood money save for the report that exposed the morally perverse creators of oxycontin.

"They've implemented a system which abides by certain invariable truths—money is the only thing that matters," Michael said, "and they remain faithful to finite resources while waging wars with countries that have an abundant source of black gold lurking underneath their sovereign soil. But alas, national borders mean nothing when this is the case as they will create any means to procure it."

The blood money on the smart walls transformed once again to the twelve-inch television screens. "Like father, like son," said one news report. "George W. Bush swears he had reliable intel on WMD's—" Michael cringed.

"The systematic acquisition of natural resources is just one way those in power keep their power," Michael said. "The private bankers have become the new kings—an oligarchy of depraved individuals are now the unelected leaders of the world and keep whole nations in debt and, therefore, under their thumb."

The channels changed in flowing waves to economic reports where dizzying displays of numbers and signs flashed on the screen to be deciphered. "The FED has increased the money supply once more to combat inflation—" one news report said. *That's absurdly nonsensical,* Michael thought.

"Perhaps because the economic jargon is so difficult to understand—by design, mind you—the masses don't even comprehend every dollar created in the ether has an attached debt to it upon its immaculate conception. Therefore, debt is intrinsic in the system itself. In all my time incarnating on earth, it's the biggest scam I've ever witnessed, sir."

The individual television screens dissipated into the 4D format. A desert sun saturated Michael and the old man in ancient rays as the floor screen displayed an aerial view of a skinny man with a crown of thorns digging into his head. He struggled to carry a wooden cross.

An angry mob spat on him and hit him with stones from the four walls. Michael's stomach churned as he vividly remembered that day so long ago and the sacrifice he endured for humanity. A Roman soldier whipped the skinny man; he fell forward and rolled on his back. "Why has thou forsaken me," the man said, looking up from the floor screen as blood leaked from the thorns, into his eyes.

"Yes, it's a sad situation—this Babylon banking money system—which creates money out of thin air and attributes interest to it upon its inception. Dark alchemy, it is," the old man said. "I was elated when you kicked the money lenders out of their temple of usury. Even though," he adopted a regretful tone, "it ultimately led to your demise. But I'm more concerned with what you will do differently?"

"I'll do an UBUNTU[1] society," Michael said, "like in the olden days before we destroyed the last cycle with the flood." His eyes lit up. "There will be absolutely no money, no barter, no trade, no value attached to anything. Everyone will contribute their natural talents and acquired skills to the benefit of all in the community. In this way, abundance will run rampant, and everything will be free."

The passion of Christ faded and gave way to the twelve-inch screen format. Two tramps dressed in rags fought over a coveted corner on one screen while children begged for food on another. Michael could feel the hunger pangs of the thousands of malnourished children looking back at him with their sickly eyes batting to fend off pesky flies, unable to exert the energy to swat them away.

"They can split the atom but can't figure out how to feed the needy. More people die every day from starvation than any other time in history," Michael said, "while a staggering one-third of the world's food

---

1.   For more on Ubuntu, read *UBUNTU Contributionism—A Blueprint for Human Prosperity: Exposing the global banking fraud* by Michael Tellinger

stores are thrown out every year, not because it spoils but because people don't buy it." Michael shook his head in disgust. "Because of this concept, scarcity prevails over abundance. It will be the converse in my society."

The old man smiled happily, thinking of such a world. "Will the children attend school?" he asked.

"Yes, of course, sir, a variation of it, anyway," Michael said. "But the current paradigm of education in the mad world they live in has nothing to do with teaching and learning. It's about indoctrination, not education—a methodical machine which systematically mass-produces future worker bees, taught not to ask too many questions or even think for themselves."

"School. Work. Death," the old man said.

Michael nodded in agreement. "I'll champion a society that teaches them how to access the full potential of their brains, which are the most advanced machines in the universe if only used in coherence with the heart. But as it is today," Michael shook his head, "when they can't control their minds, their minds end up controlling them. It saturates their very essence with an onslaught of negativity and judgment, and they lack the guidance and ability to turn it off. So, their best asset becomes their worst enemy." He nodded knowingly. "They emphasize the strength of the body on earth, but the body has limitations whereas the mind is quite literally limitless—again, it will be the opposite on my planet."

"I wish I could've seen that in action, son," the old man said. "And of religion."

Michael scoffed at the mention and instantly regretted it. But the old man was smirking with smiling eyes, and with his dimples burrowing deep into his cheeks, he motioned his left hand in a circular motion for Michael to continue.

"Forgive me for saying, sir," Michael said, "but religion surpassed its usefulness a very, *very* long time ago." He gauged the old man's demeanor, but it remained as impartial as the universe. "It's intended purpose is more detrimental than the results it produces."

The old man contemplated this. "How so?" he said.

Michael thought of his many incarnations and attachments: he had been men of science, philosophy, and astrology; he had imbued his essence into the pervading ether of the *Akasha* and whispered into the great minds of writers, inventors, and explorers. But due to the uncompromising free-will policy of the universe, his most impactful incarnations had to do with men of the cloth.

Michael despised religion, but his job as head archangel was to influence the direction humanity went, not dictate it. As such, he had spent many lifetimes trying to implement certain ideologies that could potentially benefit humanity. His execution was always flawless, and he had even sacrificed his life on more than one occasion—the thought being if he was martyred, all the better—but humanity would invariably dilute the message as time went on.

"Well, sir, if religion were a business," Michael said, "it would've gone out of business eons ago."

As Michael's thoughts changed, so too did the channels. They were suddenly surrounded by men of all manner of faith, killing in the name of their appointed god. The Crusades, the inquisitions, the conquistadors—Muslims killing Jews, Jews killing Christians, Christians killing Native Americans, Native Americans killing each other—all in the name of God.

"The collateral damages from war, outright genocide, and the incurable division it yields," Michael said, "isn't worth more than the value from those losses." He shook his head emphatically. "It simply wouldn't be sustainable, sir, and would've gone bankrupt before it even got off the ground."

"And why do you think that is, Michael?" the old man asked, trying to guide Michael on the right path of his own accord.

Michael thought about it for a moment before answering: "If there is an us, then by definition, there must also be a them, and anything that separates the masses will inevitably destroy them, sir," he said. "Christians, Jews, and Muslims. Democrats, Liberals, and Republicans. Rapists, murderers, and Packer fans."

The old man snorted and laughed loudly as a cratered cheese head manifested on his head. He tugged at the collars of his green and yellow Aaron Rodgers jersey and then dabbed playfully. Michael laughed and then fell silent.

"I have often wondered why you allowed so many different religions, sir."

The mercury flickered in white and black static before the word "HBO" popped up on the screens. "Welcome back to Last Week Tonight with John Oliver," said the host of the satire news show. This particular episode focused on how easily the host ordained his own religion. He named it Our Lady of Perpetual Exemption, exposing a fundamental flaw in the system and poking fun at the hundreds of new churches founded in America each year that receive tax exemptions.

"Ah," the old man said, "but you know I only made one and the rest splintered from source, if not imagined entirely anew by man's enviously vivid imagination and adoration for power."

"So," Michael said with a shrug. "I won't give them a source, sir."

"None?" the old man said, trying to hide his surprise. "What an interesting concept."

"No sir, I'll give them a holistic lifestyle. A healthy mind, body, and spirit doesn't require a belief in the supernatural. Man can be wicked for a belief, but a lifestyle will not birth a suicide bomber. Like their medicine, nature will be their religion."

The old man smiled and nodded. "And of government?"

"It can go the way of religion, sir."

"So, no religion and no government? But how will I ever get my money?" the old man asked, joking. "No government is possible with small populations but not feasible with billions of people. No?"

Michael thought of his campaign trail when he incarnated as Abraham Lincoln and how he went from town to town on his soapbox, wooing every crowd he spoke to. *It's just not the same,* he thought, *nothing but a popularity contest to see who can earn the most money.* The ship's AI interfaced with his thoughts, and the television screens changed channels.

"Could this election be the first time a presidential nominee raises a billion dollars?" the news anchor asked on the television in front of Michael.

"Contributors sponsor both sides of the spectrum and have who-ever wins deep in their pockets," Michael said. "It's a despicable exhibition of democracy, sir."

"Tell me how you really feel, son," the old man said with a smirk.

Michael laughed. "Did I mention they're corrupt," he said. "In a world where money is king, anything can be bought, sir."

"So, what then, shall you do differently?" the old man asked solemnly.

"I must admit, sir, it is here where I am at an impasse."

"Well, let me ask you this, son," the old man paused a moment, "what is Legion's prime directive?"

"To hit critical mass in enlightenment after boasting a population of ten billion souls, sir, and to that end, modern governments are the antithesis. They're all about control, and really, are nothing more than lackeys for the corporations and banks. They conduct unspeakable acts upon their citizens as a premise to launch illegal wars. There are whole generations who've grown up knowing nothing but war. Tragically, it has become the new norm, and when the homeostasis of a society is perpetual warfare, their demise is inevitable."

"Yes," the old man said in slight agreement, "but war is another topic, entirely."

Michael recalled his attachment to John Lennon and the message of love he had tried to convey. But as he thought of the humanity of 2026—it was hard for him to *Imagine* they'd ever received the message.

They don't even dream anymore, he thought, *just generation upon generation of conformers—conformers and settlers.*

"I believe it's all relative and intertwined, sir," Michael said. "War casts shadows of religion, country, and money because religion, country, and money are all benefactors of war. Nothing is more profitable than war. So, they seek it out like madmen all under the umbrella of spreading their subscribed ideology."

Circus music blared from the ship's PA system, and the television screens changed once more as Michael and the old man were bombarded with an onslaught of propaganda. As it does to humanity every day, the news outlets attempted to lull them into a hypnotic trance, repeating the same script repeatedly.

"WMDs, Terrorism, Patriot Act, War, War on Terror, 9/11, Twin Towers." Thousands of broadcasts perpetuating the fear-based agenda.

A circus indeed, Michael thought.

"Top-tier government officials lie about weapons of mass destruction and prey on the patriotism of their citizens in a well-orchestrated scam that engulfs a nation in patriotic duty," Michael said. "Those same elected officials walk through a revolving door of fascism into their private sector for defense contracting, weapons manufacturing, big oil, and the like. They bomb whole countries with impunity and then rebuild them, and with every bullet, bomb, and nail used, they see a profit."

A moment of mercury static danced on the screens and then breaking news—

"Dick Cheney's ties with the huge multinational conglomerate Haliburton are just now surfacing—" Michael tuned out the disturbing reality.

The old man rubbed his chin with his thumb and pointing finger. "I see," he said, "and how could they possibly get away with such atrocities?"

Just then, ripples began oscillating and transforming the Cheney debacle into news broadcasts from across the planet, all reporting on the same event—9/11. Thousands of broadcasts in hundreds of languages reporting on the moment the planes crashed into the towers.

"The same people who control the governments," Michael said, "control the media, sir. They use their minions in the so-called free press to incite an agenda that subscribes to systematic racism, race-baiting, fearmongering, and the like. Divide and conquer is the name of the game. Which boggles the mind to the uninformed, but to the savvy, they know, if you control the media, you can get the people to believe just about anything."

One by one, the news broadcasts melted back into the six-screen 4D format, and suddenly, Michael and the old man were thrust into the streets of New York City on the evening of September 11th. Two heaps of rubble smoldered ominously a few blocks away, and directly in front of them stood World Trade Center 7, perfectly unharmed save for scattered fires on a few of the top floors. A loud series of layered pops accompanied by dust showers emanated from the skyscraper before it collapsed unto itself at freefall speed. A flashing clock on a building across the street read 5:20 p.m.

"Indeed, you can, son," the old man said, scratching his head, "like how two planes brought down three towers on September 11."

An acute throbbing suddenly pulsated in the middle of Michael's forehead, where his third eye chakra was located. His empathic abilities stretched the gamut to intuition as well. The old man reached over and siphoned off the negative energy distilled by the haunting probability that 9/11 was an inside job.

Michael's chakra went from deep black to vibrant indigo and the dark energy distributed into the old man's aura. The sensation tingled and then went numb before returning to homeostasis.

"They wouldn't have been able to convince the masses if not for the media regurgitating the diabolical script on repeat, effectively brainwashing the lot of them and filling them with a patriotic vengeance," Michael said. "And it's right there in the official report for everyone to see … or not see."

"Ah, yes," the old man said with a grimace. "The infamous third tower."

"The third tower that didn't get hit by a plane and fell nine hours in the same exact fashion as the other two. Yeah, the infamous, phantom third tower that's not even mentioned in the 9/11 commission report."

The old man shared in Michael's shock. "Yes, I didn't think they'd get away with it," he said, nodding his head, "but, alas, you are right, Michael." He paused. "A monopoly on the media is paramount in swaying public opinion and a vital asset to those who wish to keep the masses in bondage—perhaps their most valued asset."

He clapped his hands loud and clasped them tightly. "So, no government, then, eh," he said, "no government, no media, no economy, no religion, no jobs? Everyone will just be sitting in their caves, doing nothing then, am I to presume?"

Michael knew the old man's wit and stifled a laugh. "Well, not exactly, sir," he said, "I'll do the Atlantean model—but the whole planet."

"Ah yes," the old man said firmly, "the Atlanteans—our finest hour."

"Yes sir," Michael agreed.

Of all the other cycles and all the other civilizations, the Atlanteans were the only ones who evolved high enough to reach ascension. Legion had poached them and put them on another planet to see how they would fare independently.

The old man laughed. "It's funny," he said, "all the legends speak of Atlantis being struck with fire and smoke and sinking into the ocean in one night. Yet nobody considered that perhaps they didn't sink at all but took off into the cosmos." The old man paused for a moment, contemplating a world where the Atlantean way of life stretched far and wide. "What a pity."

The liquid mercury activated, and suddenly, Michael and the old man were on earth circa 10,000 BC. Torrential rains melted the snow and ice that blanketed the landscape, and swaths of water drowned the lands. Thousands of spaceships ascended into the sky on the ceiling screen until they looked like distant stars. On the walls, hundreds of spaceships loaded the last of the Atlanteans for their exodus to Zeta Reticula.

"Yes sir, indeed, it was a tragic loss," Michael said with his arms extended, "but, if you recall, that was my idea."

"It *wassss?*" the old man said. But the dumbfounded way he said it seemed off to Michael. He suspected the old man was feigning the lapse in memory for some reason. *But why?*

"Yes sir. Following the fall of the souls Lucifer recruited, I had the foresight to predict we were going to have to step in with the flood and, wanting to save the best asset we've ever created, we allowed them to ascend in isolation."

The old man seemed perplexed. "Highly unorthodox, indeed," he said incredulously. But Michael sensed the old man remembered more than he was letting on.

"Yes sir. But it worked," Michael said proudly. He just then realized the last time he checked their progression was before his previous incarnation, twenty-five years ago. The AI interface recognized this realization and displayed a live feed of people living in harmony on a foreign planet.

"AAR module," Michael said, "what's the population of Zeta Reticula?"

The live feed continued, and a robotic voice said, "Zeta Reticula has eight billion souls, sir."

That sounds about right, Michael thought. "And how have they fared since my last progress report?"

"They've flourished impeccably, sir," AI said. "Their ascended master hasn't had to lift a finger thus far. They are what Legion has declared an unprecedented anomaly."

Michael brimmed with organic pride.

"No country?" the old man asked.

"They are by and large community-oriented," said AI, "but there is no sovereignty as there is no need for such a construct."

A world without borders and flags, Michael thought, *is the only route to achieve true peace. A world where anyone anywhere is considered your countrymen—the country of humanity.*

"No government?" Michael asked.

"It is how it was twenty-five years ago, sir. They have UBUNTU communities run independently based on the individual needs of the community."

A world without governments waging wars and extending their ideologies to an unwitting populace, Michael thought, *is the only route to true freedom.*

"No commerce?" the old man asked.

"No industry?" Michael asked.

"See for yourself," AI said.

The mercury pixels rippled and then on each screen displayed a world where cooperation was the prevailing model, not competition. A world where abundance was so rampant, possession and envy were foreign concepts. A world where there were no socioeconomic class divisions because there was no money, and thus, there was no strife, no crime, no poverty, no hunger, no suffering.

When money is subtracted from the equation of life, Michael thought, *so is greed, pain, and all other fear-based models derived from competition.*

"No wars?" the old man asked.

"No sir," AI said.

Of course, there aren't any wars, Michael thought, *without money, religion, and the bravado of patriotism fanning the flames of indignation, there is no need for war.*

"How have they come along technologically?" Michael asked.

The screens displayed machines working tirelessly around the clock and how technology had freed up the time the vast majority would be working.

"If you're looking for a planet that uses technology for the betterment of every sentient species on that planet," AI said, "then you would be hard-pressed to find another in all the cosmos better suited than Zeta Reticula."

The old man threw his hands up in defeat and uncharacteristically stammered: "But, I thought, well, I mean, that's to say," he said clumsily, "didn't we leak these technologies to humanity, years ago? Didn't you attach to Tesla?" But the old man said this in such a way that Michael knew he was putting him on.

The walls left Zeta Reticula and the individual screens melted into the six-screen, 4D format, thrusting the room into 1940s decorum. They suddenly found themselves on the thirty-third floor of the Hotel New Yorker as a team of G-men clad in black suits broke into room 3327 and ransacked it. They had arrived empty-handed but left with totes of boxes filled with all manner of innovative genius.

A lifetime spent fighting big business, Michael thought, *didn't do my attachment to Tesla any justice—they just waited for him to die and then stole his life's work.*

"We did, indeed, sir," Michael said, "but governments and big businesses suppressed our efforts at every ... single ... turn." He enunciated the last words slowly for effect. "The common theme of this conversation, if one were seeking one, would be humanity's proclivity for greed."

The Hotel New Yorker disintegrated back into the twelve-screen format, and on every screen was the same news report. Although Michael could stomach no more negativity and tuned it out, he could still read the flashing headlines—CEO OF GM RECEIVES $22 MILLION BONUS WHILE CUTTING 15,000 EMPLOYEES.

The old man agreed with a subtle nod. "AAR module," he said, "is there any manner in which the Atlanteans fare worse than humanity?"

"Negative, sir," AI said. "They are a family of one."

"As it should be," said Michael and the old man in unison.

"Activate AAR shadow mode," Michael said, activating the ship's modality to display a live feed on what they were talking about. Michael continued:

"They meditate en masse, exercise regularly, and their diet consists of natural, unaltered food." The walls mirrored exactly what Michael spoke of. "So, disease is at a minimum, and there are no created ailments for the profit of pharmaceutical companies because there is no money. And they have so much culture, sir, which—"

"Ahah," the old man exclaimed. "I have found the weak link in your alleged utopia."

The AI's after-action review module communicated with the old man's psyche and went back to the multi-screen format where angry mobs held signs that read *George Floyd was human too, Black Lives Matter,* and such. They screamed at Michael and the old man from the news broadcasts. Michael's stomach churned as absolute negativity leaked from thousands of news reports that propagated seeds of division and negativity in a systematic agenda to divide the masses.

"If you're going to say there's no racism because there's only one race," Michael said, "we poached the Mayans, a tribe from Israel, a small community from Roanoke Island, North Carolina, and other peoples from all corners of the earth." Michael paused. "They are color blind, sir, and without blinders of hate and bigotry, they see only the intrinsic beauty in every man, woman, and child—as racism is largely a learned behavior."

"I see," the old man said. "So, what do they do for recreation?"

"Return to AAR shadow mode," Michael said. "They listen to orators and watch plays. They conduct ceremonies and rituals to commemorate nature on the equinoxes and solstices. They talk and laugh and read and play. They make love, paint, and write."

Michael took in the utter love and positivity emanating from the live feeds. He was so happy and proud, and he realized it was the first time he'd ever felt like the old man. Angels aren't wired to consider the species they have been assigned as children, whereas all ascended masters assume the role as mother and father of the species they champion.

For the first time, Michael felt a connection he had never felt and considered that perhaps humanity wasn't innately bad; they just needed better guidance.

Maybe, just maybe, he could be the one to conjure their latent potential forward and help them finally ascend.

The old man saw the wheels of hope percolating in Michael's mind and cleared his throat.

"I'm sorry, sir," Michael said, "I was just thinking."

"Would you like to share with the rest of the class," the old man said with a knowing smirk.

Michael nodded and thought aloud. "By no stretch are they perfect, and on occasion, they disagree and squabble, but they always find amicable ways to resolve their issues and very rarely does it result in violence—as violence is largely a learned behavior."

The walls precisely mirrored this.

"They stare at the stars and wonder what their purpose for creation is," Michael said in prideful awe, "not knowing they are the living embodiment of it. And the family unit is impeccable, sir. They are so very tight, which makes for a tight community, which in turn makes for a tight planet. There's never been such an overwhelmingly positive display of micro to macro consequences. It's staggering, sir."

The live feeds flickered, and then an algorithm rebooted the screens. When they turned back on, holographic images of eight billion Zeta Reticulins projected into the room. Families spent quality time in phantom images, which bled over billions of other families doing the same thing. Not one family stood alone, and Michael thought it appropriate as they were all connected by an invisible force. It seemed as if one family's closeness and happiness leaked to the next family and, therefore, the furthest family away, for they were all tethered together as one unit.

"Return to default mode," the old man said resolutely. The translucent walls returned. The old man rose slowly from the cloud couch and put his hand on Michael's shoulder. He gave it a light squeeze. "You are ready, Michael," he said with finality.

He closed his eyes. They rolled into the back of his head and fluttered about curiously, but Michael had seen this happen one thousand and ninety-eight times before. He knew the old man had just set the wheels of his own demise into motion.

The old man opened his new eyes for the first time. He closed them slowly, acclimating, then gradually faster. He looked at planet earth, and his eyes swelled up. "It's even more beautiful now," he said in a whisper.

"Did you just do what I think you did, sir?" Michael asked. He looked at the old man's eyes, static on his natural brown.

The old man nodded innocently as the distinct glow that surrounded him perceptibly dimmed. At the same time, Michael's aura had gotten just a few shades brighter as he absorbed the powers acquainted with an ascended master.

Michael became dizzy and wobbly. His heart ached with a conflicting desire to scold the old man and embrace him all at once. Michael was hurt. He was sad. He was angry and confused. "But sir," he said in a cracking voice, "you had so much more time."

"Oh?" the old man said, still gazing upon the earth.

"At least another hundred years, sir."

"That's but a whisper in time, Michael," the old man said playfully. He shifted his gaze from the earth and saw Michael's puppy-dog eyes swelled in tears. The old man hated to see Michael just so, but he was on a mission—his last mission.

Knowing he didn't have much time before he could no longer articulate his outgoing orders, the old man went to work. "Your orders, once I supernova," he said, "are to initiate the total reset sequence protocol."

It took Michael a second to shake off the orgy of emotions and contemplate the implications of the orders. "But sir," he said, confused, "we're not supposed to leave earth unless an unforeseen emergency presents itself."

A similar occurrence had happened millions of years prior. Humanity was on Mars at the time, and they had discovered nuclear warfare there as well. It seemed in every cycle; humanity invested more energy creating newer and better ways to kill each other than anything else. If only they could channel that creativity into more productive methods, they wouldn't have destroyed their atmosphere and had to flee to earth. It has been their home ever since.

"The whole point of me self-destructing this premature is to spare humanity from flagrant suffering," the old man said. He shook his head. "It's over, Mikey," he continued in prideful defeat, "there's no point in delaying the inevitable. These past few cycles of sheer negativity have thrown the earth into a great imbalance. She must heal herself." He paused. "When I supernova, I want you to compound the destruction with the total reset protocol. Do you understand me? Humanity mustn't suffer for more than a few hours. We must rip their tooth out, root and stem, lest they suffer intolerably."

Michael considered the logistics behind such an order. It was possible, of course, albeit highly unorthodox. "But, sir," he argued, "we're not supposed to—"

"Never mind what you're supposed to do, son," the old man said sternly. "As an ascended master of Legion, I have full autonomy, and *these are your orders.*"

Michael couldn't fathom why the old man would give such an order.

The old man saw Michael's suspicious looks, and he knew Michael thought this was the desperate act of a deteriorating mind. Although the old man was currently in command of his wits, he knew his coherence was slipping away with every passing second.

"This was a thoroughly calculated decision, Michael," the old man assured. "I've already conferred with engineering, and their scans indicate Mars's negative energy has long been purged, and humanity has a better chance at attaining ascension there than on earth—which they have made incredibly sick," the old man said. "Now promise me."

Michael conceded to a dying man's wish: "I promise, sir," he said in a low whisper.

The old man clapped and clasped his hands tightly. "Splendid. Now, you must also promise me you will achieve these events that you spoke of on Zeta Reticula, on Mars. Let not another angel or ascended master deter you from the path of which you have just laid before me."

Michael nodded slowly, but as he contemplated the probability of breaking such a promise, he resented the old man for putting him in such a position.

This is a lose-lose, he thought.

The old man wasn't satisfied with Michael's unsure nod. "That's not enough, Michael," he said definitively, "you must promise me."

But again, Michael answered only with a conspicuous nod.

The old man unclasped his hands and put them on Michael's shoulders. "Say it, Michael," he said with deliberate sternness, "you must say you promise."

Michael shrugged the old man's hands away and paced about nervously. He felt resentment, anger, and sadness build up in his chest before erupting from his mouth. "Who am I to promise such results I know not of," he said. "You're an ascended master, and you couldn't do it, nor could any before you, and you ask this of me?"

"I have every faith in you, Michael," the old man said. "Now, promise me."

"I cannot do as you please, sir," Michael said defiantly. "I will not."

"Promise me, Michael."

Michael was astounded by the old man's presumptuous stance. He personally had no faith that he could achieve the mission because humanity would invariably self-sabotage his efforts. He sensed the old man was delusional to put so much trust in him.

"Is it not enough you have destined me to be a failure," he said, "will you not be pleased until I have become a liar, as well?"

The old man was getting dizzy and wobbly. He knew he only had a few more moments to make Michael believe in himself—to make Michael see what he saw in him.

"You and you alone have had the answers all along, son," the old man said. He grabbed Michael's hands and led him to the middle of the room. "Activate AAR shadow mode," he said. The walls went blank and then back to default mode, waiting on words to shadow.

"You had the foresight to move the Atlanteans, and they thrived in isolation. You know a species will not reach ascension if they are unable to overcome racism, so you reintroduced them to different races, and they have thrived in unity, son."

The old man saw a faint hint of hope, a twinkle in Michael's eyes as the walls mirrored what the old man spoke of, and indeed, Michael saw them living in a proverbial utopia and a spark of hope lit in the essence of his soul. The old man knew how powerful hope can be.

All you need is a spark, the old man thought.

"I have no doubt Zeta Reticula will achieve the committee's purpose in record time," continued the old man, "and it will undoubtedly be the new blueprint for running a planet." He grabbed Michael's arms, raised them to the side, and spun him about in slow circles so he could take it all in. "This was all your doing, son," he said, "you've already done it once. Can't you do it again? With a new planet and free reign."

The old man had the same knowing twinkle in his eyes as when he was pretending to forget earlier, and Michael had a sudden revelation—he realized it was all a charade.

"You lied to me, sir," he said, clutching his chest.

"Whatever do you mean?" the old man asked innocently.

"You've been planning this the whole time. Haven't you?" Michael said. "*You played me.*"

"Played you?"

"You used me."

"I motivated you, son," the old man snapped. "After the failed third cycle, I knew, statistically speaking, we weren't going to prosper in the succeeding cycles, and I love humanity too much to perpetuate the same problems."

The AAR shadow modality was still operational, and Michael realized this really wasn't the desperate attempt of a failing mind but a well-contrived plan that went back twelve thousand years.

"So," the old man said, "I decided to do something drastic, and I gave the one person who knew humanity better than anyone else full autonomy and just look at what you did with the opportunity—the Atlanteans are going to ascend, Michael."

Michael shook his head. "I don't want this," he said stubbornly. For as the old man had just pointed out—no other angel knew humanity better than Michael, and he genuinely didn't think they deserved to ascend.

They're far too dangerous, Michael thought. *They can't even coexist amongst themselves. What will happen when they have entities pure of heart to exploit?*

"The burden is already yours, I'm afraid," the old man said, sullenly.

"How am I to even convince anyone I'm the new ascended master?" Michael said, tugging hopelessly at strings.

"You mean despite your newly acquired powers and distinct glow?" the old man said, with raised eyebrows. "Azrael has been made privy to my plan for some time now."

Michael didn't wish to see any backdoor deals between his twin flame and his favorite ascended master, so he put his fingers on the screen and moved them diagonally a foot apart. As he stared at the massive blue marble, he recalled Azrael's unsolicited showering of sirs, and then it made sense—it all made sense.

The old man felt his chest tighten, and a sense of urgency enveloped him. "Please, Michael, you must promise me you will end their suffering," he begged, "you must—you must—you—ahhhh—"

The light vanished from the old man's eyes. He swatted at the air and went about in circles like a mayday plane crashing to the earth. When he hit the ground, Michael could hear bones cracking followed by a hissing sound as the door opened.

"What the hell just happened, sir?" Azrael said. "There was just an unscheduled earthquake in Japan. A massive tsunami is rapidly approooo—oh."

As Michael cradled the old man, his skin slowly atrophied like a grape left out in the unforgiving sun to dry. "He's decided to self-destruct prematurely," Michael said.

Humanity broke his heart, Michael thought resentfully. *They broke his fucking heart.*

"He didn't want to prolong their suffering any longer than was necessary, sir," Azrael said. "He knows he's failed. He's known for some time now." Azrael walked over to his twin flame and embraced him.

"He did what he did because he believes in you, Michael, and so do I," Azrael said. The old man contorted on the ground, and Azrael said, "Activate self-destruction module."

A hatch in the floor yawned open, and an apparatus that looked like a transparent coffin crept up with mechanical precision.

"Help me get him into the container, please, sir," Azrael said.

When they tried to raise the old man, he kicked, punched, and flailed spastically on the ground. He screamed hysterically for Michael to come to his aid, but when Michael reached for the old man, he sunk his teeth into his hand. Michael recoiled and looked down at him with a broken heart.

"Don't touch me, you scoundrel," the old man screamed in a panic. "Where is Michael? I demand to speak to him at once." He squinted his eyes aggressively. "Do you know who I am?" he said. "Where is Michael?"

Although Michael was only a few feet away, he may as well have been in another galaxy entirely.

"We must get him into the pod before he supernovas, sir," Azrael said. Then with a sense of urgency, "He is no longer your master but a ticking time bomb."

From the old man's solar plexus an orange glow started emanating—his essence, leaving his body.

An obnoxious alarm indicated an ominous detection, and a disembodied voice boomed from the PA system. "Dangerous energy detected," a robotic voice said, "please place in the module, or destruction is imminent."

Michael went for the old man's arms, but he chomped at Michael's hands once more. "We don't have time for this, sir," Azrael said. "I'm so sorry, sir." The apology was just as much directed at Michael as the old man. For he knew how much his twin flame loved the old man so.

"Destruction is imminent," the robotic voice warned, "dangerous energy detected. Please—"

With no regard to his old, frail body, Azrael picked the old man up and flung him into the pod. Once loaded with the dangerous payload—which harbored enough energy to destroy whole galaxies—the swinging door collapsed unto itself. Michael stood by, crying helplessly; he couldn't bring himself to hurt the old, beloved man.

As the old man examined his new environment, a frantic paranoia engulfed his intellect. He hit the pod lethargically like a sloth fending off a pesky fly. The pod pulsated in a fabulous rainbow-colored hue every time he made contact as the remnants of his powers were being transmuted into energy, and like a dying star, he was going to collapse unto himself.

Gabriel, the archangel, came rushing into the room. "What the hell is happening?" he inquired. "There are earthquakes and tsunamis and voooo—oh." He saw the old man frolicking about inside the pod. "*Already,*" he said, almost admiringly, "he could've had another hundred years."

"At least." This from all three angels in unison.

Michael touched the pod lightly and gazed upon his favorite ascended master. "He didn't want to prolong their suffering," he said. "Speaking of which,"—*they're not going to believe this,* he thought—"it's time to initiate the total reset protocol."

Gabriel snapped his head sharply at Michael. "What?" he said.

"His last orders are that we make the reset as quick as possible," Michael said. "He doesn't want them to suffer any longer than they must."

Gabriel put his hands on his hips. "That's not the procedure, Michael," he said in a smug tone. "We're supposed to save some for posterity and then restart."

Did he forget I incarnated as Methuselah? Michael thought.

"I know the SOP, Gabe, but he doesn't want any of their current social constructs bleeding into the next cycle."

"But, Michael, it's not—"

"Just *fucking* do it, Gabe," Michael snapped.

Gabriel thought about it before responding. "No," he shook his head, "the old man no longer has authority. Who did he pick as his successor?"

"Him." Azrael patted Michael on the shoulder as he made toward the door. "I'll start it, sir."

"*You?*" Gabriel said. Michael answered only with a subtle nod. "How's that even possible?" But even as the question left Gabriel's lips, he noticed Michael's pronounced glow and witnessed his eyes change color, and Gabriel knew it to be true.

"How would you like to relieve Lucifer in the Dark Knight for the duration of my tenure?" Michael asked, referring to the archaic black satellite which orbits the earth. Lucifer had been stationed there ever since he helped the dark ones infiltrate the soul regenerator machines. It was, in fact, the most despised of assignments among the archangels and the closest thing they had to solitary confinement.

Gabriel fell silent as he could think of nothing worse than the possibility of being isolated for 25,920 years.

"Right now, as we speak even," Michael said, "humanity is in great peril. We must first end their suffering, and then I'll explain everything to you if I must." He resented Gabriel for making him explain. "But for now," he said contemptuously, "will you please get the crew to prep the ion thrusters?"

Gabriel nodded and walked away with his nose hanging in the air.

Alas, Michael was alone with the old man. He had the expression and demeanor of a scared child, hiding under a bed from a terribly frightful monster. Michael thought the look appropriate and reasoned that the terribly frightful monster was humanity at large.

The old man scanned the clear pod, which was much lower than Michael would've preferred, and as he thought he'd like to sit, a chair manifested out of thin air. The manifestation was quick and concise and an irrefutable indication that he was, indeed, the new ascended master.

Just as he sat, the old man seized and contorted and even outside the thick pod, Michael could hear the tearing of flesh as bones ripped through the old man's caramel-colored skin. Through the exposed gashes, revealed the old man's true essence—a blinding light—which winked through the cracks like sunlight under a canopy of dancing leaves. But Michael knew what was happening—

Energy can't be created or destroyed, only redistributed. As such, following the natural order, the old man was due to implode, and the bulk of his essence would be transmuted into the new ascended master while the remaining energy would be shot down in a particle beam to wreak havoc on the earth like a scorned ex-spouse.

Michael wished the old man would stop fighting the process and spare himself the agony, just as he did for humanity.

Above the old man's unearthly screams, Michael heard the hissing door again. "The ion thrusters are ready, sir," Azrael said, "just waiting on your command."

Michael nodded and put his face to the glass pod. "Why is he fighting it?" he wondered aloud. "Why is he holding on?"

Azrael hovered over his twin flame and gently placed his hands on Michael's shoulder. "He said he wouldn't expire until he was assured that you'd put your hatred for humanity aside and achieve the mission, sir."

Michael locked eyes with the old man, and a mutual adoration that had tethered the two souls together made him feel at home in the old man's company. Michael decided his love for the old man vastly outweighed his hatred for humanity, and all at once, he vowed to honor him by achieving the mission.

"I swear on my life, sir," he said in a low whisper, "I will get the inhabitants of Mars to the fourth density within my time. I—I promise, sir."

Just then, as if a lingering remnant of the old man were waiting on the promise to be incanted into the universe and release him of his torment, the old man smiled a knowing smile. Then a brilliant light emanated from his mouth and eyes and ears and his body vortexed unto itself before vanishing in an immense blast. Michael's body soaked up the energy, vibrations, and frequencies, and he felt his powers increase at the subatomic level. He relished in the sublime knowledge of the universe—so much knowledge.

Michael saw the Fibonacci sequence, fractal patterns, golden spiral ratio, and sacred geometry everywhere he looked. When he gazed upon the earth, he marveled at the creator's artistry, and where there should've been nothing but empty space, he beheld a kaleidoscope image of the dark matter that connects everything—a webbed matrix tethering the earth and humanity to the cosmos—the *Akasha*.

Beyond the substrate of the physical world, in his mind's eye, he saw the world from the perspective of the person whose eyes to which he was currently tethered. The perspective changed along with the eyes.

Michael closed his eyes and listened to the sounds of the universe—a divine melody composed of all nine solfeggio frequencies and the Schumann resonance.

The door hissed again. "Sir, there's been a pole shift," Gabriel said. "Africa is the new North Pole."

The immense knowledge Michael had just been given hijacked his autonomous system and deciphered the geometric equations. He acclimated to the foreign ability just as quickly as trying on a new pair of glasses.

"Activate destruction and custodial protocol," Michael said.

The floor directly below the clear pod opened, and the old man's remaining energy was released in a particle beam and sent shrieking toward the earth. The energy released would erupt volcanoes, spawn floods and tornadoes, and awaken the Leviathan and all manner of destruction would ensue. Then the stone giants scattered upon the planet's surface and underneath her oceans would reanimate. They'd wait out the destruction for forty days and forty nights and then conduct their custodial purpose, ridding the planet of any evidence of civilization that wasn't set in stone.

"That will be the last pole shift humanity will ever have to endure, sir," Michael whispered into the empty pod. "I promise."

The seat disappeared at the same time Michael raised from it. "Okay, gentlemen," he said with a resurgence of confidence, "I know we're supposed to let the destruction settle and fester for a bit, but wadasay we put those poor bastards out of their misery?"

A command center manifested out of thin air when he turned

to face the translucent wall, and he sat down in a captain's chair that molded to his physique brilliantly. A speaker dropped from the ceiling, and Michael spoke into the ship's PA system.

"This is your new captain speaking," he said, "under article 34892-Alpha/Zulu—humanity has been deemed hopeless to reform. I have no recourse but to invoke the total reset protocol." He let the implications settle for a second. "Activate Lunar Module Command."

The floor opened, and a small drone flew about. It hovered over Michael and scanned his body for the ascended master's energetic signature, confirming his authority. "Hello, sir," the robotic voice said, "what are your orders?"

"Prepare to initiate ion thrusters in T minus 60 seconds."

"Destination?" AI asked.

"Mars," Michael answered.

A deafening alarm wailed incredulously, accompanied by a series of rotating red lights. "Commencing countdown," the ship's AI system said, "engines on. Fifty-nine, fifty-eight ..."

The earth's moon hadn't been moved in millions of years. The subsurface quarters shimmied this way and that as the ion engines charged.

Michael thought of the conversation he had just had with the old man and how dearly he held him in his heart. His only wish was that he would fulfill his promise.

"Thirty, twenty-nine, twenty-eight ..."

I will, sir, Michael thought.

"Three," *I promise,* "two," *if it's the last thing,* "one," *I do,* "lift-off."

Static electricity fused with molecules hanging in the air as the charge completed and earth's moon rocketed within Mars's orbit. Michael watched through the translucent wall as the earth became smaller, and smaller, and smaller yet. He knew the biblical destruction would be thorough enough to spare everyone a quick death.

But Michael had been around long enough that he didn't dwell on this last failed cycle. His focus shifted to the task at hand, and he started formulating a game plan; starting from a blank canvas, they would terraform Mars, and then he would scour the Legion database to assemble a vanguard of willing star seeds, lightworkers, and other volunteer souls, in tandem with the incarnated angels to help guide humanity on the path to ascension once and for all.

Epilogue: Betty Hill's Original Sin

AFTER THE THIRTEENTH CONSECUTIVE DAY of having these dreadfully vivid nightmares, Betty Hill sought support from a hypnotherapist. Under hypnosis, she recalled the encounter with the gray beings, and she realized they had lied to her. From the last dream Betty had, she knew they weren't post-biological humans from the future, but the dark ones that Lucifer helped, the ones that Legion removed their souls.

Because of their fall from grace, they were excommunicated from source and couldn't escape the entropic grip of the material world.

To remedy this, the fallen angels decided to use earth as a lab and humanity as lab rats in a controlled experiment to modify hybrids and genetically harvest souls. But they couldn't circumvent the free-will policy of the universe until the Oracle found a loophole in the system— they only needed permission from one human if that human were to be immersed in the quantum field, which would connect them to all.

Betty recalled how the rest of the regressed memory played out.

The medical examiner placed the syringe in Betty's navel and extracted her eggs. Then they went to meet her husband, Barney, and as they made their way, Betty noticed a whole farm of massive cylindrical tubes which functioned as artificial wombs where beings were being grown.

You are our first, the leader thought, *but you will not be the last. After we incubate your eggs, we'll place them inside one of them.* He pointed to the beings gestating in bubbling liquid. *And then find a way to get our souls back.*

Betty was appalled. "Souls," she said, confused, "you didn't say anything about souls." Betty was a God-fearing woman, and she tried objecting, but the medical team grabbed her and dragged her down the ramp, kicking and screaming.

The medical examiner waved his hand, and they found themselves back in their 1957 Chevrolet Bel Air. They couldn't account for the last two hours and were thirty-five miles south of their last known location. They saw a massive UFO with beings waving in the windows when they looked up.

Sitting there on the hypnotherapist's couch, she just then realized how much like Eve she really was. For just as the serpent tricked Eve into eating the forbidden fruit, so the dark ones tricked Betty into allowing them to use humanity as unwitting cattle.

Her one mistake was responsible for the phenomena known thereafter as alien abductions.

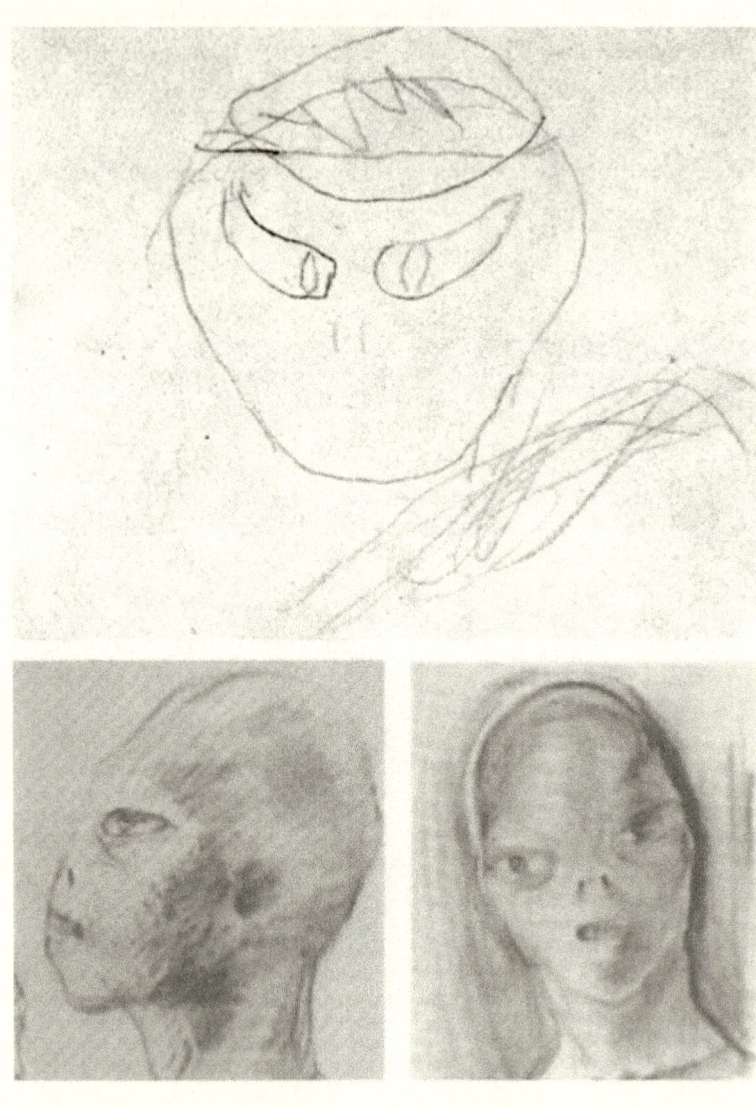

THIS IS HOW IT LOOKED WHEN IT WAS ABOUT 200 FEET
HIGH.
↓

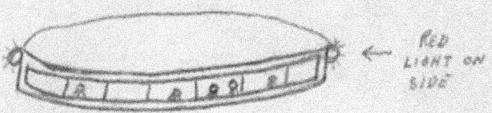

← RED
LIGHT ON
SIDE

THIS IS HOW IT LOOKED AFTER SHIFTING OVER HIGHWAY, DESCENDING
TO ABOUT 100 FEET OVER FIELD.
↓

← RED
LIGHT ON
END

FINS THIS SLID
OUT FROM
SIDE WITH
RED LIGHT

www.ingramcontent.com/pod-product-compliance
Lightning Source LLC
Jackson TN
JSHW022301170925
91139JS00001B/1